ALSO BY LAURA PRITCHETT

THREE
KEYS

THREE
KEYS

A Novel

LAURA PRITCHETT

DELL
NEW YORK

A Dell Trade Paperback Original

Copyright © 2024 by Laura Pritchett
Book club guide copyright © 2024 by Penguin Random House LLC

Published in the United States by Dell, an imprint of Random House,
a division of Penguin Random House LLC, New York.

DELL and the D colophon are registered trademarks
of Penguin Random House LLC.
RANDOM HOUSE BOOK CLUB and colophon are trademarks
of Penguin Random House LLC.

ISBN 978-0-593-72420-0
Ebook ISBN 978-0-593-72421-7

Printed in the United States of America on acid-free paper

randomhousebooks.com
randomhousebookclub.com

2 4 6 8 9 7 5 3 1

Book design by Diane Hobbing

Image on title page by AdobeStock/michalsanca
Image on part openers by AdobeStock/PictureSyndicate

Dedicated to my three keys: Jake, Eliana, Michael
and to heroine explorers everywhere

PART I

THE
FIRST KEY

STARS AND BIRDS

How quickly she'd become animal. How fast feral had descended. The upkeep of the body seemed beyond her—hair tangled, teeth filmy, a real need to shower. It was absurd how fast a foggy *lonely* had descended too. How, exactly, was she to occupy herself for the next three months, not to mention the rest of her empty, empty life?

Ammalie ate a pear with one hand, her driving hand, and combed her hair with the fingers of the other as she drove past the dried grass outside Cheyenne. *Empty, empty, empty.* She jerked her fingers through graying tangles—*dry as the grass outside*—which she'd done for most of the entire circuitous drive from Chicago. Finger-combing was simply not the same as with a brush, which she had forgotten to pack, and then subsequently forgot to buy on each of her stops. She'd had the seemingly brilliant idea to grab an extra plastic fork from the café in Chadron, Nebraska, but it broke nearly immediately after trying to use it in her unruly hair somewhere right on the Wyoming-Nebraska border in a town called Ditch Creek, which was as absurd as the fork. Was it a ditch or was it a creek? How could its status be so poorly defined?

She was acting kind of crazy and she knew it. Self-awareness was not reserved for the highly educated white-collars of the world, though she suspected they thought otherwise. *Anyone* with half a plastic fork tangled in her hair should get some help. Anyone who'd left her humble-but-comfortable home in a rush in order not to lose momentum or let reason seep in, and anyone who likely hadn't brushed her hair fully in a week or a month before that, well, that person was. not. well.

She didn't care. She could care *less*. She could care less than caring because she'd hit rock bottom, end of a rope, the place where maxims or axioms—or whatever one called phrases about phrases—no longer applied because the world no longer made sense. Bits of sweetly-worded wisdoms simply did not apply to chaos. Last night, prone in her sleeping bag in her car, she'd listened to a podcast about people who'd experienced a recent breakup or death of a partner, and how they had reduced executive functioning. She snort-laughed at the truth of that. Yes, her neural and behavioral changes were wildly evident. No MRI images needed here. Husband dead, son launched, job she *liked* gone, a world running amok, a planet lurching through space and being mistreated all the way.

Without a doubt, her brain was not working right. But the real mystery was: How did *others* continue to pierce the fog with clear and focused thoughts? And why couldn't she be one of them?

She spit the half-chewed pear pieces into a plastic cup containing the remains of sunflower seed shells. The pear was underripe, it was going to give her a stomachache, she should listen to nature. Then she reached for her water bottle, and, in doing so, spilled the pear bits and sunflower seed shells all over her cupholder and floorboard and her mail, which is when she acknowledged once again how *very* wide was the gap between the goal of "Be Interesting!" and the "Being Interesting Is Fucking Difficult!" truth.

It was a chasm, really.

She blamed it on the people who made videos on van-living and strong-women-solo-traveling. She blamed it on Frances McDormand. How delightful it would be to put them in jail for misleading the public. Living on the road was not as easy as it looked, and she ticked off the missing essentials in her mind:

> The frequent need for a pair of scissors, tape, fingernail clippers.
> The frequent need to pee.
> Ice to keep food cold.
> Heat source to keep feet warm.
> Something to do during long dark hours.

Room to move around, to stretch legs, to bend at the waist. She was not born a hunchback, after all, and she felt a pang of sorrow for those who were, and then felt a zing of shame, since she should be grateful for a straight spine that required bending when living in the back of a car.

Oh, and yes. And someone beside you. So that when you saw sunlit sandstone cliffs and mammoth bones and heard wind whistling through caves, as she'd done in South Dakota, there would be someone to *ooh* and *aah* with, which made the *oohing* and *aahing* comfortable and fulfilling instead of stab-your-heart-out depressing.

These were essential things.

She scratched at her scalp and dandruff swirled in the air, caught by the sun. Disgusting. This air was *dry,* no joke. Perhaps her scalp was emitting the particles of fog in her consciousness, an indication of her unclear thinking and the reduced activation of network areas of her brain. Her whole head, inside and out, was a dry-hot mess. What she needed was a brush, soap, and water, which is when it would get better. *She* would get better. Life would clarify. Make sense.

Soon. Maybe tonight. Tonight, she'd be turning a key to the rest of her life.

DENVER WAS AN unsurprising hell—no one, not even a nutcase such as herself, delighted in the trauma of speeding, merging, honking traffic. She felt like she was in a flock of berserk geese, all of them nearly flying into one another in a moment of panic. But soon after, she was on the exit that took her into the mountains, and then, yes, it was like freaking angels singing. Early October, the aspens bright yellow, lit up by a fall-tilted sun that was playing hide-and-seek with storm clouds.

She pulled up to a rest stop with a sign that read KENOSHA PASS, parked in the gravel pullout, and sat, dazed. *Beautiful, truly beautiful; now we're talking.* This is where calendar photos were born. Golden leaves, green pines, blue peaks, buttery sunlight slants. She closed her eyes and rested, heard herself make a gurgling sound as she fell into a brief moment of sleep. This was a new skill set of middle age that kept surprising her—a lifelong insomniac who could now zonk out in a car. It was a brief moment, though, and when she opened her eyes, she was surprised to discover that the sky and weather had undergone some kind of seasonal surgery. Now it was blustery, the sun hidden, and there was a hint of spitting snow.

She let out a dramatic sigh—she had noticed her new penchant for those too—and gave up on her daydream of a sandwich in a sunny splotch on a fallen tree. Instead, she stayed in the car and ate and read the Colorado sign's details, something about South Park Ranching and Kake's Charcoal Kilns, which she knew nothing about, did not care about, and never wanted to care about, though she had the vague notion she should. If she had been with Vincent, he would have found a way of cajoling her into caring, if only because he cared, which she would have found annoying but maybe simultaneously endearing.

The parking area was crowded—mostly with people in their twenties or thirties and unaware they were in the best years of their lives, brazenly heading into the mountains despite the dandruff-like snow—the planet having the same dry-scalp problem she did, apparently. Something about these hikers' tenacity both annoyed and endeared them to her, and she took inspiration from their bravado and sighed and got out to pee, which was her version of living it up bravely, she supposed. There was no Porta Potti or outhouse, so she crouched between the two car doors, even though someone might see her bare ass briefly as they whizzed by on the road. Arrest her, already.

She had become an animal. This lunacy could put her in jail. *Jail!* She should think this trip through a little better. Mari kept telling her so with an increased pitch and vigor in her voice, and Mari was right, and Mari didn't even know the whole truth. The trip was dangerous on several levels. Dangerous because she couldn't think too far in advance—*Just one key at a time,* she kept saying. Dangerous because Powell or Apricot might come looking for her and see what a mess she was. Dangerous because she was about to break into a house, dangerous because she knew she was flipping out—and that worst of all, she was flipping out for the first time in her life, which meant she had no experience in how to handle it.

SHE CONSIDERED THE tangle of keys dangling and clanking on their key ring, turned the one that started her car, then turned it back off and did the drama-sigh. "Learn to live a little, push yourself a little, eh?" she said, and forced herself out, bundling up with hat and mittens and scarf, muttering a scattering of cusswords about the cold, the curses somehow feeling deeply satisfying and absolutely necessary.

She was asked immediately to take a young couple's photo with a JUST MARRIED sign soaped on their window—first some shots with the mountains behind, and then some that included the parking lot, because the two women were trying to fit in the sign that said 9,999 FEET, which they clearly found amusing, giggling and falling into one another with laughter, something about one foot shy of five digits, and she had to relent and smile at how in-love people found nearly *anything* amusing. Plus, she suspected they were high, the pot shops being plentiful in this state, maybe the 9,999 kind of high. *Very* high. She might be a bland-white-bread-middle-age-invisible woman, but she wasn't stupid. She started humming a Billy Joel lyric, "She's been living in her white-bread world," as she tried for several angles in an effort to cut out the cars, including her own dirty beast, since they made the photo ugly, although youngsters these days could probably just fuzz out the ugly of any photo, a skill set she had not yet cared to embrace and would die without embracing.

When they were satisfied and offered a giggly thanks, she had the audacity to say, "May I suggest to you? May I suggest this is the best part of your life?"—another song lyric and surely one they would not know—and before they could respond, she started walking quickly up the trail. Her thighs were reluctant almost immediately, her lungs reluctant very soon after. "Hi," she said to a man who was jogging down the trail and surprised her on a corner. He moved on quickly with a snarly grunt.

"Hi," she said to a young couple, who acknowledged her vaguely.

"Hi," she said to the next man, and the one after that, and the one after that, and none acknowledged her at all, as if she were a ghost, though the next one said, "Have a nice walk," and actually looked her in the eye and smiled.

She hiked on, cold but happier now because of that simple smile. She stepped aside for the line of teenagers who were coming down the mountain at a fast clip, and then again for two gray-bearded men, and then again for two women runners, and then again for an athletic middle-aged guy who looked so much like Pierce Brosnan that it probably *was* Pierce Brosnan, and she wondered for the first time in her life who would name their kid Pierce, and she then decided to name the nighttime blues that came often at dusk "The Pierces," because that's what they did to her heart. The heart that was flat-out and obviously lonely and broken.

On her way back, as she neared the parking lot, a man approached her and stood in the middle of the hiking path. "Why, good afternoon," he said, in what struck her as a rather formal and serious greeting, though she was secretly happy to have someone acknowledge her existence on earth.

"Heya." Her eyes went from his to the chubby face of the blue-eyed toddler in his backpack, who said, "Ball ball" and pointed to the visible moon in the now-clear sky. She raised an eyebrow; clearly, the kid was as brilliant as the Colorado weather was changeable.

"True that," she said to the kid.

The dad ran his hand over a very unruly, wiry beard, and she wondered if all young men had wiry beards and if so, at what age they began to come in better than this Brillo-pad-looking thing. In a soft voice he added, "You checking out the Colorado Trail?"

"No, just stretching my legs. On a car trip."

"Us too. My wife is napping in the car. She's exhausted. I'm trying to give her a break by just wandering around the parking lot here. I keep checking to see if she's awake, but no."

Ammalie nodded. "It's more tiring than I thought it would be. Driving, I mean. It's exhausting, and I've been thinking how all the views, the space, well, it's . . . kinda *loud*. Can space be loud? Everyone makes travel seem so easy, and it's kinda not. It's just not. People are such liars. And I don't even have a kid to occupy," and then she added, "besides myself, I guess, ha."

Now the man was crouching to tie his hiking boot, and so she was face-to-face with the child, who was puffing out his cheeks, then making popping noises while digging his little fists into his brown curls. "Hi, kid," she said.

He popped his cheeks at her in response.

"You look happy to be alive," she said.

He popped his cheeks again.

The dad snorted as he stood. "Kids are good like that. Kinda like dogs. None of the trappings of worry. Such as, money. Such as, dying. Such as, not crashing the car. You know what I notice? There's a lot of crosses. I mean, there are lots of crosses alongside the road. Especially in New Mexico."

"That's the direction I'm heading. I saw lots in Nebraska and South Dakota and Wyoming, though. Crosses and snow fences. I know what you mean." She drew a big breath in. She hadn't really talked to anyone for days. "I was thinking, on my drive. Snow fences are there to prevent death, you know? And crosses mark the death that happened anyway. How human it is! This need to protect life, or mark death if it happens."

He blinked at her a moment, as if deciding whether to continue this conversation. "I hadn't thought about that," he said at last, scratching the wiry curls on his chin again. "What *I'd* been thinking about is the ribbon of roads, which are built on wagon tracks, which are built on walking paths, which are built on animal paths, and what a very human and animal need it is. To travel.

Yeah, we are just *wired* to travel. We like to move. And if we can't? Like, city kids living in poverty? Like I used to be? Well, people will find ways to travel in their brains, aka drugs, and that might be why we have such a problem. Or we start stealing so we *can* travel, also a problem. I almost got pickpocketed at my local grocery in Las Vegas last month by a kid. I grabbed his arm and he said he needed a bus ticket, needed to get home, he was sorry, but he *needed* to travel. Humans are basically just animals with a few extra words."

She snorted agreement.

The man flashed a smile. "I call these thoughts 'Road Thoughts,' kinda like 'Deep Thoughts,' which I used to watch with my dad, and he's like the same age as you, which means you're old enough to remember from *Saturday Night Live,* right? Heh. Anyway, nice chatting with you."

She laughed and felt a momentary wave of connection, and when he stepped out of her way, she waved goodbye to the lip-popping youngster, who balled up his hands and waved backward, at himself. That kid would be middle-aged and creaky with his own cultural references someday, or, at least, one could only hope.

SHE DROVE ON and dropped down into South Park with its blue crags of what she'd read were the Collegiate Peaks—who would pick *college* names for such untamed, uncultivated, wild landscapes, especially when such beautiful words were available? Mount Princeton, good f——ing grief. But it was towering and granite-faced and impressive, and it also signaled that she was getting close.

Snow swooped across the road in ghostly bands—spooky. Being alone suddenly spooked her out. Life spooked her out. Death spooked her out. Probably she should turn the car around. Chicago and a familiar home and her humdrum life were maybe not so bad after all, though those too had been spooking her out.

But no, *onward,* damnit. She just had to think. If the key didn't work—what would she do then? Why, she'd continue to sleep in the car until she worked out a new plan. But no, that wasn't realistic, or desirable, because she was cold and achy and hungry for a real meal and wasn't sure she could take sleeping in the Grey Goose for another night. It was harder than she had thought to be crouched on hands and knees all the time; yes, the sleeping bag and puffy air mattress had been well thought out, but it was still the back of a car. Moving everything over to one side so she could lean half the backseat forward to create a horizontal sleeping area was a drag. Getting out to pee in the middle of the night was a drag. Crawling around inside like a crab was a drag. Having cold feet was a drag—she needed a microwave to heat up a rice pack, rice packs being one of the best inventions known to humankind. Heating up one thing at a time on her tiny butane camp stove—first water for coffee, then a can of soup, then more water for tea—that was a drag. She'd gotten better at it—what a newbie she'd been—but truth be told, so much of this was a *drag*.

On the other hand, the Grey Goose was doing fine, running well despite her two hundred thousand miles, and recently named thus because geese were adaptable, strong, went everywhere, and, when left in peace, were good, steady long-distance fliers. Plus, they headed south in the fall, which is exactly what she was doing.

Yes, it was just fine. Sure, her life did seem deserted and untenanted, suddenly—yes, that was the word—an untenanted life. And sure, she seemed to have an aimlessness of soul. And sure, there was a fogginess that had moved into her brain. And sure, she was still grieving Vincent, guilting over Vincent, even after more than a year! But she had the Grey Goose, she had some keys, she had

America to drive across, she kinda had enough money to make it work, and she had herself, and so, surely, it was just not *that* bad.

She pulled at her eyebrows and earlobes to stay awake. She wondered about Powell and his pot-growing and if he'd go back to school and how he was grieving for his father. She wondered about Apricot, what she'd do when she found out that Ammalie had left her home, and if any of her older-sister instincts would kick in, and how the cancer was. She wondered how Mari was faring through her divorce. She wondered how Levi was. "Levi—pronounce it like the jeans," he had said upon meeting her. Levi, a man like no other. Levi, the customer who made her heart thump. But she had to learn to stop thinking about Levi, she'd never even had a relationship with Levi except for in her mind, and Levi couldn't care less about how she was doing, and it was ridiculous where her brain went.

This was the crux of her new life goal: to change her brain. Like, really *change* her mind. Change what her brain was occupied with. Because, frankly, she didn't want to die this way, daydreaming about an imaginary life—and if Vincent's death had taught her anything, it was that death did not wait around for you to get it together. Life was not what happened in your daydreams. Life was what happened in your *life*. And if your life was stupid and dull, well, that was your own damn fault.

She pulled over for gas at a station in a cluster of buildings that were surrounded by an expanse of pale-yellow dried grass covered in a dusting of white, and this enormous meadow was hugged on all sides by mountains, and the mountains were being hugged by dark clouds that were surely sending down snow. She filled up the gas tank and although she had enough food, she let her hoarding-OCD-ness take over, and she bought three more cans of soup, an extra half-and-half for her coffee, and another sandwich. Back in the car, she didn't even bother putting them in her cooler; she was close enough now. Within the hour.

She glanced at the time and did some calculations in her mind as she chomped on the last bits from the enormous bag of Chex mix that she'd made to save herself money. It was important she get to the cabin before full dark, but certainly during the early evening, when most people would be settling in at home and eating dinner or watching TV. If there was one thing you could count on in life, it was people's patterns.

She figured she had a half hour to kill, so she tried the one person who would offer comfort instead of require effort, and who surprisingly picked up. "Mari! Why aren't you at work?"

"Hello, friend," Mari said. "Because I'm home sick."

"Sick with what?"

"A regular cold that feels surprisingly lousy. Where are you now? Wyoming? And I actually looked at the map you sent. Why are you going in such a weird, convoluted way?"

"Because I want to see this great country of ours! And I'm in Colorado. Looking at blue mountains that are turning white as I speak, and I'm almost to my first real destination. I miss Arlo. And am in need of a pep talk."

"*Arlo?* Who's Arlo? You mean that dog we had years ago, in college?"

"I miss Vincent, I miss Powell, I miss you, but I was also just missing Arlo. I'd love to be road-tripping with Arlo. It's kinda scary, being alone. I look disgusting. You should see me. I feel disgusting."

"I think you're allowed to miss whatever you feel like missing. I thought you didn't really like dogs. Actually, you *did,* didn't you? *Vincent* didn't like dogs. Too much hair to clean up. And you don't *have* to be alone and disgusting, you know. You could have waited and planned this trip with me, for instance."

"I never pressed Vincent about dogs because I've been tired. Everything in the past years has made me tired. I'm going to get untired. By life. It's like a workout, but for the soul. That's what this *solo* trip is. Like those vision quests young kids have to do in some cultures to become a man or whatever? This is my version of that. I'm just delayed by several decades."

Mari breathed a snorfly laugh. "You've been alone too much. You're such a weirdo these days, freaking the fuck out and driving across America despite never having done such a thing, nor ever expressing interest in such a thing. How's the Grey Goose? And whatever else you've named today?"

"My camping stove, I've named it Dude. I am so much more efficient! I can set up my camp table, start Dude, make coffee, watch the sun rise, and without as much misery as when I'd first started, and then I tell Dude thanks—"

"Oh god, you're talking to a camping stove—"

"—and then I get gear packed up and I'm on the road before anyone notices my presence. I also fully know how to use pepper spray. All these years I've been carrying it around but never tried to use it—"

"Oh my god, you're using pepper spray—"

"—but I tried it last night in Nebraska. Works great. I bet the rock outcropping didn't appreciate it, but I was smart enough to not be downwind from it. I truly have learned a few things."

There was an audible, exaggerated sigh. "That sounds so horrible, I can't even express how horrible all that sounds. That's what hotel rooms are for."

"Bleh."

"Convenience and comfort and *safety*. I think maybe you shouldn't be talking to your camping stove. In fact, I think sleeping in the back of your car and talking to Dude, a camping stove, and practicing with pepper spray, well, those are sure signs you should come home." Then there was a pause and a sneeze. "I have already told you this, but I think we can all see your psychology at work here. Vincent didn't survive, and so you are in some sort of survival mindset, and, you know, Ammalie, it's not the apocalypse. There are still hotel rooms and coffee shops."

"It's a *challenge,* Mari. Like, some people *choose* to run marathons. Some people choose to sail across the ocean. Others choose to hike across glaciers. I have no idea why—all those things seem stupid. But those people exist. Explorers. It *all* sounds miserable. Why would they do such idiot things? But this trip is born of the same impulse. I want to prove I'm tough and competent and interesting and therefore beautiful, so that even if no one else loves me, I can love me."

As she spoke, she was staring at the floorboard of her car, at the scattered mail and sunflower seed shells and pear bits, and realized that the envelope containing her car tags was among the mail. She had until the end of the month to put them on, but she needed to remember. She'd once been advised by Apricot, who was a klepto back in high school, that people only got caught when they did *two* illegal things at once, so having up-to-date tags on her car would probably be wise.

"I love you, Ammalie," Mari was saying. "So does Powell. So does your sister. So do lots of people. You are so not alone."

"Also, I want to be fortified for the twists and turns of the rest of my life. Isn't that a good line? I came up with that on the drive."

"That's lovely."

"Fortified with adventure. The way not to get depressed about getting older is to remain a curious learner. Education is fortification. I heard that on an angry talk-radio show, which I forced myself to listen to for a few minutes because of this same impulse—I must try new things, even if I find them confusing! And it's only been ten days! Well, fifty-five years on the planet, which included a year of unexpectedly living alone, and *then* ten days."

Mari sniffled and sneezed again. "Just so you know, you've always been competent. Mother, wife, waitress, human being, all that jazz—your life here was enough."

"Naw." Ammalie felt the sting of truth pounce on her heart. "Naw, that's just not true. Too passive, in action and in communication. Too floaty. Too tired. Basically, I've been a lazy person. Letting Vincent do all the decision-making."

"Maybe because Vincent insisted he do all the decision-making—"

"Or because I let him—"

"—Or because he liked it that way, Ammalie! Cripes, you sometimes drive me *crazy*." Mari's voice verged on angry now. "You've been working your whole life, and, might I add, at a job you stayed at because it was convenient for Vincent and Powell; you could have gone back to school, you could have done anything—"

"I liked waitressing; some people actually like it." Ammalie felt the bark in her voice and took a breath. "And I liked getting out of the house at night, in those early days, so that Vincent had to do the nighttime parenting; heh, the *only* way to get some men to engage is to leave the vicinity." But she knew she was telling a half-truth. It had simply been the easiest path.

"No, you did it because it made life easier for Vincent, who wanted life made simple for him. You married a mildly controlling man. Or not so mildly! I know you hate hearing that, Ammalie, but he wasn't always good for you." Mari sneezed again, and then again, and then there was the sound of the blowing of a nose.

"I am telling you, I actually *liked* waitressing. People-watching and good-enough money and come *on,* Mari, you know it was a cool place! Low-key! And that Burt was the best. And needed me. And also, you don't sound so good."

In agreement, Mari let out a hacking cough, and then managed, "Well, I'm going through a divorce, I have a cold, there are nuclear weapons, and all that stuff we used to protest together still exists, and it gets me down because it *should* get me down and we're *all* tired."

Ammalie crunched a peanut from her Chex mix in her teeth. "Remember our dating days? Music and beer and lots of boy-friends. Surely we had colds then, but that's not what I remember. We were having too much fun."

"Yes."

"We didn't realize."

"We did not."

"The world was lighter, and yet, we felt everything so deeply. But talk about reckless! We'd fall in love with married men. We'd have flings. We'd say, 'Well, I can't control my emotions!' That was our excuse for everything."

Mari snorted and finished the thought. "You can't control emo-tions. But also, not a good idea to let them control *you.* That's what maturity teaches you."

"I hate being a grown-up."

"Yeah."

"Maybe we went too far with that, though. That responsibility thing. I'm going to go back to letting my emotions control me for a brief while." Ammalie scrunched her face, as if saying this truth physically hurt. "You wanna know the hardest thing? Being the only one responsible. Like, the added need for competency. No room for error, no copilot, no one to turn to with a look that means, *Well,* you *figure it out.* But also, the bigger tragedy is this: For the first time ever, I feel I've figured out how to live, but there's no one to notice. I know how to autopay my bills. I know how to cook on Dude."

"I know how to light a grill!"

"Operate my iPad."

"Which cords go to which things."

"And where those cords are."

"Exactly," Mari said. "We've figured out how to *be*."

"And I'm finished parenting, which has rendered me into a more patient, understanding, compassionate person."

Mari went quiet, and Ammalie put her forehead against her steering wheel. When, for the love of god, was she going to stop saying stupid things?

"I wouldn't say you're finished parenting," Mari said. "Powell still needs you. Even if he is being a shit."

"I know," Ammalie said. "Thank you."

Mari coughed. "We're awesome, we know it—that will have to be enough. I gotta go make tea. What's your word of the day?"

"Empyreal. The highest heaven. Pertaining to the sky. That was yesterday's word, but it's prettier than today's word, which is plaguey, as in, plaguey, as in, vexatious."

"Nice. Have an empyreal time, my friend. Don't be plaguey."

"Mari? It will be weeks before I call in."

Mari's voice was suddenly plaguey. *"Weeks?"*

"No cell service where I go next."

"Weeks?"

"It's a sweet off-grid cabin I rented!" Ammalie heard a tremor of nervousness in her own voice. "I know you love and support me. And I love you."

Mari made a sound of resignation. "Okay, friend. I get it. I guess. Go forth—"

"—and kick ass. May the force be with ya and all that jazz."

Ammalie smiled, grateful for how old friends shared your history of phrases or axioms or idioms that made sense to you both.

WHEN SHE CALLED Apricot to say the same thing—no cell for weeks, this being the real turning point of her adventure—Apricot, in her trademark loud, gruff voice, said, "Whatya gonna do if you choke on an apple and there's no one there to whack your back?"

"I promise to chew my food well."

"What if you cut your head?"

"I'll bandage it."

"What if you have . . . I dunno, a stroke?"

A buzzing ring filled Ammalie's ears at such a high pitch that she could barely hear Apricot saying, "Jeez Louise, I can't believe I just said that, Sis. It just sounds *scary.*"

"It's okay, it's okay," Ammalie found herself saying, though tears were rising, not so much over the comment about strokes but because Apricot was speaking the truth. It had all been scary, and suddenly seemed more so, but what she said was, "You wouldn't think it was scary if I was a man."

Apricot made a concession-like sound. "Men. They get to have all the adventures. And then you're doing what? Going to New Mexico to drop off some pottery shards?"

"Arizona."

"To put back what Vincent took years ago? To a place he never invited you to?"

"Right. And . . . yeah, he felt like a shit for picking them up. He always intended to put them back. It will bring his soul peace. It's one thing I can do for him."

Apricot's voice sounded huskier than ever. "You coulda mailed them back to some official, probably."

"Naw, *I* need to put them back. But listen, how are you feeling?"

"Never better, and you take care, kid," and with that, her sister hung up.

Ammalie turned off her phone and stared at the bug-splattered windshield. Calling Powell would be a mistake, she knew, but the low ache in her heart was unmistakably called *missing someone.* She missed him terribly. And yet she also knew that the best way to get him back in her life was to leave him temporarily alone. Not totally alone, but she'd back off, which is what he'd clearly asked for. Indeed, he could not have been *more* clear. So she started the car and drove on.

She was soon at the turn she needed, a county road that darted its way into the mountains. Before making the actual turn, she steered into a gravel pullout. Several cars gunned past her and one driver flipped her off and she realized they'd been behind her for some time—she'd zoned out and forgotten the cardinal rule of being a polite driver and letting faster drivers pass you whenever possible. She hated drivers like that.

Her heart started thumping like a rabbit's foot. "Hey, Thumper. Chill," she murmured, which is what she said when it got like this. Before real panic could hit, she gunned the Grey Goose, took the turn, and drove straight into the mountains. She just had to keep going. She drove by a little cluster of cabins, then past the stretch of forest service lands, and then there were long stretches with very few signs of human life, save the barbed-wire fences. The road turned to gravel, and then bumpy gravel, and then really rutted gravel. She remembered all this on the edges of her memory. Soon she'd see the blue sign of a dancing Kokopelli that would signal the turn.

She started to cry. She supposed it was the memory of this place, coming with Vincent, or maybe the relief of having made it this far, or maybe just stupid perimenopause or whatever the fluctuating hell her body was gallivanting around with. She swiped the tears from her face harshly; she had to drive, after all. Night was not far from descending now, it was full dusk, the blue hour, *l'heure bleue,* and yeah, she should've fucking taken French courses and become a chef or a lawyer or anything but she hadn't and now snow was spinning right at her into the windshield. To the sides, aspens were white-barked and staring at her with their dark eyes. *Change your daydreams, change your actual life,* they seemed to be saying to her. *Otherwise you'll end up breathing bitterness in that last sacred breath of yours.*

CHAPTER 2

The key didn't work. She stared at it, tried again, jiggled it, reversed it, tried the bolt, and then started all over again. It. just. didn't. work.

She had to pee and couldn't think with pressure in her bladder, so she went in the pine-needle-strewn driveway in the near-dark, one hand on the cold Grey Goose for balance. In the twilight, she scanned the dark shape of the fancy wood-and-stone cabin. No flowerpots, no stumps of wood, no decorative rocks.

Where would *she* put a key?

Think think think think please think.

She smelled the rank sweet stench from her crotch. Gross. Another night in the car? Or should she drive hours into a town and rent a room? Why had she thought a key ten years old would work? On the other hand, why not? *She* hadn't changed her lock back home in Chicago in ten years. She pulled up her yoga pants, walked to the door, and put her hand above the doorframe. No key. She picked up some snow-covered decorative rocks and squinted in the last of the light. No key. Maybe it was on the corbel of the porch—is that what those slants were called?—but to check, she'd need more height. She got the cooler out of the car and stepped onto it and stretched up and moved her fingers along the wood.

Key. Yes, key.

Cold and smooth. She pulled it into her palm as she stepped

down. Ha-ha! She loved humans; they were, in fact, incredibly predictable. She turned the key and let herself in, stood in the doorway
looking at the silent home, then dug out her headlamp from her
backpack and moved quietly around. It was much as she had remembered. She glanced at the fireplace longingly, but she wouldn't
build a fire. No light and no fire smoke, nothing that could be seen
from a distance. She did turn up the thermostat, though; the electri-
cal bill wouldn't reflect a small surge for another month, and there
was no way she could sleep for another night being so cold. She
would not turn on any lights, or do anything visible from afar, and
she'd move her car around back, but the house was isolated enough
that no one would notice a headlamp or a candle, of that she was
certain.

She was only going to do things that were invisible. She was
going to embrace the invisible part of being a middle-aged woman,
by god. If that's what life and culture was going to throw at her,
well, fuck. She was going to take it to the extreme.

She warmed a can of soup on Dude—dangerous, she knew, but
it was a roomy house—and then ate and then felt bad about cooking inside, putting another person's home in danger. But she moved
on, put everything away in its plastic tub and her sleeping bag on
the couch, and then took another wander through the rooms, pan-
eled in beautiful beetle kill wood. She whispered aloud her excuse,
so that it would be at the ready, already voiced, natural-sounding:
*It was an emergency. The cell phone died, she'd started feeling woozy
on a hike, she remembered this house. She had stayed here once with her
husband—he was dead of a stroke, yes, it was so sad. She was so sorry.
She just wasn't herself, wasn't feeling herself, this was so unlike her.*

All of it was true, except the cell phone part. She paused at a
bookshelf and stared at the Scrabble game caught in the beam from
her headlamp and felt an old familiar pain—familiar from the last

year and a half, at least—move across her chest. It felt like an actual creature—which is why she called it the Sea Creature—that moved around and occasionally pressed against her heart. She supposed it was just that no one was here to play Scrabble with, although, to be honest, had there been, she might not have played anyway, and would have wished that she was alone.

To distract herself from the shelf of two-player games, she reached for one of the old books, *Hunting-Fishing and Camping* by L.L. Bean, who she hadn't realized was an actual person, not just a catalog from which to see pictures of nice flannel shirts. She flipped through it and found a line about how traveling into the open spaces and challenging oneself teaches people to forget the mean and petty things of life.

Exactly, she thought. That was the plan.

Only when she had put everything back exactly as she'd found it, and her own stuff was nicely consolidated next to Fluffiest Red, her sleeping bag, did she allow herself the hot bath. She ran the water and undressed and climbed into the tub and sighed. This was no ordinary tub. In fact, the tub was the whole reason she had picked this place. It had stayed in her memory as heaven, not because the tub was so fancy, although it was one of the extra-deep ones, but because of how it was positioned: next to enormous windows, a whole *wall* of windows, with moonlit pines and aspen and stars, so many stars, stars and stars and stars.

Surely this was the best way to stargaze—warm, floating in hot water, looking out glass.

She sank deeper in the warm water and kept her eyes on the stars. She was safe.

The particular beauty of this cabin was its bathtub and its isolation. Not a single neighbor, which was the opposite of her entire life experience. Indeed, it had been advertised as being on a hundred acres of mountain land, and she felt like she needed all hundred of those acres.

After some time, she put her distance glasses on and really considered the nighttime sky. Orion's Belt was easy, and his shoulders, and his bow, and Cassiopeia's W, and of course she could find Venus, because Venus was always near the horizon, never in the center of the sky, because it went wherever the sun went, like a partner who wouldn't let his lover out of sight. She didn't know the lesser-known constellations and determined to learn such things now. There was something so settling about them, because who cared too much about small infractions and wrongs when one realized what a small blip in time we all were?

She had the vague notion that she could make herself have an orgasm, which would be the first in more than a year and a half, her last being with Vincent one lovemaking Saturday morning, but that seemed too blasphemous to even wonder about. But also, the sad, honest truth was that it was equally blasphemous to have her body atrophy more fully into menopause and away from something she had liked about herself. She had loved sex. She had loved being sexual. And she and Vincent had really had a pretty good sex life, and she'd never considered how it would feel without sex for more than a year. She really missed it; there was a dead, heavy sorrow sitting in her pelvic region, probably right in her stupid fluctuating uterus, probably the same creature that sometimes moved up to her heart was floating there. "Sea Creature," she said, "I don't want you in my heart *or* pelvis—fuck off. Go somewhere else. Big toe, maybe."

She couldn't masturbate, though, she was too tired and too sad, and so after a half hour of soaking and staring at stars, she climbed out of the tub and dried her body—so pudgy!—with her travel towel and brushed her teeth, put on face cream, and put the items right back in her backpack so that if she had to leave fast, she could, and without a trace. At the last moment, she opened the drawers and found a hairbrush in the third one down. A clean, new-looking brush! A miracle. As she ran it through her wet hair, she focused on the pull on her scalp, how it was so much better than a fork, so much better than fingers. What a fine invention! She decided to steal it. After all, if someone had appeared in her life so in need of a brush, she would have happily handed one over. She'd only steal what she herself would have happily given, had someone asked. She had to assume people would be willing to part with little things, such as if someone stayed in your house and used a bit of electricity, because, well, she simply had to believe that humans would give that much, because *she* would give that much.

Appropriate Poaching, she decided to call it. And in each instance of poaching, she'd do something to right her karma. Offer some gift.

When she was truly bed-ready, clean and warm and relaxed—the first time in days—she looked again in the mirror. She touched the little scar on her temple, now a white thin curl, and then ran her fingers over her thinning eyebrows and pushed back her walnut-colored hair—or what used to be walnut-colored hair but was now being overtaken in haphazard ways with gray and also a lighter color that was the remnants of dye from months ago. It felt nice to be touched, even by her own fingertips. She considered her face and her almost-masculine jawbone and her green-and-brown-flecked eyes, breathed in, and said aloud, "It's been a tough year or two or lifetime on you, kid, but not really, let's face it; but also, you're going to be okay."

She climbed into Fluffiest Red on the couch, and as she quieted her mind and hoped for sleep, she thought of Vincent. Of being here with him. They'd rented this place on a "Grand Road Trip"—

something they'd tried to do every third year. The in-between years were reserved for "Bland Road Trips," which weren't really bland, but it rhymed with Grand, and those trips were the ones they stayed local to save money. It was the third-year trips that were much anticipated and much planned. This trip, they'd come the last year her mother was alive, so young Powell was with her for two weeks, and they'd had the luxury of a vacation of two adults sans kid. It had been glorious, frankly, because sometimes parenting was overrated. Exploring Colorado, hiking sand dunes and blue peaks, talking uninterrupted in the car. When they'd left, she'd accidentally had the key still on her key chain, and somehow, year after year had passed and it was still there.

She had even joked with Vincent in the years after: *I could go back and just let myself in.* She preferred that phrase, *letting oneself in.*

He would smile at this old joke, and eventually, his smile was automatic—the result of its being said too many times, the result of them being too many years together. In response, he would usually bring up their next adventure—planning trips was one of his great obsessions and joys.

She'd made a good choice, coming here. *Well done, you, well done,* she thought as she stared up at the pitched ceiling. This cabin was perfect, being situated rather far back in the Sangre de Cristo Mountains, but more important, she had some assurance it would be empty. She'd contacted the owner about renting it, but he'd told her it was no longer on Airbnb, that his family had become sprawling enough—with grandkids and kids and so on—that he kept it solely for them. And then she emailed him a chatty message inquiring after his family and he had responded with an *I'm just out the door now, in fact, we're all going to Mexico on October first—a big family affair to celebrate my Big 75!* and she knew enough about him to know he meant a private jet, a private house, that he had *that* amount of money, and so she'd written back, *How nice, how lovely, have a really grand adventure, please.*

When she closed down her email that night, she sat in her empty, still house and felt her empty, still life. She'd had a big fight with Powell in which he'd said she was boring and he hated her; then she'd had a boring phone call with her sister about the most mundane of all mundane things and couldn't tell her about the fight because they just didn't discuss real things; and she'd been unable to stop the loop of a daydream of kissing Levi, the regular at the restaurant who felt anything but regular in her heart for literally no reason. Plus, another Chicago winter was coming. Three days later, she found herself on the road.

Now she had to admit, she did feel . . . happy. Sure, she was invisible, irrelevant, and a criminal to boot, and she could maybe end up in jail, but her previous life felt like a jail too, and this felt like, well, *youth.* The curious and slightly naughty and fun-loving Ammalie still resided within.

Three months, three keys, three adventures involving breaking into some truer version of herself. Already, she knew it was going to be far harder than she'd guessed to find a certain clean crispness of body and soul. But at least she knew what she was running from, knew what she was after, and, to top it off, she was washed and warm and had a home to stay in. It was a start.

CHAPTER 3

She woke in the last moments of dark to a creak in the house which she determined to be only a creak. Mumbled "Good morning, honey bird" to herself, and dozed as she watched the sun brighten the snowy mountainside in the distance before she got up to make pour-over coffee using the actual stove in the cabin because she was going through the fuel canisters faster than she'd anticipated.

Her legs were achy, and she realized it was not so much from the drive or the hike yesterday, but rather from being bound in the sleeping bag; she needed to move around more than the bag would allow, and she vowed to unzip it from now on. Perhaps even move to the bed, though she liked being in the main room, where she could see someone pulling up.

But the real question was not the couch or the bed—it was whether or not to stay at all. Was this crazy? She looked out the front door window at the dusting of snow, meaning any tracks she'd left yesterday as she pulled the car to the back would be hidden, and any tracks of someone new would be seen. There was no trace of anyone, including her.

Stay? Or go?

The answer: She'd get in shape. She did a plank to the count of ten and then five sit-ups, and stretched. This day, this very day, was the beginning of a new her. A really really new her.

She got dressed and put on a coat and went outside and sat on a flat rock covered with lime-green lichen and leaned back against the brown-orange bark of a ponderosa and raised her face to the sun. The snow on the trees was unfolding itself into water, dripping in the quiet. *That* was beautiful, like a little chime. She considered the low-growing sage and pine cones and small rocks and dried grasses at her feet and sipped her coffee. The whole scene emitted what she could only describe as *mountain smell*, sagy and piney and fresh. Different from *restaurant smell*. Or *house smell*. Or *Grey Goose smell*. Certainly better than any of them, especially when mixed with the smell of her coffee.

It warmed enough for her to remove her jacket, and the sunlight on her arms felt like a lemony kiss—she thought the phrase absurd, but that's what it felt like. She stared at her appreciative arms and all the sun damage on them, the white spots and dark freckles and a few small red weird things that had popped up in the last year. "You gotta accept this," she said to her arms. "It is what it is. The alternative is worse."

To her right was a pile of what she guessed were elk droppings and an ancient cow patty and a very long nail that looked like one of the earliest nails ever made by humankind. What had such a nail been used for? How did nails get made by hand? When did people stop making them by hand? And what should she do with her day? And what was she *doing*?

Far away, she heard a gunshot, or what sounded like a gunshot, and she stilled, listening for more and feeling a little panicked. Hunting season, maybe? Wasn't October the month her father had gone hunting with his friends? Now her ears were tuned in, and she heard the faraway sky-buzz of a jet and birds calling to one another and the plunk of something falling softly on the duff, perhaps a pine cone. She heard what sounded like the yapping of a dog down by the dirt road, and dripping snow, and what she heard most of all was the silence. The world could be so quiet, really.

She heard herself do the drama-sigh; she was definitely becoming a sigher and needed to stop, so she took out her journal so she could reroute her future. No more sighing. Meaning, no more living a life in which she found herself sighing. She wrote,

New Life Goals for Ammalie So She'll Stop
Dramatically Sighing:

Body is just fine because it has to be. Butt dimples just part of deal. But also,
Could you pleeeeeeeeeease get serious about caring for it?
Meaning, exercise. Meaning, learn. Brain and body <u>active</u>.
Taken together: Take the remainder of your life <u>seriously</u>.
YOU ARE GOING TO DIE!
Be a good mom for Powell. Friend to others. Take care of the defenseless.
DO NOT GET ARRESTED.
Forgive yourself. He would have died anyway.

She held the journal in her lap and decided to stay. And to fully own that decision so she could stop fretting. Decision made. She'd not turn on a light, she'd use minimal hot water and heat, she'd right her wrongs, she'd let go of any last shreds of guilt. She had her excuse ready to go. She'd sit with her berserkly contradictory emotions and come to terms with *all* of them or somehow let them float away into the Colorado sky. She'd find peace—some good-enough, attainable version of it—and that would be that. Her goals were as clear as last night's stars.

• • •

THE SKY WAS somehow so curved that it reminded her of a blue bottle. The air was clean and damp from the melt, the world was as silent as Chicago was loud. Empyreal. She hiked on and moved up the mountain, coming across something that might be bear dung, then the prints of a rabbit and perhaps a fox in the snow, still left in circles under the trees. She was startled by a deer who was startled by *her.* They considered each other, and she wished she could flick her ears as the deer did, though she did stomp one foot in response to the deer's stomp.

Whenever she heard movement, she sought it out; it was always the birds, either ones down low in the grasses or ones up high in the pines. There was also the low roar of something, which she realized was uninterrupted wind moving through the mountains. She watched a raven that seemed to be following her, or at least tracking her, and yakking with a shrill repeated sound that reminded her of a frog. "Yo, eyes in the sky," she said up in its general direction, and it took off, black wings against blue sky.

This is so glory-fucking great, she found herself repeating in her mind, by which she meant: that I can just *go.* One of the hardest parts about relationship—or at least, her relationship with Vincent—had been the pacing. Vincent had always been so slow—she'd always been waiting, ten or a hundred times a day. He'd kept her waiting in the most mundane of ways: To get into the car with everything. To turn the actual ignition. To back up. To park. To sit longer at a meal than she wanted. On a hike, as he stopped to look at rocks. At a grocery store, he considered all the options. He even had long pauses in his sentences when he spoke.

God, she'd tried to be patient, hadn't she? How many times a day?

And perhaps had he sometimes been slow on purpose? To exert some control?

Or had she just imagined that?

A few times, they'd had bad blowups about it. She had simply wanted to move at the pace that she wanted to move. Wasn't that a legit request? Why was he so comfortable making others wait?

Well, now she could. Move at the pace that felt natural.

She wanted to be truthful! Admit it was nice to not have him alongside her! To be so unfettered! And then, as she turned back to look at the empty cabin, she supposed that this was not what she had wanted exactly. Both were true at once. If there was one thing that Vincent's death had taught her, it was that incompatible feelings coexisted all the time.

This is what it is. Miss him and be relieved. This is what it is. I'm alive and he's dead. This is what it is. Her mantra corresponded to each footfall in the forest, with a faraway dog yap sometimes chiming in.

SHE DID NOT go back to the cabin when she'd first had the impulse to do so or even when she'd started cussing with exhaustion and frustration; she kept pushing on because today was Day Uno of her New Vida, which was also going to include learning some Spanish because she was tired of being a white-bread midwestern woman who was unaware of too much. At some point, it was her fault. It was embarrassing. It was small. She would *not* be a Karen, as Powell accused her of being. Or was it a Becky? She couldn't remember names that she didn't assign herself, but anyway, the point was: She'd admit her failings, her privileges, and try to do better. And she'd start now, and mark it by having a Long-Hike Day.

She moved quickly through the aspens, their shimmering yellow leaves still dripping snow. This was close to the same hike she'd done with Vincent. They'd left the cabin and headed up in this general vicinity, though they'd gone much slower, he stopping to finish sentences or to tell a story, which is something he often did, as if walking and talking were not mutually compatible. She stopped twice for photos, and once to stretch, since her back hurt from all the driving and sleeping in her car. Just like the high-country weather, her emotions changed fast, and just as with the weather, she could see them.

"Vincent, hey Vincent," she said softly to the sky, which felt absurd, but how else could she address him? "Love basically is being fascinated with someone, isn't it? And you had lots of fascinations, but I wasn't one of them. You had geology. Stargazing. Bird-watching. Family history and ancestry. Weather stations. The history of the Civil War. Vikings. Viking footwear. Viking sail-making. My god, you even had a stamp collection! All those nights in the basement! I could go on and on and on and you were always down there, ya know? Doing whatever. Anyway. Now I'll find my *own* damn interests."

The raven squawked at her specifically, and the wind blew generally, and her own mind worried for her sanity. But talking aloud felt *physically* good. Crazy, perhaps, but so what? When had society decided that talking aloud to oneself was a sign something was off?

She cleared her throat and started again, loudly now. "I'm feeling shitty these days, Vincent! Grief over aging, grief over you, grief of a job lost, grief about the planet, grief over war—plus my body is still doing whatever the fuck it's doing. But I can get clear if I. just. start. telling. the. truth. So, first and foremost, I might have saved you if I'd been better prepared. Don't give me that *no, no, no* bullshit, because truth was, I might have. I just stood there and I got you water! Water! If I'd called 911 sooner, well, *that* would have been helpful! You didn't need water. I am really, really sorry about that. Please tell me that you died thinking of the truest and best version of our love? That you weren't bitter?"

Her knees buckled then. Of their own accord, almost. As if she needed to be kneeling to say this. She knelt fully and peered at the sky. "Vincent, there's one last thing I need to tell you: I was going to leave you." She paused and then started again, more calmly. "I was waiting for Powell to be out of the house. And Mari and I were . . . planning on doing it together. She's leaving Maximo. That sounds weird, I know! It *is* weird. Two friends timing it so they could go through divorce as a team. But it just became apparent that we were both wanting a divorce, so we decided to do it together, just like we decided to have kids at the same time, remember? Except that she couldn't ever get pregnant, or stay pregnant, so I did it alone. And now she's doing the divorce alone."

She paused. "So, that's the hardest truth. I felt . . . well, we were a sinking ship, and I was close to drowning, so I had to swim away, and I figured you probably felt the same. But I never wanted you *dead*. I really somehow thought you'd be in my life, and wow, I've gotta say, it feels so very strange, to have wanted you gone, but not *this* gone. I had lost you already, you being in your basement all the time—and then I planned to lose you again, divorce-style—and then I really lost you, via death! That all feels really fucked!"

She felt interrupted by something, and so cocked her ear, but all she heard was a bird cawing nearby and a dog yipping far away and the drips of snowmelt on trees. Then she realized she'd been interrupted by a *smell*—the strong vanilla smell of a ponderosa pine. She turned and looked at the tree she was kneeling near, which was rather enormous, in fact. The orange-brown-red bark was actually quite beautiful, and she moved closer so that she could lean her nose into it and pick away a small flake. Then she saw it had a barbed wire wrapped around the trunk, down low, and that one of the loops of wire was reaching out in her direction. She pushed the wire back toward the bark, where apparently it belonged.

But *why*? *Why wire*? Why was there barbed wire around the tree?

Her eyes followed the ancient remnants of strands of barbed wire that were tangled in the undergrowth and then disappeared under the earth in two directions. The tree, apparently, had once been used as a corner fence post.

Well, okay. She stood and turned to go, thinking *Poor tree, it's being strangled, that sucks, people cause so much damage,* but then swung herself back around and studied the tree for real. The loop of barbed wire was clearly digging into the bark. But trees just adapted and did their own thing, right? Although the tree had never *asked* for barbed wire. She felt confused by humanity's sloppiness, but also annoyed that she cared about the situation at all; it was not her problem. She tried to get clear on the situation by listing the basic facts on her fingers, one by one:

Was the wire cutting into the tree's bark?

Yes.

Was the wire needed?

No.

Would the tree do better without the wire?

Yes.

Should she do something about the wire?

Yes.

Was she too tired and lazy to do something about the wire?

Yes.

Should she allow that to be the case?

Fuck, no, she supposed not. Not on the first day of her new life.

She shrugged off her pack. In her emergency pack, she found her multi-tool, which she'd never really used, so she spent time flipping things out and then back, muttering "Huh!" with each new revelation. A screwdriver with a switchable bit! A bottle opener! A knife! And of course, the main tool, which was the pliers and wire cutter, too small for the job at hand perhaps, but certainly the best option. She wedged the blades between one strand of the wire and squeezed.

Nothing. She squeezed so tight that her hand ached; her face scrunched with the effort. Still nothing. She tried again, pressing every bit of strength into that hand, and pressed it into the tree so as to get a good angle, and then a fury took hold and she squeezed all of her anger about everything with a loud and long *stupid fucking fuccck youuuuuu* to everything. But the wire did not cut.

She stopped, rested her forehead on the tree, which now smelled like a whole vanilla factory. Tried again, and then again, and the third time one strand split. The second strand was easier, and the moment that it flew backward—she had to leap out of the way—she could have sworn she heard the tree breathe. She felt a surge of glee—she'd done something right!

She stood underneath the tree and gazed up at its branches meeting blue sky, put her palms against the bark, then hugged the tree and smelled the vanilla gift it was offering back. "I'm sorry you had that strangling you," she whispered into the trunk, and she didn't want to get too woo-woo about it, but she felt the tree thrumming with relief.

Finally, she stepped back and put her mouth on her rasped knuckles, tasted the blood, and winced. They really hurt, a burning-type hurt, and her eyes burned with tears. *With freedom comes pain.* Or at least that's the wisdom she arrived at as the Sea Creature sadly swam around her chest when she pulled out her first aid kit to bandage her aching hand.

CHAPTER 4

Some dog's yapping was unmistakable and insistent and was accompanied by the occasional yowl. Or maybe *yowl* wasn't the right word; she'd never quite heard such a sound. It was back down the road, and always in the same spot, and her brain couldn't figure out a plausible reason for the ruckus. As she sat and drank a glass of red wine, she scanned her memory: There were no houses on the road for such a long distance, and, as far as she remembered, there were no campgrounds here, it being private and not public land.

How far did sound travel? How worried should she be?

She didn't want to drive to go check, of course; someone might see her and take note of her license plate or general presence. Plus—two glasses of wine and snowy, isolated roads and it would be dark soon. Nor did she want to walk that far, though how far was hard to gauge. So she ignored the dog and the human who was presumably with it and hoped they'd just go away. Besides, she'd already done her good deed for the day.

But the yapping did not go away. And dusk was coming.

"No, no, no, no, and fuck and fuck and fuck," she muttered, because checking on this dog and its likely human owner would require so much work. The human would notice her presence; everything could potentially get fucked up; it would ruin everything. But what if the dog—or the person—needed help? She could not, in good conscience, leave a dog yowling so wretchedly in the night.

She groaned and stood. It would be good practice, she supposed—

packing up her stuff, leaving the house as she'd found it. Besides, it would occupy her—what other great thing did she have to do? So she packed up, loaded her car, and drove for ten minutes down the dirt road, taking it slow since icy patches on shady spots made her feel precariously close to the steep edge, and she pictured her and the Grey Goose toppling down a mountain, rolling, rolling, rolling. She saw no dog. The barking continued, though, when she pulled over to listen. Finally she saw movement in the trees, not too far from the road, a midsize dog lunging in her direction but held by a rope or something that kept jerking it back. She looked all around through the forest for a person, but there was nothing else moving. As she had with the wire-bound tree, she felt only confusion. What was she seeing, exactly?

She sat in the car for a moment to assess—always best to sit and watch, she figured. But she didn't see anyone, so she got out and turned on her headlamp and walked closer, close enough to see the dog up close—white chest and gray mottling and very fluffy; perhaps a mutt with a lot of border collie?—and then saw that a stream of blood was meandering down the white fur on the forehead and was also smeared across the floppy gray ear. Christ almighty, it was hurt! It was tied to a tree. It was still quite young, not quite puppy-young, but not yet grown, its paws being too large to fit the rest of the body. A teenager of sorts. A bloody, skinny, half-grown pup.

When she approached, it lowered itself, cowering, and then rolled to its side, submissive; and, squinting, Ammalie could see it was a she, and that there was no blood on the underside, just on the head.

"What's up with you?" She glanced around—white aspen and green pines and deepening blue sky—and then carefully approached wearing thick leather work gloves from her Survival Bucket, but the dog was clearly not going to bite her. It was tied or tangled with an old rope collar to an aspen tree. She freed the dog, and then, because the dog didn't move, she brought over her water bottle and her camp kit bowl. The dog sat partially up and lapped the water furiously as Ammalie scanned the area, and then tried to scan the dog's head.

Had the dog been tied up by a hiker?

Had the dog escaped from a nearby home and gotten tangled? But no, the rope had been tied in a knot around the tree.

The longer she stared at the cut head, the more her brain started to make sense of what she was seeing. She reached out to wipe away the blood with a bandanna, and while the dog ducked, it didn't snarl or wince, and so she poured water on the blood and gently swiped again on the forehead, above the right ear. The dog had been cut with something sharp. Cut purposefully. Cut with three straight lines! They seemed to form a K, or something similar, and it confused her even more. Cut to tattoo? Or to punish?

"What the *fucking fuck*? Who would do this to you? And *why*?" she whispered to the dog, and the dog looked up from the water bowl at the same time her heart really started thumping. Fear, but also a surge of anger blasting with hot fury in her chest and cheeks—truthfully, she'd have liked for about half of humanity to be wiped from the face of this special planet; whether it was nuclear warheads or abused dogs, there just wasn't time for this shit anymore.

She ran her fingers over the dog, feeling bony ribs, and paused on the dog's haunches at a raspy area. She parted the fur to peer by headlamp. Surely, by god, those were not cigarette burns? She bit her lip. She should *go*. Something here was fucked up. Tears flurried into her eyes. Where was the nearest humane society? Or veterinarian? What should she do? And god, why couldn't she think? She felt so foggy-headed and confused. The only clear thought she had was a certain knowledge that she wasn't thinking through stuff the way she used to; some sense of perspective or clarity was lacking. So she tried listing truths:

> One: The dog was hurt, though not in a life-threatening way, but it shouldn't sit bleeding out here all night long.
> Two: There seemed to be no human around, which was good.
> Three: The dog might be associated with a bad dude who might show up, and that was not good.
> Four: Night was now closing in. The vet clinic would be closed, and what was the nearest town, anyway? That little cluster of buildings near the gas station? Surely there was no vet clinic there.
> Five: She'd had the wine, and shouldn't drive.
> Six: Yes, she was going to drive the dog back to the cabin. Obviously. And then she'd take it from there.

She dug her fingernails into her head to think, which is when she heard another sound. A low male voice, something about *Where the fuck are you, you bitch?*

"You fuck," she hissed in the direction of his voice. The words came out of her before she could stop them, and she slapped her palm over her mouth. Then she whispered to the dog, "Not you. *Him.*" Then she and the dog both cocked their heads in the direction of the man's voice, which now sounded like a vague string of cursing, though she couldn't make out any specific words. But it was clear that a man was walking through the trees and coming toward her as dusk was turning into cold night, and now her heart was really going berserk. She wrapped her fingers around her pepper spray with one hand and put her other on the soft nose of the dog. *Shhhhh, shhhh.* The last thing she wanted was for the dog to start barking again. Then a clear phrase came out of the forest, much closer now: "Where'd you go, you *fucking fucking fucking* bitch? You bark all goddamn day and *now* you're quiet?"

Without further thought, Ammalie untied the rope and gathered the dog in her arms at the same time she heard the man. "Where are you, you *fucking bitch*!"

You fucking bastard, she thought, but she kept her mouth closed this time as she lifted the dog slowly, bending at her knees, trying to ascertain if she had the strength to do this. The dog was heavy and bulky and she stumbled forward, but quietly. She couldn't look over her shoulder at the same time as walk in the dark, so instead she just winced and prayed and coaxed herself, *Just go go go go go.*

By the time she got to the Grey Goose, she was gasping, but the dog had thankfully stayed quiet except for some low grunts. She'd left behind her water bottle, but it didn't matter—this littering was justified! She heaved the pup into the Grey Goose and winced again as she started the car—anyone would be able to hear that!—and at the same moment heard gunshots. *Boom, boom, boom.* She ducked, instinctually, but drove off, fast, no headlights, wheels spinning the dirt, glancing in the rearview mirror, though no one appeared on the dirt road in the darkening sky.

Then the road turned, and she was out of view. She turned on her lights. "Glory hell!" she yelped, and she could not think and so drove past the cabin and to the top of the ridge. She was hoping to throw anyone off the scent that she was staying there, and also just needing a quiet minute to fucking *think.* And to get her heart to stop thundering. When she found a pullout a good distance past the cabin, she put one hand on the dog and powered up her phone for the first time, and stared. She'd been hoping to go a full month without it—part of her being a true female explorer and all—even if there was cell or Wi-Fi at the cabin, but something about a lit-up phone just brought security, and that was what she needed now. The feel of it in her hand helped her breathe. Beside her, the dog panted. She panted. They panted in unison.

She tried to slow her heartbeat as she read her texts. A few from the usual suspects—Mari, Apricot, the car place reminding her she was due for an oil change—and one call. But wait, *what*? She stared at her phone in confusion as she listened to the message.

Somebody named Officer A. Alzone. The police had called *her*?

"This is the Park County Sheriff's Office," the message simply said. "We're wondering if you can give us a call immediately. Again, this is Officer A. Alzone."

What, what, what, what, what? Oh god, she'd been caught breaking into the house. Or stealing a dog. *Already?* But that didn't make sense!

She had all her stuff in her car. She should just go. Except that she'd wanted to wipe down countertops—to erase fingerprints as well as be polite—and do a once-over on the house. Although the police didn't have her fingerprints; she'd never been arrested for anything, had she? Just that one time in college for underage drinking, but they hadn't taken her prints.

And she was a bit tipsy!

And also, *how* had she been caught? Who had seen her?

The darkness felt stunning, the trees and sky being nearly indistinguishable. The cold felt stunning; she was shivering badly now. The dog's injuries felt stunning. The phone call was stunning. Her slowness seemed stunning. She was sitting in the car in the dark, shaking even though she'd turned on the heat, when the phone rang, startling her so much that she yelped. She looked down. The same number: the sheriff. *Oh no oh no oh no,* and she started to cry and thought *Just fucking do it, face the music,* and answered before she could back out.

"This is Ammalie," she sniffled. She put the phone down and on speaker.

"Ammalie Brinks?"

"Yes."

The woman on the other end of the phone sighed. "We've been trying to reach you—"

"I'm sorry. I'll leave right now. Can you tell the cabin's owner— also, the dog, well, it's hard to explain, but the dog—there's a guy, a guy who I think is bad—"

"Were you on Kenosha Pass yesterday?" the woman interrupted her, briskly, and clearly annoyed. "Your vehicle is a gray Subaru, Illinois license plate RME909?"

"Um, yes." Ammalie squinted hard at the dog, as if that might squeeze out the confusion in her brain. She touched the greenstone and brass key on her necklace and then reached out to push her hand into the dog's fluffy neck fur. The dog whimpered, and then three gunshots sounded from far away. "Yes. It's me. I'm Ammalie Brinks and I'm so sorry—"

"There was a series of car break-ins, including one that—"

"Uh, there's somebody shooting and I found a dog—and wait, my phone, wait, what?"

"Car break-ins, including one that went badly—"

But more gunshots had Ammalie pressing the gas, U-turning on the dirt road so fast that rocks spun, and she gunned it. The phone lost the signal of its own accord. She drove back to the cabin, car bumping mightily on gravel ruts. It seemed crazy to drive back *toward* the danger, but at least there she could lock the doors. Now she felt furious and strong. It was her goddamn house—kind of. And she deserved to feel safe there. And who the hell hurts a dog?

She wanted to strangle whoever it was. *Lock the door, lock the door, lock the door. Safe, safe, safe.*

SHE PULLED INTO the area at the back of the house, walked the dog in, locked the door, cleaned off the paws quickly by the light of her headlamp. When she let go of the collar, the dog walked inside, but slowly, head drooping, not trotting as a dog normally would. Ammalie moved fast, putting down bowls of water and leftover rice with slices of turkey, which is all she had. The dog gobbled and drank and then lay down right there, by the food, and closed its eyes, and so she ran and found it a thick blanket, the hard floor not looking comfortable at all, and coaxed the dog onto it. The pup put her head between her paws and closed her eyes, as if that was all there was to be done.

Ammalie gathered a knife, a baseball bat she'd seen in a closet, and her pepper spray. She also had her car keys at the ready, not only to drive off if need be, but so that she could press the red alert button on them—her car had been made the first year they were available and she always figured that an annoyingly honking car would be a good alarm; someone might eventually come see what it was about. She also had her phone on, next to her, and set to Wi-Fi calling, so that she could call 911 if need be, though that, of course, would lead to other problems.

She sat on the kitchen floor beside the dog and stroked her neck and gently touched the cut on the head, trying to calm herself. It was painful to see, the soft fur streaked with blood, but she could tell the bleeding was stopping. Ammalie ran her hands over the dog's ribs and legs and watched the dog's reaction—no wincing, no pulling away.

"Horrible people are out there," she said to the dog, who thumped its tail on the floor. "I'm so sorry."

She bit at her fingernails and then picked at the skin around them. So, the police were coming. Surely they could ping her cell phone or triangulate it or whatever it was called, and they were coming.

Well, fine. She had her story ready to go. She'd make sure the dog went to a shelter. Surely she'd be arrested and fined or whatever, and she'd call Mari, who would call Maximo's brother, who was a lawyer, and Maximo himself was a paralegal, and in the end, it wouldn't be so bad, would it? Who would really put a middle-aged grieving possibly-crazy woman in jail for very long for simply staying a few nights in a house?

The Panics were coming. She had to do something repetitive and calming or her fingernails would soon be shreds. In the Before Days, she would have counted tip money, lining up bills, or perhaps opened a drawer and straightened the items, or, if at work, wrapped the silverware in cloth napkins. She needed to touch things. Line them up. Make sense of them. So she looked around the room and her eyes settled on the small first aid kit she'd used to bandage her hand, and then the other two larger ones she'd brought in and set by the door so they wouldn't freeze.

Her Holy Trinity of first aid kits, each with its own specialty.

My god, yes, that's what she needed. Safety. Preparedness. Tangible help. She laid them out on the floor by the window, where moonlight was streaming in, and put the lanterns and headlamps nearby, and then unpacked each one, lining up its items outside the container, and the dog walked over and joined her, curling up near her thigh.

"Car camping enthusiasts should be jailed. But so should first aid kit makers," she said to the dog, if only because talking felt calming. "All of them, everywhere. They should be jailed for offering a false sense of security, by offering items that are almost of no value. For example, now. Your cut head. Nothing in a stupid premade, store-bought first aid kit would be all that useful. No Band-Aid would be of any help. What one really needs is gauze, a *lot* of gauze, not some stupid package with *one* wimpy piece of gauze." She held up the enormous package of gauze she'd put together herself and showed it to the dog. "What one really needs is a long bandage to wrap around the head, possibly in a couple of directions, depending on the length and location of the cut, because heads are round and hairy or furry, depending on the creature, and Band-Aids won't stick. You see what I'm saying?"

The dog thumped her tail.

"Why do we live in a world where first aid kits are so inadequate?"

The tail thumped.

"Why do we live in such a world at *all*?" Her voice was so distraught that it worried even her, so she went for something calmer. "Do border collies have tails? Or are you . . . an Aussie? Or a mutt? I don't know much about dogs."

The dog thumped her tail even more.

"What do you want to be named?"

The dog cocked her head and then put it back between her paws.

"Stupid, stupid little Band-Aids, sure, you might want a few butterfly Band-Aids, especially if your forehead would scar, like mine did after my accident at Avogadro's Number—that's the restaurant where I waitressed—but seriously, if you were out in a forest and got hurt, literally the last thing you would care about is a paper-cut-size Band-Aid. Like, I bet ninety-nine percent of the tiny Band-Aids are never used by anyone, anywhere, at any point in time. Except for perhaps children, but only because they like to stick them everywhere, but that's because they are being used as stickers." While she talked, she lined up the items, first one way, then another. "All first aid kit makers should be sued for stupidity. But of course, what I really mean is that all dog abusers should be sued and jailed and perhaps swiped off the face of the planet, though very few people are brave enough to say that and mean it. I mean it. Rapists and child abusers and animal abusers. Gone. I'm sorry someone did this to you."

She put ointment on the small round scars—some were healed and some were pink and new, and while she wasn't sure what they were, she *was* sure they were sore and painful. Then she ran her fingers across the dog again, feeling for broken bones or other injuries, and remembered that once upon a time she'd wanted to be a nurse, which is what her mother had been. Too late for that now. She'd be dead of old age before she got through school.

"My emergency kits are the most perfectly organized and complete kits known to humankind. I have three of them, each unique. Here's what you need, what every car should have." As she listed each item, she picked it up and showed the dog, and then leaned down to put a checkmark on a list she'd made for each container:

> Water bottle: You need a way to carry it.
> Pan to boil water: Water is fairly useless if it will kill you.
> Matches: To make fire to do so.
> Water purifying tablets if you cannot make a fire.
> Water itself: Humans' weak spot, as anyone in Flint,
> Michigan, could sadly attest to.

She heard herself make a gasping intake of breath. My god, that man was out there. He might burn *her* with matches or cigarettes, cut her, abuse her. She shook her head, *no,* as if to shake off the fear, and continued:

Freeze-dried meals, to sustain one during mini-crises,
humans having annoying caloric needs.

Bags of beans and rice, to sustain one during long-term
crises—ditto.

Fish hooks, wire, rope, to sustain one during really long-
term crises—ditto.

Updated medicines, both prescription and the few actually
helpful OTCs—pain and infection being a biggie.

Space blanket, tarp, heat packs; warmth a biggie since
humans' caloric needs aren't really enough to keep them
warm.

Knife to cut things, and, conversely, duct tape to bind them
together.

Pepper spray—for bad people and the occasional bad
animal.

Journal and pen—because clear thinking is essential.

Flares

"And this," she said, fingering her greenstone Māori necklace with the thick key, a gift from Vincent when he returned from New Zealand and asked her to marry him. "Because emotional survival matters too. We all need a charm or something. I've turned into a prepper, and preppers know about emotional needs too."

She stopped lining up her items and looked out the window at the dark silhouettes of trees lit by moonlight. She tried to breathe. In through the nose, out through the mouth. A few months ago, she'd read an article about an inmate who died of dehydration as he'd been screaming for water. This had led to a short obsession with reading about death by dehydration. Dehydration death, she knew now, was torture. Cells shrink, organs fail, delirium sets in. It's terribly painful. And the presence of water didn't always solve the problem. Eighty percent of global diseases were waterborne; a child died of water-related illness every twenty seconds. She wished she could forget facts like that, but she couldn't.

"I brought Vincent water in his moment of death," she murmured, staring outside, listening intently for any sound that would signal danger. "A glass of water that didn't save him, but it saved you, didn't it? You wouldn't have made it much longer. Nothing here would have saved Vincent," she whispered. "But I saved you."

As if in response, the dog got up, walked to her bowl to lap water, then walked back, turned in a circle, and sat down with a thump, and so Ammalie hugged her, and took a big, wavery breath. She was okay. They were okay. If a man came, the dog would start barking, and she had her pepper spray and knife at hand.

"Travel Pouchy is smallest and is for my backpack," she whispered, holding it up, needing desperately to be touching things, to be speaking. "Duffel Pouchy is for my duffel bag, and contains not only a first aid kit but travel comfort items, such as eyedrops, dental floss, tweezers—things you won't die without, but which make life drastically more comfortable. Okay, I'm feeling better now; it's passing." She scratched the dog's neck, could feel the calmness return to her voice and heart. "And for the grand finale, this bucket is called the Survival Bucket and is the most important thing to grab in a moment of need, okay? You could survive with this thing for a while." Just touching the plastic bucket made her feel better. Having the dog around made her feel better. Having Fluffiest Red beside her made her feel better. Having walls around her made her feel better. Because out there was real *danger*.

"See how ready I am? See how safe we are? I'm going to name you Lady Shackleton, because he survived and that's the best survival story known to humankind, and *Endurance,* his ship, was just found. We all know his *wife* probably prepped the trip—women do all the work! And they didn't get to explore—what bullshit! But times have changed, it's time for women; and we're better explorers, because we're not off to ransack some country or plant a flag. No. We're seeking wisdom and internal truths in addition to the physical journey. Different plotlines all together. So don't worry, we're going to be okay. I hope no asshole is looking for you. My guess is not. I bet he's lazy, and I bet he's a coward. Did he have a car? Was he hiking? Does he live nearby? I myself am not going to sleep very well tonight. That I admit. But don't worry, I have it covered. I'll pepper-spray the hell out of him."

She buried her face in the dog's soft fluff again and started to cry, and the dog licked her hand, and although this was all more than she'd bargained for, at least, well, she had a *story*. An event. An interesting occurrence about something she *did*. And when was the last time she'd really had one of those?

CHAPTER 5

Lady stood up and yawned in Ammalie's face, and so she woke to rows of canine teeth in her view, dog breath in her nose. With unmistakable and universal body language, Lady conveyed she wanted out, which sent her heart thumping as she sat up. What if that man was out there? Ammalie jogged from window to window, looking out, and then opened the door cautiously and with pepper spray in her hand. The man had been in her dreams all night, a dark shadowy looming figure that kept her awake during the darkest hours. She listened with every fiber of her being, but now the sun was lighting the mountains, and soon Lady was back of her own accord, panting and tail-wagging. Ammalie looked out at the forest one last time, then bolted the door when she closed it.

Then Lady was following her around as she made rice for the dog and a big pot of vegetable soup for herself. She cleaned the kitchen so that it was as she'd found it, except for the extra soup in the fridge and freezer. Only then did she have the idea to look for dog food, and sure enough, in the hall closet she found a lidded bucket. She gave some of the kibble to Lady and stretched and journaled and waited for the police. They'd called her, they'd triangulate her cell, and although what she was doing didn't seem that wrong, she supposed breaking and entering was a big deal to some.

In the afternoon, she went outside to see if she could chop wood—there was a woodshed with an ax, but after lifting the ax a few times and having it waver around, she had to snort at her lack of strength. Plus, of course, chopping would create noise. Instead she resorted to stacking the existing wood more neatly. She'd try to leave this place a little better than she found it. Lady followed her around, calmer than she thought a young dog should be, and indeed, Ammalie felt calmer than she thought *she* should be. Surely, the police would come. But until then, she'd continue on. So be it.

There were still many hours to pass in a big long Day Two of her New Vida and the rest of her life, so she went back inside and climbed a steep set of stairs to look in the loft, where there were twin beds and a closet, and in the closet were some tubs marked ART SUPPLIES, JEWELRY-MAKING SUPPLIES, CAMPING SUPPLIES, FLYTYING SUPPLIES, and MISC, and it made her happy to know that everyone, everywhere, made their own essential kits of various sorts. She was taking down the jewelry-making supplies when she heard a car door slam.

"No," she said, as if that would make it go away, and then she hugged Lady to her and said, "Shhhh, shhhh, don't woof, it's the police or the bad guy, maybe they'll go away. They can't just walk into locked houses, after all. That's unlawful entry. But oh glory, fuck, fuck, fuck." The reality of it all was hitting her, and she sank to the floor of the closet to hug the dog. Someone was opening a car door; she could hear music coming from the car. Oh, god, what had her plans been? And police don't play music, do they?

Didn't she have a Plan A and Plan B? Plan A was to state her excuse and run past someone and speed away. Plan B was to hide. Or no, Plan B was to surrender. And if the person was bad, she supposed Plan C would be to fight. But with what? Jewelry-making supplies?

She could hear that the person was still at the car since the music was still going. Fine. Fuck it. She ran down the stairs, followed by Lady, grabbed everything she'd placed by the door, and ran upstairs right at the moment that someone fiddled with the key and lock and entered the house. She slipped herself and the dog into the closet, panting, hugging her things to her. Lady didn't seem to be inclined to bark at all—in fact, she hadn't barked since the barking that drew Ammalie's attention in the first place. Maybe her throat was sore. She was, however, content to lie down and put her head on Ammalie's lap when Ammalie sat crisscross on the closet floor in the corner.

Ammalie's heart was thumping—*shhh, Thumper, shhh*—and she put her hand to the greenstone necklace. Oh, god, what was she doing? Oh, god, what would jail be like? Oh, god, this hiding strategy was worse because now it was clear she was purposefully trying to evade the law! She had to immediately pee, and before she could stop herself, she did, which Lady gently sniffed. She looked down at her wet crotch and the dog's nose as she listened to some shuffling downstairs.

"Don't bark," she breathed into Lady's fur. "Don't bark." She breathed in to the count of seven, then out to the count of seven—or was it supposed to be seven and four? Or four and seven?—and tried to think it through:

She'd wiped down the tub, so there would be no residual water.

She'd rubbed the bathmat to erase footmarks.

She'd left the kitchen clean, no evidence of food, except the containers of soup in the freezer and fridge. All trash had been taken out to her car, and the car was behind the house and in a pocket of trees. Only one small window faced that direction, north, so the car was not visible from the house, and a new dusting of snow had fallen. There were two containers of water and food on the floor for the dog, but they were by the trash can and maybe out of sight?

Then she heard humming.

A woman!

She felt the energy notch down an octave. A woman, a woman, a woman! Thank god! She likely wouldn't be killed. *Women should run the world* was her first thought, and her second was, *Hollywood was definitely one of the Great Offenders, right up there with first aid kit makers and travel-video makers, because people never peed their pants in movies.* She had even peed when she'd found out Vincent had died. And why didn't she put a bucket in the closet for just that purpose—she hadn't thought it through! And water! And some food! Why hadn't she prepared for this scenario?

Calm down, Thumper, calm down. She put her head on Lady's shoulders. There was more humming, the sound of items being plonked into a trash can, so, okay, she'd run downstairs, surprise the woman, apologize, run out of the house with the dog, get to her car, and drive quickly. Keep driving and never be found. All would be well.

She felt with her fingertips in the dark closet to make sure she had the keys, her purse, her backpack with her laptop and journal and first aid kit. She'd miss Fluffiest Red, but she'd just take the backpack and purse.

Then she smelled salvation.

Window cleaner.

Oh, hallelujah. This woman was a housekeeper! She'd be gone in a few hours! Not an Airbnber, not a stray family member, not someone staying the night, and not the police. Glory, glory. The cleaner surely would not be cleaning this loft, and if she and the dog could just stay quiet . . . quiet . . . quiet . . . She hummed it in her own mind over and over. *Be quiet. Be invisible.* And that was not so difficult. She held still until she heard the sound of a lock and a door.

* * *

THE HOUSE CREAKED but lapsed back into a silence that lasted long enough for her to tiptoe out and peek down the stairs. No car in the driveway. A bit of new snow showed only the tracks of one car, coming and departing, and so she let Lady out from the closet and she went bounding down the stairs, happy to be free.

Amazing!

She snorted in delight. Amazing that she was actually, literally, wildly invisible.

She was *this* minimally existent!

She put her hands on her knees and bent over, laughing out the stress, laughing out the joy, as the dog circled her legs. As she stood up, she felt a wave of dizziness hit her; the room tilted ever so slightly, but she grabbed onto the counter and laughed again. She had planned for such a thing—living without much evidence of living—and it had worked!

She was a superhero, except she had to pee again! She ran into the bathroom. It was newly cleaned; she could smell it. She put her wet undies and yoga pants into a plastic bag, changed into fresh clothes from her duffel, then looked around the house. Yes, the soup and dog food were gone—damn—but that had been the only evidence. Then she saw something new on the kitchen table. It was a sign that said, WELCOME, KAT. In smaller print it said, *Mr. B asked me to confirm you'd arrived safely on Monday. Please text the number below when you arrive (I leave Tuesday for a vacation and want to know you're all settled). Enjoy.*

The dizziness calmed even more as her blood pressure righted itself. She had until next Monday—nearly a full week—to skedaddle. *And you know what?* she thought. *I'm going to take advantage of every last minute.*

* * *

SHE BOUGHT DOG food, a dog bed, and dog toys in the first town that had a real store, which was an hour away. Then she got groceries and wine. Only then, with her car loaded, did she drive into a parking lot and turn on her phone. Her brain had been circling and circling around car break-ins. What did she have to do with that?

When she was connected to the right person, she said bravely, "So. This is Ammalie Brinks. You called me, but I was in the wilderness and my phone cut out. I'm sorry."

"Oh, yes," the woman said. "We wanted to question you about some theft from vehicles at Kenosha Pass. We're seeking to identify owners of the cars parked there during this incident. But the person in question has been caught. With the help of some photos you took, actually. But unless you had something stolen or that is missing, we don't need your assistance anymore."

Ammalie breathed out, in. "Sorry, I'm . . . I'm feeling slow today."

"You took a photo of a newlywed couple? In the background was your car and plate, which is how we tracked you down. Two cars down from you was a Nevada plate. The occupants of that vehicle were caught with a great deal of stolen items in their car."

"A Nevada plate? I met a man—with a cute kid—"

"That would be the one, yes. He and his partner."

"But no. He was out hiking with the kid. I stopped and talked to them!"

"Yup. While he hiked and kept watch, the woman was going through people's cars. She's a pro. Knew which car doors opened, had the latest in technology. Just so happens one of those cars was my daughter's car—she was out hiking with her boyfriend—hence my extra interest. Not only that, but they stole some meds, nearly killed someone. Bad situation. Heart trouble. Consequences. There are consequences to actions." She said this fiercely; it was clear that no one should mess with this woman's daughter or people's health. "Thank you for your time. Sorry to bother you."

"But, wait," Ammalie stuttered. "You don't need me to—you don't need me? For . . . anything?"

"Not unless you're missing anything."

She found herself laughing. "I guess my car looked too shabby to bother with."

"Or you might have just been too visible from the road or something. Anyway, we have all the evidence we need. The women you'd photographed? They are the ones who first called it in. A whole bunch of wedding gifts missing, some very expensive. They showed us the photos on their phone. We had four license plates to go by, one being yours, one being the thieves—"

"But," Ammalie rambled on, "it's just that . . . a woman breaking into cars *while* people were hiking? She just . . . it's just so *brazen*."

The officer burst out in a hard, bitter laugh. "Well, not all criminals are hardened-looking men, you know. Too many cop shows! Some are women. Young women with a kid and a husband. And bad ethics." She made a tsking noise. "Breaking in, stealing stuff."

Ammalie suddenly felt quite dizzy again—one of the worst sensations ever to be invented by the body, and clearly brought on by stress. She pushed her hand into the dog's fluff and then steadied herself on the steering wheel. "But . . . were they homeless? Did they need the money for the trip? Maybe they needed gas money?"

The woman snorted. "Doesn't matter, now does it? Stealing is stealing. Taking from someone else is *wrong,* now isn't it? I personally think many Americans have forgotten a few basic rules on how to live. Have yourself a nice day. Thanks for taking those photos," and before Ammalie could stutter out any more confusions, she'd hung up.

* * *

"Mari," she blurted into the phone. "Mari, Mari, Mari, I'm having a real adventure here!"

Mari blew her nose in a surprisingly loud honk. "I know, I know. We discussed this. A hero's journey. Frodo after the ring! Odysseus! Luke and the Death Star! Ammalie and the American West! But just admit it. It would be easier to be home, watching TV, and getting take-out, and then, well, dying, as we all do. Why are you calling? You said it would be weeks."

Ammalie laughed. "I'm having fun and I wanted to tell you. I'm sitting in my car, watching a horse galloping across a field, and every once in a while it just bunches to a halt at the end of the fence, as if objecting to the fence, then it turns around and goes the other way. Poor thing! But also, so beautiful. All these snowcapped mountains. It is kinda wild. Wild and glorious."

There was a stretch of silence. "I wish I wasn't sick. Maybe I'd cancel all my appointments and come visit you. You're starting to convince me. And after all, don't heroes have companions fated to go along? Wise counsel? Yoda? Princess Leia? Mari the Great? Didn't we learn that in Dr. Henze's class way back when?" Then she added, with a bit of nostalgia in her voice, "That was the best class."

"Exactly, exactly! Mari, I'm on a *heroine's* journey and that means it's an *internal* journey for self-*actualization* and that frankly is far more exciting than hiking across Antarctica and I have a *dog* and the most amazing views of the nighttime sky and I sorta tried to *chop wood* unsuccessfully but I did *save a tree*!" Ammalie could hear the delight in her voice. She was so relieved she could nearly cry. The police were not after her.

"So many questions have I," Mari said dryly. "And I'm glad you didn't go weeks without calling me. And yes, we all know that women are more interesting. Obviously. Enough with the battles and the rings, who the fuck cares! We need new stories! How about wise living on Planet Earth?"

"Exactly!" Ammalie watched the horse trot up and down and fling itself into the occasional rear. "But you? How are you?"

"As you know, we all get bitter or better as we age—and I am hoping for better. Maximo has moved quietly into the basement. No big fight. No big objection. Which made me think: I don't think I'm getting bitter or better. I feel . . . flat. We feel flat."

Ammalie watched the horse, the mountains, the horizon. "Exactly. Me too. Mari, I have a serious question here. You'll be single again soon. You ever think about falling in love again? A man giving you that look? That look that makes you feel not-flat? And then you realize it's not gonna happen? Because we're not thirty?"

Mari paused. "Maybe."

"Maybe, or yes?"

"Maybe I'd love to feel love again. A partner to witness stuff . . . That seems like a good idea, like something I want, yes."

"Yeah, but do you *daydream* about falling in love?"

"I'm too preoccupied."

"Come on, you do so daydream."

"Okay, maybe."

"But here's the tricky thing! In your daydreams, are you the age you are now?" When there was no answer, Ammalie continued. "The truest truth about me is this: My daydreams are not about a fifty-five-year-old me. They are about an earlier me. Are we at an age when daydreams need to *change tenses*?"

Mari coughed and honked her nose. "Explain yourself."

"When I was twenty, my daydreams featured a twenty-year-old fabulous version of me! In my thirties, I dreamed of me in my thirties! But not now. Now, I have to imagine a *previous* version of myself. This is the main difficulty of growing old, isn't it? Suddenly your daydreams become pure fiction!"

"Aw, Ammalie—"

"I am no longer physically the same person I am in my head. That's a hard thing to reconcile! That's all. That's all I want to say. I'm just being real." Ammalie's happy energy suddenly twisted as fast as a storm, and tears flurried into her eyes. She could hear the thickness in her voice. "I've lost my job. My son doesn't need me. I'm not married. I no longer attract a gaze. Not that I should have ever needed that. But somehow I did. Who am I relevant to? Huh? Life is more lonely than I thought it would be."

"I'm sorry. I'm so sorry," she heard Mari saying over and over, because somehow Mari knew just how badly she'd been hurting.

Ammalie sniffled. "Aw, thanks, friend. I guess I just don't *want* to daydream about being a wise woman, a helper, a sage, an elder, a crone. I want to daydream about being thirty and hot. The truthiest truth here is embarrassing. I want a *man* to notice my competency and adventurous self, and I want a *body* that is attractive to a *man,* and I want a *man's* arms wrapped around me, and I want a *man*. Ugh, it's so horrible to say. I'm such a petty, vain, empty, *reliant* soul." She hung her head and looked at her soft, pouchy belly and the stains on her cheap shirt and snarled at them.

Mari chuckled. "I love you. Clichés are clichés for a reason, I guess. They exist because there's some truth in them. Midlife crises are real. You are not alone in this. Look at the amount of money women spend on youthful serums and surgeries! I'm glad you're doing this trip, Ammalie. It's an important time in our lives. I know I kid you about it, but I think there's something inherently important about what you're doing."

"Thanks," she sniffled.

"Another real-life thing I've been wondering, Ammalie. How are you affording this? A cabin in Colorado? Did Vincent's life insurance stuff get worked out finally? I thought he didn't have any after all?"

Ammalie watched the horse, now standing and satisfied, and then glanced at Lady, sleeping in the back. "Yeah. He did. Got it worked out. That's how I'm affording the rental." She simply could not tell Mari the full truth, which was: She simply wouldn't do it. Spend money from a man she was going to leave, whom she hadn't helped in a moment of need. If the money came through, it would go to Powell. And meantime, she would . . . well, live for free, by breaking into people's houses.

"Vincent would have wanted you to have it, to enjoy it. Don't forget, Ammalie. You have lived a good and beautiful life here. Powell. Me. That's *enough* of a life. Society tells us it's not enough, but it is. It's a friggin' lot of work. And it's enough. You *have* enough. You *are* enough. But you go do you, Ammalie. Go forth and kick ass," which is what Mari had said for the last twenty years, and, as woo-woo as it sounded, Ammalie could feel her hug from across the airwaves.

Mari didn't realize it, but she *was* Ammalie's companion, fated to go along on the heroine's journey. Mari, Lady, her old self—all rooting her on. Those were companions enough.

CHAPTER 6

The rest of the week floated by in what she thought of as an unprecedented series of pools in a river. Her whole adult life she'd been in rapids, but now she meandered, floated, circled around lazily like an aspen leaf caught in a slow eddy. She read three novels she found in the cabin, all set in Colorado, plus the L.L. Bean book on how to hunt and process game, and one book called *Great Colorado Bear Stories,* which made her feel better about bears, since Colorado's bears were black, not grizzlies, and shy, and only four people in the entire state of Colorado had been killed by black bears in recent history, and two of those had been feeding them. The main message of the book seemed to be *we do not have to be so scared,* and she tried to take that to heart.

She stretched and did yoga and planks. She and Lady went for hikes or wanders, as she called them, depending on their speed and length. She saw no signs of the Bad Man, heard no gunshots. She had moments of calm and moments of fear, the latter mainly consisting of thinking of Lady's owner and his hate-filled cussing, and how remote she was. In defending something that clearly needed defending, she had put herself in danger—which reminded her of all the good people everywhere on earth who had stood up for justice and peace at the expense of their safety and well-being, and that made her anxious too. Perhaps she was hormonal, but it made her want to cry.

But *onward*! That was her motto. She made a batch of granola, the ingredients for which she had—oats, nuts, seeds, cinnamon, oil, although she forgot the honey and borrowed some from the stocked cupboard, deciding that honey was within her Appropriate Poaching Rules. So far, she'd taken a brush, electricity, and a cup of honey, which were things she'd be happy to give to someone in a similar situation, which made it not *really* stealing.

Most important in her week was her journaling, and particularly her New Journal One-Third Rule: one-third about understanding the past, one-third about noticing the present, and one-third directing her gaze at the future. The last third was hardest because it was vague. To combat this, she made lists of things she hoped to do with her time left in life, such as see Powell well into adulthood, take a trip to Greece someday, and learn to make something, perhaps jewelry or pottery. Learn Spanish. Learn about the arts.

She didn't have any professional goals, really. Going back to waitressing wasn't a dream; it had just been oddly easy and *fun,* with flexible shifts and good for their savings account, and besides, Burt had been a great boss even when she'd first started as a college student, had taken her under his wing. Altogether, the job was a unique gem that most people spent lifetimes seeking: friendly coworkers, good tips, lots of regulars, and a really truly good boss, and all that was so frigging *rare* that it had just been hard to leave. Should she have done something that challenged her more? Probably. But life challenged her enough. Parenting was hard! Life kept her busy! But what about her *passion* goals? Something that gave her life purpose? Until now, she hadn't thought about it.

Perhaps she'd go back to school?

Work in a fire tower?

Volunteer at a nature preserve or an animal shelter?

Nothing specifically called to her. Her future sounded like old TVs, making that disturbing white noise.

In the afternoons, she began beading bracelets from a kit. Many of the beads were fluorescent plastic, but there were some small silver ones and blue glass and tiny rectangles of pale orange. It appeared that several jewelry-making kits had been tossed together—the cheap kid ones found in box stores plus tiny baggies of beads from elsewhere. There were tools of all sorts—small pliers and wire clips and the hoops needed for making clasps. There were three different manuals, two for kids and one for adults, the kid ones being the most helpful.

By the end of the week, she had a vague understanding of wire wrapping and attaching various types of clasps, and she'd made a dozen bracelets and had come to an understanding of how colors fit together in the way she liked best—not too random and messy-looking, but not too orderly, either. She alternated three blues with one orange and one or two silvers, perhaps an odd bead thrown in, tied together with loops and latches she learned to make from a small booklet. She chose her favorite—the one she'd most like to keep—and left it on top of the bead kit, for someone to mysteriously find someday.

Her days stretched in a way she'd never experienced but always imagined. She watched the aspen leaves begin to fall. Twice the snow spit and once it snowed enough to stick. The days became slightly shorter. She wandered around her life, stopping to do planks or stretching or journaling or just staring out the window.

Nights were hard. Dark came early, and she was limited by her headlamp or flashlight. A dullness sometimes came over her then, and she felt both too lethargic to do much and yet too antsy to sleep. She drank wine and sat in the dark, or she had a beer and stared from her sleeping bag, now unzipped so she could thrash. She grew nostalgic about her youth, about young Powell, about the early years with Vincent, about Levi at the restaurant and how simple her crush had seemed back when she put her simple head on a simple pillow in her simple life to daydream about them kissing. She blinked at the stars from the tub, and they seemed to blink back. These dark hours were the ones she had to sit with, learning to be comfortable with being uncomfortable.

One night, she started a puzzle, headlamp on and flashlight positioned on the table strategically. She worried about how long it would take her to put away if suddenly someone showed up, but threw caution to the wind. She found herself addicted, stayed up late, and dreamed of fitting pieces together. She figured there was something poetic and profound about how her consciousness was trying to piece together presence and absence.

She flipped through her books on the night sky and birds, the names of everything drifting in and out of her brain. She focused on memorizing two from the bird book—she hadn't actually seen them outside, but she liked the pictures in *Sibley's*—the yellow-rumped warbler and the painted redstart. She watched the ravens, who seemed to watch her back and to greet her with a deep croak anytime she went outside.

Each day, she got faster and more efficient at bundling her sleeping bag and putting it in a pile next to her plastic bin of cooking things and her cooler, so that if she ever did see or hear a car coming, she could pack up her stuff and get it out to her car in minutes. Something about the routine of this felt satisfying and calming. She'd also smeared dirt on her license plate, obscuring the *R* so that it looked more like a *K* and covering most of one of the 9s. She hoped it looked natural, as if the car had been splattered by mud, and she wasn't sure how effective it would be, but something about trying to cover up who she was felt good.

Maybe, she realized, she was overdoing this Getaway Business. Maybe she really was going crazy. Maybe she didn't have a fork in her hair at the moment, but she had the metaphorical equivalent in her soul.

But still, something was working here. She *needed* to do this. At various moments in the day, she realized she was having *fun*. She remembered a book she'd read as a kid, something about two kids living in a museum at night, and the way they hoarded coins they'd pulled from the fountain. She forgot why they were in the museum in the first place, but she remembered that, like her, they seemed to want to stay and explore and remain undiscovered.

On Sunday afternoon, she did a once-over on the house, using rubbing alcohol to wipe away smudges from every surface, and then packed up the Grey Goose. She was undecided—should she grab her sleeping bag from the car and stay one more free night in the house and leave before dawn? Or put in a few hours' driving on the next leg of her trip and car-camp somewhere on BLM land? She'd learned BLM meant Bureau of Land Management, not the movement—and this land was free and unrestricted, no national or state park passes or camping registrations required, a gift to Americans by America that she figured most Americans, especially those on the East Coast, didn't know about.

She was standing outside, considering these two options and being mesmerized by the glimmering gold leaves, when she heard the crunching of tire on gravel.

The word exploded from her. "*Fuuuuuuck.*"

But she had to laugh. She felt oddly calm. Almost amused.

She couldn't leave now, there was no time, so she stood, firmly and confidently, Lady next to her. She smiled inanely as an old Toyota Tacoma with a WILDER RANCHES sign painted on the door pulled up. A lean woman with blond hair pulled into a braid swung out of the high cab. She looked to be in her sixties and of the West—silver jewelry and jeans and a flannel shirt and actual scuffed-up cowboy boots. They were the working kind of boots, not the dress kind.

"Are you Kat?" Ammalie said with a bravado she did not feel.

"Uh, yeah," the woman mumbled, reaching down to pat Lady, who was nosing her in the crotch. "Kat Wilder."

"Welcome. I've got the place cleaned for you."

"I came a day early." Kat ducked her head and put a hand to her neck. "See, I—I—I . . ." She trailed off. "I'll come back tomorrow, as planned. I just wanted to . . . see the place, get my bearings."

An understanding crept into Ammalie's mind—oh goodness, *Kat* was nervous! *Kat* was breaking in a day early! *Kat* hadn't planned on seeing anyone, had been hoping to sneak in, which is something she and Vincent had joked about doing once at an Airbnb, hoping to stay an extra day without the absent owner noticing, since they knew where the key was and that the owner wasn't around. It was the poor recognizing the poor.

"Oh, no worries, just stay. You're here!" Ammalie extended the gold key in her palm. "What's an extra night? Here's a key."

Kat's face registered surprise, then relief, then a genuine smile. "Okay, well, thanks. And I'm supposed to leave it on the corbel?"

"That would be perfect." Ammalie smiled happily, as if she said that all the time.

"You don't mind that I'm a day early? It's just that . . . see . . . the thing is, is . . ."

"No worries at all."

Kat stood there and then limped forward. "I didn't expect anyone to be here." And then, nodding to her knee, added, "Old injury. Fell off a horse."

"I'm just on my way out; I came to check on things for you. I'm a . . . neighbor. The owner asked me to come. The cleaner has already been here. Have a nice stay."

Kat nodded but then opened her mouth to say something. "But wait. Won't you stay for a cup of tea?"

Ammalie blinked in surprise. "Oh, no, I couldn't. Enjoy."

"Because today is the day of my recovery anniversary. Off of heroin. It's kind of a big deal. I tend to . . . feel a lot on this day. Hence my early arrival. I was feeling twitchy and . . . I don't know. Unsettled."

"Oh, I'm sorry," Ammalie said, feeling it sincerely. Twitchy and unsettled was something she could empathize with, even if Kat's was surely worse. "Well, not sorry about the sobriety, of course. Congratulations on that."

Kat reached down to pet Lady, who was circling their legs with a stick in her mouth that kept whacking them on the legs. "Thank you. What a beautiful dog. It's complicated. Every year I go somewhere new and beautiful to remember my friend, who didn't get clean in time and whose death keeps prompting me to keep my act together. These past years have been tough, though; everything in the world seems more complicated, and I'd sure as hell like to zone out, get some relief. Your dog has a cut—"

Ammalie saw Kat squinting at the slice on Lady's head, taking it in, drawing her conclusions, and her brain swung into the easiest lie. "I rescued her from a shelter recently. Obviously, someone was . . ."

"Jes*us*!"

"I know."

"That's horrible." Kat bent down to the dog to examine the cut more closely, and she glanced up at Ammalie with a fierce look in her eye.

"I know, I know. I'll love on her forever. To make up for the bad."

Kat nodded approval. "Some people are real shits. The older I get, the more I want to do my part to . . . I don't know. It's not that I want to do them wrong. It's not in my power for one thing, ha. I guess I just want to help the good guys." She ran her hands across the dog, exactly as Ammalie had done. Her fingers found the round wounds on the dog's butt, and she sighed. "She seems otherwise okay."

"That's what I thought. You're a vet?"

"No, but I'm a rancher." Kat stood up, stretching her back. "Look, speaking of doing kindnesses, maybe you could not mention my early arrival? Or no, that's a terrible thing to ask! He's your neighbor."

Ammalie made a gesture at her mouth of turning a key and then throwing it away. Meanwhile, she really looked at Kat, who indeed looked like she wasn't feeling well for reasons other than sneaking into a place a day early. "Let's sit outside; it's warm. We could do a few turns of Scrabble on the picnic table before it gets too dark. I don't have time for a full game, but first one to fifty points?"

Kat let out a bark of laughter. "I'd love to."

What the fuck are you doing? Don't tell her any personal details, keep it to the weather, she said to herself on her way back in. *What kind of crazy are you, Ammalie?*

But it was not crazy. It was a delight. Over Scrabble and tea, with golden aspens quivering, she heard the story of a childhood in Hawaii and Colorado ranches and wild horses and mustangs, which Kat had spent years trying to protect. Kat spoke of her home in Salida, and seeing mustangs in captivity in the prison program in Canyon City. "Mustangs and men, captured but not tamed, I like to say. It's quite a thing. There's a lot of pretty innocent dudes there, and it strikes me as unfair, and I'm a little tired of so-called justice in this country. I myself have lived a wild life, and when I got clean, I had to adjust to a different kind of living. Just like those horses and men, though some of them don't deserve to have to, you know? I'm hoping to find a band to belong to."

"That sounds lovely. And necessary."

When Kat asked, "Do you have a special someone?" Ammalie shook her head no. "Just a guy I have a crush on, but that's just something that will live in my brain."

Kat nodded as if she understood. "Me either, not at the moment. I miss . . . hands. Someone touching me. But a partner comes with strings. And I want the strings less than the hands, ha! I have my own strings to untangle first."

Ammalie snorted. "That sounds smart."

"You wanna know what I've been comparing my emotions to? A tumble of necklaces and earrings that get all bunched together in your jewelry drawer. I need to sort them out, and lay them side by side, so I can see the beauty of the individual pieces again."

"I like that."

"I don't believe in God." Kat looked up at her. "I believe in grace, or in clear moments, in moments that glitter, like a jewel."

Ammalie felt a wash of gratefulness for a woman who said real things, who saved mustangs, who saved herself. So she responded in truth: "That's what I am doing, I guess. I need bits of jewels too, and my old life could no longer satisfy." Ammalie glanced up and saw that the sun was now below the tree line. "I need to go. I'm sorry, but I do." She handed Kat one of the bracelets she'd made, which were in her jacket pocket, with a few humble apologies about its rudimentary style.

"It's beautiful," Kat said, holding the bracelet in her palm. "It will remind me to sort my jewelry, so to speak."

When the two women hugged tightly, it felt like two souls connecting for one moment, which was one pure treasure.

WHEN SHE PULLED out of the driveway, Ammalie sang a string of joyous cusswords to Lady, who sat in the seat beside her, taking it all in with a panting smile. The curses were a release of nervousness, an acknowledgment of the weirdness of some future time when the homeowner might have a strange exchange about a mysterious person who stayed for Scrabble, the one who had scraggly graying hair, or the moment he found the stacked wood or a necklace or a note about a missing puzzle piece.

Oddly, she wasn't scared. There was no camera at the house. Kat had never seen her car, since she was inside unpacking when Ammalie pulled out of the driveway. Humans were capable of not noticing, or not caring, or explaining things away in their mind, both small stuff and big.

People were truly capable of zoning out. Which is exactly what she'd done these last years, of course. There was plenty she'd not noticed, surely.

Still, it was stunning how easy it was to get away with this.

And if anyone stopped and questioned her, well, now she could just say she was exploring, driving along and looking for public land access for camping. An older man drove by in a black minivan and tipped his hand up from the steering wheel—a local rancher, she assumed, in an odd choice for a vehicle. She lifted her fingers from the wheel at the same time she saw him squint at Lady and tilt his head. She pressed on the gas and drove faster, glancing in her rearview mirror, but the minivan had gone on. For one thing, it was a narrow, snowy road, no good places for a turnaround, but for another, he was likely on his own way, somewhere, in his own life.

Real food. That was her first stop, and so she drove to a coffee shop in a cluster of buildings alongside the highway and ordered a coffee and lasagna to go, not wanting to leave Lady in the car alone for long.

Communication. That was next. Her phone revealed a text from her sister, and she decided not to respond, which was normal—she and Apricot often went weeks without check-ins, even since the diagnosis. Nothing from Powell, and she felt a surge of bitterness or anger or sorrow, she wasn't sure what, rise and bloom in her chest. After the funeral, Powell had checked out, which is the opposite of what she had hoped and tried for. Since her repeated texts and calls clearly only irritated him, then made him blow up big-time, she'd been trying for silence.

Mari, however, had left many texts.

All well? What tense are your daydreams?

Hey, I'm at Avogadro's! Which is reopened now after the fire! Burt recognized me, says hello, says a customer has been asking about you. Wondered if he can give out your number?

Hey, a guy named Levi is here at Avogadro's. Handsome Black middle-age guy. He wants to know where you are. Can I tell him? Please advise.

Ooooooohhh . . . Is he that regular you liked so much? How come you never told me he was Black? Not that it matters, but maybe it does? Just because, well, our neighborhood. Our lives. Not the stuff of our youth. Not what we dreamed of. I'm the only POC around & so get to deal with all the dumb Day of the Dead questions! America is so weird. I won't give out number till you give me the ok. How's the dog?

Now that you mention it, my daydreams are about a younger me. That is sad.

Ammalie sat in the car, engine running for warmth, and closed her eyes. So that she could feel what she was feeling. Because it was a burst of warmth. Of magic. She felt the Sea Creature surge up happy in her chest. Levi. Levi was looking for her!

Such a simple small thing, such a dumb thing, but it *filled* her with some youthful excitement, expanded her whole chest. She hadn't felt this in so long! She had the vague echo of a memory of this sort of feeling, and she touched her chest and laughed.

She texted back: *Safe and sound but leaving for a new place. Yes, Levi was the nice regular. He looks like Denzel Washington. Handsome, don't you think? Do you think it's weird I only ever dated white men? Well, I hardly dated. Then I got married. So maybe I didn't have the chance. Always had a crush on Levi and maybe him on me, but I think I just dreamed that because I wanted it to be real. But there was . . . fondness. But honestly (I can admit this only to you), I was always intimidated by him—he's too cool, and I'm too, well, uncool. As you know. Tell him I'm on a spiritual journey of sorts. Or on vacation. I'm not ready. Get his number and tell him I'll reach out. I'm secretly happy to hear he asked about me. Even though he was just a customer. But still. It's nice. I want him to be happy.*

Immediately Mari responded, *Call me,* but when Ammalie tried, the call dropped twice, and so she responded, *Sorry, can't, will when I have a signal, at a small café in the middle of nowhere, but larger towns coming up.*

Mari wrote back, *You always compare men to actors. Is there any man who does not look like an actor? Are you lonely?*

As a reply, Ammalie attached a photo of snowy mountains lit by alpenglow. *I have plenty of company, including myself. Vincent only looked like Vincent. You look like Rita Moreno. You are a good friend. Xoxoxox*

Then she texted a vague *Hope you're well, love you* to her sister and son.

There was a call about extending her car warranty and one from a vague friend from childhood, checking in, having just heard about Vincent's death. There were some emails from friends, both close and peripheral, but nothing required a response. She sipped at her coffee and stared at her phone. It used to be so important—the dings kept her addicted and grounded—but now she felt no great need for it at all. Before she left, she texted Mari one more time: *Hitting the road again. With the dog. Will call soon, I promise. I'm happier than I've been in some time. Thank you. It's working, this plan of mine.*

CHAPTER 7

The next morning, after splurging for a room in an old mom-and-pop hotel on the side of a road, she drove south toward Taos, a historic town she'd always wanted to see. She chomped on an apple with her driving hand, finger-combed her hair with her other, and sang '80s songs as loudly as she could. Randomly, when she had service, she asked her phone, "Where does the Rio Grande rift start?" Taking the time to do this was something explorers would do. To simply allow the space for curiosity. Deep canyons had to start somewhere, after all, and she knew the Rio Grande Gorge started with a rift, but where did that rift *begin*?

Somehow, seeing the beginning of a tectonic chasm felt important—perhaps it would give her insight into her own shifting, her own fault line. Google Maps led her across a flat landscape dusted with snow that ended in a desolate dirt parking area with an expansive view of the Rio Grande winding its way across flatland. The area had one old car parked in it, which felt like a beacon. She pulled up next to it, got out with Lady, bundled up, and started walking alongside the slow-moving river, which was beautifully caught in the in-between stages of freezing over, a dark stream of running water in the middle, ice on both edges.

And there it was: Up ahead, the land started to sink. Or, rather, small red cliffs started to rise up alongside the river. It depended how you wanted to look at it, either the land sinking or the cliffs rising, but either way, this was the very beginning of what would become one of the world's most famous and deep canyons down-stream.

"Empyreal," she said, and it was. She picked her way along the ice and rocks with Lady trotting nearby, and then they both stopped suddenly. The large tracks of a cat—mountain lion? bobcat?—gave her pause. Her heart thrummed and her ears went on alert and her eyes scanned the cliffs, now as deep as she was tall, but all she saw were mud swallow nests clinging to rock.

She considered turning back, but she had Lady, and also she could see three figures in the distance, and the presence of other people made her feel at ease. As they neared, she nodded a hello, as did they, and they were about to pass one another when she cleared her throat. "Hey, do you know what that is?" She pointed across the river to several tall columns made of stacked stones.

A teen with a shock of black hair with dyed blond edges spoke first. "Old remnants of a *mojonera*."

"From the late 1800s." The man was broad-shouldered and wore a thick flannel shirt. "Provided shelter for those watching sheep. Also a directional marker—a cairn of sorts. And also, maybe, humans just need a landmark, a place to feel safe, or to land, no?"

"Interesting," she said, and meant it. "And this is exactly where the Rio Grande Gorge starts, this is the rift that turns into that big, deep canyon near Taos?"

All three nodded, and she said, "That's way cool," and they nodded again.

Then the woman spoke. "Can you imagine those early explorers? Encountering a huge gorge like that? They had to cross it somehow. And this is the spot. This area is known as the Vargas crossing. Of course, they were relying on the people already here, who knew such things." She had graying black hair pulled into a cascading ponytail. "De Vargas was an explorer, and like everyone, he needed a way to cross the chasm. I think we forget how hard it must have been, getting across these landscapes."

"You walked the bridge across the great canyon yet?" the man said.

"Not yet. Going there next."

"People jump to their death there," the teenager said in a matter-of-fact voice. "There are telephones. You know, so you can make the call. It's super scary. The bridge sways and stuff. Gives me the squeebie-jeebies."

The woman reached out to ruffle his hair. "It's true," she said, quietly. "Two types of people go there. For such contradictory reasons too. Either to jump to their deaths or to be awed by the beauty. The second is the holy choice," and she made the sign of the cross.

The kid nodded downstream. "And this is a holy place. There are petroglyphs in that direction. On the right. This area has a pretty interesting history."

"Pride," the woman said softly, and although she didn't say more, Ammalie knew her to mean that they had pride in the area, and that Ammalie should too. "For six or seven generations, the pueblos here existed without Spanish influence," the woman said. "Which is why the language and customs in this Colorado–New Mexico area are so different than the rest of the Spanish-speaking world."

"I'm the tenth generation. That's pretty amazing, actually." The kid raised his eyebrows at her, as if to see if she'd challenge him on the point.

"I think that's beautiful, that history. I wish I knew more about this area. I have so much to learn . . ." Ammalie suddenly felt shy and out of practice, unable to converse.

The man was staring at Lady, who was trotting around everyone's legs, occasionally whacking them with a stick she clasped in her mouth. Then he tilted his head to the bright blue morning sky. "It's one of the last warm days we'll have for a while," he said. "Here comes the winter of discontent. People are always more trouble in the winter. My life is about to get more complicated."

The kid laughed. "He'd know," he said to Ammalie. "He's the mayor of this town."

Ammalie wished the man would stop looking at Lady—either because he might recognize her or might ask questions about the injuries—and now he was reaching down to pet Lady's head. She tried to distract him with a question. "What does that involve? Being mayor, I mean?"

The man snorted. "It's unpaid volunteer work and mainly consists of doing miserable things like dealing with wastewater."

Ammalie was surprised. Did mayors of small towns really not get paid? Were things in this country still so . . . unofficial? But what she said was, "That's what you're doing today?"

"No, no wastewater today. Today, I'm walking out my annoyance. Today, I was contacted by a gentleman whose granddaughter was dating a guy who broke parole. When the police chased him, he ran into the gentleman's house. The police knocked and there was no answer, and the door was locked, so they *knocked it down*. Now the grandfather wants eight hundred bucks for a new door. While I understand his desire to have a new door, I understand that my community does not have the funds to pay for a door. Such funds will come out of budget for a new playground, and, after all, the parole-breaking is not the town's fault. And so it makes me sad. So I came out here for a walk with my amigos here."

"He comes here," the woman said, "because if he walks in town, everyone stops to ask him something."

"Everyone needs some peace," Ammalie said. "That's why I'm here too."

"May you find it," the man said. His eyes were on the dog in such a way that she suspected now that he recognized her.

"I better go," she stammered.

The man gazed down the river. "These mountains, they're made of volcanoes. Not the same as the Rockies right over there; those are uplifts. This is a very special place, if you know what to look for, and there are hot springs along the river. You just have to know what you're seeing, otherwise you're hardly seeing anything at all." His eyes met hers. "It's a good dog you have here. Go in peace, amiga."

His gentle voice wishing such a thing—such a simple, true thing—and offered in such a sincere way made her breath catch. He knew something about the dog, and he was signaling his approval. She waved goodbye and kept walking, Lady trotting on beside her.

Though she kept her eyes on the rock walls, growing in height and making her feel smaller, she didn't see any petroglyphs. She walked for a long time, eventually turning back to her car, feeling disappointed. But maybe not finding them was for the best; she didn't feel worthy or in the right place emotionally to see and appreciate such a thing. She didn't know enough about the Native peoples—Southern Utes or Taos Puebloans? She didn't even know!—to have the honor of seeing their art. She needed to learn more. That was part of an adventure, after all. And for now, the dusting of snow and the river and the blue sky and the sunshine were pleasure enough.

Before she left town, she left eight hundred-dollar bills—half the cash she had—in an envelope at the post office with the clerk with a note that said, *FOR THE MAYOR, FOR THE DOOR, EVERYONE NEEDS A DOOR.* She also hoped it would serve as a bribe or thank-you of some sort—to leave her and Lady alone.

It's possible, for example, that he had taken down her license plate.

She kept thinking of his voice. He had wished for her to go in peace with such *sincerity*. It did seem like grace. Like a prayer. As if he acknowledged the world was hard, and that he was worn out by it himself, but also that in doing the right things, peace could in fact be found.

VINCENT HAD DIED in the month of April. It had been sudden: Powell had just come home for spring break and informed them he was dropping out of college, that it was all too much for him, and that, furthermore, he loved them and all but he didn't want to move back home, he was renting a house with three other guys.

That night's dinner had been awkward; they were all angry, each for their own reasons. Powell sullen for meeting with resistance. Vincent furious about the wasted college money and lack of discipline. And she was angry at the weariness that kept plaguing her, which Vincent's anger contributed to, and which, in turn, made her angry at him. It seemed with each passing year, she was just getting more and more tired—and she couldn't tell if it was normal body aging or if it was something more psychological or emotional in nature.

That night, she and Vincent had been arguing. Or perhaps not arguing but working through something little, something about the house, although underneath that small argument were all their old and nebulous and much larger battles . . . he being in the basement all the time, either for work or hobbies, she being annoying (or at least he made her feel that way, as if her very presence on earth was interrupting him). Vincent reached up and touched his head. He'd had a headache for a week, but then he said, "I'm not feeling so great," and then said it again but it was slurry, as if he was drunk. At the same time, she was struck with a hot flash—they had just started—and was focusing on the sensations of that, confused and miserable.

Then Vincent murmured something like *I don't feel so great* again and then he spoke something else, a blur of a noise, and he was looking down at his right hand. She helped him into a chair and said, "Let me get you some water," and she got him a glass of water, and then she stood above him, not moving quickly at all, being so slow, and it had taken her a long time to connect the dots. Then his face looked weird, and his left hand was moving but his right arm looked limp, and *that* was when she called 911.

She yelled for Powell.

She yelled for Vincent to stay.

Then he said something, and she couldn't be sure but she thought it was, *My head got torn.*

So, life ended.

It. just. ended.

It ended with: I don't feel so great. My head got torn.

She had taken so long to react. She had been the slow one.

As she drove on the Rio Grande Gorge Bridge, which he'd always wanted to see, her eyes smarted with tears as she wondered yet again about Vincent's last breath. She hadn't seen it, of course—he was at the hospital. She wished he had died from a different cause, one with his brain still working, so he could have left her a note or a word. But no, a stroke—he'd not been conscious when he'd died—and perhaps he had really died as he sat in their living room.

She tried to remember the exact last breath she *had* seen. Having called 911 and now on her knees in front of him, saying, *They're coming, help is coming, it's going to be okay, help is coming,* and then running to unlock the door for the paramedics, and then back to him, and then Powell there, saying, *Dad? Dad? Dad?* and both of them kneeling near him, and then the paramedics were moving him to the stretcher, moving the board out the door. Gone. Everything changed so quickly and she and Powell just stood there, stunned and stupid in the silence.

She felt the Sea Creature zing down her spine, causing her to shudder. A horrible memory—though not remembering felt like a cop-out, like cowardice. So she thought of his last breath. She thought of first aid kits. She thought of snow fences. Of crosses alongside the road. She thought of *mojoneras.* She thought of water. She hoped he had found peace. Died in peace. She thought of all the ways humans endeavored to find peace and what a worthy and noble journey that was.

THE RAGGED TAXIDERMY on the walls at the café in Taos shouted *Creepy death!* but the green chili shouted *Fucking alive!* She sat outside, bundled up and warm enough in the sun, her nostrils flaring with spice. Apricot simply had to be called. Of the three keys in her life, this one was the most rusty and needed to be jiggled in the lock of communication.

But honestly, how painful. The conversation was as it always was: boring chitchat about neighbors and the weather and Apricot's recent purchases, which included a chair that massaged your back *and* had an internal heater, simply amazing. When she realized that Apricot wasn't even going to mention the cancer, Ammalie brought it up, but Apricot's impatience was clear. "I told you, Ammalie. It's like the safest kind of leukemia you can have. It's a super-slow progression and I'll likely die of something else before it gets bad enough to treat. Sometimes I feel like I have the flu, that's it!"

Apricot's voice was so snotty that Ammalie didn't even bother to mention any details of her trip. Something bitter in her was fed by keeping her own secrets. Perhaps it was anger, perhaps annoyance, but it all came down to the fact that Apricot had quit trying to communicate for real long ago. Ammalie didn't have the energy now to fix the problem. But even as she hung up, she knew that somewhere deep inside was still the five-year-old her holding her older sister's hand, and the two of them caught in fits of laughing, and how they'd skip through the neighborhood, which was just being built, and they'd sneak into half-finished houses to draw with chalk on plywood or play games of hide-and-seek. Entering those homes had seemed so natural; perhaps that's where she'd gotten this current idea.

She had to admit that sometimes, memories were enough of a key to your heart. The key might be rusty and unused, but it still opened a lock. Or had the potential to.

After quick texts to Mari and Powell, both of whom were at work and couldn't take a call, she sent them photos of the huge Rio Grande rift she'd just visited. Before leaving, she went to the restroom, and as she peed she stared at the license plates decorating the walls. Thank god there wasn't taxidermy in the bathroom—now, *that* would be a horror movie. But the plates were interesting— a mishmash of colors and states and logos. Some new, some old. She tilted her head and considered the various colors and styles. And then she dug her multipurpose tool out of her backpack. Her hands simply did it. Took a New Mexico plate off the wall.

She stared down at it and considered. It was stealing, sure, but there had been two calls from an "unidentified" number on her phone, no message, and probably scams, spams, swindles, *flimflam,* which was her word of the day. But still, it made her suspicious. Could be that the dog owner had tracked her down. Or the homeowner. Or the guy in the van she'd passed. She wasn't dumb: Any police officer who ran a plate would see this one for the fraud it was. But on the other hand, if someone was looking for an Illinois plate, and, well, they saw New Mexico instead . . . a New Mexico plate with new tags, surely that would help?

People were tired. People were lazy. People liked to see what they wanted to see.

She slipped the New Mexico plate into her backpack and left.

When she walked to her car, she glanced at her own plate, just to be sure what sort of screwdriver she'd need when she found herself alone.

ON HER LAST stop before Key Two, she pulled up at the Bosque del Apache National Wildlife Refuge exactly on time. It was again *l'heure bleue,* the hour when the sandhill cranes and snow geese would land for the night in the lake. She'd planned and executed this important moment like a pro, and it was perfect exactly in the way it had once been unperfect: A decade ago, Vincent and she had missed a morning liftoff and the evening landing on the trip they'd gone on specifically to see such a sight in Indiana, him taking his time leaving the hotel room in both instances, slowing them down on *both* ends of the day. She had hated him then, believing his puttering had been on purpose, though he denied it. She considered now that he likely *had* slowed them on purpose, perhaps as a way of silently getting her back for some slight. He could be like that. He had often wanted to control the pacing of things, would do subtle things to exert his control, but always in ways so small that it was hard to exactly define, or fight against, though still, she hadn't spoken to him the entire way home. He had known, after all, that there's *only* the morning liftoff and evening landing, and timing is important, and he managed both times to be "running behind." Small moments of selfishness. Or flat-out unkindness.

She breathed out, tried to let it go. She'd been as disappointed then as she was delighted now. She climbed out of the Grey Goose and bundled up in coat and mittens, leaving Lady inside, and stood in awe along with a few other tourists at a magical moment. She tried to form the words that captured it:

A *multitude* of snow geese.

A *cloud* of snow geese.

A *blizzard* of snow geese.

A slow-moving *tornado* of snow geese.

A fucking amazing amount of snow geese.

The birds came in groups, circling and landing in the lake. Her mind scanned itself, looking for words to explain it, but it was impossible. It was beyond words. And then it was over. She stood quietly, taking in the surroundings of lake and carcasses of cottonwoods and leafless trees. A few smaller groups of snow geese landed, and then a smaller number of sandhill cranes did the same, sounding like garbling frogs or something very ancient. Then the tourists left. Then she was alone, standing in the near-dark.

She breathed a sigh of accomplishment, of wonder, of joy. She'd wanted to do something, and she'd done it. Simple as that. She got back in her car and drove down a nearby dirt road and parked on the side and slept in the back of the Grey Goose in Fluffiest Red, with Lady curled at her feet. Though she was crampy and her period had started yet again and she was cold, she could feel the surge, a cloud, a blizzard, a happy tornado circling in her heart. She was lifting off herself.

PART II

THE
SECOND KEY

ICE AND WATER

Thar she was—the old trailer, battered and alone, one window covered with a black tarp undulating in the wind like an eyepatch gone haywire. "Ahoy, ahoy," Ammalie murmured, struck as ever by the weird things that came out of her mouth, seemingly on their own. Since never had she ever uttered the word *ahoy*.

But that's what she felt like: a pirate caught in a terrible storm. The seriously rutted dirt road required steering to the far right, or the far left, or just gently entering the potholes and washouts straight on, cringing as she waited for the scrape of metal on rock. Excitement surged up her throat, though—her body might be bucking on the dented road, but her heart felt like that of a kid waking up to the best birthday gifts ever, because here was the solitary white oval of a vintage travel trailer with a faded turquoise strip and a faded red lightning bolt, straight out of the fifties and cute as could be.

Next to it sat a picnic table and beside that, a clump of trees she knew to be desert willows because of the educational signage at the last rest stop. A line of bushes spread west to east, meandering along what must once have been a creek bed, and to the right, toward the setting sun, the dry creek led to what appeared to be a low rocky canyon with some trees she couldn't identify. Everything in the three other directions was simply endless, endless, *endless* rolling land, made extra-endless because of its pastel dullness, and extra-extra-endless because of its sparsity, which made the whole landscape appear as if it was barely hanging on to existence as it clung to the sky. This was what was meant by desert. Not the sand dunes kind of desert with camels walking through, but the desert of the American West, the desert of Arizona.

"Freaking bizarre as Mars," she whispered, and Lady whined, and the Grey Goose jolted in agreement. She tried to find the words to name what this landscape even *was*: yellow-pink rocks and yellow-pink dirt, basically, but what else? Dry scrub, dry yellow grasses, dry bushes, tall yuccas that rose to strange heights and reminded her of women with flowing hair and arms waving and warning her away.

She parked far from the trailer, so as to have the *Just looking around, my husband stayed here once, la-la-la* look, as opposed to the *I'm invading your place* aggressiveness about her. She felt calm and collected, but upon climbing out of the car, a yelp of primal fear came hurtling out of her mouth before she could stop it. Cripes almighty! What *was* that thing? Some creature was cowering in the brittle brush and mesquite, staring at her with grumpy round black eyes, and then she realized there were *more* pairs of black eyes, which caused her to screech again.

What the hell? Her brain scan resulted in nothing. She couldn't place these creatures at *all*. Didn't something like this live in Africa? Or India? Raccoon monkeys—was that a thing? She had a momentary wave of confusion—where *was* she? Did she have Alzheimer's?

She watched them until they reluctantly wandered off, sometimes throwing annoyed glances over their shoulders and eventually disappearing toward the rocks and trees, as if they were riding off into the sunset. Ammalie clicked her tongue in consideration of the situation while the Grey Goose clicked noises as the engine cooled. Her yelp seemed to be still echoing. She hadn't uttered a sound like that—of pure surprise and fear—in a good long while. Or maybe ever. That fact made her snort, which made her laugh softly, perhaps out of nervousness, or perhaps because she was now living a life with moments worth yelping about.

She picked up her phone to google "raccoon monkeys in Arizona" but saw that there was no service, so instead she let Lady out of the car. The dog tentatively trotted around, sniffing, but often looked back to Ammalie for reassurance. Inspired by Lady, Ammalie sniffed too. The air smelled like . . . well, desert. Like dried grass lit by late afternoon winter sun, like cottonwood leaves, like skin. Maybe a hint of creosote. But something sweet too, and she had the sudden memory of the smell of her father's cherry tobacco and how they would walk the dirt alleyways of Chadron after dinner together, him smoking a pipe, and her heart pinged with nostalgia.

Well, she'd made it. She leaned against her warm car, biting her lip, pulling her jacket around her, considering. In front of her was her second key: a trailer named Dart. It was not shaped like a dart at all, but an oval. It had faded red and turquoise paint on battered white-and-black lettering that spelled out DART in the lower left. And that black distinctive eyepatch for a window. Perfect. Her eyes rested on the small rocky outcropping to the west, since this was the only place anyone could hide and not be seen, and was the only place of interest, really. But it was quiet and had no signs of life, nor did the rise of land beyond it. If she squinted, she could see a blur of gold at the base of the distant mountains—the leaves of willows or sycamores or sumacs or cottonwoods perhaps, evidence of a much lusher place. She assumed that was Cave Valley, another place with a confused identity—was it a cave or a valley?—but regardless, she knew it was famous for its biodiversity and wildlife corridors. She had read on the road signs that it was a strange confluence of several ecoregions and the recipient of more moisture than the rest of the dry state.

And this? Well, this was *not* that. This was on the edge of that. This was the Badlands. Funny how two opposing landscapes could be so near each other. And also, this was the opposite of the treed-in safe feeling of the Colorado cabin. But maybe here she was equally invisible? Just a different *kind* of invisible? She was glad for Lady's presence—the dog perhaps had been a gift from the universe, and she reached out to gently scratch her fingers through soft fur until she became clear on two things: She'd give it a try despite being spooked, and she'd prove to herself that she was just fine with being unseen.

HER PLAN WAS to just sit for an hour and observe. Look for tire tracks or signs of life either up close or far away—cars, flashes of light from houses, hikers, anything. It's true there was no house in regular sight, but with her binoculars, she could see what might be a cluster of trailers or small homes to the east, and beyond that, occasional glints of light that told her it was the rural highway she'd taken to get here.

A roadrunner with a lizard in its mouth ran by—that was startling! Lady didn't even notice, being occupied with sniffing and wagging her tail at the base of Dart—but Ammalie stared after it, mesmerized. Vincent had told her about those—roadrunners—when he'd returned to Chicago with a key and some photos of this place. He'd put the key in a padded envelope and asked her to mail it on the way to work. He'd not wanted to mail it without checking the postage, unsure, because it was a *key,* after all—and she'd agreed, since she drove right by the post office on the way to Avogadro's Number. For some reason, she really wasn't sure why, she'd committed one of the few dishonest things she'd done in the marriage—she didn't mail it, then lied and said she had. She just didn't feel like it, and surely the owner had a spare, though she wondered later if it had been some passive-aggressive thing, to punish him for going on this trip without her. Or maybe she was just a key klepto. Or maybe she was just lazy.

Why had she been so curmudgeonly? Or actually, had she been the exact opposite of that, but her emotions had no place to land? Had she grown curmudgeonly because *he* had been that way to *her*? Was she really such a child, with a *Well, I'll show you* sort of attitude? But it *had* hurt her, when he'd planned the trip with a friend from Dark Sky and never even considered asking her along. Maybe because he assumed someone had to stay home with Powell, or maybe because he wanted to do things solo, or maybe because the lodging was not up to snuff. He'd complained about it, even, about how he had the "most remote, most rustic accommodations" of anyone in the stargazing group, an old trailer tucked off in the flatlands, far from the observatory, requiring that he drive on a terrible road to meet the others, but it had been free, a gift from some Dark Sky appreciator, and the money saved had been enough for him to get the flight to Phoenix and make the trip happen in the first place. She remembered feeling a mean kind of glad that he'd had to suffer a little—he who had increasingly been checking out of her and Powell's life.

She had no guarantee it would be empty, though Vincent had remarked several times how remote and rough it was—a broken hinge on a window that made it hard to vent the place, a bathroom that was . . . an interesting experience, a composting toilet. The man who owned it lived in Texas and once or twice a year came out here in his new fancy RV, but he stayed on the other side of his fifty acres, the prettier side with trees and a stream and where he had hookups. He offered this place for free to stargazers and volunteers, though it was so inconvenient that Vincent had wondered if anyone really ever stayed there at all. "It would be a great little escape place for emergencies," he'd said. "You know, like if zombies attacked, this would be an ideal shelter. We'll definitely go there if zombies come."

He'd been right about that. Zombies would never bother with this place.

She pulled out a turkey sandwich and ate while leaning against the car, absorbing the buzzing space of vastness while Lady galloped around, sniffing wildly and, at one point, letting out a bark, which was the first time she'd heard Lady bark since the day they'd met. A weird bird, one that looked like a cardinal but was not, startled and flew toward Ammalie from a perch in the willow, perched again, then flew over her again, clearly curious about *her*. Funny, that. How wild creatures watched humans more than she'd ever realized.

THE KEY TURNED, the door swung open, and she was struck with the idea that probably a key was not needed at all, that a simple strong pull would have opened the door. Comically, this made her feel unsafe, since *she* was the one breaking in, and she had to snort with amusement as she stood at the threshold, taking it in. She took a step forward but kept her leg out so that Lady could not enter—she had dirt on her paws, after all. Dart was not as broken-down as she had imagined—someone had been keeping track of it, which made her feel vaguely uneasy. To her right, there was a mattress with a light blue sheet and blankets folded at the base, with the exception of a small quilt, tossed haphazardly and touching the floor, so she instinctually rearranged it while looking out the large window above the bed. Directly in front of her was a small kitchen; to her left a little sitting area that could function as another narrow bed. There was a small shelf with books about stars and the local area, and there were also various items lined up—binoculars, a headlamp, a lantern, some beautiful rocks.

At the back of the trailer was a small closet, intended as a toilet, she supposed, but she didn't want to deal with whatever that entailed, so she went outside and squatted and peed where Lady just had, then went to rotate the propane lever on the tanks outside, went inside, and turned on the heat valve, which was right inside the door. It started to click; hurrah for propane, hurrah for heat! She closed her eyes, *Thank you, Texas Guy.*

She looked for a fridge, but there wasn't one—there was just a shelf where a fridge might have once been, and a red cooler sitting on the floor below it. Damn. She'd been hoping for some sort of electricity, whether solar-powered or wired or just magically available, as it often seemed to be. Now that she was fully in Dart, she could smell the faint acid smell of mouse piss, and she was surprised, actually, that there wasn't more of what she'd always called "mouse dirt." Indeed, the cleanliness of the trailer surprised her. It really wasn't bad.

Vincent had mentioned there was no running water, so she had bought and filled four five-gallon containers, which took up all the available space in her car. She knew also that there was some emergency-use water underneath the trailer, but since the containers had probably sat for a long time, and likely frozen and heated, Vincent had not wanted to use them and neither did she, microplastics and all. They would, however, be fine for a hot bath, which she wanted desperately.

She lugged the drinking water out of her car and plonked the big containers on the picnic table and kept her eyes on Lady, who had been venturing farther and farther from the trailer ever since their arrival. It was good for dogs to run, she figured, but Ammalie wanted to keep her in sight. She bit at some dried skin on her lip. "Okay, it's not going to be easy," she said to the weird bird, who was still hopping around. "But I probably won't die, right?" To quell her anxiety, she sat on the picnic table, got her journal from her backpack, and made a list:

Things That Will Be Difficult and I Need to Overcome
Like a Badass Explorer Would:

The Space: Cramped.
The Safety: But who'd arrest me for breaking in *here*? What criminal would be wandering around out *here*?
The Cold: How bad will November be?
The Electricity: Specifically, food preservation.
The Water: How long will it last? Not long. Trips to town required.

The first two items were psychological and wait-and-see situations. The third, fourth, and fifth were biological and practical, and after some time, she'd know the answer about temperature, preserving food, and how fast she was going through water. That was the point of true exploring. Leif Erikson and Vasco da Gama and Robert Scott had to figure all this out too—as did every woman in noncivilized areas, which was a shit-ton of women, and *she* had a grocery store an hour back! And she could always just *leave*! It's not like she was going to *perish*.

Ammalie scratched Lady's under-neck. Perhaps there was some sort of KOA campground to stay at once in a while—to shower, fill up water jugs, stock up on ice? Also, she practiced what she'd say if anyone discovered her. Sure, she'd play the sympathy card—*her husband had come here alone, had recently died, she was in grief, he'd always wanted to return some pottery shards he'd found here . . .* But also, really, who would find her? She only knew of this place because Vincent's file folder called PLACES TO GO had a printout of an email sent from the owner long ago: *Look for the big tree with a lot of bird feeders next to a white rock at the corner of a barbed-wire fence, head south for ten miles, high clearance such as a Jeep recommended, take left after the fireplace ruins, head south again at the rutted road marked with blue stake and the dead willow . . .*

Well, she had promised herself a true adventure, one that pushed her limits, so here she was. Success! And indeed, when she glanced westward, a gasp swooshed from her lips. The setting sun lit the valley in shafts of light, and the bottoms of the clouds were pink-orange swirls. She held up the binoculars and could see that in the distance were indeed the cliffs of Cave Valley—she recognized them from a photo. A true oasis. She put the binos down and watched as the clouds grew upward in great puffs, their lower halves increasing in color in funky, psychedelic ways. Fucking magic. If she'd been a woo-woo sort of person, it would have seemed they were billowing to welcome her to this home.

HOT WATER. SUCH a simple delight. And the work of procuring such a basic substance was its own delight. She'd boiled water in three pots on the trailer's stove, carried the hot water outside, and added it to cool water in a tub she'd placed near the picnic table. All the water came from dusty plastic containers under the trailer, which were heavy and cumbersome and icky on the outside, but she felt strong and capable inside and out. All the hiking at the Colorado cabin had put her in better physical shape than she'd been for a while—and there was something enabling and pure about taking care of a basic need without the help of much technology or conveniences. Or a man.

Inspired by a photo she'd found on a website for broke college students, she'd bought a high-grade, thick plastic storage tub back in Chicago, and she'd even practiced bathing in it in her kitchen, with bubbles and a candle to boot. Sure, she couldn't sink back like in a real tub, and instead had to sit upright with her knees pulled up, and draining it had been a drag, though here she could just tip it over. On the trip, it had served double duty as her main storage container for nonperishable food—crackers and cans of soup and dried fruit—and so now all those items were stacked on the picnic table so it could function as her bath.

When she stripped naked and stepped into the warm water, the first stars fizzing against the early twilight sky, she knew it had been a brilliant idea. Food storage by day, bathtub at night. She sighed and reached for a gin-and-tonic she'd prepared. *Empyreal Heaven.* Lady sat beside her, content, occasionally licking beads of water off her arm.

This was living. This was interesting. This was a true and real moment. If only to her, and that's all who really mattered. She'd remember it forever—and that was not true of many of the nights of her life. How sad that most of them blended together, had been spent in front of a TV. She looked upward at the stars, blazing like nothing she'd ever seen, and whispered the Spanish verse that had been on her *Learn Spanish, Niños!* audio program:

Mira el cielo,
la primera estrella,
Mira la luna,
tan grande, tan bella!

So she did look at the sky, the stars, the moon, and yes, it was big and beautiful. But more grand even was the feel of her lower back muscles relaxing, her cramps subsiding, her sure knowledge that though far less celebrated, women had always been more competent and tougher explorers than men, given that they were also dealing with menstruation and the idiocy of so much societal fucked-up-ness, such as Isabella Bird hiking the mountains of Colorado in the Victorian skirts and ridiculous shoes of the 1870s. Ammalie considered now that while she was amazing, Isabella still had whiteness on her side, and her story had been told, and she wondered now about all the other women unsung, unnoticed, equally or even more badass. She raised a tipsy toast to the moon, to strong women everywhere across the globe and across time, in all cultures and societies, and felt a kinship, knowing that *all,* whether rich or poor and regardless of living conditions and race and ethnicity, had craved the experience of a warm bath. That they all deserved one under the stars with some sort of delicious drink because by god, women were fucking amazing.

When the water started to cool in the chill, she stood up in the tub, gingerly stepped out into her flip-flops, pulled her faded beach towel around her, and headed into Dart with her battery-powered lantern. The water she'd left should be boiling by now. When she opened the door, Lady darted past her legs, making her stumble, which caused her to stub her toe on the Dart's red cooler. Ouch! Instead of moving forward, as an empty cooler would have, her toe made contact with heaviness. *Why a heavy cooler?* she heard herself think, and when she pulled up the white lid, she heard herself think, *Why . . . ice?*

Why ice?

Heavy cooler—why ice?

She stood straight, felt the wave of zapping fear sluice through her, felt her body burn with hot terror at the same time she felt the frigid air. Lady parked herself outside the bathroom door and started barking.

Why barking?

At the same time, that door *opened*. At the same time, a man stepped out.

Her scream never came. Her mouth only opened in a stunned, terrified, silent O. But inside her head was a noise louder than the one that came when she got the news Vincent had died, a thousand more voltages than when she'd seen the raccoon monkeys, a pure and shattering screech. On the outside, she stood, silent, clutching her towel with one hand and a pot of boiling water with the other.

His HANDS WERE up, palms out, as if calming a horse. That much she could see by the light of the lantern and the flame of the pro-pane stove. He was not moving toward her, and, if anything, his body language indicated he wanted to back away and run, but there was nothing to back into except the trailer wall, and he could not move forward since she was blocking his exit. He looked about thirty and had a tattoo creeping up the side of his neck and was barefoot. She clutched the towel with one hand and the boiling pot with the other. She took this all in in a second in the dim light, and in the second second, her hand was lifting the pot of boiling water.

"Hey, lady," he said, simply. "Jesus." Then, "Jesus, thank you, you're not the law?" Then, as an afterthought, "Do not throw that water at me . . . I was hoping you'd *leave*." He kept his eyes on her but reached one arm down to gently redirect Lady, who was nosing his crotch.

Ammalie heard an enormous sucking in of air as she tried to fill her lungs. As she did, her eyes darted around the camper, as if the small dim space would reveal yet another human. She put down the pot, turned off the stove, put her hand out as if to indicate *stop,* and then picked up the pot of hot water again as she backed out of the trailer. "Stay there. Do *not* move! You . . . You've . . . been in that bathroom the *whole time?*" Her voice was a hiss, but she had the sudden image of her sitting in the Colorado closet, waiting for the housekeeper to leave. "I'm going to put on clothes and I want. you. to. stay. where. you. are." She could not see him now, but she kept backing up, still clutching the towel in one hand, the pot of hot water in the other, and moved in the direction of the picnic table, which held her jacket and clothes. She was shivering terribly and her heart was gallopy and her mind was so slow, and occupied with one great question: *Where is the car key?*

She scrambled first into her sweatshirt, then her coat, then her hiking pants, then pulled on her shoes without bothering with socks, then put on her winter woolen hat, and it was only then that she allowed herself to look at the trailer door, where he was now sitting on the steps with a lantern, running through Lady's neck scruff with one hand, resting his head against the palm of his other in the universal sign of exhausted despair. "I was hoping you'd go," he said, finally. "Whoever you were. Like, check on the place and *leave.* I thought maybe you were . . . Who *are* you, anyway?"

She stood near the table, one hand near the pot of water and the other curled around the pepper spray in her jacket pocket. "Where is your car? Why are *you* here? Why are you barefoot?" Then she added, still in a hiss, "You have *ice.*" Ice meant so much: that he'd been to town, that he was hiding a car.

He didn't answer, didn't shrug, didn't do anything except rub his hand over the scruffle on his chin. She touched her pant and jacket pockets—no keys. Glanced at the picnic table—no keys. Keys, keys, keys, where were her *keys*? Ah, in the front pocket of her backpack, which was on the bed in the trailer behind him.

"Okay, let's . . . let's start again," she ventured. "My name is . . . Kat. Kat Wilder." Her voice sounded ridiculous to her, as if she were trying to converse with a grizzly bear to buy time. "If I can just grab my things behind you, I'll go."

He stood, turned to eye her belongings inside, and mumbled something along the lines of "Sure, sure, jesus, lady, you scared me."

She was struck by how thin he was. Not in a starvation kind of way exactly, though . . . maybe? He was built lean . . . all muscle, youngish, and slight of frame, but that wasn't all. He simply wasn't eating enough. He was in the vicinity of good-looking, she thought, with slightly crooked teeth and a thin jaw, but mainly looked a bit unhealthy in both body and spirit. She had the idea that she simply had more calories and reserves of energy residing in her body than he did, that she might be able to take him down. Also, he looked, well . . . frightened, so frightened that he might cry. Also, he smelled bad, and she could now see he was filthy, not only his jeans and pullover but his matted dusty brown hair and the embedded dirt in his skin.

His voice was weary and yet also still full of some existential wonder at having company. "Look, lady. Can I sit down at that picnic table and explain?" At the sound of her name, Lady ran back up to him, tail wagging, and nudged him again in the crotch for a pet.

"I just need my backpack," she said. "Which is right behind you. And my sleeping bag. Just move aside. Now! I need you to let me by you."

He walked away from the trailer door and sat at the far end of the picnic table in the dark. "I'd appreciate if you didn't tell . . ." he trailed off and then started rambling top-speed. "You wanna beer? I can tell you one thing right now. I may be a lot of things, but dangerous to you is not one of them. I got a mom and sisters and all that. I'm not that kind of guy. I have never understood that kind of guy. Can't even wrap my head around it. I understand your fear, I do, but I'm not that guy. So you don't have to worry about that. You may wonder why I'm here, and that's legit, but me being a threat to you is off the table. I hope you're not a threat to *me*."

She started to shiver in earnest as she stared at the dark forms of his bare feet resting on the rocky ground. Weren't they cold? Didn't they feel the rocks and cactus? But she also breathed a sigh of relief. Surely he couldn't run fast with bare feet. She ducked into the trailer, got her backpack, unzipped it while keeping her eyes on him, felt for her keys, put them in a pocket of her down jacket. The moon came out from under a cloud and she heard herself whimper, a pent-up noise of fear escaping, and she felt some pee wet her thigh.

"Lady, seriously. I will bring you no harm."

She walked out of the trailer, fingers curled around the keys, the pepper spray can grazing her knuckles. Now she could take a moment to consider him. He'd pulled up his hood and sat hunched in the cold, so she grabbed one of the many blankets on the bed and tossed it in his direction, then tossed the big pair of wool socks she kept in her backpack at him, and grabbed another blanket for herself, and then the extra lantern. Only then did she really truly breathe, a rattly thing that reminded her of a rattlesnake. "Ah," she said finally. "You are running from the law. *You're* squatting here!" At that, she started to laugh—a release of anxiety more than humor—and then the laugh abruptly ended and was replaced by tears that burned her eyes.

He didn't answer, but cast his eyes off into the dark with a look of sadness. She walked over and sat down at the opposite corner of the table, opened her cooler, grabbed two beers, and put one in front of him. "Okay," she said. "I have pepper spray and a knife with me. Just so you know." But instead of opening his beer, he put his head in his hands and sighed. "Aw shit," he mumbled, and then she heard, "It's *over*. My time has come. I need a clean minute to wrap my brain around that," and then he started to cry, head in hands.

She waited. Looked around as if the dark sky would give her some clue as to how to respond. Finally, she ventured, "I'm squatting too. But I'm not on the run from anything except my boring life. Though that felt pretty dangerous, I will say. I think I was in real danger of becoming a TV-watching alcoholic and wasting my days and then dying. I always believed I'd die young, I don't know why, but regardless of when I do, time is shorter than we think, and I only get this one life, you know? And believe me, wasting the time we do have is a serious fucking danger." The words came out of her before she could stop them, but somehow they seemed true and necessary.

He looked up, surprised. "You're not this trailer's owner?"

"I am not. Some wealthy man in Texas owns this trailer."

"And he doesn't know you're here either?"

She paused. "He does not." Then, "What's up with your feet? Why aren't they cold? That's weird."

A smile darted across his face. "My sisters always say the same thing. They hate me for it. My feet, I don't know what to say about them, they just don't get cold."

"They don't get cold? I've never heard of such a thing. All I *ever* have is cold feet; even in the summer my feet feel cold. It's like my feet have an air conditioner built into them, meant to torment me."

He leaned sideways to regard his feet. "I mean, I wear socks and shoes usually. But you pulled up. I grabbed my stuff and ran to the bathroom. But, my feet, they're just sturdy."

"I hate you," she said. "Tell your sisters I agree."

He laughed. "I got so lonely that I started to talk to them. My feet. Their names are Righty and Lefty. I can't believe I just told you that. I'm not crazy. Kat, you say?" He paused for a minute, thinking. "Kat. Well. It's nice to meet you. I'm Kit."

She snorted, assuming he was joking. Or, rather, lying; after all, she just had. Kit and Kat. But she decided not to press it. Who cared, anyway? He smiled again. "I apologize for my . . . smell and looks. I haven't showered in a good long while. I haven't seen a person in a good long while."

"Liar," she said gently. "You have ice. Ice doesn't just appear in the desert. Where's your car?"

He started to say something, stopped. "A s— A family member."

She opened her beer, took a swig, and looked at the stars. "You're on the run and hiding out and a sister or someone brings you food and ice." She nodded to herself, knowing it was right.

"An unidentified person," he clarified. "Maybe it was a UFO. No one else is involved."

She nodded an okay. "Well, don't tell me what you did, because then I'll know, but do tell me—was it really bad? Did you kill someone? Never mind. Tell me. What *did* you do?"

He shook his head no. Then said, "I'm from Wisconsin."

She wasn't sure what to do with that piece of information, so she nodded, pulled her blanket around her, looked at the stars, waited.

"I don't know much about the desert," he said. "I'm from *Wisconsin*. I don't know how to live here. Or how to, say, get to Mexico."

She snorted with the clarity of the irony here. He was going the opposite way of so many people. So many people traveled to *find* safety, and here she was, traveling to lead a *less safe* life.

"Or how to live a life under the radar?" she asked.

"Yeah, I don't know much about that either. To answer your question, monkey-wrenching, I guess you'd say. Of the noble sort. A kind of earth justice, shall we say. No one hurt, physically. And let me say right here that I'm not trying to be political. Not left, not right, not nothing." He stood, as if deciding to run, then sat. Stood again, then sat. Pressed his fingertips to his eyes. "Except I notice that we're fucking ruining our one home! Do you understand how rare and irreplaceable this planet is? It's a floating blue ball in space that has just the right conditions to support life and we are fucking it up! It is a horrendous crime, a form of torture and abuse. What we're doing. Let's just leave it at that." This last bit was said with a thickness to his voice, and she knew he was still crying.

She chewed on her lip. "Well, good for you. Probably. Maybe. No doubt it's complicated."

He turned to her, his eyes showing surprise. "Thanks, lady," he said, with real emotion. "We're running out of time, lady. Planet is, I mean. What you said about your life goes for Mama Earth too, you know."

When she breathed out softly, the sound coming out of her mouth was still shaky. "That's the dog's name. Lady. Lady Shackleton. I stole her from a bad guy. So I guess you could say we both have justice on the mind. Justice that goes beyond this country's laws."

"Right on, man." When he reached out to scratch Lady's ears, she could see his arm shaking as her voice had.

They both took a deep breath at the exact same time and for the exact same reason. As they did, they caught each other's eyes and there was a recognition. "I call them the Shakes," Ammalie said quietly, and he nodded, understanding.

"That was scary," he said.

"A lot of adrenaline."

He nodded and pinched the bridge of his nose, then opened his eyes wide, as if that would help him gain some clarity. She could see by the bright lantern-light that his eyes were also green, like hers, but his were like some old rock around here, and they were very sad. She felt the world tilt a little, the result of two gin-and-tonics and the beer and the bath and the adrenaline. "I should go," she said. "If the law is looking for you . . . Well, I'm not wanting to get caught myself. I'm on an adventure and was just looking for a place to call home."

"This world is fucked," he said, and she assumed he meant whatever environmental destruction he was trying to protest.

"Yeah," she said. "I'm trying to protest the fuckery myself. By going a little crazy."

"Right on." He smiled a smile so genuine and young that it made her heart crack.

"How do you stay warm? The propane wasn't on." She herself was quite cold, and she suddenly and desperately wanted a fire. Her eyes drifted to the firepit near the picnic table, but it seemed unwise to build a fire in a place so visible from afar.

He followed her gaze, read her thoughts, then jutted his chin toward an outcrop of rocks. "I make fires over there. It's protected, I don't think anyone can see it. I don't want to use up the propane, except in case of a major emergency or something. I'll make us a fire, if you want."

"You saw me naked," she blurted out of the blue. She was truly surprised by this fact and her voicing of it. She tried to explain. "You are the first man besides my husband to see me naked in about thirty years. Can you believe that? I go to female doctors and female massage therapists, so, truly, you are the first man . . . *Wow.* That's *insane.*"

His eyes went from her to the tub. "Well, you had a towel. And, oh, now I understand! You were taking a bath under the stars!" He was staring like a hungry animal at the big plastic tub of water glistening in the moonlight, then he turned to smile at her with real warmth and respect in his eyes. "Right on. A hot bath would feel kick-ass. A hot bath and a fire. Nothing more fundamentally better than that, right?"

"I'll heat you up some water," she said, rising. And that's exactly what she did as he went to build a fire in the small rock enclave. Then they switched places—he to the bath, she to the fire, and when she caught sight of his naked body from the corner of her eye as he stepped in, she let her gaze linger, both out of curiosity and concern for his slight frame. An old line of poetry floated up in her mind: *I've been warmed by fires I did not build.* The peace she felt looking at him, and then at the stars, and into that fire—it was solid, and it was real.

SHE SLEPT IN Dart's bed with Lady curled alongside and stars blazing outside. It was the chill that woke her but it was the word *blazing* that was the first to enter her mind. *I am freezing under burning, blazing stars,* she thought, which is when she remembered Kit. Her nose was cold and her breath came in mist but she kicked off her sleeping bag and pulled her jacket on so she could stand and look out the window at the lump of him barely visible in the dark. There he was, sleeping on a camping pad on the picnic table, which is what he had proposed; surely he had to be far colder than her, given that he had no shelter. She wished he'd slept in her car, as she'd suggested. Or on the other couch-bed. Or, in *her* bed? Was that crazy? What was wrong about two bodies curled beside each other? People in other cultures shared beds, out of necessity and comfort, did they not? Why did Americans insist on being so *alone*? Or was it just her?

Lady raised her head and sighed happily as Ammalie snuggled back in. It was still very early, the sky gray and full of night, so Ammalie sat up and reached above her to pick up the lantern and a book on local history or stars, but her eyes landed on a spiral notebook that said GUEST BOOK. She flipped it open to the first page. It dated back to 1990, which made her snort—there had not been many guests, or they had not been very verbose. There were a few faded signatures early on, one person left a Rumi poem about lions and tender stars, and there were some notes from people who'd come to see the dark sky. Then, near the end, she saw . . . Vincent's handwriting . . . no . . . but yes, it *was* Vincent's handwriting.

"Oh!" Her hand went to her heart, to buffer the Sea Creature's sting. "Oh, jeez, oh, oh."

A note from a ghost. Lady nosed her as if to comfort her, but tears rose without warning. A bad cramp echoed through her insides at the same time, as if in response. She swiped at the tears so she could see. The entry was short:

Here with the Chicago group of Dark Sky-ers. Missing wife and son—but not missing cold and snow. Thanks for Dart's magic. I've connected with a part of my past here, shrugged off some deep sorrows. Trying to reset. Cygnus is my favorite. Albireo.

What part of his past? What sorrows? She scanned her brain. Were they going through a tough patch then? Had his self-induced isolation been depression? Besides the normal Chicago winter depression, which they joked about every year? Besides staring at stars, had he come to process some old injuries, done some introspection? What had he said about this place? Why had he never let her *in,* never really spoken, never had any zest for real connection? She could remember that he had connected with some friends—friends whom, despite living in Chicago, he rarely saw. Ammalie remembered feeling vaguely grateful at the time that he was a man who *had* friends, who made some attempt to cultivate and keep friendships, since it seemed so few men did. Sure, she'd felt abandoned at being left alone with Powell, but mainly because she was *tired.* Always, she was tired. Why did people live lives that made them so *tired*? Or was it just parenting? Or was it just her?

Cygnus. Albireo. She didn't even know those words! She looked on the shelf and pulled down a book on stars. Its thickness was intimidating, and she nearly put it back, but she cajoled herself into action. One key to the universe at a time.

Cygnus, it turned out, was a constellation lying on the plane of the Milky Way, deriving its name from the Latin word for *swan,* and contained the Northern Cross—a celestial waterfowl swimming through the river of the Milky Way. The swan's tail was composed of a variable star, meaning its brightness changed over time as its surface expanded and contracted, and the swan's head was a star called Albireo, a favorite among astronomers because when seen through a telescope, it revealed itself to be two stars together.

She put the guest book on her chest and stared at the soft waking sky through the window. Vincent had perhaps done the same. Two stars, connected.

She felt nearly as naked as she had been last night. She hadn't had sex with a man other than Vincent in decades. There was no doubt in her mind that she wanted to—she'd occasionally wanted to even while married; who didn't?—and now, with the hardest waves of grief and confusion and guilt gone, she could clearly identify the desire. She could admit the deepest truth, if only to herself:

Two stars were better than one, and she wanted a *man*. Her body flat-out burned with the ache of desire, though it's true that had turned more into an *echo* of desire, as if that part of her remembered what orgasm and satisfaction felt like.

As she drifted back to sleep, she wondered vaguely, and without any seriousness, about Kit. Too young and too injured and too occupied with other priorities. And yet. Two humans. In need of comfort, of touch, of humanity. When had sentiment become a bad thing? When had basic human desires become so taboo? She wished she weren't bleeding; she was so tired of *that* part of her body. But the other part flickered and burned, steady as a star— that was one thing she knew for sure.

CHAPTER 9

Mother. Lover. Crone. She felt the tug of all three simultaneously in different chambers of her heart, causing the Sea Creature to fling itself around in a pinball-game flurry of confusion. As Kit cooked eggs and warmed tortillas and offered small talk and deflected questions with flashes of a shy smile, she found herself worrying about his skinny body and bare feet, like a mother would. But also, zip-zapping lust—she was, after all, sitting on the bed beside the kitchen, and he could take three steps, lean her back, and be on top of her. Oh to feel *that* again. And yet, what a disaster that would be—her puffy-stomached, menstruating self did not feel like a good match for him. Perhaps she should be mentoring or assisting him, be wise counsel, be wise elder, but that did not feel like a good match, either.

What a stupid, contradictory time of life this was. And yet, no. Not stupid. Lucky.

Meanwhile, she did what all humans have done when confused— she chatted. They shared small talk as they shared breakfast. The raccoon monkeys could have been ringtails or coatimundis, different but both bizarre. The wild pigs were javelinas. Yes, the weather was mild, the sunsets beautiful. He'd been here for about a month, though he wouldn't answer more on that subject. One of his favorite places was the Colorado sand dunes, near the town of Salida, which, did she know, meant exit? She shared that she was from Chicago, a husband dead of stroke, a son growing pot, a lifelong job waitressing gone. The restaurant had burned in a fire, and there were enormous delays in getting it reopened, which it had just done. But she was finished with all that. Without husband, son, or job, her life felt as empty as this big landscape, so she was looking to fill it up with Things That Were Real before her time on the planet was up.

She didn't share her real name, or that this was her Second Squatting. She didn't share that she knew Kit could track her down later by license plate, or that knowing that made her feel uninvisible and therefore fragile. But also, she hadn't done anything *that* wrong. In fact, it was all laughable. A small series of small crimes. Compared to what he had done—and he only shrugged at all her suggestions—she was not even a potato in the bag of small potatoes.

As they cleared the dishes, she threw out some words, just to see if he'd flinch.

"Oil and gas? Construction? Billboards? Did you do it alone? Or with a group?"

But he only shook his head *no,* though he finally added in a kind voice, "For your own good, and for the safety of others, I shall remain quiet on the matter. But I will say this: The world is full of cowards. Because of that, the poor suffer, animals suffer, the planet suffers, and we need a revolution."

To which she said, "I'm in agreement. But first I'm starting with a revolution of my soul. The personal is political, after all."

After breakfast he bundled up, including shoes, and lifted his arm to raise a red tool kit, as if that explained something, and walked off into the desert, toward the first rise of a rocky outcrop back near the road. *Well, that was weird,* she thought, squinting after him. She stood hands-on-hips for a moment, unsure, and then wandered the property, making sure to stay away from the direction he'd gone, so as to give him privacy. She didn't want to seem like a squatter *and* a stalker. Whatever he was doing—making a food cache? making a bomb to blow up a dam? carving toy animals out of sticks?—she wanted to leave him alone.

Lady galloped around her; clearly, her natural instinct was to get as much exploring done while still sticking by her human, which was perhaps surprising, given her history. But Lady evidently trusted her, and vice versa. Ammalie followed Lady's cue and did some mindless wandering herself. She saw a lot of scrub, cactus, an elf owl that she could identify only because she'd flipped through the bird book over coffee.

She bent over to pick up bits of broken beer bottles, the green and clear glass glittering in the sun on the cold earth. Humans were slobs; what kind of idiot smashed beer bottles on purpose? Or shot at them? Her favorite items in the Colorado bead kit had been a few pieces of tumbled glass, and she'd tried doing some wire wrapping, which was the easiest way to incorporate glass into jewelry. She put these shards into an old lunch baggie in her backpack. She didn't know what for—they were too jaggedy to use for jewelry— but she felt the need to get them off the soil.

When she got back to Dart, there was no sign of Kit. His backpack and cooler were still inside, and she resisted the urge to snoop. Instead, once she was sure she was alone, she swapped the plate on her car. She found the envelope with new tags on the floor of her car, buried under other mail and wrappers and banana peels—and then put the tags on the New Mexico plate. She didn't want any more calls from sheriffs, or Lady's owner, or even that mayor. She didn't want to be associated with Illinois and her old boring life.

No more wasting! She left a *GONE EXPLORING, WILL BE BACK, SECRETS ARE SAFE WITH ME* note and drove toward Cave Valley Regional Park. Her plan was to go for a hike and see this famous landscape, and on the way home find some store with gas and ice and food to gift to Kit, as well as scope out potential places for future water and ice needs. When she got home, well, perhaps he'd even . . . move into Dart with her, sleep on the thin couch that could serve as a bed, or, yes, even better, lie down beside her. Oh, god, to rest her cheek on naked chest. She wondered if skin itself could be lonely.

As she turned onto the highway, an official-looking car appeared behind her. Border patrol? Sheriff? *Go away,* she thought, glancing in the rearview mirror. She glanced back, then at her speedometer. Nothing would actually happen. If she didn't speed, there would be no reason an officer would run her plate. It reminded her of a game she and Apricot used to play, pretending bad guys were after them, hiding one place and then another, darting around their backyard, and it occurred to her that Apricot's diagnosis and Vincent's death had caused her to revert to childhood. Perhaps playfulness could solve her adult problems. Lady seemed to agree, putting her head out the window with what appeared to be a smile on her face.

She wondered with a pang about how Apricot's cancer was *really* doing. Her sister, at some point, would *die.*

And Mari's divorce—how that was *really* going, in the secret recesses of Mari's heart?

And Powell, who seemed the most distant of all. That was her true sorrow. How was he, *really*? But she'd been overbearing; his yelled request that she please *leave him the fuck alone for a while* was clear.

The car behind her turned off, and soon the scrub of the Chihuahuan Desert gave way to the green life of Cave Valley. She chomped a pear, this one overripe and juicy, so she had to slurp it down fast. She thought about tossing the pear carcass toward the edge of the road, which banked down to an arroyo, but then worried that perhaps it would land on the road, and a bird would eat it, and the bird would get hit, and *that* kind of rule-breaking seemed off-limits. She did have a moral compass, after all. Instead she plonked it into her coffee cup holder.

Once she was actually in the park, the traffic increased, and she wound up a mountain with a surprising diversity of trees—plenty she didn't know but some she did; she had been making an effort, after all. Sumacs, walnut, willow, pine. And sycamores, with their golden bark, still dropping yellow leaves. Towering rocks jutted out of the mountainsides and caves; patches of lichen on rocks glowed in startling colors.

A shady trailhead caught her attention; there was only one car parked there, an old Subaru, older than hers even. She was disconcerted to see a man standing by it, but breathed easier when she saw he was with a blond curly-haired kid, maybe around eight, which, as everyone knew, was the Most Perfect Age.

"Hi, New Mexico," the kid said as soon as she got out of the car. "I'm Lulu from Seattle and we just got done hiking."

"I'm Ammalie," she said, glancing at her license plate, cursing herself for giving her real name.

"Emily?"

"No . . . uh . . . Ammalie." Still, she couldn't stop herself! What an idiot she was! "It was the most interesting thing my parents did."

"Ammalie. What's it mean?" Lulu bounced from foot to foot, her blond curls bobbing with each bounce.

Ammalie slung her day pack onto her back, an indication that she needed to go. She didn't want to converse with anyone, and if she did, she wanted to encourage low-hanging conversational fruit, which meant not revealing anything. "In German, Ammalie means work, which yes, is what I've done my whole life. But in Scots Gaelic, it means *water*. Which is what I'm doing now. Moving like water." She said it happily and offhandedly, but as soon as the words were out of her mouth, she felt a sting in her heart, which was followed by a cramp in her side. Water. She'd brought him water.

"Do you have kids? Do you have a husband?" Lulu was blurting out questions nonstop while the man was loading the car. "What's your dog's name?"

"One son. Powell. He's in college. Well, he'll soon be back in college. Maybe. Lady Shackleton, that's the dog's name."

The man turned around and raised an eyebrow. He was athletic and handsome and looked about seventy with blue eyes that really *did* twinkle. Ammalie immediately got the sense that this guy was happy; his eyes and his aura radiated humor and joy. Maybe he was a Buddhist monk. Maybe he was on magic mushrooms. "A bunch of explorers," he said. "Powell, after John Wesley?"

She raised an eyebrow back at him. "Why, yes."

He looked down at Lulu. "Powell was that field naturalist who scoped out the Grand Canyon on the first raft trip down the Colorado River. Well, the first trip we know about. That I know about. Surely Indigenous people did it too, and we need to remember our history has been incomplete. But what a crazy trip! All sorts of mishaps! They barely made it out alive. And Shackleton too! Nearly died. Exploring can kill you! Or nearly kill you!"

Lulu sucked in her cheeks and scrunched her nose. "But *we're* exploring."

He nodded. "But safely, kiddo."

Ammalie was delighted by the exclamation-point energy that this man clearly had zipping around in his soul, and decided a simple conversation would do no harm. "My husband was a fan of Powell," she offered. "He was just back from New Zealand and was in his Adventurer-Obsession phase. Scott, Shackleton, but most of all, Powell. As I'm saying this, I am realizing they were all men. There need to be more women explorers."

"Well, wasn't Ammalie Powell's wife's name?"

She was impressed. "Close—it was Emma. And his sister was Nellie."

"Like ever, they were probably the unsung heroes behind the hero."

She snorted. "Exactly. Women always become invisible." She winked at Lulu. "Never let that happen to you."

He reached out his hand. "I'm Dan."

"My grandpa is a bird-watcher," Lulu piped up as she hopped around.

"Birder," Dan corrected. "Since so much of birding is actually listening! Sometimes there's not that much watching going on at all." Then he cocked his head and made an exaggerated stance with his arms spread wide, as if praising the forests. "Hear that?"

Ammalie listened to a bunch of chirping.

"That's a yellow-eyed junco!"

"I hear it!" Lulu cheeped herself.

Dan looked crazed with delight, one eyebrow quirked. "Did you? Do you? Hear it?" And though she was not sure she could distinguish one sound from the other, she closed her eyes and tried. They listened for a while, and she opened her eyes to find Dan's eyes lit up with some deep delight as he gazed at the trees.

She said, "Um, hey, maybe I can ask you a question? What are birds doing when they rub their beak back and forth on a branch?"

"Feaking. All birds do it. Cleaning their beak."

"Clark's nutcrackers, their beaks look like they've been dipped in raspberry juice," Lulu said, confidently. "But they might change the name. Because bird names are always changing—people don't realize that—and this time it's because some of those birders were racist."

"But also because . . . ?" Dan prodded.

"Because DNA and stuff and knowledge *evolves*. We shouldn't be afraid of change."

"Exactly."

"Grandpa, do that thing where you make the noise."

"Pishing!" Then Dan did exactly that—making a pishing sound with his lips, over and over, much longer than Ammalie thought he might, and Lulu whispered, "The birds will come in to see what it's all about."

Sure enough, a few birds fluttered overhead, including a small one with some yellow that flashed by. Lady also ran over and sat below Dan, clearly enchanted by the noise as well.

"A painted redstart!" Dan gasped.

"That's awesome," she said lamely, glancing up. "I was just reading about them."

Dan was doing a happy dance, silent but with glee, and she was delighted to see anyone showing such . . . exuberant joy.

"New Mexico, that's where we'll head after Arizona," Dan said, glancing at her plate. "I'm getting Lulu out of the house for a month so her parents can work, and doing some homeschooling from the road, and we're having fun, aren't we, now? You just gotta adapt."

Lulu bent down to pick up a rock, which she held out to show Ammalie. "My mom has cancer so she's super immune compromised and I always seem to get sick so I can't be around much, and even if I was home, I wouldn't go to school, because maybe that would kill her, and anyway, I like online school. And she'll get better."

"Oh!" Ammalie said, startled by all this sudden rapid-fire talk. "I'm sure she will. What a grand adventure you're having."

"This place feels like a big soul-sigh, if you know what I mean. What happened to your husband?" Dan asked it nonchalantly, but when she faltered, he said more gently, "You referred to him in the past tense."

"He died."

"I'm sorry," he said, and seemed to mean it. "How long have you been alone?"

She bit her lip, a bit annoyed. Here was a human who was maybe getting *too* real. "A little over a year and a half."

Dan tilted his head. "Good for you, getting out. Alone. Travel is simply good for the soul. My wife has been gone for about five. I miss her. But life is short! We must embrace it all!" Then a weird thing happened: He winked at her.

Her brain did a slow rumble. Had he flirt-winked at her?

Meanwhile, Lulu was rambling off mountain names—*Hieroglyphic Mountains, Cave Creek Mountains, Chiricahua Mountains, isn't that a cool name, Coronado National Forest, Coronado was an explorer!*—but Ammalie's brain was still registering the wink, glancing at Dan, catching his eye, witnessing a raise of the eyebrows now, intentional.

Yes: It was *that* sort of wink. That sort of eye-catch. An invitation to be sure.

How very . . . forward! How very . . . insane! How long it had been for her!

Out of habit, she looked down at herself. The button-down blue shirt was hiding some of the pudgy middle—she'd actually put her best shirt on for Kit—and her hiking pants fit looser after her time in Colorado, and she'd brushed her hair—with an actual brush, not a fork—and braided it into one gray-brown braid down the side, now that it was long enough to do so. Not bad, actually. But still . . .

She stood up a little straighter and looked back up at him—yes, still sparkling blue eyes—and then over to Lulu, who was chattering on. *Madrean Sky Islands, that's another cool word, oh, and also the Dragoon Mountains, whoever named stuff around here was smart!*—and Ammalie forced her gaze back to Dan and sure enough, his eyes were there, so she went back to Lulu. *Soooooooo many places are named boring Englishmen's last names, like Mount Everest, like, give me a break, but not here, everything around here has better names, like Pinaleño Mountains and Dos Cabezas Mountains.*

Because Lulu was looking up at her now, expecting some response, she focused on the blond, bouncing kid. "Amen. I was in the Collegiate Peaks a few weeks ago," she said, collecting herself. "And I thought that was the stupidest thing ever, to name gorgeous wild mountains after . . . you know, stuffy colleges. Literally, I can think of nothing dumber. Come *on.* I think things should be named after what they look like, or remind you of, or something amusing or clever."

Lulu was delighted, which made Ammalie delighted, which made Dan delighted.

To Dan, she ventured, "Uh . . . where you guys staying? I . . . I'm looking for a KOA or something similar."

"Don't know of one of those around here," he said. "We're at Cave Valley Cabins, down the road there. Nothing fancy. Simple and clean."

"There was a pig outside our cabin this morning," Lulu said. "It smelled weird."

"A javelina," he corrected.

"A bunch of birders stay at these cabins," Lulu chimed in.

"Grandpa says there's a whole spectrum of birders, some snooty and some just normal people. We're the second group."

"I myself am trying to learn the birds. Birds and stars."

"A house wren is my favorite, because they're so small with such big noise. Did you know the males build a bunch of nests—and then the females pick one? They pretend to keep up those other homes to distract predators. I love that, pretending to have other homes!"

Ammalie startled. Pretend homes. Exactly.

Then she felt a pang for Powell. She missed him, the young him. She was glad for Lulu's chattiness; soon enough the forces of society or the universe might render this kid mute and sullen, as they had done eventually to Powell. She still needed to figure out why and how that had happened, and why the ages of thirteen to fifteen had been so . . . much less fun than she thought they'd be . . . and the ages from fifteen till seventeen seemed to be so much more distant than she thought they'd be . . . and things had just started to get better and good and then . . . well, now he didn't want to talk at all. She had tried and tried. Invited him on trips or to dinner or on walks a thousand times. She longed to know if ever the real relationship, the friendly conversation, would return. How to make that happen?

But wow, she *missed* him. She put her hand out to steady herself on the car and pinch the bridge of her nose to stop the tears. By then, Lulu was chatting away again and Dan was looking at her with some warmth and some concern, but then their momentum swept them away and they climbed into the Subaru and left. Lulu offered her a friendly wave and Dan offered her a smile and a look that only a true flirt could give.

* * *

THE HIKE MEANDERED alongside a dry creek bed and strange rock outcroppings that glittered with quartz. Lady was leashed and trotted nearby as Ammalie repeated the names of the trees over and over—placards had been placed to educate: creosote, paloverde, oaks, all of which seemed to have their own scent. The leaves of one tree looked exactly like stars falling to earth, and she was surprised that so late in the year each leaf was still caught in various phases of turning from green and yellow. She had lunch on a warm rock that had another big rock behind it, creating a perfect chair. She read from a novel by Kent Haruf set in Colorado and decided that next up she'd buy a novel set in Arizona. That's the least tourists could do, she thought—read one novel set in the state they were visiting. Then she napped a little, Lady beside her.

When she woke, she dug the shards of pottery from her pocket and stared at them, resting in her palm. Vincent had never been specific about where he'd found them, only that he pled temporary insanity. He was so delighted in having found something—a key to the past!—that he'd picked them up. He wanted them for his own. It wasn't until later, spurred by a talk at the local library about the importance of leaving artifacts, that the guilt began to gnaw. How selfish that had been! How small-minded! What if everyone did that! What good were pottery shards sitting on his office shelf? He needed to right his karma. He needed to put them back. He suggested they go together someday to return them.

Someday.

What an easy word to say. What a bizarre assumption.

But she couldn't do it, it somehow didn't feel like the right place, and so she put the shards back into her pocket and hiked back to the car and drove the car off the mountain. As soon as she was at the park gate and had reception, she called Powell. He didn't answer, so she left a message.

"Hey, Powell, I miss you truly. Was thinking about you when you were eight or so, when we built forts and went on adventures around the neighborhood. I just wanted to say that I'm sorry I wasn't more of an explorer for you later. I was thinking that often I didn't rouse the energy to do things, and Dad would sometimes suggest trips and camping, and I argued that you should just be allowed to go to the pool or flop on the couch, which is what you wanted to do back then, but now I realize I was just being kinda . . . lazy, I guess. I was *tired*. You were too young to know you had options beyond the pool and the couch. It takes some spine, some energy, to get people out and exploring, and Dad was great at that, and now I feel bad that sometimes I was a weight. Not always, but sometimes. I just wanted to say that. I love you. Go explore life. Conjure up the *oomph* you need to go have adventures. It does in fact take *oomph*. I hope this makes sense. I'm not wanting to be a nag. But I am still your mom, you know. I love you so much. I really, really, really miss you."

She let that all sit. It was the truest thing she could say, and it was important.

She texted Mari: *All well, you? Love you. Despite not communicating, I am really thinking of you. And hoping all is ok. I'm in remote Arizona. Adventuring.* Then she texted Apricot an obligatory photo of Cave Valley and drove on.

She knew the pattern of her people: Powell might text something back in the next day or two, Mari would get back to her as soon as she could, Apricot likely wouldn't for weeks, and then only out of obligation. As kids, they'd adored each other—at least, that's how she remembered it. But in their teen years they grew annoyed with each other, and then the adult years sent them spiraling further apart, and then they really rifted with the death of their mother and all the work that involved. Which was too bad—that had been their chance, perhaps, to find the laughter and friendliness of the early years. There were certain things that only Apricot knew, things only siblings growing up in the same household could know. Small things, but still, those things were a part of who Ammalie *was*.

She resumed driving, and right before she hit the edge of the desert, where the mountains were about to change into flatlands, she passed a little dirt road with a sign that said CAVE VALLEY CABINS. She slammed on the brake, jolting Lady forward, and pulled in. "Sorry, Lady," she said, reaching out to hold her in the seat, then scratching her jaw, which Lady seemed to love. After a stretch of winding road, and after crossing a wooden bridge, she came upon a cluster of small log cabins. A sign pointed to the lodge, a wooden building with dozens of bird feeders outside. She saw the old Subaru pulled in at one of the cabins and smiled; Lulu had been a little bit of unexpected bright in her day, and Dan . . . well, Dan. She didn't know what to make of that.

She scanned around for a water spigot. Her eye rested instead upon a HELP WANTED sign in the window of the office. She paused a moment, considering. She'd thought about getting a job at her destinations, but the problem with a job was that people would want forms—IDs and Social Security numbers, and it's not that she couldn't do that, but she didn't *want* to do that, her whole goal had been to live under the radar, to be invisible, to have some time on earth where she was mostly untracked, unavailable to others, and could move at her own pace and rest until she felt rested and *not* work.

Also, she had trained enough servers and waitresses herself to know what a drag it was to train someone, only to have them leave. She didn't want to be that person. But on the other hand, she needed to think about the reality of the trailer. Small, claustrophobic, without electricity, and, well, *occupied*. And although she had enjoyed daydreaming about some flirty romance between Kit and her, she needed to get real. She should leave Kit to his own . . . adventure. Besides, he was fifteen years too young, and Dan, well, Dan was fifteen years too old, although she had to admit to the irony of that opinion, given that she was the one who was angry at culture's rules about appropriateness in general, and about making assumptions based on age. Apparently, she had some unpacking to do of her own assumptions. Who said she couldn't take a lover twenty years older or younger? No one. She was limiting herself in ways she was barely aware of.

She did a U-turn, left, and drove on, back toward the desert. At a lone gas station, she grabbed some overpriced canned goods and sandwiches and dog food and gallons of water, bought gas, and drove back to Dart, the right front wheel making an unhappy noise, the rutted road surely not helping, but her heart jumping around with some vague excitement. She and Kit would have the sandwiches and chips and ice cream she'd bought. She even had honey sticks filled with weed that she'd bought in Colorado. Perhaps he'd like to get high with her—it had been a long time since she'd done that!—and they'd talk and laugh and embrace the floating coziness that weed generally offered.

She'd hear something of his life. She'd see that smile. She'd feel connected to a man for some brief moment in time. That was enough.

THE SEA CREATURE stabbed one good zinger into her heart before slinking down into her stomach, drowning, when she found Dart empty. Not only empty, but *empty*. No ice cooler, no sleeping bag, no tarp, no tool kit, and nothing but a clean composting bucket and wood chips in the trailer bathroom. No Kit hiding there. Worst of all, no note—though hers was gone.

She sat down at the picnic table and ran her fingers through Lady's fur. Bundled up in a coat, she was warm enough, but she turned her face up to the sun, as if doing so might warm her heart, too. Suddenly she didn't feel well. Perhaps losing all that blood in the past days, perhaps eating canned food, perhaps the stress of squatting in someone's trailer only to find someone there, perhaps the sorrow of seeing Vincent's handwriting, perhaps missing Powell, perhaps coming across a man who awoke some old feeling but then had disappeared into the desert. Yes, perhaps having people suddenly go missing was just breaking her. Or maybe it was just low blood sugar.

She poured herself a whiskey and ate a few potato chips and watched the setting sun. Fuck the universe. It all just suddenly *hurt.* The Sea Creature wasn't letting up, zigzagging and stinging her heart: One zing of nostalgia for eight-year-old Powell. Another sting of regret for not realizing how special that time had been. Another zap of sadness knowing she'd not be a grandmother, probably, given Powell's realistic fear of the future. Another zing for kids like Lulu never being born, because climate change had made some understandably unwilling to bring someone else into the world. Several zings for finding Kit gone, without a word. A small series of zings in her lower belly for a body going haywire and menopause signaling the end of something, though, of course, she didn't want a child *now,* though technically, and insanely, her doctor had told her she still *could.* She snorted sadly, thinking how absurd it would be to use a condom now, at this late stage in life.

Lady, who was sitting on the picnic bench too, pushed her head under Ammalie's armpit, as if trying to get her to stop drinking. But Ammalie raised her whiskey in a toast instead and said, "Lady, what can I say? It takes the bite out of the gloom. It reduces the pain."

As if in response, she began to cramp badly, enough to gasp and lurch forward. She put her forehead on the picnic table. So fucking unfair—her period should be winding down—the whole setup was complete fuckery! She stared down at the grain of wood and said to her armpit and Lady's nose, "Hey, Lady? You ever feel like you have a new and improved heart? You've figured out how to live? You feel you've just been born? But then you discover you're getting old and life is fragile and you could *die*?" Then she began to cry in earnest, her body heaving, and Lady nosing her armpit while she mumbled sorrowful truths.

WHEN SHE WOKE at her Midnight Alert Hour, as she'd named it, she sat up in Fluffiest Red and glanced around Dart, lit by moonlight, and moaned. The wind was gusting and the trailer rocked and creaked, the plastic in the window swooshed back and forth, and, god, she felt unsteady herself. And cold. She was still drunk. And high—she'd gone ahead and done that on her own—and not only had it *not* been fun, all it produced was sweaty feet and dry mouth and endless-seeming munchies, which had required that she eat an entire bag of chips. The trailer started to wave—and it wasn't all from the wind.

Jesus, why was she always making such bad decisions? She pulled up her sleeping bag and pulled Lady closer to her and gazed at the cupboards in the little moonlight-lit cabin. The cupboard handles were so ugly. Her heart was ugly. She was an ugly person. She lay there, panting, recognizing a general anxiety, a general loneliness, a specifically bad headache.

To distract herself from pain, she considered her day tomorrow, which was spookily open-ended and empty in a spookily empty place. What would she do? There wasn't enough room for her yoga mat inside the trailer, but she could get her exercise by going on a hike. She could journal and study plants and stars and then she'd . . . She wasn't sure.

She didn't feel like doing any of those things.

She considered the dark outside and registered her fear. How very different life was without bright lights. She thought of the streetlights of her neighborhood in Chicago, evenly spaced, and the glow of light from the city itself in the distance. Although she found the light and noises of the city a constant low-grade annoyance, this silence-except-for-wind was weirdly annoying too. She hadn't realized silence could be so loud that it zinged your eardrums. And suddenly it was all *very* spooky—she had to admit it. No one knew where she was except Kit, and maybe he was not a nice man after all.

"Ammalie," she heard herself whispering, "I know you want to be a brave explorer, but this is stupid, this just isn't gonna work."

She fell asleep and dreamed of the restaurant. Of teaching another server, which she had done countless times. In her dream, she told the woman all the waitressing wisdoms: the side work of busing tables, rolling utensils. How the kitchen was loud, so when you said something, the cooks had to reply "Heard." How when you went around a corner you said "Corner" and when you were behind someone you said "Behind." How "open counts" were the number of people with menus open, how you might walk around and tell the kitchen staff that there were "sixteen open" and they'd reply "Heard." How big round plates were called "rounds" and French onion soup was referred to as "fo." She spoke of the need for efficiency. Speed.

At first light, she woke to the dream, and her hand was on her scar on her right temple—the result of a tray tipping, her losing balance, a broken wineglass hitting her head as she hit the floor, and a gash wide enough that even the good surgeon couldn't quite make it invisible. No one had been at fault, not exactly, but it's also true that perhaps she'd been moving too fast that day, and perhaps she'd been daydreaming or vaguely unhappy. In any case, now it felt like a marker of her work, her speed, her not really living her life, of being checked out and oblivious.

It marked something else—the moment she'd decided that getting a divorce was the sanest path possible. Her boss had driven her to the hospital; she'd called Mari to pick her up. She hadn't called Vincent, since she knew he was at a Geography of the Midwest meeting, but more because she knew he would find her very request annoying, her interruption annoying, her very presence on the planet annoying. It didn't even occur to her to call him, in fact. Comfort and help were to be found elsewhere. He had ceased to be interested in her life. And Mari was right—the only interest he did seem to have was in bossing her around, making small directorial comments about how she could do this or that better. The situation was not only bland, it was quietly toxic. A bloody head, and she'd not even considered calling her husband. *That* was revealing. And she knew then that if she let it continue, *she* would be to blame.

CHAPTER 10

Her mouth was tangy, her hair a tangle, her teeth filmy, her brain fuzzy and unrested. *Oh, how fast the feral descends.* She sat up slowly, sipped at water. Lady sat up too, and whined a sad whimper, as if telling Ammalie that she too saw the problem here.

Now the trailer was surprisingly hot, too hot. In her drunken blur, she'd turned the heater to high at midnight, which was insanely stupid, given the limited propane. She struggled out of Fluffiest Red—lordy, she was going to suffocate—turned off the heat, and opened the door for a breeze and to let Lady out. No sign of Kit. Just the Grey Goose, sitting there valiantly, frosted. Chilly air rushed in, and she went from being too hot to too cold almost immediately. She closed the door and pulled on long underwear and bundled up.

She'd make up for her Lazy Living—drinking too much, pouting—by doing something spectacular. She dully gathered her items: backpack, water, Travel Pouchy, first aid kit, a cheese sandwich, a container of dog food. She'd go as far as she could in one day—perhaps ten miles. Just to push herself. Just to see if she could do it. She would no longer feel squishy and sad, inside or out. One hike, and then she'd leave. Move on to someplace new. Where? She did not know. Hence the hike. It would give her time to think.

Should she text Mari the coordinates? Should she leave a note? *Just, go. Get going, you. big. baby.* She had Lady. She had food and water. She had a plan. Shackleton didn't text people. She had a coat and hat and gloves and food. Self-reliance was a lost art.

She headed first to the rock outcrops where she'd last seen Kit near the rutted dirt road. There were footprints in the sand, to be sure, and the firepit, and a small cave she'd not seen before, where, she supposed, a cooler could be placed and kept in the shade. But there was no sign of a cooler or anything else. No sign of camping. Nothing being built. She kicked at the dirt, wondering what he had meant about monkey-wrenching. Like, putting sugar in a politician's gas tank? Like, blowing up a switching station at a gas rig? Like, sending some evil substance to an Exxon official who was burning up the Amazon jungle? Like, blowing up part of the Nestlé plant that was pumping water from an aquifer for stupid plastic bottled water near the Great Sand Dunes of Colorado, which he'd told her about? Suddenly the possibilities seemed endless, and she had to admit, she approved of nearly all of them.

She needed to forget about Kit, she needed to forget about Levi, she needed to stop wondering about Dan's intent, she needed to stop hoping for love, she needed to stop navigating her life around men, she needed to *change her brain*. She needed to be a strong solo explorer. She hefted her backpack to her shoulders and set off to the south, breath misting from both her and Lady's mouths. She knew this was called Bootheel country, and it did feel like a bootheel; rather, her soul felt trampled like a bootheel. She had to step between barbed wire twice—surely she was trespassing on private land, but no one was in sight. She moved up what looked like a deer path, which reminded her of what the thief in Colorado had said—that roads were built on animal paths, that they had a wisdom about the best way across valley or slope.

She hiked on and paused, suddenly aware of how easy it would be to get lost. Okay, she had to be smart here. She took small bits of twine from her backpack and tied them to trees, snapped photos of the landscape around her. She could still see Dart, could also see how it was positioned in the long flat valley, a solitary dot in a huge landscape.

After an hour, the land began to incline more fully with rock outcroppings and more trees. Her legs pushed her up; her head was clearing and she wasn't out of breath and she felt strong and capable. Despite drinking too much and her mushy soul, she *was* in better shape than she'd been for . . . well, a decade, at least. She stopped to get her bearings often—the bluff to the south, the distant peaks to the west, the location of the sun, and petted Lady, who was trotting happily beside her, darting off occasionally to smell something but always coming back.

She stopped under a paloverde tree so they could both eat lunch, and she estimated she'd been hiking for a little over two hours with a few breaks, so perhaps had gone five or six miles, and now she'd have to double back, which scared her a little. Why'd she come so far? Well, nothing like putting oneself into a situation to force a push into new territory!

The sheer expanse was the stunner here—the land stretched so far that she felt she could even sense the curve of the earth. That, and the solitude. She was truly alone, and the hairs on the back of her neck pricked, even with Lady panting nearby. Planet of the Apes, that's what it felt like. But it had been invigorating— and she'd not been too cold, nor was it windy. The air was crisp, her cheeks pleasantly chilled, her lungs and heart and leg muscles strong. She was *alive*.

She closed her eyes and tried to feel the place, the joy of the place, to practice her gratitudes for sitting here. It didn't matter that Vincent would love it, or that Powell should someday see it, or that Apricot would never bother to even wonder about it, or that she'd tell Mari about it. It didn't matter that Levi or Dan or Kit should see her out here. It was just her. Ammalie. She was the one whose eyes sought out the cactus wren on the cholla, she was the one who sensed that the air was cooler in the draw where a creek normally ran, and she was the one who could *smell* the sunlight in the sunny patches. She tapped her hiking boots on the ground. She meditated on her feet, about how they connected her to the planet, about all the steps they had ever taken for her.

As she chewed her apple, she felt too the expanse of *time,* and tried to recall the history of this general area—Cochise, the great chief, and the Hohokam people, how this land had been taken, *stolen,* from them, violently. She remembered something about Pancho Villa and Geronimo, but she thought too of the women, the untold-of, unsung, strong, and kind women. She could also understand why so many people came here for vision quests or mystical experiences. She could *feel* how magical this place was— Chihuahuan Desert to the east, the Sonoran Desert to the west, the Rocky Mountains to the north, and the Sierra Madre to the south. The place had a vibe, a storied history, a crazy topography. It was a *place of interest,* as the placard had declared, and her getting here made her a person of interest.

As she gathered up her supplies to head home, a texture caught her eye. Smooth human-made something under a nearby tree— something out of place. She approached carefully: It was a filthy olive-green plastic storage tub, similar to the one she kept her food in, but much older and battered, upside-down with a very large rock on top of it. It was alongside an animal trail in a wash. She looked around for a minute and then walked right up to the tub. On it were words, scrawled in black marker and sloppy hand-writing: GO IN PEACE, TRAVELER. PAZ.

She took off the rock—heavy and nearly all she could manage—

and lifted the tub. There were three dusty gallon jugs of water and two very rusted cans of beans titrated tightly together. She considered it for some time, was aware of how slowly her mind was working. Ah, for migrants, for those who were walking up from the Mexico border. Two of the gallons had writing on them. One had a peace sign and the other said AQUA PURA.

Huh. Someone bringing water. To keep someone alive. Exactly what she'd done, only *this* water was useful.

She put the tub back, adding the freeze-dried snacks she had in her pack, put the rock back on top, and turned around, retracing her steps, feeling surprised. Surprised that a water drop would be this far north. Was that normal, to have water drops here? Also, perhaps she was less alone than she thought. There were people wanting to be unseen everywhere. Her bitterness about middle-age-woman-unseenness suddenly felt deeply, deeply silly and petty—here she was, moaning about growing older, being alone, being without a job, sad about dumb things like her eyesight deteriorating and the necessity of five different kinds of eyeglasses, but who had the capacity to get all those glasses, and all this while someone else was wanting to be invisible to *survive*. To *live*!

No more of this, she thought. *No more of this whining. You're embarrassing even me. How lucky you are. Not another word of whining.* Then she glanced at the angle of the sun and figured she'd better pick up the pace. Tiny rocks under her feet rolled like BBs and she had just enough time to glance down at them with curiosity when her right foot started to slide, her body tilted backward, instinctually tried to correct itself and lean forward, and then, horribly, she felt the pebbles under her left foot give. Air. *Ooof.* She was aware of her feet floating in air, time speeding up, her ass hitting hard ground, a zing in her tailbone, and a twist sending her sideways into a long-fallen branch and the rock beneath it. A moment of

quiet. Of startle. Of Lady's whine. Of the sound of pebbles still rolling downhill. Then the pain hit.

She sat up and covered her mouth with her palm to hold in the
moan and rising vomit, then moved those fingers to her temple.
They came away bloody. "Oh, okay, no thanks," she said to them.
"Oh, fuck." And to Lady, she said, "It's okay, girl, it's okay," because Lady was trotting around her, whining.

Awe. That was her main emotion. Awe that life was so predictable. She had forecast such a thing when packing the first aid kit,
and such a thing had happened.

Then, more pain. In her tailbone and in her head. Lady whined;
she whined. She put her hand back up to her head and looked. A
palmful of blood. Head wounds just bled a lot, right? But warm
sticky ooze was seeping down her cheek and neck and she looked
down and pulled her shirt away to find a thin stream already between her breasts. It had all happened so fast.

Stay calm. Ammalie, stay calm.

My head feels torn.

Stay calm.

With shaking hands, she got out her first aid kit and unwound
the long piece of white bedsheet she'd rolled long ago. Breathed
in, breathed out. Put a thick piece of gauze and applied pressure to
the wound. Flung it to the side when it was pure red, then put new
gauze on, held it tight as she quickly wrapped the bandage around
her head. Over this she put her baseball cap, in order to hold it all
tightly to her head, though there was a piercing pain, and her teeth
were chattering now, and not from the cold.

She rinsed the blood from her hands with water from one of
her bottles, made sure to drink the rest of it as she swallowed two
ibuprofen. Her hands were still sticky, especially in between her
fingers, but she didn't want to waste more water. She sat there until

she felt she was okay, and then stood slowly. It was fine. The world wasn't wobbly, though there was a stinging burn and an ache in her head, two separate sensations.

"Ut-oh," she said to Lady. "Ut-oh ut-oh ut-oh."

She turned and stumbled down the path, in the direction of Dart. Her heart throbbed along with her head.

Think, Ammalie. It had taken her a few hours to get here, and then she'd paused, and if it took her a few hours to get back, she'd make it in daylight. Barely. But if she had to stop and rest, then it would get colder and dark, and although she had a headlamp, the idea of tripping or stepping on cactus or animals . . . oh, god, there were bears and jaguars. She tried to pick up her pace, but she stumbled, and slowed.

Slow, Ammalie, slow.

Her brain whirred and blurred. She felt high again—were the edibles kicking in *now*? She touched her greenstone necklace and the key that hung next to it. She hummed a song. Some creature moved in the bush beside her and her yelp sent her head into a new level of thrumming.

"Oh my god," she mumbled to Lady, trotting alongside her and also looking tired. "Oh, god. What have I done? I need . . . help. I'm so stupid, I'm so fucked!"

Against all odds of the universe, a calm, quiet voice responded. A voice that was not her voice, but more like an echo of a voice, as if coming from a different plane of existence, as if coming from others who had been here. *Keep going.*

Oh, god, she *was* going crazy. She *was* high! She touched her ears, as if they were the problem. Auditory hallucinations. She'd heard of such a thing. The pot . . . the loss of blood . . . the loneliness . . . she *really* had broken. Into *shards*! She didn't realize how many breaks there could be! No one had ever bothered to tell her that when you thought you'd hit rock bottom, there were way more bottoms to go!

She sat down and started weeping, hiccupping and wiping snot on her sleeve. She was woozy, then nauseous, then trembling from cold and fear, then woozy again. She'd bled through her tampon and pad and could feel warm wet turning cold in her crotch, where there was also cold pee, and so she struggled with her pants and her backpack and supplies and managed to deal with all that, and then rested again. Now her head was bleeding through the bandage. Her tailbone zinged wildly from her fall. Her head felt like a balloon about to burst.

A contorted ironwood tree next to a dilapidated barbed-wire fence was nearby; she got up and stumbled over to it, sat on a rock at its base, heard herself whimper. If she had been hiking with someone, this would be so different.

She wanted one of her three keys.

She wanted to go back in time.

She wanted to do things differently.

Head resting on the tree, she could gaze at the sky. Now the sun was tilting to the horizon and the temperature was dropping. Though it was still light out, the moon was up and visible and something was fluttering above—*bats,* she realized. She murmured the children's poem while staring at the first stars and applying pressure to her head by pressing her palm into it. If she could just quit resisting this . . . If she could just accept this place, and the night, and the unexpected situation . . . She had some sense that this was not her plan, but it was okay . . . If she could just rest. She was cold. She pulled Lady to her and hugged her, and Lady stayed still, quietly panting.

Some part of her brain told her to move, and another part told her to stay. As ever, two opposing truths existed at once. *Get up.*

Move on. Onward. Rest, rest, you need rest. Some indeterminate amount of time went by, and then she heard Lady woof.

When she opened her eyes, she saw a figure, and oh, fuck, she was hallucinating or had a concussion.

"Hey, Kat." His voice was low and full of concern.

"Kit?"

She reached out and poked him hard in the stomach to see if he was real. He gently held her hand. "Where'd *you* come from? What are you doing out here, Kat?"

"I was on a hike. I fell."

He was on one knee in front of her, holding her hand, then shining a light into her pupils and putting his hands on her neck. "I've been watching you for a bit . . . hoping you'd make it on your own, I guess. You seemed to be doing okay until now." He sighed. "Debating. My life or yours?"

"Why is it one or the other? Why'd you leave?" Her voice was whiny.

"Can you walk? It's getting colder. Push on. Like Shackleton, eh? You can do it."

He reached out to pull her up, and they took some small steps. He had a backpack on, a cooler in one hand, a nearly empty gallon jug of water in the other, but he set the water down and abandoned it so that he could use one arm to prop her up. In the other hand, he held her backpack. For a long time, they shuffled in silence, and she found herself counting things in three to the fall of a footstep.

Step—by step—by step.

Key—by key—by key.

Pow-ell, Mar-i, Apri-cot.

Step—by step—by step.

One—and two—and three.

As they stumbled on, Lady trotting by their side, her mind loop-ily thought back to the vague time after Vincent's death, the way so many people had commented on how well she was doing, but how one co-worker had asked bluntly if she'd encountered a Dark Night of the Soul, to which she'd shrugged and wondered *What does that even mean?* She understood it now. And she was in it. Her dark night was actually in a dark night, and no, she was not okay.

As if in response to this thought, Kit said, "Hang in there. Talk to me. You doing okay?"

"Ah, that's why I did this trip," she murmured by way of answer. She halted and pointed up at the Milky Way, at the swan, Albireo. Now she knew: Because she and Vincent *had* connected when they traveled, and in order to truly let him go, she needed to feel connected to the best moments with him, so as to really tell him and her guilt *goodbye*. It was the better way to go. To consider the best moments, not the bitter ones. But simultaneously, she needed travel to connect with her own independent self, to say *hello* to herself, the most genuine version of herself. She said, "To break into other people's lives until I found mine."

"Okay, cool," he whispered back.

"And it's easier because I'm white. We're *white*. Do you know what that gives us?"

She could feel him pause, then nod.

She started to cry. "I haven't had to walk across deserts. Or worry when police pulled me over. And you haven't either. To inhabit my true self, I need to recognize these things. I've been breaking into homes. I need one person on the planet to know that I'm doing this illegal thing. And you're *it*. And I need someone to know that I was trying to be courageous, but also, I was always taking so much for granted."

She thought he'd object or wave away her comment, but he did not. He was nodding, murmuring, *Right on, lady. Cool, cool. Keep walking, friend.*

DART AND THE Grey Goose reflected in the moonlight like a lighthouse, an odd beacon of light in the desert. The hoots of the owls and the sounds of coyotes no longer startled or scared her—her nervous system was overloaded—and Kit and Lady were with her. She was shaking hard now, though, and Kit had his arm around her waist, both propping her up and trying to keep her warm. He'd put his winter cap on her head, and his jacket on her shoulders, though she didn't quite remember when that had happened.

Her mind floated. To big things, important things, things to distract her from the pain. Like, she hadn't cared so much about the United States–Mexico border situation—the proximity principle and all. Chicago was so far away. She wondered how humans could better tune in to issues beyond their purview? And do more about the things they clearly saw? Like, children in schools being shot. Like the destruction of the planet. Like the rights of women fading away.

She needed to go someplace other than her hurting body. Than this cold night. So she also touched the greenstone necklace for comfort. Vincent's engagement ring, of sorts. He'd bought it from a Māori co-worker in New Zealand, whose father made them. Next to it, he had put a thick, small key, which he'd said he found on the property he was living on, and that he found particularly beautiful, but that since it didn't fit anything, he'd . . . well, *taken* it. He thought it was as pretty as the stone itself—after all, an old key was a piece of art.

But the greenstone and key were more than an engagement ring.

They were also meant to mark the loss of their baby. Though being on birth control, she'd gotten pregnant on one of their early dates, and before she knew of the pregnancy, he'd left for New Zealand on a long-planned trip. She'd emailed him—one of the first emails of her life, this being in the '80s—and told him of the pregnancy, unsure whether to get an abortion or not. He confessed to having a lover there and being unsure himself, and both agreed it had been just a fling, and yet, now there was this . . . situation. A baby.

She'd waited for her brain to decide—and then nature decided for her. Right at the two-month mark, she miscarried, which was a relief and extraordinarily physically painful and somehow very, very sad. Contradictory strong emotions blasting her all at once. She was twenty-two at the time, alone, in college, with a dead father and a mother she wasn't very close to, so when Vincent arrived with a proposal and a necklace, she said *yes*. When she told him there was no baby, he proposed again, and again she said yes. And she'd worn it since, touching it whenever she needed it, such as now. Because even if love had dissipated, and even if the commitment to marriage had perhaps been born of fear more than true connection, it all had originally felt so hopeful and real.

She thought, *I want to love again. I want to hope again.*

She thought, *I want the world to be better for everyone, for women and children, for people of all countries, I want better solutions.*

She thought she heard a voice from the dark, a whisper. "Just do *something*. Any good thing. Keep going."

IN THE TRAILER, she mumbled "Thank you" as she climbed into her sleeping bag in bed and Kit said, "No problema," but she had been thanking the universe, Lady, herself, and, sure, Kit too. She turned on her side and stared at Kit's filthy jeans, since that's what was in her line of sight. He was moving around Dart quickly. First, propping her up by bear-hugging her and pulling her upward and leaning her against the trailer wall, then heating water, putting a cup of tea into her hands. He was rewrapping her head and then unzipping the bottom half of the sleeping bag and pulling off her socks and checking her feet, then massaging them, then bundling them up with new socks with hand warmers jammed in. He was pouring dog food into a bowl for Lady. He put a sandwich into her hand, and when she didn't eat it, he tore off a hunk and pressed it to her lips until she started chewing.

"You want medical attention? I can drive you. The wound— well, it's not the gash I imagined, given how much you bled. It's not too deep, but it's *long*. Like, super long. Maybe about four inches. Dang, lady." His voice was soft and he kept on chatting, perhaps to calm them both. "Starts at your hairline, goes back toward the crown. You have all this *hair* in the way. It's hard to see. But it's stopped bleeding, I do think you'll be okay."

But they both knew what he was also saying: If you're fine, I prefer not to go into town, so she said, "If I need to, I'll take myself in the morning." Then, "Kit, how old are you, anyway?"

"Thirty-nine."

"You look younger."

"That's what people say."

"You're a grown adult."

He nodded, confused. "Just like you."

"You been doing this for years, or is this a new thing?"

"New."

"Because you got to a place in life where you knew you needed to do more?"

He nodded. "You could say that."

"Just how much trouble are you in?"

He groaned and sat back. "I'm trying to figure that out myself. I know I need to take responsibility, but also, I need to say that what I am doing is right. I will say this. I'm sorry I left. I just didn't want to put my . . ."

"Sister."

"Yeah, my sister. In jeopardy. I don't want to go to prison, though I will if need be, I guess. But one thing I can't do is put *her* in danger. She's only bringing me food. She's got two kids! So I needed time to think through a plan. I went to this . . . predesignated site we have where I leave an empty cooler and she leaves me a full one. Believe me, I wanted to come back and hang . . . I wanted to stay. With you. You seem like kinda a nut, an interesting and intriguing woman . . . And this sucks, being out here alone! I'm not a natural at it. It's not like I've got a long history of backpacking in the wild! I'm just figuring shit out, man, and I could use some company. I'm lonely. But I just couldn't do that to my sister . . ."

"I get it," she mumbled. "She's one of your keys." She reached her hand up to touch her bandaged head, if only to make sure her head was really there. The pain roared, and she remembered that she'd hoarded some antibiotics and so dug them out of her backpack, took one, and then got up to pee and change her pad. Then, she got back in bed and closed her eyes.

A firm hug.

A shower.

A real meal.

A more comfortable place.

Heat.

She wanted all this—for herself, for Kit, for everyone.

She reached out to touch Kit's arm. "I'm so glad you found me."

"What if I hadn't, Kat? I was camping out there. I heard this noise. Scared the shit out of me."

"Well, this wound is not going to kill me."

"No," he said.

"If a cut this size was on my arm, I'd just bandage it."

"Yeah, me too."

"It just bled a lot because it's on my head."

"I think so," Kit said. "But I'm not a medical professional."

"I don't have a concussion."

"You don't seem to."

"You talk to your feet?"

He paused. "What?" Then he laughed. "Oh, yeah, I mentioned that to you. Righty is quite a chatterbox, quite bossy and obstinate. Lefty, on the other hand, is quiet and meditative, a peacemaker. What can I say? I'm going crazy out here."

She snorted. "I love it." Then she added, "I wouldn't mind if you stayed the night. To keep an eye on me."

He let out a gust of air. "Well . . . I dunno, lady." He smiled. His voice was encouraging when he said, "You stole a dog from a bad guy. You're squatting here and you've been breaking into homes. You changed your license plate, I see. *You* might be a little crazy. But I need to tell you, you're now harboring or helping a wanted fugitive who is a target of a federal investigation. You're in new territory here, Kat. That's why I should go. There is a warrant issued for my arrest. I'm telling you this so you can choose."

"I choose you stay."

"Kat, listen. There are three ways outta this. Are you listening? If ever someone questions you. There's something called a justification defense, in which you can claim you felt the government was not justified in going after me. The other thing you can say is that you felt threatened by me, or that you had a lack of knowledge. Okay? So pick one of those three. If ever you need to."

"Got it," she said. "I'll pick the last one. I don't know nothin'.

Yes. Lack of knowledge, that seems like the one." She took his hand and looked up into his eyes. "Kit, just tell me. Overall, what do you *want* for the planet? What's the goal here?"

He paused. Made a wistful hum. "I guess it comes down to one word. *Wilder.* I want things to be a bit wilder, so that the wild things can *live*. Like, ninety percent of the weight on the planet is made up of humans and their stuff and the animals that feed them. There's hardly room left for anything else! That's wrong! We need things wilder. That is my mission. That is my word."

"The planet to be wilder," she said.

"And people's hearts."

"And our time on earth."

"Exactly."

"Wilder," she repeated. "Truer." She felt satisfied. "I need to sleep now." She could barely form words. "You have my promise. You have my friendship. I swear it on all good explorers' graves. But do stay with me tonight. Next to me. Then you can stay or leave, I get it. But I need to not be alone at this particular moment in time."

CHAPTER 11

Head, knee, butt.

Joints, muscles, nerves.

Plinks, zings, chimes.

Pain came in so many flavors of lousy. But then there was this: She woke to her face pressed against Kit's arm, her own arm thrown over his chest. *Companionship for the skin* was the phrase that drifted across her mind as she drifted back to sleep. She woke the second time to desire. The old ancient human glory surpassed even pain, which seemed unbelievable, but there it was, thrumming. *Survival of the soul trumps all.* That was the phrase that floated in her brain when she opened her eyes to find his weathered-rock-colored green eyes looking back with a fond and concerned expression. Before her reasonable brain could step in and ruin everything, she leaned forward and kissed him on the cheek, and then when he didn't pull back, kissed him on the lips, and when she pulled back, he leaned into her and kissed her. A soft brush of a kiss, but with just enough pressure to signal that lust existed alongside fondness. Then they smiled at each other and then she fell asleep. The third time she woke, she was alone. Coffee was next to her in a thermos and underneath it, a note.

> K, I need to leave for good. But it's to protect people and it's
> done with regret. Wish we were both less alone. And I've
> had some lovely daydreams about you. But, onward, before

it gets messy, because what else? That's what you said in your sleep last night. "Because what else?" This planet is all we got—remind people of that. For the wild, K.

She felt the vacuum of sadness drop through her body. But better to feel it, to let the disappointment sting, and then to remember the kiss, surely the gentlest, softest kiss she'd ever received.

From bed, she looked out the window and watched the wind whip the dirt around, and then she got up, dressed, checked the bandage, threw on a winter cap to keep the bandage in place but also to conceal it, put Lady in the car, and drove without thinking much to the Cave Valley Cabins. *One problem at a time,* she thought. *Just. Go.* But it was a softer, calmer directive than it had been in times past.

She pulled up to the office and was walking toward it when she saw a kid dart by with blond curly hair poking under a red cap. "Lulu," she found herself saying. "You're still here!"

Lulu wheeled around and trotted back. "You're the woman from the parking lot who names things! We'll be here for a long time. My grandpa is friends with the owner. They fought in a war together a long time ago. Are you staying here?"

"No. I'm staying in a little trailer. But it's small, and it gets lonely."

Lulu scratched at her wool cap. "You have some blood or lipstick on your cheek! I wanted a veggie burger for early lunch so Grandpa Dan is making me one. Want to share?"

"Aw, I don't want to eat your lunch." She thumbed off the blood and could hear the lack of sincerity in her voice; she was too exhausted to object to much of anything at the moment, and literally, there was nothing she wanted more than a burger, and so added,

"Actually, that sounds really fun, can I accept?" and watched Lulu run off, blond curls and red hat bouncing.

A woman a little older than she was, but much brighter and cheerier and full of zest, emerged from the cabin that said OFFICE. She wore a coral fuzzy coat and matching lipstick and had blond-white hair tucked into a knitted hat of various shades of peach. She was holding a big white bag of what was presumably laundry and was humming a song.

"Excuse me?" Ammalie said. "I don't suppose you want help if it's just for a few weeks or so? No pay, just in trade for a place to stay? I assume you want something longer term?"

The woman raised her eyebrows and said, "Yes, something longer term."

"I myself wouldn't want to hire such short-term work, I agree," Ammalie plunged ahead. "But I'm traveling through, could use something to do, a bed to sleep on. I'm honest and a hard worker. I don't want pay. I want a bed." It all came out in a rush, and in the awkward pause that followed, she started to add something about its being a bad idea and then stopped talking altogether.

The woman looked at her with a tilt of her head and raised an eyebrow at something; perhaps, Ammalie thought, she still had a smear of blood on her cheek. "Sorry, I just . . . don't think it would work."

Ammalie bowed her head. "I understand."

"Nothing personal."

"When I was a waitress, we hated hiring short-term people. All that training."

"You waitressed?"

"Twenty-some years." Ammalie's eyes went to the bird feeders, which were being swarmed by birds of all colors and sizes, and found herself musing, "You know, everyone kept expecting me to become some kind of professional, to move on to something else. But don't you think they were making some assumptions? About what we value? I valued flexibility. And ease. And it was a good gig and I could parent during the days and work nights and it helped my husband launch his career."

"Oh, I wasn't criticizing!"

Ammalie smiled. "Sorry. I just feel lately like I have to defend my choice, even to myself. Anyway, I never did actually intend to let so much time slip away. But it did. Slip. That's why I'm traveling. Living it up." Ammalie heard her voice trailing off at the end; she felt too tired to complete sentences and the birds were too mesmerizing. It was cold enough that her words created a puff of mist, and she watched it drift away from her and toward the birds at the feeders.

"What else did you do?"

"Mothered." She touched her greenstone necklace. "Mothered and waitressed and was a wife. It's not much, is it?"

"Well, actually," the woman mused, "it kinda is. Or can be. If done well. I'm Rita. Did you do it well?"

Ammalie nodded slowly. "More or less, yes. I did. I tried. I suppose it's fair to say that my customers, my husband, and my son felt loved, attended to, acknowledged . . . and sometimes even delighted!" She added this bit with a surprise in her voice, because *she* was surprised with the truth of it. It *had* been true. Sure, she wished she'd had a little more . . . spunk, but really, she had put in a lot. Day by day. Moment by moment. She had given.

Rita bit her lip. "Okay. I'll write down your license plate and come after you with the law if anything goes askew around here." She glanced at the car, as if to do just that, and then added, "Oh, but wait, is that a dog I see?"

Ammalie turned around to see Lady in the car, looking out the window at them expectantly. "That's Lady Shackleton."

"Ah, no dogs on the grounds, sorry. They scare away the birds. And birds are why people come. Love the name, though. Beats 'Scout.'"

Tears blurred her eyes. Lady was so pure and good. And Ammalie was so tired. And why did things contradict like this? "I understand . . . totally. That makes complete sense. She's not my dog, actually. I found her. She had . . . blood on her head. And . . . cigarette burns or something on her rump. And no tags. I just took her. I didn't know what to do . . ."

Rita was still staring at the dog. "Rex used to have a dog that looked like that."

"Rex?"

"My brother."

Ammalie stood there, feeling awkward. Headachy. Miserable. "Thanks, though. Nice place you have here."

She turned to go and saw Lulu and Dan approaching. Dan waved her over. "We already grilled you a veggie burger, so you can't say no," he yelled. "Come on over. Rita, I can grill you up one too!"

Rita lifted her bag of laundry, as if to say *I've got things to do,* and chuckled and whispered, "Watch out for him, he's a flirt. Known him for decades, he's a friend of my brother's, and his flirtatiousness has only gotten worse with age. But his heart is gold."

Ammalie smiled ruefully. Ah, so it had not been *her* in particular he found attractive. But that was fine—she didn't feel good enough to do anything except survive. Which involved eating. She followed Dan and Lulu over to their cabin and glory glory, the smell of a cooking burger. Better than a flirty moment, better than sex, better than an orgasm, and almost better than a gentle and unexpected kiss. She was so hungry. Not only for a hot meal, but for something she did not cook, some offering as an act of companionship or humanity. She nearly cried over the need for it. She slid into the picnic table and closed her eyes and turned her face toward the sunlight, blue sky, bird chatter.

"Thank you," she mumbled.

"Thank you to the sun that grew grass and the cook and the person who built this picnic table and the person who made ketchup and the person who grew tomatoes and the tomato plant itself," Lulu chimed in, and when it became clear she wasn't going to stop with her gratitudes—which were endearing—Ammalie smiled and turned her eyes to Dan.

"I'm sorry," she whispered, "but I'll have to eat fast, but only because I don't want to leave my dog in the car for long. But I am so, so hungry, and this smells so, so good. Thank you." Then she nodded at Lulu and said, "Lulu, that was a good list. Thank you for reminding me to be grateful. A lot goes into everything, doesn't it?"

As they ate, Dan cast occasional worried glances her way, and did not wink, and Lulu chatted happily as they rotated the condiments around. Somehow ketchup and mustard and pickles and lettuce had never, not once in her life, seemed so amazing. Dan kept opening his mouth as if to say something, and then finally said, "You know, let me grill you up another burger for the road . . . You look . . . pale."

She shook her head no. "Thank you, but I need to go. I'm so grateful. You can't believe how grateful." She caught his blue eyes so he could see she meant it. "But I do sincerely need to go." She was sliding out of her seat when Rita approached.

"So, you say the dog is not yours?" Rita stood above them, hands in her coral jacket, and then reached out and ate a pickle slice. "So, like, you do not have a forever relationship with that dog?"

"Well. I mean . . ." Ammalie felt a flush in her cheeks. "I love Lady, if that's what you mean. Who wouldn't? I'm not returning her to whoever did that . . . I kind of stole her . . . but also I guess I don't feel like burdening a humane society either. Although . . . I don't know . . . I just, I just . . ."

Rita flashed a smile. "Oh, without a doubt, I'd steal a dog from someone who was abusing her. Breaking the law for the right reason is something I can get behind. Laws are more like guidelines. I'm just saying, I went and looked at her, hope you don't mind," Rita said. "You're right. About the burns." She glanced over at Lulu, as if to encourage silence—no one wanted to be talking about an abused dog with a child around. "What do you think about her staying at me and Rex's place?" Rita nodded her head north. "We live over there on a bordering property. The old family ranch. Rex could use the company, frankly—he's a little sad these days. And the dog could run free. And you could stay here, as we discussed, working for a free bed."

Ammalie blinked. Teared. Blinked again.

Rita waited for a response, but since she didn't get one, she continued. "So, okay, here's the deal. Things are slow in the hostel room because it's winter—so those beds aren't being used. Trade you a bunk bed there. You'd likely have the place to yourself the whole time, but you might need to share. Let's do one week and see how it goes. You can visit your dog anytime. And, of course, when you leave, the dog goes with you."

"Oh, yay!" Lulu squealed a noise of delight.

"I didn't know people did hostels," Dan said.

Rita bobbed her head. "Rex and I consider it our gift to humanity. Everyone needs a cheap room. We used them ourselves in Europe and New Zealand and Australia, when we were young, traveling together; seemed like a good idea. Needs to be more of 'em in this country. Everything has become available only to the wealthy—including recreation." She ate another pickle. "Just to get clear, my expectation for a free room would be about three or four hours a day. Be at the desk in the morning for a few hours—I like my mornings to myself; guests will be checking out, so all you have to do is take their key and wish them well. They're all paid up, generally. Then spend an hour or two in the afternoon cleaning. Serious cleaning. It's hard work. Takes muscle. For that, you get a free room, no paperwork, no pay. Hours are flexible if you need a day off or something, as long as you make up the time."

"I can help!" Lulu chimed in. "Can I? Can I please?"

Ammalie blinked again. Her headache was pressing down, but her heart was lifting. "Deal. Can I come over tonight?"

"I don't see why not. But I'm on my way out. I lock up the office in the midday, so I'll have to explain things to you later. Took down your plate, just in case you're a criminal." But she winked, and the smile on her face was warm. "If it's okay with you, let's go put your dog—what explorer was she named after?"

"Lady Shackleton. Lady for short—"

"Excellent! Remind people that there was a woman behind the man! Lady and the Tramp too, though I guess that makes you the tramp!" Rita laughed a burbly cascade of notes. Not only were her jacket and lipstick coral, her whole *self* seemed coral-bright. "Well, let's put Lady in my truck. You okay with that? You can visit her daily. See how she's doing. We'll see what Rex thinks. But certainly, it will be fine for a week. This is just a test run."

"Oh good! We can tease the birders together!" Lulu was clapping her hands. "Rita and I do it all the time. She's really funny. Did you know that wild turkeys contain more ancient DNA than any other creature? Did you know that TVs, which are turkey vultures, can smell carrion from a mile away? Did you know that every single feather of a yellow warbler has yellow on it?"

"I did not." Ammalie's head hurt so much, but she could also feel the sparkling light of amusement and relief. "And learning from you is way more interesting than reading a birding book. I mean that." She handed Lulu a yellow bracelet she'd made at the Colorado cabin, which was still in a tangle with others in her jacket pocket. "See you in a while, crocodile."

She thanked everyone, departed with Rita, leashed and walked Lady to Rita's truck, along with the food and bed and toys, and hugged her around the neck. "I'll check on you soon, okay?" she whispered into Lady's neck while hugging her wiggling body. "I need something easier, for just a bit. This might be a good solution for both of us."

THE GUILT SEEPED into her body, pinging around with the physical pain. Guilt for not calling her people, who deserved *some* attention, after all—even if she felt strangely reluctant. Agatha Christie took eleven days of mysterious absence, after all! And what about all those male explorers, leaving behind families and obligations for *years*? Was she not allowed a few weeks to herself? But still: It didn't seem right. She stopped at a hill on the way out where Rita said there was cell reception and indeed, she could see bars on her phone.

To her relief, there was a text from Powell. *Thanks for nice message, Mom. I actually think you are remembering wrong. We did plenty of adventures. Remember how you forced me to go camping in the backyard? But no worries, I will explore and have oomph! Speaking of: I met someone! Dad's Bday next week. Miss him, it's weird he's just GONE, you know? That's so stupid. It's just so stupid that I don't even know what to say about it. Thanks for giving me some space, I just needed it.*

Yes, death was stupid. Yes, it was ironic he had demanded space, and it had hurt her, but now she seemed to be the one increasingly in need of it herself. Suddenly space seemed reasonable. And a girlfriend—good! She'd been convinced Powell could benefit from a partner; most humans were happier in a relationship, with someone to witness and share the day, and she suspected that he in particular needed someone intimate. To figure out how to really talk, communicate, be in relationship with—which was, of course, something she needed to do as well. She hoped he had tons of sex in his life, premarital—and in fact, they had a running joke that perhaps he'd never get married, and then none of it would be premarital at all! Their joking came in response to her own strict upbringing, which had tried, unsuccessfully, to make her feel guilty about unmarried sex. Her own young life had been filled with so many religious rules. She could have used more experimentation, openness, heartbreak . . . because maybe then she'd have been more focused and involved with the marriage, or in marrying the right guy.

She texted back, *I know, I'll call on his birthday. Good for you. Be kind to your lovers' hearts and to your heart. I never had many rules, but remember the three I did have: 1) No drunk driving. 2) No serious drugs. 3) Be kind with hearts, and safe with sex, and no unplanned children. Three of the most no-duh rules to live by—but DO live by them— because the consequences are enormous. I love you so much—adventure on!* She noted with a fond snort that he hadn't asked about her trip at all. Ah, the teenage brain. Although she hadn't been much better; she'd been totally in her Ammalie bubble.

There were several texts from Mari that had come in during the last few days—Mari was a true friend, and Ammalie hadn't been very reciprocal of late. The last one caught her eye: *Nothing new with me and Maximo. Holding pattern. Levi called me, he seemed sad and concerned. I did not give out your number but I said I'd pass on the message. I think he assumed you were friends, and he feels a bit slighted. Friends don't just run off now, do they? Haha, jk. Where ARE you?*

Her heart felt like it was schoolgirl-skipping down the street. What *if*? What if he'd assumed they were real friends all this time? And why did she have trouble believing that? Because, well, it was part of the restaurant culture. People cared for each other, sure, but it was only within the context of the restaurant, not outside it. And what if there was more—although, was that weird? And why was she overcomplicating it with her yearning daydreams? Was she at fault for ruining a good friendship by turning it into something romantic in her mind? In the course of humanity, how many friendships had been stamped out because of the wish for more?

She texted back some basics to Mari, knowing that neither text nor emoji was the way to communicate anything real, but at least Mari would know she was alive. She added a final text: *More Real Stuff to come, trust me. Stay tuned. I love you.*

She texted Apricot a *How ya doing?* and stared at the phone, wondering if she should say more, but decided against it. She only had so much energy, after all. Instead, she sent a photo of her pretending to hug a cactus. Surprisingly, Apricot texted back an immediate *Where the hell are you again?* She simply responded *On an adventure* and turned off her phone. Part of "Be Interesting" was not feeling obligated to fill people in on the details.

Her voicemail was bleh: one from her eye doctor, one from a dentist, one from her doctor's office—it was time to schedule her annual exams, Pap, mammogram, blood work, blah, blah; the business of living seemed endless; staying out of feral-dom seemed endless. The other was from the Chaffee County Sheriff—hadn't she worked that out already? She deleted them all. She needed the world to leave her *alone,* she needed time, she needed to heal.

She'd leave Dart perfect. She cleaned and swept and straightened the sheet, pausing for a moment to remember Kit's kiss. She left some cash in an envelope with a K, GOOD LUCK scrawled on it, just in case he returned. Money always helped—and if he didn't find it, someone in need would; no one who stayed in Dart had many resources. Right before her departure, she wrote THANK YOU FOR THIS UNOFFERED-BUT-MUCH-APPRECIATED GIFT, FROM A MYSTERIOUS VISITOR WHO NEEDED YOU in the guest book, right after Vincent's writing, so that their handwriting could be together. As she went to close the book, she realized there was one entry after the blank page—the page had been skipped—and the writing was in soft pencil, so soft she hadn't seen it. "Lovely. Fine weather. Cheery place to talk about things past and future, the remoteness clarifies the brain. Cheers, Apolena." She was startled by the name—it had been Vincent's grandmother's name, and she'd always loved it. Had she had a daughter, that was to be her name. It was also the name of an older librarian back in Chicago, and Vincent and she had talked about it, how it seemed to be a Czech and Slovak name, some version of Apollo.

Her head was thrumming now, but there was satisfaction that Dart was well tended to. She stepped backward out of the camper, locked it up, kept the key on her key ring, and drove away.

Though she craved a shower and to get settled, she spent an hour driving back toward the nearest town for gas and groceries—it was truly annoying how much humans needed calories and fossil fuels. Energy, energy, energy. The store was tiny and the choices were limited, and she put all the remaining vegetable-based canned soups in her cart. Chunks of meat in soup should be added to the list of Great Offenders, right up there with Frances McDormand, she thought, and indeed, perhaps she'd stop eating meat anyway. At the last minute, she added iodine tablets and colored pencils because they were near the door. As she checked out, she asked the cashier to mail a few postcards she'd written a few days ago.

She pulled into the cluster of cabins right at dusk. The office was closed but Rita had left a note with a key pinned to the stick board. *Let yourself into office, go to door in the back, make self at home, see you at nine to show you the works. You'll have to jiggle the key, but don't worry, it works.*

SHE HELD THE key in her palm and considered it. This one had been gifted. Offered openly. It brought a flush of tears. She turned the key, heard the click, and let herself into a room behind the office that had three sets of bunk beds and a bathroom with a well-appointed and spacious shower.

My god. It was heaven. It was a home.

She unpacked and found a plastic bag and tied it around her head. She was exhausted but she wanted to be clean, and oh, the glory of a hot shower. She lifted the bag on one side to wash one half of her head, since it had now been a long time since she'd washed her hair and her scalp seemed to ache with the need for it. She felt a sting as water trickled into her wound, and she wished she knew what she should do, wash or not wash the area, but decided it was safest to let it be for another day or two.

In Chicago, she had gone to the hairdresser every six weeks for a cut and a dye, nothing fancy but just an attempt to get to the walnut color she used to be and was not ready to let go of. She went for occasional pedicures and facials. Once every few years, she splurged on a spa getaway that included laser treatments for her face and saunas and massages. She had once been a woman who showered daily and pampered herself in a humble way; now she was a woman who simply craved soap on her head—even half her head would do!—and was delighted by the fact of warm running water.

She took a bottom bunk and nearly cried with the delight of the space. She put out her yoga mat and stretched. She checked her head, which was now just humming rather than thrumming with pain. She charged her phone, filled her water bottles, and heated soup. Then slept deeply because she was *meant* to be here. No one could approach her and accuse her of anything. This bunk was publicly hers, and it was delicious.

CHAPTER 12

She masturbated first thing upon waking. It had been a long, long time, but it happened without thought, her body more in charge than her brain, which was still fuzzy from deep sleep. She vaguely imagined a mixture of Kit and Dan and the feel of hips near her hips, a chest above her chest, the movement of muscle and tendon of bone he scissored into her, thrusting, good, the rising power of desire. The pulsing *relief*—glory, glory, how long had all that been stored up—and sparks swept up her spine and across her belly.

Content, relieved, melted. That's how she felt. With her hand still between her legs, she let her mind drift to Levi. What *was* it about him that had occupied her night after night, daydream after daydream? Why had her imagination latched on to him? She didn't particularly want this obsession but had to admit the interest was somehow *real*. When she'd first gotten to know him, he was called the Regular by the other waitresses; although there were a couple of regulars, he somehow got to be *the* one. He came in nearly daily for lunch, and sometimes on the way home from work for a piece of pie or a crème brûlée.

He looked about her age, dressed nicely, was dark-eyed and -skinned, with a streak of gray that ran down a nicely kept beard, and he exuded a certain calm confidence. He was a little thick around the middle, which he teased himself about; she remembered him saying, "'He was not portly yet'—that's a line from Faulkner! What a great line! Not portly *yet*. As if we all get there. Ha!"

She knew the things he spoke of and those he did not. For example, she knew that his wife had had macular degeneration and though nearly blind, had still volunteered with the kindergartners doing crafts, loved listening to audiobooks and NPR, and had passed away a few years ago. These things he told her. But she also knew, just from body language or subtext or however people come to know such things, that he sometimes delayed going home. She knew things that were likely private, such as that he popped some sort of gummy when he left for the evening—weed, she assumed. She knew he worked as a professor of history. She knew that something about his past or his constitution made him prefer this good-but-informal diner as opposed to the fancier places nearby.

She knew that because he was Black, he likely had experienced all sorts of moments which she had not, and the privileges of being white often occurred to her while she watched him during quiet moments. Though he was unaware of it, he had been a teacher for her in that way—reminding her of her taken-for-granted experience. That she didn't think much of anything when seeing a police officer, for instance. Or that when she turned on the TV, mostly white main characters filled the screen, and so she felt represented. She became aware of how the news often seemed to report on a situation differently depending on if the suspect was white or Black. She began to notice the articles in the paper about disparities in medical care according to race. Because of him, she began to *notice*. What she should have already noticed. But maybe that was one reason for the crush—he was a teacher of sorts, and surely nearly everyone fell a little in love with those who opened their worldview.

But also maybe it came down to this: He looked at her quietly, and with seeming admiration and interest. Maybe it was just the way he looked at her. Nothing more. Amazing, how much emotion could grow in a heart simply as a result of a gaze. How was it that humans were so swayed by nearly nothing?

Over the years, her brain conjured up ways that they would have to end up sleeping near each other. A horrible hailstorm where they couldn't leave the restaurant! A blizzard! Her brain was like a Jane Austen novel. In her daydreams, they didn't even kiss or have sex most of the time; it was just him holding her, warm and tender, and their having real conversation.

Honestly, she suspected that he felt something similar. Perhaps that's why these daydreams had started. She'd noticed a spark. Yet, she should get him out of her brain. Mutual attraction left alone— well, that was the safest way to protect it.

Levi, Levi, Levi. Where was he? How was his job? Was he lonely? How was his teaching? Did he like it? She did have some tender and lusty feelings for him, and what to do about that exactly, she did not know. But at least she'd had an orgasm to start her day. She was coming alive again.

SHE LOOKED OUTSIDE the main office window to find three javelinas wandering by in a light dusting of snow that had arrived overnight, four ringtails in the trees, and what seemed like a million birds of such various size and color that her eyes felt confused—so much to track! She felt as she had at Bosque del Apache, that her relationship with birds was something that would *grow,* that it was a living thing.

Rita pulled up and the birds scattered with her bustling arrival. "Lady Shackleton is happy as can be," she announced upon seeing Ammalie. "Although she chased all the chickens. We're going to have to teach her to cut that out posthaste. But Rex loves her.

L-o-v-e-s her." Rita spelled it out and smiled sadly at Ammalie. "I knew he would. Reminds him of Froggy, a dog he had long ago. But don't worry. We understand that she's your dog."

Ammalie was relieved; Lady deserved better than sitting in the car all day. Or whatever else would have been in store.

Without any preamble or pleasantries, Rita launched right in and explained that when her husband had died, Rex had come from his home in Mexico to help with the cabins—this while she showed Ammalie the laundry machines and cleaning supplies and explained which cabins would be turning over when. Then she did a little bit of role-playing, such as, when customers left happily, the response was to sincerely say you hoped they came back, and when a customer left with some complaint, the response was to say, *We'll take that into consideration, thank you, and safe journeys.* "The thing about letting someone on your property," Rita said, "is that you *want* them there. You want to feel good about having them there."

"I understand." Ammalie ducked her head, vaguely ashamed.

"We run a good place here," Rita continued. "They are simple, rustic cabins, and we advertise them that way. And I won't be much influenced by the privilege I see more and more of. Many people are spoiled brats, and that goes for all ages and political parties and ethnicities, et cetera, et cetera. Take it or leave it, I say."

"Gotcha. It's a beautiful place."

"We have free speech in this country but not frank speech. I speak frankly, just so you know," Rita said.

"I wouldn't know what to complain about myself." But at the same time, Ammalie felt a flush of shame—over the one or two times she had left a so-so review at one of the places she and Vincent had visited, her reason being that their trips were rare and so she wanted them to be special and so, yes, little things like a broken coffeemaker had, back then, in that other life, felt like a big deal.

This shift in perspective was perhaps what she loved most about this New Her. She was much more chill. Much more flexible. "I was listening to a radio show," she ventured. "About a thought in Buddhism about there being three poisons—ignorance, aggression, and passion. And passion doesn't really mean, you know, sex. It means a passion for getting what you want. Like, as they put it, you have an allegiance to comfort. You want things the way you want them, at a high cost. You want your coffeemaker to work. You need a pillow a certain way. I wonder if we have a little too much of that?"

Rita blinked. "Exactly. I like you. *Allegiance to comfort*. Get over it, people."

"I'm on some sort of quest for . . . not heading in that direction as I age."

Rita nodded, then added, "Don't get me wrong. I love this place and most of the guests. I'm just a little frayed. My husband dying taught me one thing, which is, try not to live a life where you're so frayed all the time." She smiled at Ammalie. "That's why I'm glad you're here, for even a short time. What happened to your head?"

"My husband died too, about a year and a half ago," Ammalie said quietly. "And my head? I was out hiking and I tripped and my head hit a branch and a rock."

"I'm sorry to hear that," Rita said, catching her eye sincerely. "Very sorry. About the death and the injury."

Ammalie put on a brave smile. "His death taught me to go out and *do* things. Upset the routine. Live a little. Expand, while I can. That's why *I'm* here."

"Good for you. Works out for both of us. You a birder?"

"No."

"Birders." Rita said it twice and then said, "Woooo-ee," without further explanation. She beckoned Ammalie outside and started filling the bird feeders from seed kept in enormous trash cans that were pinned shut, the obvious implication being that Ammalie should learn to do the same by watching.

"I like birds," Ammalie offered tentatively. "I'm learning."

"Well, don't wear that jacket." Rita raised an eyebrow. "As a novice birder, you will attract great disdain. From the others. For example, for wearing bright clothing, like your jacket, which is too red, they'll think you're scaring the birds away."

"But you're wearing coral!"

"Only around here. I wouldn't if I was out birding. I, for one, am not birding. I am human-ing. I love watching the bird*ers,* and I'll tell you, there's quite a range. First, there are the life-listers that keep a meticulous list of every bird they've ever seen, and many of them overlook what the bird is doing; they just want the check-mark. It's very competitive. The 'List 'em and Leave 'em' types. They are incredibly detail-oriented people, the OCD types of the world. I do not like them."

Ammalie snorted with a genuine laugh. Oh, the joy of honest people!

"Then there are the birders who are life-listers and not obnoxious. They have no problem being kind. David Sibley—you know Sibley's books, yes?—he's in this category. A good guy. I met him once, in a field. He said to me, 'Why, there's an olive-sided flycatcher on a nest,' and, like a magician, just set up a scope and invited us all to see. A good man, a generous man."

"I love that," Ammalie said, picking up a scoop to help fill the other feeders.

"Me, I like the casual birders. They want to figure it out, see what the bird is doing, and simply share that with another person. Half the time, they have the bird's name wrong, or partially wrong, but they revel in birds, they feel *joy*. Dan is that sort. Lulu will be a better birder than Dan any day now. Then, of course, there's the vast majority, who know very little about birds, nor do they care."

Ammalie reached into the can and ran the birdseed through her fingers, the soft globes pouring through. "I might be in the very-beginner category, trying to move up. And the birds themselves, do you have a favorite?"

"Well, obviously, vermilion flycatchers and phainopepla are the best. I mean, just listen to those *names*."

"Lulu likes house wrens. I like snow geese and ravens."

Rita raised her eyebrows. "Interesting combo."

"Also sandhill cranes."

"Yes, cranes. And great blue herons. Four hundred," Rita said, out of the blue, and without further explanation.

"Four hundred?" Ammalie prompted.

"There are four hundred species of birds here, residents and migrants—do you know how many that is? It's a lot. Birders come from across the world. Bullock's orioles are maybe the best, I forgot about them, and don't let anyone tell you otherwise. Those dangling sock nests!"

They walked inside and Rita showed her where linens were kept and where some emergency supplies were. "You'll do just fine. Call me if there's any problems, although I rarely pick up the phone if I don't feel like it. I'm really not cut out for this job."

Ammalie nodded her understanding, still delighted.

On her way out, Rita turned and added, "Just to warn you again, there will be some rude ones, and it has been my experience that these rude humans are especially rude to middle-age or older women. You want my two cents? I'll give them to you anyway. Hold their gaze and stare. Make them speak to you the way they'd speak to a strapping, handsome man, or a gorgeous young woman. Don't let them do that belittling thing. Don't you let them get away with it. I try to be apolitical, being a host and all, but you'll get it from all sides and from otherwise-seeming nice folk. Do. not. let. them. speak. down. to. you. Or worse yet, not see you."

Ammalie startled. "Exactly! Rita, exactly! I'm so noticing this tendency. I'm newish to middle age . . . I'm just now seeing it. Back at the restaurant, people were mostly nice to me. And I wonder if it's because, well . . . I was young and kinda . . ."

"Attractive."

She shrugged.

"Honey, you're going to notice it more and more. Don't stand for it. Do what you can to reeducate people. Step directly in front of them and force them to hold your gaze, if you must."

Rita ended the tour of work by showing Ammalie a little golf cart that could be driven down the dirt pathways from cabin to cabin with the clean bedding and supplies. She told Ammalie to start the day by cleaning the cabin called North Star. Then she was gone, a whirlwind calmed, and Ammalie stood there, touching her head, taking in the cluster of cabins and blue-sky day.

She drove the golf cart down the dirt path that wound itself through the property, learning the gist of the cart and the property. She felt oddly gleeful. She was a grown woman and still somehow delighted by the thrill of a small motorized vehicle. And also because the cabins had wonderful names, which she listed over and over in her head.

Moonsquin
While-Away
Evensong
Epiphany

She singsonged their names; they all sounded like not only good places to be but also good internal places too, as if each one offered advice on how to spend the day.

HER HEAD HURT but her body enjoyed actual physical labor—not planks, not lunges, not walking, but necessary and useful labor. Scrubbing and vacuuming and changing sheets. Maybe that's why she had liked carrying plates and trays—she liked moving with purpose. All of it left her panting and occasionally grunting, but she felt strong, felt her arm muscles working as they had when she'd been waitressing. She felt the strength in her core when she lifted and flipped the clean white sheets over the bed.

For the first time since she'd been on the road, she played music on her phone while she worked. She'd been living in such silence, she realized—but that's because she had wanted to hear a car pulling up, her ears always attuned to danger. Now she put on her favorites, old folk songs and new folk songs. Lyle Lovett and John Hiatt and Townes Van Zandt and Eva Cassidy and Nanci Griffith.

Her sister had been the one to help her fall in love with music, plinking the piano and teaching her Carpenters tunes. *Sing, sing a song, sing out loud, sing out strong . . .*

She wondered how Apricot was doing, felt the pang of the rift between them—the endless dealings with the mess their mother had left. There hadn't even been any money—so it wasn't that—it was instead just the separation of tasks, the "Did you call the bank and ask if she had a safe-deposit box?" and "Who canceled her Netflix subscription?" and "Did you take the millionth load of junk to Goodwill?"

It had taken more than a year and there was so much stuff— stuff was such a burden!—and nothing good resulted except that

Vincent had witnessed it and heeded the inherent lesson, which was, as he put it, "to get one's shit in order," and he had done just that. He put all their accounts on a spreadsheet, set up life insurance policies, discussed and wrote down their burial-spot wishes (a green burial if possible, and if not, cremated, ashes scattered illegally along the river, their favorite place to walk), wrote a will. They'd sat down together to discuss everything. Then they'd cleaned out the garage, pared down the detritus of life, and organized cabinets and drawers. It had been calm and comforting to do, actually. It took months, but it was a good set of months, and they'd frequently had sex afterward and a nice glass of wine—something about the mutual work increased the mutual attraction. Come to think of it, their Death Prep months had probably been the best months of their entire marriage.

So, in a way, her fight with Apricot had helped her marriage—had created a period of peace and ease. And, of course, all that work had helped her enormously upon his death.

Apricot was not Apricot's real name. Her real name had been Heidi—Ammalie and Heidi, from old Dutch relatives—but Heidi had gone to the trouble of changing her name in her twenties, which was when she wanted to make it big as an actress and figured she needed a memorable name. The acting thing had lasted about two years, with a local theater community performance or two, and then Apricot had become a real estate agent. But the most interesting thing about her life was her obsession with garage sales and amassing all sorts of high-quality random items. Such as, when she heard that Ammalie was going to go on a road trip of sorts—Ammalie had kept the details vague, just saying she needed some space to grieve and pay tribute to some of her memories with Vincent—she sent her some of the items Ammalie was using now. The travel pillow that collapsed into nearly nothing, the efficient camp stove, the tiny kit of high-quality silverware and cutting board and kitchen items that tetrussed amazingly well into the smallest possible space.

She loved her sister, she did, and she worried about her health. It's just that their infrequent phone conversations had lapsed into vague topics that would be the same things you'd discuss with a stranger, all of which rendered a real relationship nearly impossible. It was after one such call that Ammalie had looked around her kitchen and thought, *This is my boring chitchat life,* and her eyes had fallen on a box of keys, particularly one with some red nail polish, mostly worn away by time, that being the key to the Colorado cabin. That was one of the several small moments that had hatched this big idea, so she supposed she had her sister to thank for that too.

THE BEAUTY OF this job was that she had task after task to do, and there was none of the decision-making of having a completely open day. Rita came in to briefly inspect her work—not that she didn't trust Ammalie, she said, but just that she wanted to discuss standards. She approved the sheet-tuck and the toilet and the tub and the windows and pointed out that it was easy to forget cleaning inside the microwave. Her final piece of advice was to always check one last time under the bed, because if there's one thing that creeped people out, it was finding some item, not their own, underneath where they'd been sleeping.

Since there was only one cabin that needed cleaning until later in the day, Rita asked Ammalie to rake the walkways and stack up twigs and fallen branches for a future bonfire. "If you need any extra work gloves, there's a big lost-and-found box under one of the bunk beds in your room," she said.

Ammalie felt her heart lurch upward. She was so tired of wearing the same few outfits—cars were small, after all, and so she'd limited herself to two pairs of pants and four shirts, and she hadn't realized how much she'd come to hate the sight of them for no other reason than that they were the same. Repetitiveness was depressing. Green sweatshirt, gray flannel shirt, maroon T-shirt, thermal turtleneck, red jacket.

As she'd hoped, the box held all sorts of treasures, some ugly and some rather cute, especially a purple-blue athletic jacket, which she pulled on. She started a load of her own laundry—everything was grimy now—and then took the time to write Powell a card, one that would arrive on Vincent's birthday, she hoped. She didn't explain the trip or her current life, but rather just wrote a small list of favorite memories that she had of Powell and Vincent. She could have gone on and on, but she was limited by space, and besides, it would accomplish what she wanted, which was to let Powell know she was thinking of him. Then she wrote Mari and Apricot each a postcard, telling them a few of the things she most appreciated about them.

Finally, she took a quick break and checked her scalp. Her head certainly ached and had a long lumpy raised area, but the pain was bearable, and there was no more blood and no pus or signs of infection. She dabbed on fresh antibiotic ointment and gauze and pulled her tight-fitting cap over it all. Bodies and hearts were strangely fragile, and yet also strangely capable of repair.

As AMMALIE FILLED the bird feeders that evening, Lulu ran out in a puffy pink jacket and hat. With sidewalk chalk in hand, she followed Ammalie around, making quick chalk drawings on the small bits of sidewalk or flagstone as they went. Together they watched the birds, particularly an acorn woodpecker, but the most amusing thing about Lulu was simply the speed at which she talked, darting around like a bird herself.

"Do you have any sisters or brothers?"

"One sister. I was just thinking about her, actually."

"Where does she live?"

"New York."

"What does she do?"

"She sells houses."

Lulu sucked in her cheeks and gazed directly at Ammalie's face. The honesty of the gaze made Ammalie want to ask about Lulu's family, but not if it caused pain. She kept the question vague. "Tell me about your life."

"I have a mom and dad and Grandpa Dan." Then, "I miss my mom and dad. Sometimes at night I get super homesick, but they call at eight p.m., and I might go home for Thanksgiving."

There was more to the story, obviously—she could hear it in the little pauses in Lulu's tumble of words—but she didn't press. "I'm sure they miss you too."

Lulu singsonged on. "I'm going to be a nurse and save people. And if I like it, then I'll go back to school and be a doctor. But also be a birder. You hear that sound? That's a white-breasted nuthatch, I think. I call them the nasal-nose bird."

Ammalie closed her eyes and turned her face toward the sun, feeling the simple delight of the joy of this kid. "I love that. I can think of no other profession that is so immediately helpful. My mother was a nurse. It's a great gift, to be a good nurse or doctor."

"My mom's cancer is not a horrible kind. So don't worry. But the nurses help her the most."

Ah. Ammalie had often wondered if people went into professions strongly influenced by their parents—either what their parents had done, or the opposite of what their parents had done, or what would piss their parents off the most, or, as in this case, the profession that would most help their parents. Mari, for example, had become a physical therapist because her mother had been in great neck pain all her life, and so Mari had grown up knowing about C2 and C3 and stretches and exercises. And Vincent had become an accountant because his father's business had gone under, and he'd always said that if only his father had given him control earlier, it could have been saved—which is why, she considered now, he'd ended up believing that bad things happened when you lost control.

Yes, it was true that Careers Were Greatly Influenced by Parents, and she decided to add that to her list of Basic Truths About Human Nature. Meanwhile, she asked Lulu if she could borrow some chalk, and knelt down on the bit of sidewalk pathway, and together they drew swirls of color.

CHAPTER 13

"Storm moving in, they say!" Rita said one day, after a series of lovely days in which Ammalie settled into the routine of this new life. "Weather is what keeps us in our place!"

Rita had just swung herself through the door with a gust of very cold air, and Ammalie rushed forward to help with the armful of firewood stacked so high that it rendered Rita's face invisible.

"We are *not* the most powerful force on earth," Rita huffed. "Not that you can trust a meteorologist! But they try. We humans just try. We need to be gentle with one another. Assume good intentions. I say just let the one cabin go today; instead, won't you help me find all the snow shovels and bring in more firewood? Lady Shackleton is fine, by the way."

Ammalie stacked some of the firewood and then glanced outside at the hard bits of gray snow falling, and it reminded her of the snow at Kenosha Pass, which seemed a lifetime ago. But it also made her think of Kit—please, god, may he not be out in the desert. She had planned to go back to Dart soon, with extra supplies just in case he was around, and either way, to leave them in the trailer for any future person in need.

In the meantime, she helped Rita, working as quickly as possible. They built a fire in the lounge's small fireplace and lugged in more wood and stacked it alongside a wall. She found three snow shovels and dropped one off at each of the three closest cabins, during which time Rita shoveled the bit of snow that had already accumulated. During her lunch break, Ammalie fixed a quick grilled cheese with pesto, and as an afterthought, filled her coffeepot and water bottles and extra cooking pans with water, just in case. She was about to go fill the bird feeders when the lights blinked.

Flickered on. Flickered off. Went out.

It was so anticlimactic. No big storm, no big wind. Just no power.

Rita knocked on her door and poked her head into the dorm room. "Something must have happened up the road. I'm heading out. Rex says he's not feeling well and I need to check on him. Before I go, I'll knock on people's doors and tell them what they already know, which is, the electricity is out. What they might not know is that we're on a well. And that means there's no water, either. So they're going to have to save any water for drinking, and they're going to have to flush toilets the old-fashioned way, by dumping ditch water in the bowl and relying on gravity. Snow, ditch water, whatever. I'll need you to hold down the fort, won't you? If the electricity comes back on, please fill every container you can. I wish I had some iodine tablets, for snowmelt. Drinking water will be the real emergency here. That, and the cold. Please calm everyone; no need for too much panic. People will rise to the occasion, eh? Because they have no choice. Humans are funny that way. And this will pass soon enough. Just a wee storm."

Ammalie waved goodbye and glanced at the sky—thick gray, with a dark, billowing cloud bank taking over. But she was smiling. After all, she'd rehearsed the survival sequence of events a million times in her mind to put herself to sleep. Yes, water. When it wasn't available, you had to know how to move fast, fast, fast to procure and store one of life's most necessary elements. She remembered reading a story about 9/11, about a woman near Ground Zero who had had the foresight to fill her bathtub with water as soon as she heard the first news report, and when the water was cut off soon after, she was able to fill her neighbors' water bottles. One small act had helped so many. And iodine tablets? She had plenty of those.

Ammalie supposed many books got read that day, by windows, and with the muted light of a sun thrumming through the clouds. Or perhaps the guests did puzzles. Or played games of Scrabble—there was a faded maroon box containing the familiar tiles on a shelf in her room, and once again, she felt a pang of not having a partner.

The snow let up, then began again, now at a slant because the wind had picked up. The house creaked, some damper started clanking, and then the wind became a howl. She picked up the landline—dead. Checked her cell—no signal. Tried the tap—no water. But worst of all, the room was getting colder. She picked at her fingernails, thinking of Kit, but she was being overly motherly. He was an adult male who had sisters and a support system, and, even though he had not shared it, it was clear he had some sort of plan.

She had to help the people *here*. She bundled up and, gasping with the effort, she delivered extra blankets and sleeping bags and several iodine tablets to each of the cabins that were nearby. Her idea had been to drive the golf cart to the more distant ones, but the cart got stuck in the snow after the second stop. This surprised her—there wasn't *that* much snow on the ground yet, just a few inches, but apparently golf carts weren't created for snow. She furrowed her brow and stared off toward the more distant cabins, but truth be told, she wasn't even sure if anyone was staying in them. She didn't have a complete list of occupants and hadn't yet met everyone. And now she was freezing herself and the wind was taking away her breath.

Everyone she did talk to seemed worried but also sturdy. They knew that the heat was baseboard electric and that without it, it would be cold tonight. Sure, not *Antarctic* cold—this was Arizona, after all—but cold. She went to bed in Fluffiest Red with a hat on and breath misting out, chilled and uncomfortable, but sure that she'd wake to blue sky.

TERRIBLE, HORRIBLE, NO good, very bad day was the thought that popped into her mind when she woke, from a children's book she used to read to Powell, but no, this was not funny, this was not charming. It was white and a whiteout. The clanking of winds had woken her in the dark, and she'd sat up, hugging her knees and trembling with cold, and now it was howling like a live creature.

She forced herself out of her bag and looked out the window, her breath immediately fogging the glass. *Oh, fuck, fuck, fuck,* she kept muttering, as if cussing would help her move through the chill, would keep her from having to hunch over and clutch her coat around her. The cabins were not visible—nothing was visible. Squinting during a short lull, Ammalie could see the outline of big downed branches fallen into deep snow, bushes flattened, a bird feeder hanging broken near the window.

She felt alone, and she felt worried that everyone else felt alone. Dan and Lulu, for example—even if they'd wanted to, walking from their cabin across the white expanse would be difficult, perhaps even impossible. Leaving a shelter would be an act of stupidity.

She built up a fire in the main room, careful to keep it small because of the limited wood. She placed a pan of water near it, and once she saw steam, she poured the water into her thermos, which she put at her feet deep in the sleeping bag. An hour later, she forced herself up to do that again, then did a halfhearted workout to get her blood moving, windmilling her arms while looking out the window. A lone small deer stood under a pine, head down, wet, covered in white, surely miserable, and she wished she could open the door and welcome it in. She dully ate cold leftover spaghetti, was grateful for all her filled water containers. She peed in a bucket. Pulled all the extra clothes from the lost and found onto her sleeping bag next to the fireplace.

Anxiety had a life of its own, roaring and rearing, howling like this very storm. She pressed her fingers against her forehead. When she felt her throat tighten, she thought about taking an old anxiety med she had in her purse, or drinking a glass of wine, but then decided against it—those would mess with her body's ability to respond fully to the cold. To occupy and calm herself, she listed what she'd do if the water came back on, over and over, like a mantra.

Pan in sink—ready to be filled!
Bucket in shower—ready to be filled!
Taps. are. on!
Turn on stove—boil water!
Flush. the. toilet!
Coffeepot ready!
Rice pack in microwave!

But the power did not come on. It got colder, and her nose started to bleed. With the smear of red on her hand, fear bloomed fully and darkly. People in Texas had recently frozen to death while sleeping, and she started crying as she remembered the heartbreaking story of a child who had gone outside to play—snow being rare in Texas and all—and how when he came indoors his parents had no way to warm him up. There was simply *no way* to warm a human up without a heat source, that was the bitter fact, and they only had thin blankets, and lived in an old trailer, and he had *died*. The unhoused froze to death in startling numbers. Hikers at the sort-of-nearby Grand Canyon had died in a blizzard in which over three hundred inches of snow had fallen.

And despite the images of cactus, Arizona was high desert. Once, she'd read, it had reached forty below. And then her mind whirred as fast as the sheer white outside, fast and fierce. Every member of Robert Scott's polar expedition froze to death! Everyone here was going to freeze to death!

She picked at the skin around her fingers. Swiped away tears. Sat in her sleeping bag and fiddled with all the items in her first aid kit. She set out the Scrabble tiles and then spelled the word *cold* and gave up. She wanted to do something, but it was too cold to do anything. She fell asleep, woke with a bloody nose again, stanched it, then forced herself to sit up, wave her arms around, stomp her feet. She needed to get blood going. She was hungry, despite having eaten. Her muscles were tight, the hairs on the back of her neck raised, a searing tension ran up her spine. Her feet thrummed with sharp pain. And yet she knew: It was cold, but not *that* cold. It would get colder.

You're fine, everyone's fine. To prove this, she listed the scariest moments of the trip. The first night in the Grey Goose, in Iowa, everything disorganized and new. The second night equally bad, somewhere in South Dakota, which she'd gone out of her way to see. She'd spent the night in the parking lot of a church in some small town, scared and unsure of the whole idea, and she'd sat in the car and drunk too much wine and stared at the blues and greens of stained glass lit from the inside, having a hot flash and yet quite cold. She'd slept sitting up and woke headachy and stiff, and when she'd returned to her car after peeing in nearby trees, there was a note on her windshield—*TRAVELER, IF YOU NEED EVEN JUST ONE THING, COME ON IN*—and a flush of tears had overwhelmed her and she'd turned to the window of the church and waved, unsure if anyone could see her, but wanting to offer a sign of gratitude.

She wished she could ask for help now. She needed heat. She needed a lighted window.

She breathed into it. Tried to focus on what she did have. Fluffiest Red. Dude. Walls. Life. Breath. Water. She was not alone in a desert—and with a pang, she started to cry again for those who were. *My god,* she thought. *There are in fact people and creatures out there, dying.*

And then the electricity flipped on. "Glory to the heavens hallelujah!" she yelped, and scrambled out of her bag, tripping and moving fast despite her lethargy. She pushed Start on the microwave and coffeepot and electric kettle, splashed water on her face, all as the pans in the kitchen sink and shower were filling. She flicked the light on and off, on and off. A signal to the others: Come here.

She barely got it all done right before it flickered off again. Then she sat on her bunk bed. A bark of laughter escaped her chapped lips.

By god. Yes.

It had gone exactly, exactly, *exactly* as she'd planned. And it had resulted in two pans of water, hot coffee, a clean face, a warm rice pack, a cup of tea, and a signal. She'd used her minute of water and electricity as best she could. She put the rice pack at her feet, then stomach, then feet, all of her body parts arguing for it. She sipped at the hot drink and said, *Feel this simple good thing, Ammalie.*

She hoped the others had used the time wisely too. And speaking of: How to help them? It wasn't clear. There was no doubt in her mind that the main road was impassable and dangerous—if not from the snow itself, then by the complete lack of visibility. There was no way Rita and Rex could safely get here. She was in charge. She needed to take charge.

Could she get to Dan and Lulu's? Or to her car, which was closer, to blast the heat and charge her now-dead phone? But really, what good would that do? It seemed increasingly dumb to her that all the humans were far apart, each in their own cabin. Sure, at first anyone would want to stay in their cabins. Privacy. Comfort. The awkwardness of cramming together. But this night could get *cold*. The situation had changed. It was no longer a night of inconvenience, an annoying trip-changing storm. It was the other kind of storm. A potentially *life*-changing storm. If they were in one room, they'd at least be generating heat, and checking on one another.

Another memory of a kids' book floated up. *Little House on the Prairie*. Pa tying a rope between house and barn so that he didn't get lost in the snow. At the time, it had seemed unlikely to her, pure fiction. Now she saw the truth of it. Those kids' books were a damn series of survival manuals!

The howling and clanking seemed to lessen, so she stood up and looked again. She could make out the dim outline of the other cabins through the orb of muted sunlight and the sideways-blowing snow. Maybe she *could* make it over to the cabins? She jogged around, opening and closing doors and cabinets, looking for rope, but only found bits that were too short. Even tying them together wouldn't work—the cabins were too far apart. She couldn't see how much snow had accumulated, so she opened the door quickly and saw that the wind had created a drift as high as her kneecaps. Not terrible—certainly she could walk through it—but walking through deep snow would be exhausting and get her wet.

What to do?

Let everyone fend for themselves in their cabins? Perhaps that was the only thing *to* do. Cabins scattered across an acre—there's no way she could get to them all.

From her Survival Bucket, which she'd brought inside when she cleaned out her car, she took the space blanket, the flares, the heat packs. It was possible she could get to Dan and Lulu's cabin, and with two adults there would be more options. Maybe, for example, she and Dan could take turns braving the blizzard and get to a cabin and lead the occupants back to the lodge, with the other adult on alert for emergencies and to watch Lulu.

Night would come soon, and with night, the temperature would drop even more. Before she could think much about it, she bundled up with every possible bit of layering and charged out into the snow, straight across the common area and in the direction of the picnic table where she'd once shared a meal with them. She could barely see because of the storm and because of the dimming light and because it was hard to keep her eyes open in such wind. And oh, god, what was that? Her heart stopped. A bear? But no. It was two figures coming toward her, one stumbling.

Dan and Lulu.

She pushed on, lungs searing from cold, gathered Lulu in her arms, turned back toward the office. She didn't have the energy to look back, but just had to hope that Dan was trailing with the jumble of sleeping bags she'd seen in his arms.

When they got in the door and slammed it, they fell back against the wall, gasping with effort and cold air.

"Oh, hallelujah!" she managed, and turned to Lulu, covered in snow. In a flash, she had removed anything on Lulu that was wet—hat, scarf, coat, boots, socks—because anything wet was a real danger. She then bundled her up with new, dry clothes, all of which were too big for her, and plonked her near the fireplace. She could see Lulu's face, ashen and tear-streaked, but her attention was directed at Lulu's fingertips as she looked for hard, white flesh and signs of frostbite. Satisfied, she guided Lulu into Fluffiest Red, shoved the rice pack and thermos near the girl's feet, warmed another pan of water near the fire, put her own hat on Lulu's head. She put another log on the fire, then placed her arms around Lulu and rubbed her spine up and down, and then did the same to Dan, who had just situated himself on the floor near her, gasping and pulling on a dry sweatshirt from the pile of lost-and-found clothes. He was scrambling to get covered, which she helped him do, pulling a big blanket across his shoulders.

"I've never been so happy to see people in all my life," she said. "What about the others?"

Dan looked at Ammalie with eyes that meant he did not know either.

So she scrambled up, opened the door, lit a flare, and sent the blazing orange ball into dusk before slamming the door again. "It's better if they come." She lit another, and another, put a log on the fire, and then another.

And then there was a knock. A couple from Tucson, then another from Germany, and after a pause, others trickled in. A mother and teenage daughter, breathless and white-faced and scared. Then three women, one limping badly. A man who'd been in the farthest cabin, his beard crusted in white. Each time the door opened the cold and snow came in fiercely, though Ammalie did her best to pull them in and slam the door as quickly as possible. They lined themselves up around the fireplace and attended to one another, helping each other peel off wet clothing, rotating boots around the fire. One person was sniffling and seemed spookily lethargic, but others were checking on her, and one of the Germans clearly had medical training and was taking charge. Everyone was wrapped in an unsettled quiet born out of real fear.

Soon they settled themselves side by side, under whatever blankets or coats they had brought with them, and on top of couch cushions and blankets, so as to separate themselves from the cold of the floor. For a few moments, there was a hum of chatter in the dark, but eventually, the room grew quiet.

Dan and Ammalie were lying on the side closest to the door, Lulu squashed between them, with all their bags unzipped so that they could share body warmth. Lulu was asleep, murmuring something indecipherable about Tonto National Forest, and Dan whispered from his bag in the dark, "She always repeats what she learned that day. But also, she's . . ."

"None of us are okay, I think," Ammalie whispered back in the pause.

"Crazy, this is crazy," Dan was saying. "Is everyone here? This is a more serious storm than we thought."

"It's everyone, I think. I'm not sure." Here, her voice broke.

She heard rustling in the sleeping bag and realized that Dan was reaching across Lulu, searching for Ammalie's hand. She put it in his, and he squeezed. She squeezed back.

"What I find ironic," he said after they had settled into silence, "is that you seem to have a strong desire to be alone. To distance yourselves from others. Which I get. I like being alone too. But you called everyone to you."

"What I find ironic," she whispered after a heartbeat, "is that I came here to these cabins to get more comfortable. And this is as uncomfortable as I've been on my whole crazy-ass trip."

Dan snorted. "I wondered. I saw that your car is set up for camping. You've been sleeping in there?"

"Yeah."

"Money a problem?" He asked it carefully, with hesitation.

"Not really. Kind of. It's complicated."

"I could loan—"

"No, no, no, thanks. It's not about saving money so much as, well, making sure I can explore in new and different ways."

He paused. "I get that, I guess. But it sounds uncomfortable . . . and maybe unsafe?"

"Well, thank heavens I'm not out there now," she said, trailing off, and to keep from thinking about Kit, or anyone else who might be in the desert, she added, "Poor Lulu. She's okay, you think?"

"I made it as exciting as I could. A good adventure and all. But to be honest, there's other stuff going on for her, and I can see it's starting to pull her down into a dark space. For example, the phone calls—she needs them. The phones are out, of course. She misses her parents, she's homesick. And you heard that her mom—my daughter—has cancer. We timed this trip to take place during the worst part of her chemo."

"She said it was the okay kind." Dan's silence said more than words could, and she added, "Fuck cancer" very quietly.

"It's about as bad as this storm," he said at last. "Pretty fucking bad."

Her eyes blurred with tears. "You're a good grandpa. She's lucky to have you."

"Thank you," he said, and she could tell his voice was thick with emotion.

She squeezed his hand again and listened to Lulu's steady breathing. Ammalie heard a rustle then—he was lifting her arm so that he could kiss her palm. She let her surprise settle and then relaxed into it as he pressed her palm against his heart.

"Thank you." He said it so quietly that she could barely hear it, and she realized that he was lonely and struggling too.

The house creaked loudly in a gust, as if agreeing with her thought, so she said, "Tell me one good thing about your life?"

So Dan spoke quietly of designing and building passive solar homes—he'd been one of the pioneering group that had helped develop energy-saving methods—and in older age, he'd started volunteering to transport bone marrow and stem cells from donors to recipients. It helped people who were dying from blood cancers. Sometimes the trips were across the country, sometimes across the world.

"You fly with stem cells in, what, a suitcase?"

"A cooler."

Her laugh was soft but genuine. "A cooler. That blows my mind. Sometimes what I think is so technical is just so . . . not. A *cooler* with *ice*!"

He snorted a quiet puff of agreement. "Saving people is not as hard as people think. Whether it's a body part or a granddaughter, it doesn't take that much."

"I don't suppose we're very good at celebrating our successes," she whispered. "So I'll tell you mine. I simply went on a road trip. And so far, I've saved one tree, one dog, helped one woman who was having a tough anniversary of getting off heroin, helped one guy who needed a hand, and someday, I'm going to plant a tree or twenty. Or something. For the planet. Since she's been so nice to house me and all." Then, she added what was really on her mind. "I'm scared."

"I'm scared too," he whispered. He took her hand and brought it to his lips again. The first kiss was on the back of her hand, the second kiss on the palm, and she could tell how very much he meant by it. "Ammalie," he whispered in the dark. "You're a fine explorer."

She understood that had a child not been between them, and if they were not in such a precarious position, they would have folded into each other, if for no other reason than to defy the laws of aging and of storms. The very idea of it was enough. She smiled a weary smile, and since there *was* a child between them, and a roomful of exhausted cold people around them, they simply held hands, his thumb rubbing her hand back and forth, back and forth, back and forth, back and forth in what was surely one of the most comforting and tender moments of her life.

CHAPTER 14

Thank the heavens, she thought, staring at the sky. Ammalie had never felt such relief at seeing bits of muted blue poking out from clouds, and never felt such relief at the sound of a vehicle. She turned to see a white pickup charge through the snow, pulling right onto what would be the lawn and right near the sidewalk she'd shoveled with some of the others this morning. Rita jumped out with a wave and began checking on the guests, like a mother hen clucking and gathering her chicks. The driver's door swung open, and Ammalie watched as a white-haired, round-faced man swung a sporty-looking wheelchair from the cab of his truck, lowered himself into it, and pushed himself up to her. It was such a fluid and confident motion that it reminded her of a bird in flight.

He placed a big sack of granola bars and chips in her hands. "If you don't mind dispersing these. Everyone okay?"

"You're Rex!"

"The mysterious brother."

She tilted her head toward the wheelchair. "I didn't know . . ."

"Yup, wheelchair-bound for about a decade now. MS. I don't get out much, but that's by choice, not disability. I don't much care for people." He winked, and she could see his resemblance to Rita, the round features and playful eyes. "It's nice to meet you, though. I've heard good things. But I guess I better assess the damage here." He rolled along the shoveled sidewalk toward the office building, and Ammalie realized she hadn't taken notice of the wheelchair ramp on one side. There were so many things she didn't *notice*! So many things she took for granted.

Before entering the office, Rex turned around in his chair. "If you don't mind letting her out for just a few minutes," he said, nodding to the truck, and Ammalie turned to see Lady's face pressed against the window and a tail flapping wildly. In a flash, Ammalie was crouching to embrace Lady, who was circling her and whining, and then nudging her nose in Ammalie's crotch in her signature greeting. Lady looked well brushed and well fed and well loved, and when Ammalie ran her fingers over the old burns and scars, she could see they were all healed and hardly even noticeable. "Oh, I missed you," she said, and realized now how much she had.

As she and Rita and Rex dealt with the aftermath—canceling reservations, checking road closures, feeding birds, helping people get back to their cabins, confirming the health and well-being of everyone—Ammalie tried to frame the experience for them as she had once done for Powell: "Peter Pan said something like, 'Life is a very Grand Adventure.' You'll remember this like no other part of your vacation!" But everyone seemed to already take it that way—humans were a sturdier lot than she'd thought, or at least, these humans were.

It occurred to her that the human spirit was a miraculous thing, as miraculous as warm sun and a clearing sky. It seemed they'd more or less enjoyed the night together on the floor, although they'd also admitted to fear and panic and backaches, and several cried, and several mentioned needing to call their therapists or friends, so she knew there was some processing to be done as well. Adventures did not come without a cost.

Later in the day, she stood outside with Lulu to give Dan time to pack, and silently they watched the resident coatimundi scale a tree and grapple with a suet cage like a pro. They laughed at his anteater-like nose, and how, like a raccoon, he used his paws so adeptly to scoop the suet into his mouth. When it was time, she blinked back tears and gave Lulu a long and sincere hug with a promise to pen-pal, for real, the old-fashioned way. It was time for Lulu to get home to see her parents, and so Ammalie did not begrudge her and Dan their departure, though it hurt. At the last moment, Dan came back from their Subaru, took her in his arms, and said, "Unless you object, I'm going to kiss you," and because she hadn't blurted out anything, he did exactly that, a kiss that pushed with desire, and she was left standing there, mouth still open with surprise, even as he backed up, winked, and turned for his car, saying over his shoulder, "Track me down if you wish. I, for one, would not mind meeting again!"

She stood in the snow, touching her lips. She'd been kissed by two men in the last week—one younger, one older, one softly, one with passion. No one could accuse her of living a boring life now. She did a little dance as she walked around, pulling the biggest fallen branches through the snow to a pile near the firepit.

When she turned the corner, she was surprised to see Rex there, gingerly standing, the knees of his pants wet, his round cheeks rosy, a small scowl on his face. "Horrible storm, worst I've ever personally seen down here. We owe you one, which is why . . ." Then, without explanation he said, "Your car."

She blinked. "Hello, Rex!" She glanced around. "Where's your wheelchair?"

"Don't need it all the time. New Mexico?"

She narrowed her eyes at him, then at the license plate he was staring at, then back at him. "Yes."

He sighed a long sigh. "Doesn't look like a New Mexico car to me. Looks like a Midwest car, someplace with a lot of humidity. Your wheel wasn't sounding right when you drove around one day, before the storm, and I've just taken the liberty of looking under her."

She found herself frowning. "*You* were under my car?"

"I can walk and move. It just wears me out!"

"I'm sorry, I didn't mean . . ." she stammered. "What I mean is, that seems so much trouble! All the snow! You got wet!"

"Rust," he said. "As in, rusting out. As in, that car has seen a lot of moisture. And I have to tell you, it's bad—the whole undercarriage is going. It'll last you a bit longer, but not much longer."

She felt a pang. Ah, the Grey Goose was aging too. "Thanks," she managed. "I guess. I appreciate it."

"That's no New Mexico car."

She shrugged. "I bought it used."

"Older plate. I don't think they make that design anymore."

She tried to look surprised. "Oh, really? I think they do . . . they must . . ."

He looked at her, steady. "I'm surprised you didn't get pulled over."

"I'm not . . . I didn't—"

He waved his hand, as if her words were pesky mosquitoes. "Something is mildly amiss here; some information is being withheld. Rita noticed it too. It's funny, but secrets have a way of floating in the air. You can often just see them, somehow. But whatever it is, it doesn't seem nefarious. It seems a gentle secret; that's how Rita put it. I do like to wonder, though. My brain can't help but come up with various scenarios. For example, I was just reading about some serious and well-thought-out damage to some oil rigs near Chalk Canyon a few weeks ago, and whoever did it hasn't been caught, despite a big search, given the significant financial loss. That's sacred land. Sacred. Too wild to drill, some say. I happen to agree. You ever been?"

"Nope."

He blinked at her. "Yup, something is amiss here and I'm not going to ask. But I'm going to tell you that I'd hate to have you get lost out here on these back roads. Your car doesn't have long. Some adventures aren't worth having. Don't get stuck."

She put her hand to her necklace and turned to go before he could see the flush of her cheeks. She'd known it was time to fly south, and now she had the push she needed. Although, true, it wouldn't be the Grey Goose taking her.

RITA HAD A surprise in the bed of the truck: two pairs of old cross-country skis and boots. "This much snow is rare, so carpe diem, we're going," Rita said. "Come on. I need a friend to join me."

So she and Rita started out, cutting tracks side by side through the sparkling white, Lady bounding alongside, stopping occasionally to push her nose into the snow. Ammalie's ski boots were a bit big and stiff with age, and immediately gave her a cramp in her right arch, but she was too happy to care—it wasn't going to kill her, after all, and that was her new baseline. The snow was perfect. Though she was no expert, she knew there was sticky snow and gluey snow and too-hard snow, and there was perfect snow, when it was warm enough outside to not be freezing, but cold enough for a glide. The swish-swish of the skis metronomed with her heart.

Rita was a better skier and charged ahead. Aha, so *this* is what it was like to have someone go faster than you through life! Ammalie realized she liked it; it was as if someone else was fueling the energy, keeping the momentum, and maybe that's what had dragged her down before, not just the literal going faster but the emotional weight of feeling like the one cutting a trail through the logistics of getting household things done, Powell to school on time, the groceries bought.

She felt a sudden rise of bitterness toward Vincent; yes, he'd had more energy for adventures and hobbies, but that's because she was the one making regular life *happen*! Yet she also wondered why she and Vincent hadn't skied more; they both had skis and knew how. They could have gone some mornings, on the days he worked from home, or on weekends, before she left for the lunchtime crowd. But enough. No more regret about what they could have done. She was doing it now.

Rita waited for her to catch up, and then they skied side by side again, each cutting their own tracks in the snow. "Thank you for your help during the storm," Rita said. "Perspicacity. Wasn't that your word of the day a few days ago?"

Ammalie nodded.

"Well, thank you for your diligence and perspicacity during the storm." Rita turned to her and flashed a coral-lipsticked smile, which seemed particularly bright against the backdrop of a landscape of white. Then, out of nowhere, she added, "I had a son and he died. In Iraq. I'll never feel fully human again."

"Oh!" Ammalie startled, both from the information and by a thump of snow falling from a tree to the ground. "Rita, I'm so sorry. That's unbearable. I can't—I can't imagine."

"Then my husband died. I just thought I should tell you. Rex and I bought this place soon after, and we've enjoyed it here." They skied in silence for a few glides, and then she added, "My point in telling you this is that there is no one. No real kin. Rex feels better when he's warm. He left a little house he had in Puerto Vallarta, in a retirement village he loved, with paved sidewalks that are oddly better for wheelchairs than most of America's. He agreed to come help me with this place for a year or two. And now he has. He wants to go back. He has MS—did he tell you that?—and he wants to die there. He wants to take Lady too. I should have known he'd fall in love. But it's up to you, of course. My plan is to sell this place next year. To the right person. You could always stay, you know. I'd recommend the next person hire you. And I hope you stay and work for me as long as you want. We can discuss a salary and all that."

Ammalie looked over at Rita briefly, then back ahead as they skied. "That's really kind. Thank you sincerely, Rita. The storm gave me a lot of time to think. I . . . have a bit more traveling I need to do, and I best do it soon. There's one more adventure required of me. But I wouldn't mind circling back here someday."

"Perspicacity," Rita mumbled thoughtfully, her breath misting out.

Ammalie smiled at Lady, who was darting through the snow, jabbing her nose into it randomly, and then racing back to them before repeating the whole process again. The plings and drips of snowmelt and birdcalls in the white expanse seemed like a certain version of heaven, something cleansed and pure. "Rita, I brought my dying husband a glass of water—*water*. What he needed was an ambulance." Her voice sounded dazed even to her when she added, "I haven't confessed this to anyone. Truly, this is the first time I've said it aloud. I haven't even told my son, although he was there, upstairs, and he knew the ambulance got there too late. I just moved too slow, because I was surprised, and I hadn't thought it through. Water."

Rita continued to glide along beside her. They had worked out the rhythm and pacing so that they could stay side by side in the meadow. "It sounds solicitous, if not effective. And understandable! After all, that's what humans do. In particular, that's what waitresses *do*. They bring you water. Right? Sometimes they bring you so much water that it's annoying." She reached out and touched Ammalie's shoulder. "I'm sorry. I shouldn't joke. I'm so very sorry that he died."

"Even if the doctors say it wouldn't have saved him, and are right, there is still something about how slowly I reacted that haunts me. I'm afraid Vincent died knowing that I was being impatient, and that I wanted the water to fix his problem, more or less. So now I try to think through things more. Like in the snowstorm."

Rita started to speak, stopped, started again. "Well, you did great. I'm also sorry for *you,* Ammalie. I'm sorry about Vincent, but I'm also sorry . . ." And here she paused and looked down at her salmon-colored scarf, as if about to say something that edged on improper. "I'm sad you're so alone. I wish someone would bring *you* a glass of water. Metaphorically speaking. You seem so very . . . on your own. Although perhaps that's by choice? And you have people?" Then she looked up with a renewed energy, perhaps trying for happy. "It's just that you don't talk about your life much. What I do know is that you've helped us greatly these last days. We'd like to give you a thousand bucks, in addition to the room. That's my version of bringing you water."

"Thanks for that." Ammalie swished her skis through the snow. "But I don't need that."

Rita burst into a birdlike cascade of laughter. "Don't be ridiculous. Yes you do. A car repair. A trip. Or the water heater will go out in your home. Or send it to your son for college. Or donate it! There's always something, and if you're being honest, you know that as well as me."

"Actually, thanks. I have an idea of something I need to do. I have it all planned out. I just need the day after tomorrow off."

"It's Thanksgiving! We expected you'd come over for a meal. Rex is a good cook—"

"Thank you. I'll happily take leftovers. But I've decided that this year, my thanksgiving will be an act of service, and there's something I really have to do." With that, she bent over and gave Lady an all-over rib rub, with a rump scratch as the grand finale, and then, as a final blessing, she ran her fingers over the scar on Lady's head.

CHAPTER 15

On Thanksgiving, right as the red sun crested Earth and soft light spread, Ammalie pulled up to the flapping-eyed Dart sitting alone in the landscape of snow that looked like a white and undulating sea. "Ahoy, matey," she murmured, but her voice was serious and sad. Today would not be a playful one. Today could be the hardest day of her life—physically, at least, the birth of Powell being the only other one that might come close.

As she had expected, there was no sign of anyone, but when she lugged in two boxes of canned goods and left them on the counter with a note FOR WHOEVER NEEDS THESE—PEACE she saw that the money she'd left was gone. Kit had been here, presumably. Knowing that brought *her* some amount of peace, though she was still stomach-sick with worry. How had he survived the storm? When she knocked on the propane canister with her gloved hand, she had at least one answer: It echoed empty. He'd used up a full canister and probably just left. The snow had mostly melted yesterday on the dark rock path that led to Dart's door, which is why no footprints were visible.

She locked the door as she left. She had to keep going, and fast, too. She had only so many hours of daylight and a big plan. And it was cold, though the sun was now warming the planet to a reasonable temperature. She drove away from Dart, down the rutted road that was no longer a road, and the path on which she had walked with the bloody head. She cut fence twice—illegal, she knew—and it conjured up the memory of cutting the fence off the tree back in Colorado. She drove until the road was too rough. The Grey Goose had been bucking like a bronc and could go no more.

Here, then, was her starting point. She stood for a moment, hands on hips, and took in the sprawling landscape, the Grey Goose ticking in the warming sun beside her. Such an enormous expanse of scrub brush and snow, and the snow was important—her foot-prints would leave a trail, which is what she'd need so as not to get lost. Even if it partially melted during the day, as it would, there would be enough tracks to guide her. This day would push her to her limits. Perhaps what she was doing was of very little use, maybe no use. She knew she was just one woman, a white woman with a limited understanding of the situation, a woman who was foolishly stepping into a situation without fully understanding it. She knew some people would judge her harshly for this, some would cheer her on, some would bring politics into it, and there were a million ways she could be criticized.

But here's what she also knew:

She had brought Vincent water, and it had not helped.

Human beings were dying of thirst and cold out here, and water and a space blanket would help.

And regardless of its virtue or not, *she* needed to do it. For for-giveness. Or redemption. So she could get Vincent's dying face out of her mind. So she could rewrite the story of this place, instead of just remembering her cut head and her fear. She simply needed to do it.

She'd worked it over and over in her mind. Yesterday afternoon, after much of the snow had been cleared or melted, she'd driven into town to the Ace Hardware, a pharmacy, and an Outdoor

Adventures store, buying them out of all the necessary items and spending all the cash Rita had given her. She ticked things off her list, emptying a few shelves along the way.

> 10 plastic bins ($70)
> 30 gallons of water ($30)
> All the cans of beans and soups with pull tops ($50)
> All the space blankets that were available ($400)
> All materials needed for first aid kits that were actually use-ful, including water purification tablets ($600)

The cashier had raised her eyebrow and sighed; Ammalie had basically emptied her out of ointments and bandages and related items. She'd spent much of last night making stupid store-bought first aid kits into actually useful ones. Now it was all organized perfectly in Grey Goose. Now was the hard part:

Ten trips.

Ten different directions.

A plastic tub in one hand. A gallon of water in her other hand. And on her back, in her large backpack, two gallons of water, three cans of food, a few space blankets, a first aid kit. It was incred-ibly heavy. But she'd prepared for that in her mind, which made doing it possible. She'd walk about one mile per drop—some drops would be quite close to the car, but some would be farther, for a total of ten or so miles for the day, which was likely the absolute max. Yes, others could do more but she could not, and so that was that. She was not an athlete, she was a regular person with a goal and one day.

Water is heavy. Very heavy. Each gallon of water weighed eight pounds, so three gallons came to twenty-four. Plus, she had her own half gallon per trip for herself. With the weight of the cans, and the minimal weight of her own necessities, the pack would weigh about twenty-six pounds for each trip. Not nothing. Indeed, her mind began to reconfigure the mileage; she'd probably overestimated what she could do. Well, she'd do what she could. She'd do this one thing, as well as she could.

Her car was the center of the clock; she'd start in three P.M. position and would end up in the nine position, thereby covering the 180 degrees of lands that rested between her and Mexico.

The first three trips were the longest but easiest. She was rested and energetic. Twice, she heard the distant sound of Border Patrol helicopters. She wished she'd brought Lady, who would have been comforting, but she'd have had to explain why and where she was going. When she found a good outcropping or edge of a trail, she left three gallons of water, cans of food, space blankets, and a first aid kit under the large storage bin, put a heavy rock on top, and then she walked back to the car and started again.

The fourth trip, she began to feel her left hip and knee. By the sixth trip, she was talking to herself, or, rather, to an imaginary critic, who warned her not to be presumptuous, not to have a white-woman-savior complex. That what she was doing was limited in scope and it should not be treated as more than it really was—a small drop in a vast bucket. Others were helping in much larger ways, putting more on the line. There were bigger things to be done, such as elect politicians who cared about international trade laws and water conservation and the well-being of those on Planet Earth.

"Yup," Ammalie said several times in unison with each step. "Yup, it's true. It's all true. My privilege and limitations are fucking enormous. But still, I think people need to live more dangerous lives. Dangerous in terms of trying to do real good. Let me do this, even if it's just for me. Even if it's selfish. Because doing something is better than doing nothing. Let me leave water where it might actually be useful."

By the eighth outing, she was making much shorter trips, but that was fine. She'd done her best. The sun was three-fourths its way across the sky, now tilting toward land, and the snow became crunchy instead of mushy. Her jeans and shoes were soaked and coated in mud. Her shoulders hurt. Her nose had started to bleed again, from dryness or exertion or both. Her left hip and knee hurt. She promised herself that she'd stop if she needed to, and simply leave the rest of the supplies at the car. By the ninth trip, which was very short, she was crying, from exhaustion and physical pain, but also just from empathy. From knowing one small part of what it must feel like to walk so far, to be so tired, worn, desperate. She was so sad. So very bone-deep sad for all those who had done this journey, and, somewhere around the world, were doing it for real at that very moment.

She thought of Powell and Apricot, who had gathered for Thanksgiving. Oddly, her sister had agreed, and without much fuss had flown to Chicago and spent a few days in Ammalie's house and cooked a meal for Powell. When she'd texted the idea, with a *Just have some aunt-nephew time, please do this for me,* Apricot had simply responded with, *Okay, are you alive and okay and what exactly are you doing again?*

She thought of Mari, who would be with her own big family, with or without Maximo, she didn't know. She thought of Levi, who she assumed would be having a meal with his extended family. She thought of Kat in Colorado, and Dan and Lulu winding their way home across the American West. She thought of Rex and his MS and how hard it must be to carry the weight of that disease. She thought of Rita and her beautiful coral lipstick and smile and her dead son. My god, life was not for the faint of heart.

She hiked on through wet-smelling sage, came across the vertebrae of a deer, and a paw of a rabbit, and bushwhacked through some willows. Here she left her final offering, took a photo of the plastic tub with PAZ in black marker on the top, then, crying, took the pottery shards from her pocket and set them gingerly on the ground. She looked up at the sky. "Vincent! Come look! I want you to see." She knelt above them for a moment, sifting some snow on top of them. "This is right," she said. "Happy birthday tomorrow. I miss you. I wish this wasn't so. I wish you were alive. I wish your soul well; I wish you peace."

She touched the pottery shards one last time, pressed them gently into the earth, and used those same fingertips to wipe the tears from her eyes. Then she stood, dusted her hands off, and walked.

As SHE STOPPED to unlock the Grey Goose, she was startled to see headlights in the early twilight and the glint of a car against the snow-mottled landscape. It was not yet dark, but clouds had made it dark enough to see the orbs of the headlights bobbing up and down on the rutted road. They looked like two flashlights on a roller coaster, beaming this way and that. The Sea Creature swam straight up and lodged in her throat.

Maybe it was Kit's sister! Maybe it was Kit! But when she put the binos up to her eyes, she could see it was some sort of civilian-style Jeep Cherokee—and oh, god, yes, it was black with a gold streak and some lettering. *Fuck, fuck, ducky fuck,* a phrase from her teen years, flew into her mind. She moaned as she eased herself into her car and sat. She would just slowly drive away. Say that she was exploring, gone for a hike. That was pretty true. And the biggest charge against her was that she had been trespassing, cutting a fence, littering. She wasn't even sure who owned this land that bordered Texas Sky Man's property—was it BLM land, or private land, or state land? Who knew. But surely what she'd done was no *huge* deal. Whatever fine there was—well, that was fine. *A fine fine* she heard herself thinking, to which she responded, *Shut the hell up and think!* Maybe he'd run her plate and realize it was stolen, so she jumped out and took it off and threw it under her seat. If asked, she'd tell them it'd just gone missing. Stolen. That was plausible, wasn't it? She could also play the Vincent card—that he'd come here as a Dark Sky appreciator, he was dead, she wanted to do a ceremony to say goodbye and return some pottery shards to the area. And that had the benefit of being all *true.*

Or, maybe, she could just sit here until the deputy left—maybe he hadn't seen the glint of her car? She glanced in the backseat. She didn't have Fluffiest Red with her, but she did have her Survival Bucket and space blanket and enough water. But then Rita would worry; *she'd* probably call the police and reporting a missing woman. And there was no way to text her she was fine.

She didn't want to look suspicious, but she raised the binos to her face again, briefly. The deputy was now walking toward Dart as if he was just looking around, not casing or stalking the place, though his hand was on his hip on what she presumed was a gun. *It's okay, Kit's not there, this guy will find nothing.*

But that was not true.

Her binos had just caught movement, someone running low to the ground from the back of Dart over to the rock outcrop. She gasped.

Kit *was* there.

Oh no no no.

What if Kit had seen her leave food? What if she had *drawn* him to this trouble? Had her water-drop efforts brought the law?

Thereby ending Kit's freedom? By doing one good deed, had she caused a catastrophe?

She whimpered and watched Kit move until he stopped and turned toward her, and then he did exactly what she had just predicted he'd do. Once in the rock outcrop, hidden from the deputy but visible to her, he waved his arms at her in big X's, and, once sure he had her attention, he then flung one arm, pointing down the road, as if he was traffic-controlling her to leave. To get the law to leave.

"Noooooo," she heard herself whispering. She wanted to avoid whatever this would bring. But of course, she had to. She had to get the deputy out of there. She had to help a friend.

She turned the ignition. Drove down the rutted dirt road toward Dart, putting on her best smile.

THE OFFICER WAS young and slender and had a handlebar mustache— good god, was she stuck in some sort of Hollywood Western?— and he walked to his car and stood watching her approach, hand at his belt. She had to distract him. Get him out of there. The Sea Creature clogged her windpipe but she stopped and rolled down the windows. "Hey," she said. "You okay here?"

He blinked at her.

"I was out on a hike," she said cheerfully. "Driving home now. Have a nice evening!" When he said nothing, she shrugged, and started to accelerate when he put up his hand.

"Stop."

She pressed the brake, tried to look nonchalant. She could see he was taking in her car, both the outside and inside. She resisted the urge to talk; better, in this situation, to stay silent.

"I'd like to see some identification, please."

She opened and closed her mouth and had the vague sensation she must look like a fish. "I'm Ammalie," she said, fumbling for her wallet. "Out for a hike. My husband once came here. Dark Sky appreciator. He died. Of a stroke. I brought him water. But he died. I came to . . . tell him goodbye. It's a long story."

He was standing, looking from her driver's license to her face, but at the mention of Vincent's death, a softer look indeed came across his face. "I'm sorry to hear that," he said, and sounded like he meant it.

A moment of nausea was followed by a brilliant idea that unfolded in her mind. "My car, wow, my car . . ." She took a deep breath. "My car isn't well. It actually got broken into in Colorado, at a place called Kenosha Pass, you can look it up, they took my plates, that's why I don't have any on right now, and anyway, what my point is, is, that my car is making a clanky sound! Creaky. Maybe you heard it? I don't suppose you would mind following me out? When you leave? Make sure I make it to the highway, at least? I'm staying at Cave Valley Cabins, which kind of confuses me, because is it a cave or a valley?"

His stance relaxed. "Rita and Rex's place?"

She smiled. "Yeah, exactly."

"Valleys have caves in them," he said, somewhat annoyed. "And I heard your car as you approached."

She snorted, trying for playful. "Yeah. Very sick. On top of the creak, I'm worried about low oil. Don't want the engine to blow."

"So you know John?" he said, nodding at Dart.

Her mind whirred. "John the Dark Sky man from Texas! That's what I call him."

A small smile crossed his lips. "Well, John asked me to come check on the place. Somebody saw some activity."

"Oh?" She kept her voice calm. "If you see any tracks, they're mine. I'm sorry, but I got curious. I just peeked inside. From the outside, I mean! I didn't go in! I just, you know, looked in the little window on the door. He said it was okay. John did. Like, I hope I'm not trespassing or something . . . I just wanted to tell my husband goodbye. It's a long and complicated story . . ."

He glanced at the setting sun, then back at her. "Looks quiet enough to me. And there ain't much to take, or reason to be here. This is as remote as it gets." He scratched his jaw. "I'm having a day. That storm and all. How about this? How about I drive you back to Rex and Rita's and you get Bob over at Bob's Gas and Tow to come tow this tomorrow? Because it doesn't sound good at all, and yeah, you don't want to burn your engine up."

The smile that she gave him was genuine, because her delight was real. While she didn't look forward to being in the company of the law, another idea had bloomed in her brain. A colorful one. "What a generous thing to offer. Sincerely! If you don't mind giving me just a minute? I'll hurry, won't keep you waiting. I know it's getting late. I just need one minute to think on what I need from inside my car here."

But even as she spoke, she was moving fast, sliding the car key off her key ring. She left it in the ignition, jotted a quick note on the back of a crumpled dirty envelope. TAKE THE GREY GOOSE, LOVE HER WELL, SHE IS YOURS. VARIOUS PLATES UNDER SEAT. MAIL THERE TOO, SO YOU CAN FIND ME IF YOU WANT. UNDERCARRIAGE IS GOING, SHE WON'T LAST LONG. She paused. It was against her code of ethics to give out other people's information, but she also had to trust her instinct. IN CASE OF EMERGENCY, CONTACT WOMAN WITH MY SAME FIRST NAME, LAST NAME YOUR STATED MISSION, NEAR THE EXIT. SHE WILL BE ALLY. ALSO, THANK YOU FOR THE KISS.

Kat Wilder from Salida.

Then she placed a few bills—she wished she had more, but she was out—on the floorboard, grabbed her backpack, and smiled as she walked toward the man.

As they drove past the rock outcrop, she pointed with enthusiasm in the opposite direction. "Wow! Wowza wow wow, look at that sky, that moon!" Just as she'd hoped, he glanced over, looking at the hanging globe, and as they passed the rocks, she felt her heart leaning toward Kit, who was surely hiding behind them.

When she was delivered back to Cave Valley Cabins—truly, she was grateful—she shuffled off to bed and curled up in a ball, and in that position ate a sandwich she'd prepared and fell asleep before she'd finished it and without bothering to wipe the exhausted and happy tears from her eyes.

When Bob the Tow Truck Driver called to say no car was at John's property, she feigned surprise. What?! My god! Where could the car have gone! I left the key in it for you, but who would steal a car from there?

When Hugh the Deputy called so as to file a missing car report, she went along. *Sure it was clunky, but I sure loved that car!*

When Rita expressed outrage and confusion, she got closer to a truth: *Truly, it was time to donate it to NPR anyway.*

When Rex raised an eyebrow, she shrugged and got to her knees to give wiggling Lady the biggest hug of her life. Then she stood and said, "You'll take good care of her? She's helped me through a tough time," and waited for him to nod and say, "Of course, Ammalie. You have my word. And my word for silence too. I don't know what you're up to, but it's likely something I'd support."

When an email arrived from an unknown email address, she

read it three times. *Contact made, all safe.* She wrote back: *I knew Kit Kat bars would be good.*

When she listened to a message left by Levi, she closed her eyes and felt the warmth spread across her heart, which ached—no, *yearned*—to be less alone. "Uhhh, just checking in," Levi said. "Course, miss seeing you at the restaurant. Just thought I'd inquire. Finally wrangled your number from them. I just thought . . . I just thought maybe we could talk."

Levi! Such a strange energy, that joy flooding up her throat, and she found herself touching the dimple where her collarbones met, as if to acknowledge the glowing feeling there. But first, she had to focus. Three important calls had to be made. She sat in Rita's truck outside the tiny brick library in the nearby town. She could have used the landline back at the office, but she'd wanted privacy.

First, Apricot: Ammalie thanked her sincerely for spending Thanksgiving with Powell and happily listened to the details about that—a nice meal together, a game of Scrabble. In a certain way, Apricot said, it had been sweet to have that time together, with just him, but also, what the hell, when exactly was Ammalie coming home? Ammalie deflected the question and added that she was going to be out of touch, then leapt off the call with a made-up excuse.

Next, Mari: They talked of the twists and turns of a fulfilling life, and how to keep on track for one. Mari ended the call with, "You couldn't have saved Vincent, but it appears you've definitely restructured your life, so, yay! But come home now, it's time," to which Ammalie mused, "I met someone recovering from a drug addiction. Someone else with MS. An un-homed man. But mainly, I've met myself, and the limits of what I can do. I've got to seek a bit more. But I can't wait to give you a huge hug, and it'll be sorta soon, I promise."

She saved Powell's call for last. He didn't answer but called back a few minutes later, and she said, "I had to talk to you on Dad's birthday," and he said, "I know, me too," and they both said, "I miss him." The silence of that truth resonated and he said, "It's been a minute," and she said, "We'll have another ceremony when I'm home," and he said, "You're still traveling? Aren't you coming back? When you said you were leaving, I thought you meant, you know, a normal vacation. Like a week or two. Like a normal person?"

She looked out the window of the truck at the little brick building, and watched the librarian turning a key, locking it up for the day. "I'm adventuring because I need to. I'll explain, I promise."

But he was not satisfied. "Mom? What's going on, Mom? I don't understand why you're there, and I'm sorry if I was checked out, but I'm checking *in* now, because, well, what are you *doing*? And also, I'm sorry I said those things in our Big Fight, which is what I'm calling it. I don't hate you. I've never hated you. Who could hate you? It just came out. I don't think you're boring. And I don't mind you checking on me."

Tears blurred her eyes. "Thanks, Powell. I mean that." She pinched the bridge of her nose. "I'm on a road trip. Haven't you ever wanted to go on a road trip? In fact, maybe you should do a big one while you're out of school. It's hard to find the time later."

"Mom, why are you in *Arizona,* though?"

"Why not Arizona? Because it's warmer here—well, most of the time! Dad came here. And I needed to do this, to tell him goodbye. There are chollas. And cactus wrens. And coatimundi. And javelinas—"

"I don't know what those things are—"

"Exactly," she said. "That's why we all should travel. Live a bigger life."

"So you're not coming home? Can I stay at the house, then?"

She felt an arch of surprise lift through her body. "Uh, well, sure. Why? What's wrong with where you're living?"

"Nothing. Well. Everything. It's hard. Rent. Roommates. Dudes are slobs. I'm sorry I was such a slob. You never complained. You just picked up all my shit. And now I feel sorry about that. I'll never leave towels on the floor again. So I can move back in? And where have you been staying this whole time?"

She decided to tell him a part truth. "I sleep in my car sometimes." She pushed through his surprised noise. "Then I stayed in a cabin in Colorado, then a little trailer, and now I'm at a little rustic resort in a place called Cave Valley."

There was a pause. "*What?* The *car?* *What?* That sounds uncomfortable. I mean, for you, Mom . . ."

She found herself barking out a genuine laugh. "Tell me about it. But actually, I am feeling quite comfortable. I miss your dad, of course. Of course we both miss him. It hurts that he's dead. Death is stupid! But I've been so busy my whole life, Powell. Working, raising you, keeping the house, which I was very happy to do. I was efficient and fast because I had to be. But for once, I have learned to move through time differently. I still go fast sometimes, but then I go slow. I sit around and watch birds."

There was a pause. "Huh. That's like me when I smoke weed. I'm able to sit still and be at peace with it."

"Exactly."

"Well, let's smoke together sometime, Mom."

She felt her eyebrows shoot up. "Um, okay? Maybe?"

He made a surprised noise himself. "Plot twist in my life! The very idea of smoking weed with my mom . . . But also, if you sleep in your car, aren't you cold? You hate being cold. Are you *safe?*"

"The Grey Goose feels very safe, and I know how to stay warm."

"The Grey Goose?"

"That's the car's name. Was the car's name."

"The old gray Subaru has a name?"

"Of course it does! Doesn't yours?"

"No."

"Maybe work on that. What are you up to?"

He laughed. "This is really surprising. This doesn't sound like you at all. None of it. My life? Mom, I know you don't approve, but, er, my weed plants are doing great. I named them all after philosophers. Sartre. Bertrand. Arendt. I'm building a greenhouse and everything."

"Don't wreck up your brain. But otherwise, I'm proud. What about the woman?"

He sighed, sadly. "Didn't work out."

"Sorry, Powell. I am. I'm glad you're trying. It's worth it." Then, because there was silence, she said, "Wanna hear the names of the ecosystems here?" and without waiting for an answer, she ticked them off. "Desert scrub, desert grassland, oak savannah, chaparral pine-oak woodland, pine forest, mixed-conifer forest."

"Good to know," he said, clearly smiling on the other side of the phone. Then, "I sometimes feel weird or uncool for saying this, but what I want most is a girlfriend. Am I allowed to feel that? Is that wrong? A *real* girlfriend. It's kinda lonely, and I know about being independent and all but *jesus,* it's harder than you think."

She let out a cascade of laughter and told him she could not agree more. Then she told him about the snowstorm, and how her new theory was that three-fourths of the year, the planet felt as if it was trying to shrug everyone off. She told him about the audiobooks she'd listened to. She told him she was most interested now in what contemporary writers were saying about how to live, about living well on Planet Earth, which, she had decided, was the foundation of the next phase of her life. Her and Mama Earth. She reminded him of his namesake, John Wesley Powell, and how Vincent had always been enamored with his adventures.

By his questions, she could tell he did not want to get off the phone. He was actually enjoying the conversation, she thought, and they ended by sharing favorite memories of Vincent's past birthdays. When she hung up, she cried a few tears that needed release. She missed Powell, she missed her home. *Homesick,* that was the word. But mainly, she cried in relief because Powell had wanted to talk to her in a way he hadn't for a long time.

She looked at the dripping icicles hanging from the library roof and turned off her phone. All had been taken care of. At the end of each conversation, she'd clarified that she'd now be out of touch for some time. It was time to adventure again.

THE FLIGHT WAS bucking-bronc-bumpy and reminded her of driving the dirt road to Dart, except it was a rutted road in the sky. To calm herself—she hadn't done much flying in her life, and didn't like it much—she thought of hugging Rita and Rex and Lady goodbye. She thought of the notes she dropped in the mail to Dan and Lulu and Apricot and Mari and Powell. She thought of the ride to the airport with Rex, who did not press her about her missing car. She thought of her first nights in the car and driving through Nebraska trying to comb her hair with a fork. She thought of all the nights she was so cold she couldn't move well. She thought of the Colorado cabin and the stars and the hot baths. She thought of the nights in Dart, bleeding and cramping in a cramped space, and she thought of the night walking with her cut head. She thought of Kit and the soft kiss. She thought of Dan and the other kind of kiss. She thought of Levi, whom she'd kissed hundreds of times in her mind. She thought of her New Keys—the three women who had taught her something on her heroine's journey. Kat an elder, Lulu a child, Rita a peer.

She thought of her homes in Colorado and Cave Valley, how she'd now think of them as refugias, which were places creatures could live during cataclysmic events. And the next refugia would be the most glorious of all. But as she looked down at the vast ocean, she could see that Planet Earth was the only refugia humans had, and as the plane bumped up and down and shifted sideways in unsettling ways, she hoped that she'd found her own code of ethics to live by, which was to create refugias wherever she went.

PART III

THE
THIRD KEY

SEA AND GLASS

A shack. With spunk. A spunky shack. She knew she'd find the battered place tucked deeply in the bush, a mile from the sea. She knew too that the gray weathered wood rectangle was separated from the line of homes on the other side of the beach not only by distance but by elevation, it being higher up in the jungle, and sitting in a large swath of private land. That meant the house was surrounded by an enormous expanse of berserk greenery and rendered invisible from Google Maps and the human eye, and although Ammalie could recognize the pohutukawa trees from photos, the rest of the green mash was a mysterious jumble of angles and circles, soft and spiky, light green and deep green. Surrounded by such lushness, this home would be invisible in the very opposite way Dart had been.

But she was not there yet. She'd be there soon. As she walked down the beach in a light rain, the backpack pressing heavy on her shoulders, her stinging eyes scanned the scattered homes and rising hill through the mist. What if she couldn't find it or recognize it? She knew it from photos only, knew it to be humble. The artwork around it would be quirky and stunning, though, since the artists who used it for a residency each left one piece of work in an act of reciprocity. Carved statues placed in trees and bushes, stone figures hidden in rocks, glazed bowls that served as birdbaths, wind chimes made of shells and sticks.

Below this shack, and closer to the beach, she knew there was a much fancier glass-walled building for the artists-in-residence to work in, and which also served as a community center of sorts during the summer months, January through April, when the town bloomed in size, though that was relative. Ki was a small town, the smallest beach town in New Zealand, in fact. It had a limited number of houses because of limited space in the cove, and it was too far off the beaten path for most day visitors from Auckland, who had easier places from which to view the roaring Tasman Sea.

And it was truly devoid of human-made noises. In the drizzle, there was only one man walking in the very far distance and one couple walking hand in hand in the opposite direction. "Cheers, Vincent, it *is* gorgeous, and I made it," she said, and was struck by a wave of something akin to déjà vu. In an alternate universe, perhaps they would have made it here as a couple for their anniversary as planned.

Early December meant it was still rainy and blustery and damp—summer was just now coming to this half of the globe. The humidity was intense, thus the chill. But mainly, it was just *so green*. She kept repeating *so green* because she was stunned. After fall in Chicago and Colorado and Arizona, her eyes had felt starved for color. As she gazed over at the bush, she felt as if the greens were lighting up new filaments in her irises, as if a new part of her brain were being moisturized. Her eyes seemed to vibrate with life in their effort to take *in* all this life.

She did a little jig in the wet sand. She felt full of spit and vinegar. She was alive and off the airplane—which she'd felt she had to hold up with her mind the entire time—and on terra firma and in *New Zealand*. She swung her arms, both to feel the air and to warm up. "Ammalie, brava, brave one, you hate flying, you are here, you did it!"

She was, in fact, very proud of herself. The Tasman Sea was

roaring on one side, the expansive blue interrupted only by an island she knew to be Sleeping Seal Rock. To the other side, the bush-clad mountain. So far, it was exactly as she'd pictured it—she had seen Vincent's photos, after all, and had since done research.

Everything had gone as planned. She'd slid out of the bus at the tourist stop near the waterfall while the group of raincoat-clad tourists went looking at eels under a bridge, and she'd left a note and a tip on the driver's seat when he was in the bathroom. *I'm Sandra, the American with the ponytail and bright-red jacket. I've met a friend here in Ki and won't be joining you for the rest of the tour. Thank you.* That would be enough. They didn't really have a record of her; she'd not needed to show her passport, since this was a homegrown, low-key tourist operation run by one guy in a van recommended on an off-the-beaten-track website called New Zealand Underground.

She shifted her backpack. Already, her shoulders ached, but not as badly as the day dropping off water in the Arizona desert, though surely some of the tweaks in her back were still from *that* excursion. It had been just a few days ago, but it somehow seemed a lifetime ago—and it also seemed a lifetime since she had flossed. Already her gums felt swollen. How fast the feral descended! How very needy the human body was! She ran her tongue up and down the back of her teeth as she walked in the wet sand.

The crashing of the sea seemed to increase, the drizzle increased, and the shrouded feeling increased. Now she was at the end of the beach facing a wall of black rocks being slammed by waves, and so she turned right so as to make her way through the brush, and with that turn, the Sea Creature predictably roared into her throat. She patted her heart as she would a little child, comforting herself. The first two keys, she'd had a moment of tightness too; now that she knew what to expect, she wasn't fazed by this leap of anxiety.

"There, there, Thumper, chill," she told herself, and sat in a small cave in the black rocks. She was exhausted and wet and her face was being hit by a strong wind, but she shifted her pack off and leaned against it. Both she and the large backpack were covered in a cheap green raincoat—two green lumps—waiting for the quiet Break-in Hour. She squinted against wind and sand to take in the tops of waves caught in the wind, spraying backward as they rolled forward, two contradictory motions. As someone who'd only rarely seen the sea, she was awed, and aware of her awe. Beginner's mind. Child's eyes.

She now closed her eyes, so as to protect them from the grit and sand blasting her, and conjured an image of Vincent. He'd been a *wwoofer* here—a "willing worker on organic farms," a common phrase here, though she'd never heard it in America. During their early dating, it had been all he'd talked about—it was a seminal time during their limerent phase and thus had sunk itself deeply into the neurons of her brain. Ten years ago, when they were still a strong couple, she'd started putting away money. It had been her secret plan. To bring him here once again. When the marriage had started to fade and her bitterness at his isolation grew, the savings account got turned into Powell's tuition, which frankly seemed like a better investment.

What a horrible thing to think. But she had thought it, and it still seemed true. And she was equally proud that thus far, she'd not needed to use any of her savings. The expenses of Colorado and Arizona had been covered by saved tip money, and New Zealand had been paid for by pawning some of Vincent's things—weather stations, telescopes, microscopes, stamp collections—and spending *that* money was something she didn't feel bad about. They were things that took him away from her, and she'd used them to bring him back. Back to her old dreams, back to the place that had once meant so much to him. She put her wet face in her wet hands. She'd made it. Even if she flew home tomorrow, getting here felt like a monumental expedition.

THE CREPUSCULAR HOUR arrived—*crepuscular* being her word of the day—and so Ammalie heaved on her pack and trudged across dunes of marram grass and across a cracked paved road and up a muddy and slick dirt road that ended at the empty and dark community center. To the left of the glass building was another sunken, hidden dirt road—or what used to be a road—that snaked up into the forest and led to the shack. This is what she'd been looking for. She started walking with a wandering gait. If anyone asked her, she'd say she was a tourist, was just poking around in the rain—*Oh, she was sorry, was this a private driveway? It was getting dark, she'd lost her way, it was so misty out, she was just tramping and was all turned around! Silly middle-aged woman! Silly jet lag, silly American!*

But no one was around. Once she reached the forest, or bush, or jungle, or whatever it was called here, she turned on her headlamp and picked her way on a muddy path that was turning into a small creek. Then she saw the little house. It was dark enough that anyone inside would have turned on a light by now, and it was raining hard enough that it was impossible to see any of the statues or figurines, but she knew it was the right place. She was shivering now, and so she slid off her backpack, opened the front zipper, and searched for her ring of keys.

Which is when it hit her.

My god, she'd left them. With Rita. She'd left her extra unnecessary belongings, including the set of keys, in a box with Rita!

"I have no key," she said to the front door. "No key. No key. No key." She kept repeating it in order to understand it, and then started laughing hysterically. Oh, she'd been so confident, so sure of herself. And here she was in a jungle in New Zealand at night in the rain with no keys! She laughed until her side hurt and she had to bend over, and then, using the headlamp, she started picking up rocks and pots or anything that might hide a key. There was a multitude of various items; the possibilities were endless.

The rain, without warning, came down wildly, in sheets. She went from being wet to soaked. She moved her backpack under the eave of the house and then stripped herself naked, leaving her bits of clothing with the pack. No one was going to show up now, and if a jeep or some sturdy car did, she'd see the headlights coming for a good long while, and by god, who cared that it was raining! She'd swim in the air! She could either resist the cold or she could just *be* cold, be *in* the cold, and after all, it wasn't *that* cold, it was nearly summer here! Everything was so glory-hell fucked that she ran in a small circle, naked, and took a rain shower, the first of her life, using a little bar of soap with enough pooled water in her palms and splashed them against her crotch and then just stood, arms out. She was a wild creature. Wild and homeless.

For many minutes, she did nothing. Just tilted her head up toward the rain, slowly circling to take in the house, the bush, the clouds, the way rain slid off the roof, the way it slid down the palm fronds, the way it slid down her outstretched arms. Then she walked to the front door and pulled and it . . . slid open. She laughed some more and looked closely at the door. What once had been a lock was now so rusty that it did not seem to serve as a lock at all. Well, this was not Chicago. This was a small community in New Zealand and locks were perhaps not required.

She called out. "Hullo? Hullo?"

There was, of course, no answer. She stepped in, making a puddle almost immediately, and now guilty of not only that, but also of breaking and entering, and in a foreign country, no less. She stood naked save for the headlamp, and then caught sight of herself. There she was, reflected in a window with the last light of the day, her dim pear-shaped outline wavering in the wavy glass. Empyreal. One-eyed, like Cyclops, her headlamp beam shining bright. "I'm Odysseus," she said, pulling a travel towel and dry clothes from her pack. Didn't Odysseus have a dog too? Didn't he hear the Sirens, just as she had heard the birds? She felt ferocious and strong and wet and naked, and the hazy woman staring back at her looked beautiful. *You got nothing on me, Odie,* she said aloud, and then snorted at the truth of it.

She looked around for Fluffiest Red before realizing that of course her sleeping bag wasn't there. She felt a pang—it had, after all, been her primary bedding for the last two months, and was it crazy to say she'd developed a relationship with it? Then she climbed into the one bed in the back of the house, a bed she knew Vincent had once had sex in, and the knowledge of this made her smile. She knew he'd stayed down in the community center with the other wwoofers, but he had told her about this shack-house and how he'd used it with his lover, pilfering a key for a place to make love, not yet knowing that Ammalie was pregnant nor knowing that their relationship would solidify. She and Vincent had been a fling and in their early twenties, after all—both of them had declared it such before his departure—and it was not until his return that they came together and decided to create a relationship that involved hope for the future.

She was starving, but somehow the craving had dissipated into a low ache that she could ignore. If there was one thing this adventure had taught her about hunger, it was that it came in waves, and if you waited for the wave to pass, you'd be fine. Exhaustion was the stronger pull, so she nestled into the blankets and put her head on a flat musty pillow and fell asleep to the sound of rain and thundering sea.

A WAILING SIREN blared and she immediately thought *Air raid* and *Where's my Survival Bucket?* and *Earthquake or tsunami—store water!* and the Sea Creature leapt into her throat and threatened to suffocate her. She pawed at the blanket and sheets, untangling herself so she could sit up. It was so dark, pelting down rain, and she was so alone.

Then she realized the blaring was far away, on the other edge of the beach, and she had a vague memory of Vincent talking about startling sirens, how they most often signaled a car crash and were a call for the volunteer rescue brigade. That's how New Zealand worked. She plonked back down on the pillow and listened. Once the siren stopped, the only noise was loud rain and distant but roaring waves. No one was here; no one was coming for her.

She had an odd sensation in her lungs and throat she couldn't quite place until she realized yet again the feeling was called *humid*—so much more humid than Colorado or Arizona; her nostrils and her skin and her lungs felt oxygenated and hydrated. Her scalp did not itch. Her lips did not need lip balm. Her eyes did not need eyedrops.

But she was damp-cold, so she sat up, dug around in her backpack for a sweater, pulled it on, then pulled a blanket around her, put heat packs in her socks and a wool hat on her head, briefly tracing the scar, still bumpy on her scalp. In the dark, she got up and tiptoed to the kitchen. It was a regular kitchen—stove, sink, dish rack, although all much older and different sizes than in the States. There was pasta in the cupboard—*There will always be pasta in a cupboard! Humans are so predictable!* she thought—and by the light of her headlamp, she boiled a pot of water and cooked it, ate it, and then slept again.

She woke in the afternoon to a hot flash and a tui bird. She knew it immediately because of the call, very much like R2-D2 or a rusty hinge. She'd listened to sounds of New Zealand birds on her phone while in Arizona, but had never heard one in person. It had been one of her great wishes to do so. She smiled, deeply satisfied, and waited the hot flash out. From the bed, she was looking out a glass door at the tops of the pohutukawa trees—another thing she'd researched—which were still glittering and dripping with wet. The house was built on a hillside, with a car park underneath, which meant she was high up, like a bird among the curvy branches that swayed up and down, each branch its own trampoline, bouncing mildly in different directions.

She could see now that the sliding glass door of the bedroom opened onto a small deck so old and saggy that it didn't look like it would support even a child, but it did support the tui, which landed briefly on a nearby branch, and then the deck railing, shimmering green-black with the strange curled white feather at the throat, which moved as it belted out a string of crazy noises, seemingly just to welcome her, and then flew off. Then another bird, also very conversational, welcomed her, and when she looked it up in the bird book she discovered it was a piwakawaka, a fantail.

Heaven. She was in heaven. Empyreal. No key required. Heaven with Strange Names. Lulu would have loved it.

In the far distance, between branches, she could see little slivers of the sea, both the band of blue that met sky in the far distance and the lines of white breakers hitting the shore with such force.

She got up and walked down the hallway to the kitchen, taking stock. Everything about the house was dated in a delightful way. Turquoise curtains and old paneling, a very thin turquoise carpet that smelled musty. In the fridge, there were plenty of condiments—mayonnaise, salad dressing, some olives stuck in a solidified oil, lemon curd, a bottle of champagne still in the box—but no real food. The cupboard was a mess—spilled spices and a grubby film over everything, and some mice scat, but there were many cans of soup, a bag of rice, boxes of tea, some coffee.

She set the kettle to boil and went to the door. From the deck, she sized up the safety situation: With the window open, she was pretty sure she'd hear a car down at the community center. Someone walking up was the likely scenario, since the driveway was steep and looked like it was only suitable for high-clearance all-terrain vehicles. No one was above her—there was only bush as far as the eye could see. A car door slamming from below—well, that's the thing she should tune into. If she heard one, she could grab her backpack and dart into the forest, circle back down to the beach, and walk herself right out of town, hitching a ride. Hitchhiking was still done here; she'd seen it done from the bus, and indeed, hitchhiking was one of her goals.

She slipped on shoes and wandered around outside. There was a wooden picnic table, weathered and beaten, and a large rainwater tank to the side of the house, and the house itself had plants growing in the roof guttering, as if it was fitting itself into the jungle. A fenced and seemingly abandoned garden was a tangle, unkempt, and she assumed that anything coming up was volunteer. Among the things she could identify was some asparagus, young and perfect, which she took inside and sizzled in olive oil and added to the rice she'd cooked. She made a cup of tea with Manuka honey and sat down at the damp picnic table with a ratty beach towel below her butt.

From here, she had a view of the sea. The rain was still paused, though the potential hung in the air as thick as the clouds, and she could see the headlights of occasional cars, very far away, on the one road that led to Auckland. She watched them for a moment, and then looked down at the great expanse of water and noticed how the grays shifted over the surface.

"Okay," she said, breathing out for the first real time since arriving. "You got this. The ultimate righting of one's karma."

It was, in fact, supposed to be a place of doing just that—righting karma. Because of Vincent's continued correspondence with the owner, Nan, she knew its history and current status. Nan had inherited it from her family, who had made their wealth cutting down the now-rare kauri trees. A wealth made from a great environmental wrong. To right her family's karma, she had turned the place into a residency for artists whose work was dedicated to the earth in some way. This was during summer months; in winter months it was closed up. The first visiting artist was likely slated for February first, but if Ammalie was wrong and the place was already occupied, her backup plan consisted of returning to Auckland.

This vague plan was based on one clear truth: It would really be okay. Maybe her retreat would involve some travel woes, expense, or uncomfortable housing, but she no longer considered those emergencies. She was finally, finally, finally able to go with the flow. It would just be *all right*. She could *handle it*. Besides: She had saved a dog, cut wire from a tree, helped a woman on a tough night, helped a man through a dangerous spot, left water in the desert for those who might be thirsty. She deserved a little residency too.

CHAPTER 17

Midday on her second full day—the first she felt awake enough to cogitate or move—Ammalie put on a hoodie that covered her head and sunglasses that covered her face and walked back two miles along the beach into town, enjoying the imprints her feet left in the black sand. The sun was seeping through low-lying puffs, the temperature had warmed considerably, and, as she walked toward the main road, she kept being struck by the strange joy of finding herself in the opposite season from the Northern Hemisphere.

As soon as she entered the only restaurant she'd seen, which simply said PIZZA on a modest sign, she smelled fish-and-chips, which is what she ordered from the only person in the place, who was a woman approximately her age but who looked far more interesting. For one thing, she was wearing Lion King leggings and a big black shirt and had a bundle of black hair partly dyed purple pinned in a messy haphazard bun at the top of her head.

As she waited for the food, Ammalie wandered to the deck outside the restaurant, where again she was the only person. She stole the sugar packets, and then, horribly, the salt shaker, putting them all in her pocket, but then put the salt shaker back. What was she *doing*? Then she wandered inside to the front door, where flyers were pinned to corkboard, and scanned the lost cats and rooms for rent and community-movie-fundraiser night, then finally went back outside to the remotest corner of the deck.

When the woman brought her plate to her outdoor table, she

nearly cried with delight. Real fish-and-chips, from fish caught right outside! "Hello. *Kia ora*. Visiting Ki, love? Welcome," the woman said, sliding the plate in front of her.

Ammalie was startled by the word choice, the accent, and the food. "Oh, yes. Yes, I am. Just briefly."

"First time?"

"Yes."

"You have that look about you." The woman winked at her playfully, and then said, "Eat your food, why don't you," and waited for Ammalie to take a bite.

Ammalie found herself wanting to talk, despite her plan not to engage with any other human. "This is delicious. Truly. Do I look like I'm filled with stunned awe? Because that's how I feel. With a view of the sea while sitting outside. All the green."

The woman tilted her head and seemed to really consider Ammalie, which made her want to disappear into herself. "That sounds right. Awe. And that green, I like to say it's the color of a baby's first cry."

Ammalie felt her eyebrows shoot up. "Why, that's lovely. So is your accent. If you don't mind me saying so. It's so . . . unique on the ears."

"As is yours, mi-love. The weather, that's what's set to be lovely. Summer's round the corner. The winds will calm. Summer is really such a jewel, a golden time. You're staying around here?"

Ammalie tried to keep her smile going. "What a gorgeous place this is. How lucky you are, to live here."

"Yeah. Too true, it's sweet," she said. "I thought you might be the artist-in-residence over at Nan's place."

Ammalie startled and said, "Oh!" but then clamped her lips shut. Surely silence was an answer?

"Ah, the last one didn't want to talk about her art either!"

Ammalie heard herself making a random "Ohhh, wellllll" sound and fingered her greenstone necklace, and a silence stretched so long that it made Ammalie's cheeks flush. She darted her eyes up to the dark eyes of the woman, who was looking at the necklace. "A gift from my husband," she murmured.

"It's a lovely piece. Oi! You're the *jewelry* maker, right? Of course you are!"

"Oh, I . . ."

"Nan said there were three artists coming this summer. A potter, a writer, and a jewelry maker, and that the jeweler was first, that you specialize in . . . what was it? Jewelry from local clay? That you fire? I thought I saw someone coming out of Nan's house this morning while I was taking my morning swim. Up above your house there's a pure lake, you know. So pure you can drink the water from it. The lower streams are unsafe—runoff from septic tanks and algal blooms, you know—but not there. It was once my people's land, and Nan knows that, and I have permission to walk on her property as I please."

"Oh. Yes. Of course," Ammalie stammered. She had the bizarre notion that if she spoke in fragments, perhaps nothing would actually be conveyed. "How lovely. Yes. Well. I love hearing about clean water—that seems a rare commodity on earth these days. That used to not be true. Can you imagine? A time when you could drink from streams? It was a basic right. Clean water. That wasn't so long ago. And it seems like the basics have been taken from us . . . and we've just gotten used to it. Yes. Well. I'm a bit . . . early . . . I . . . I'm hoping to actually experiment with . . . a new form. Glass . . . sea glass. It's new to me. I came here to learn . . ."

"Oh! Are you fusing it? Or what does one do with sea glass?"

"Well . . . see . . ."

The pause went on so long that the woman kindly offered, "It's okay. I understand. Art shouldn't be talked about too much." Ammalie figured that the woman's mind was clicking away and she was coming to the conclusion that Ammalie was perhaps stunted in some way—particularly in oratory skills—and that, being a kind person, the woman was trying to help her answer her questions. "Well, I look forward to the class."

"The class?"

"The class you'll give. At the end of the residency. You know, to the community."

"Oh, yes," Ammalie said, desperately trying to pull herself together. What a mistake—all of this! What had she been thinking? "Of course, of course! Everything is so new. And I have a bit of jet lag still. More than a bit! I'm so sorry. I'm afraid I'm not making much sense, not being a good conversationalist. I'm just . . ." And then she added, "If you could not tell anyone I was here yet. I need a few days to . . . I just need to . . . You see, to be honest with you, I have a bit of a social anxiety problem . . . I have a flying anxiety problem, I hate flying, and then I also have a social anxiety problem, and I'm trying to be brave . . ."

The woman made a kind, tsking noise. "No problem, love. Thank you for sharing that with me. Plus, there *is* no one to tell yet! Not really. Just Judy, over at the library. But she's visiting her son in Christchurch for the month. That's why I'm closed on some days, doing double duty here and at the library. Don't worry. I'll leave you in peace. I know artists like their peace. And I know about anxiety!"

"Thank you. I . . ." Ammalie went ahead and blurted it out—wasn't it better to confront danger than to run from it? "Look, I have a question. Please don't be angry at it, I'm just asking. I don't have a work visa, just the visitor visa, and I don't want to do anything illegal, but New Zealand is more expensive than I thought it would be . . . and . . . you know, I'm an artist and all. I just didn't budget enough . . . I just really didn't! Things are quite pricey here. Twenty dollars for avocado toast—I saw that on your menu; that seems like so much! Although I'm sure it's worth it! I'm wondering if I could wash dishes for my meal? I am a good dishwasher. Cleaner. I worked in a restaurant most of my life. I was a waitress and I *liked* it. I could jump in and do anything right now. If not, no worries. I'll be fine. Of course. I have enough money for this meal, I do, but—"

Halting though she was, Ammalie knew she was making a good decision. A *brilliant* decision. A decision that would counteract her very bad one of coming to the restaurant in the first place! But better to be *present* than absent. Better to embrace the lie fully than to back off and seem more suspicious in that way. Sometimes it was easier to hide in plain sight. She'd stay one week and go. A gamble, but a worthy one.

The woman was startled by the question, but answered, "Sweet as, love. I often hire people over at the freedom camping spot for a job here or there. The exchange rate isn't good for you."

Ammalie just nodded, not knowing the specifics of that, and ate another fry.

"There's always dishes. Actually, that helps me quite a lot. And the bathroom to clean. The meal for an hour. Each worth about twenty-five New Zealand dollars. Any day you want—a meal for an hour or so. But don't tell Nan. I don't think we're supposed to hire the residents. Not that you could tell her anyway, I know she's traveling now, and when she travels, she makes it clear she is *un*-available." Then she added, "I'm Aroha, by the way."

"Oh, Aroha, it's nice to meet you. Yes, let's not tell anyone anything! I'm really grateful. I can be . . . shy . . . I came here hoping for some real, true peace. I need to sort some big things out."

Aroha's gaze was so warm and direct that it made Ammalie again wish to disappear, but then Aroha looked up at a man walking in and said, "Gotta go, love. Laters, *ka kite*." Turning over her shoulder, she added, "It's a jewel of a day. Cheers. Eat. Then dive in and do what you can. You'll figure it out. Clean dishes are clean dishes, no matter where you are on earth. Tell any new customers I'm at the library and will be back when I'm back. I doubt there will be any, though, because that's Richard, and after him, it's usually no one. Leave when you're done. Just close the door. The locals know that if I'm not here, I'm not here. Cash drawer is locked."

Ammalie raised her eyebrows. My god, this *was* a small town, and an honest town, if you didn't suspect anyone would steal one of the gorgeous-looking muffins in the glass display. She turned toward the fish-and-chips and took a deep breath in.

Oh god. God, god, god.

Somehow this had all just gotten complicated.

But the call of food was pure and simple. And eating outside! Birds all around, including the little sparrows who wanted scraps, and with the sea thrumming into shore, visible between the trees. She watched a big bird that looked like a parrot ripping bark from a tree—spectacular. The clouds hung low, a hazier blue than Colorado's or Arizona's, and she realized that for the first time in a long while, not only did her scalp not itch but her soul felt moist, and settled too. And now it was warm, and she was absurdly joyful, despite the very real current problem of being caught.

After finishing an astonishingly good meal and internally thanking all the creatures and elements that had helped provide it—including the fish and batter makers and lemon growers and sunlight and dirt that grew potatoes—she went to the kitchen and donned yellow gloves and cleaned. It was self-explanatory, as most cleaning was. Aroha was up front taking an order from a lithe young woman with a cascading ponytail, and then Aroha was gone, presumably to the library. Ammalie loved washing dishes—odd but true. *It's gonna be okay, it's gonna be okay,* she hummed to herself while she worked. Yes. It would all be a Very Grand Adventure.

AT THE LIBRARY, which had a notice that said OPEN WHEN OPEN AND CLOSED WHEN NOT, she nabbed a paperback by Maurice Gee from the free shelf, and then slipped past Aroha and sat in the back corner. She logged onto a public-access computer and checked her email and sent a quick one to Mari, Powell, and Apricot, conveying that she was fine but would communicate this way for the next few weeks. She knew she could figure out WhatsApp or buy a SIM card or travel plan, but she was in New Zealand and wanted to be mindfully present during the limited time here in this green heaven.

She did turn on her phone, but only to look at her photos, seeking the ones she'd snapped of pages from the glass-jewelry-making book she'd seen in the Colorado cabin. Then she got up and browsed the shelves until she found the only book on wire wrapping specifically, and took photos of many of the pages, figuring it was easier to read photos than check the book out. She also had to remember, she told herself, that people could learn things just by *doing*.

Just try, she thought when she got home, and dug out the little baggie of green glass she'd picked up weeks ago. *Just try. Not only a house, but a life, an identity. You're an artist, an artist, an artist.* So she sat outside at the round weathered picnic table and laid out the rough shards and some twine. This was all she had. It was not enough. But maybe art was about starting—and trusting.

* * *

MIDAFTERNOON, A CAT appeared. Although it looked black at first, she could see mink-brown fur underneath the black, and although she was allergic to cats and therefore didn't particularly like them, she thought this might be the most beautiful cat she'd ever seen. She was also happy to see it had a bell around its neck, which meant that someone cared not only for the cat but also for wild birds.

"Got nothing for you," she said. When the cat jumped onto the table next to her, she stopped work long enough to run her fingers down its neck. "You're saying I need to get it together and prepare to flee? That humans are about?" She gave it a tickle underneath its chin. "You're right, I should get ready to run if need be."

She left the cat outside and scrounged around the house, putting together a go-bag. She put three cans of soup and a bag of rice into her backpack, and then dug around till she found a red shopping bag and put in matches, a candle, two old bedsheets from the bottom of the stack of items she found in a jam-packed linen closet— why did people keep so many sheets? When she looked through the kitchen cabinets to find the oldest, crummiest pot for boiling water, she saw that these cupboards too were filthy and disorganized; there was a thin layer of grime and some mouse droppings over the shelves and pans.

But if there was one thing she didn't much mind, it was cleaning something that needed to be cleaned. After her escape bags were set to go, she lugged out all the pots and pans, washed them, put them all back, and then went to the other cupboards and did the same with the spices and dishes and silverware drawer. She remembered how much she'd liked basic housekeeping when Powell was young—how she went through the rooms, putting things in order before he returned from school, straightening sheets and hanging towels. She thought about how happy she'd been in Cave Valley while cleaning the cabins. Maybe cleaning was a key to her future.

When she'd finished, she added to what she'd just named her New Zealand Survival Kit by filling a dusty duffel bag with a raincoat from the far back of a closet, a turquoise and much-washed fleece, a floppy sunhat out of a pile of many, and most important, a small blue sleeping bag that fit into the smallest sack she'd ever seen. She was hoping for socks or T-shirts, since she had only a few of each, but there was none of that. There were books, though, and she poached one called *Natural Rearing of Children* and a tube of something called Bugger Off!, a natural insect repellent.

Her new idea was this: If she heard a suspicious noise, or if anyone confronted her, she'd dart out the door and into the bush. This was the thickest, densest mountainside she had ever seen, the sort where someone could hide a few feet away; it was *that* thick. It made walking through it nearly impossible—without using one of the narrow paths, that is—but it made hiding easy. Besides, from the map at the store she now knew where to find the freedom camping spot, which was a place she could camp for free, much like the BLM lands in America.

From the map, she also knew of another small beach accessible *only* by hiking up a steep mountainside and then down, and she supposed that for this reason, it was likely close to deserted. Places without roads signaled places without people. And finally, she knew that people camped in the caves adjacent to the beach; she'd seen evidence of a fire ring on her beach walk today. So, worse came to worst? She'd just run. Since no one knew her name, she wouldn't be particularly easy to track, and she'd simply hitch a ride back to Auckland when needed. She was flexible and capable. It would be *okay*.

Really, it would be okay.

She'd have the backpack she'd arrived with, plus these supplemental supplies were near the door, ready to go. She ran through the possible progression of events in her mind: Person shows up? Backpack on her back, a New World bag in one hand, duffel in the other, and shoot straight out the door and up into the forest, then, after about three miles, make a sharp left and head to the deserted beach. Or one of the other destinations.

It was an Adequate Plan, but not a great plan. The Great Plan would be to stay here and make jewelry.

Suddenly she was very tired, so she went back to the bed, propped up the pillows, and watched the birds—a black one with crazy yellow eyes and an orange beak, another that looked like a kingfisher, another with a very yellow head. And she closed her eyes and listened to the cacophony and fluttering cascades of notes. There was one bird that was flat-out annoying and sounded like an enormous hummingbird or a high-pitched, relentless bee. Despite scanning with her eyes and binoculars next to the bed, she could not locate the source for that one, though she did discover others.

The branches of the trees were mesmerizing too. Curvy and winding, they swayed wildly in the wind, as if conducting it. Nature and all her wisdom. She picked up *Natural Rearing of Children* and felt no great interest; she was done parenting, after all. But she flipped it open and found herself snorting in delight at the tone and style of the book. "Conventionalism in clothing is a health tragedy," she read. "Especially deplorable is the modern use of synthetic fabrics which cut off air from the human skin. Rubber soled footwear cuts off contact with earth radiations."

"I suppose that's true," she murmured to the book.

She read on. "If the threatened horror of atomic warfare should ever fall upon any part of the world (personally I believe that this cannot happen, for the world is not man's alone, it is shared by animal and plant life, and their creator will continue to protect their interests in the face of mankind's increasing selfishness), then it would be a blessing for families to know how to cure injuries and ills without needing doctors or pharmacies."

"Goodness," she said, remembering just how scary nuclear warfare had seemed to her as a child.

She flipped to another section. Senna pods were a good laxative, burns should be placed in cold water and covered with a pulp of raw potatoes or asparagus or honey, bruises should be covered with a banana skin.

It was wildly wonderful. Humans' desire to prepare for catastrophe was, well, so *human*. And so necessary. Ammalie had felt such shame about it—as if she were the only one who stayed up late thinking about how to survive various scenarios. But no. Trying not to die was part of living.

This author felt like a kindred spirit, with an unapologetic worry for the future. When Ammalie read, "We all now accept the bitter fact that even if we manage to raise healthy children, there are nuclear bombs in the possession of man," she thought of Powell, and whether or not he'd have kids, given the climate crisis and the seemingly increasing potential that his children might not be healthy or live in a healthy world. Suddenly she felt she should be with Powell—she was crazy to be halfway around the world!—although she *had* been with him, and all he'd asked for was distance.

She ached, though. Her missing Powell was real. Eco-grief was real. Her desire to protect was real. Her need to be alone was real. Her need for companionship was real. Now she felt *compassion* for her Sea Creature, having to zoom around her heart with so many different opposing emotions! But even more, she felt a brief, pure moment of connection to and awe for every human on the planet, all struggling to have an arc of time so as to take advantage of their one precious life.

CHAPTER 18

Walls of windows. That's what the community center was basically made of, and though splattered and dirty, they offered a view of the surrounding jungle, visible by moonlight. The glass door had been locked, but she found the key under a pinkish rock, and let herself into the big echoey space.

On one wall, a row of tall cupboards, and behind that wall was what she presumed were small studios and bedrooms; she couldn't check because the key didn't open the big wooden door that separated this segment from the large room. But the cupboards opened, and she was delighted to find a treasure trove of art supplies. Blocks of wrapped clay, paints, canvasses, brushes, aprons, gloves, drop cloths, buckets, rags—so much potential! The last cupboard was filled with all sorts of random equipment, including, hallelujah, a Dremel tool and small pliers and dental picks and scissors and clippers, all of which would help with jewelry.

She stood in the dark room and inhaled. What was that smell? Perhaps it was oils used to coat the wood? Perhaps it was the wood itself? Or just layers of years of art in the making—paints and dyes and solvents, all infused with the smell of salt and sea. She stretched and did some yoga on a mat she found, then meditated, and then sat quietly in the predawn light—she'd decided to sneak into this area before any reasonable person would be up—and tried to focus not on the skill set of making jewelry, but rather on the impulse of it. *What's my vision?* she thought. *What am I trying to stand for?*

Perhaps there was some aesthetic energy in pairing the violence of smashing beer bottles with the gentleness of the sea. Or she could create pieces that inspired care for Mama Earth. Perhaps she could . . . She wasn't sure, and when she closed her eyes to imagine her ideal piece of jewelry, her mind was a blank. And now the sun was coming up, the first rays lighting the windows, and so she slipped out, replaced the key, and went for a walk on the beach. After an hour in the early light, she had found only a few shells, which she suddenly felt guilty picking up—didn't the ocean need them?—and so she put them back but scanned the sand for sea glass. Near the rock outcropping, where all the mussels had attached themselves, she found one small piece, green and still jagged, very un-special and yet still a delight.

On the way back to the house, she scanned the beach and road for signs of life. No one. So she slipped into the community center again, spooked by its silence, which echoed even her light footsteps. She got on her hands and knees and rummaged through all the cupboards again. Surely there would be something she could use? Something that would inspire her?

There was only one low cabinet left unexplored, different from the others, smaller and handcrafted with thick wood. She crouched down and ran her finger over the lock. She pulled hard, but there was no budging the solid door. It was the most well-made cabinetry in the room, with fitted, hand-cut dovetail joints and an inlaid top of contrasting-colored wood, and she wondered if it was made from the now nearly extinct kauri trees. Regardless, it was gorgeous, and as she ran her hand over the top of it, she saw the word NAN expertly etched into the wood. Ah, the owner's personal cabinet.

She stood, hands on hips, and gazed around the room. Scratched her chest and fingered the greenstone necklace. And looked down to see her fingers rubbing the thick key.

Naw.

But maybe?

She took off the necklace, and before she even got the key to the lock she knew it would fit. The lock and key looked like each other: thick, old, brass. A pair.

She held her breath, turned the key, heard the click, peered inside. The top shelf was stacked with faded, dusty papers. School notebooks and crayon drawings and crooked, awkward, delightful kid lettering. Was there anything sweeter than seeing the evidence of a child's early learning? She got on her hands and knees and ran her hand over the bottom shelf. *Empty, empty.* Just a fine coat of dust, which became streaked with the motion of her fingers. But in the back corner, her hand hit something hard. She ducked even lower, her cheek now nearly on the floor. There were two canning jars, and she pulled them out, unscrewed one lid, and peered in.

Sea glass?

Yes.

Two jars of it.

No.

But yes. And why not? Who, living by the sea in the '70s, would *not* collect sea glass? It had once been so ubiquitous. She squealed and spread the pieces out on the floor. Sitting crisscross over them, she breathed out a string of cusswords of joy. Their beauty was not in the mass of them but in each individual piece. The white ones were not just white—one looked like a frosted windowpane, another had a thin streak of lavender coursing through it, another looked like shell, another was ice blue with ripples. There were pearl colors and sand colors and eggshell colors.

The browns, equally diverse. Some the color of root beer, others like tea, others like earth. And the greens—the greens! Jade and pea green and apple green and pale green and lime green. There were a few with a crosshatch marking on them, and others that looked like the lids of old bottles. Some seemed to be flecked with mica, and others were solid. Dark greens, she knew, were for alcohol, since alcohol breaks down in light. The light greens, on the other hand, were likely soda bottles.

There were only a few blues—deep like a Noxzema bottle, and light, like the color of the bottle of gin she preferred. There were even fewer orange and red pieces—she'd read in the art book that orange will only be found one out of every ten thousand pieces collected. One piece was red with gold flecks, and she guessed this was likely a piece of a motorcycle or car lens light, back from when they'd used glass instead of plastic. Finally, there were even some weathered marbles—remnants of children's beach games.

The most special thing about Nan's collection, though, was that most of it was not "half-done," the term for when it was not yet frosty, or still jagged. Nan's pieces were true sea glass, which meant they were completely frosted, smooth, perfect.

She picked out twenty of her favorite pieces. She felt guilt—of all her poaching, perhaps this was the most inappropriate, because, unlike honey or a brush, they weren't replaceable. That said, the jars had been hidden, dusty and forgotten. She also figured that she could simply undo any silver wrapping she was about to try, and could put the pieces back in the jars. Nothing she was doing was altering the sea glass permanently. She could, if needed, leave no trace. Except for one thing—which was to leave the key in the lock, so that some future person, Nan hopefully, could access the contents within.

She went back to the shack and read furiously and with intense interest. Sea glass, she discovered, took about fifty or sixty years to "make"—to be tossed in the ocean until smooth and frosted, which made these pieces about as old as she was, and also made her think about the people who'd tossed a bottle or had their house swiped into the sea long ago, when she was a child. She learned it was the acidity of the water that caused the frosting—which meant that sea glass looked different if it was in Lake Erie or the Tasman Sea. Another thing she hadn't realized was just how rare it was now. In the '70s, people would pick up sea glass up by the *bucketful*. Now, though, with so much being made of plastic, there was far less of it.

She looked up from her book and pictured Nan as a child, walking the beaches and collecting sea glass. How could this little girl have known that someday, a strange woman from America would be sifting through it, dreaming of her?

AROHA, IT TURNED out, was one-fourth Māori, and informed Ammalie that the nearest art supply store of any quality was back in Auckland, where she went every other Tuesday for food, to visit her mother, and to attend a Māori gathering.

Ammalie was invited along for the ride, and she accepted. The winding drive on the extremely narrow road was too fast and panic-inducing, but safe in terms of conversation. Just as she had hoped, they simply chitchatted about America and New Zealand and joked about the road signage and quirkiness of New Zealand humor. Ammalie kept quiet and stammered a lot—which was not too hard, given her nervousness. She revealed only that she was undergoing a kind of identity crisis, which was true.

Once in Auckland, while Aroha attended to her own activities, Ammalie went into a shop filled with boxes of glorious beads and wires of every metal and size, wandering the store and poking around. For nearly an hour, she simply looked. She wanted to be patient and let ideas form. Finally, she started committing to decisions. She put an enormous charge on her credit card—something she hadn't done this entire trip, save the flights to get here. But this purchase mattered very much to her immediate future, and she felt a zinging joy in taking a risk on herself. She bought glass beads, Czech crystal beads, semiprecious stones, pliers that curved, pliers that flattened, clasps, wire cutters, tweezers, ribbon clamps, pinch clasps, with most of her money spent on quality sterling silver wrap. She chose several gauges, and a lot of it, so that she could make mistakes. She *had* to allow herself to make mistakes; she needed the freedom of that.

As she checked out, she thought, *What a gamble!* She'd have to abandon all this if she had to run—and it cost *so* much money. But wasn't all of life a gamble? Some gambles were just bigger than others—and she was in the mood to Go Big. Be Interesting. Be Bold. She was a jeweler-in-residence, after all. Artists needed supplies.

On the ride home, she kept the discussion focused on finding out about Nan and the residency, which she pretended to know very little about. She also found out that Aroha was single, childless, and had a small dog named GingerBeer. Besides her shop, and taking care of her mother, she spent her time volunteering at the Māori cultural center and guiding hikes at the regional park. She also loved adventuring—glowworm caves and the islands on the other side of Auckland were favorite destinations. She declared herself a content woman, which meant that her life had enough content, a line she'd heard was from Shakespeare: To be con*tent,* one must have *con*tent.

Ammalie felt a tug of shame or sorrow or jealousy, she wasn't sure which. She and Aroha were the same age, approximately, but worlds apart, because Aroha had exactly what Ammalie wanted. To feel secure that one was living a full life, one with a seriousness of purpose and with some fun to boot.

Before Aroha dropped her off at the base of the driveway, it being too steep and rocky for her car, she said, "You know about the dick, yes? Don't go out on the dick."

Ammalie bit her lip to keep from snorting. "Ahhh—the dick?" She scanned her brain but arrived at nothing.

"Aye."

"The dick?"

"The thing outside the house."

"Oh! The deck!" She burst out laughing. "You New Zealanders. You flatten vowels, and you miss your *r*'s."

"So, like *lova,* I should be saying *love-er*?"

"Lover, yes."

"Aye. Lov*er*." Aroha enunciated the final *r* with emphasis, rolling it on her tongue, and gave Ammalie a wink.

Ammalie flushed, and to recover, blurted, "My dead husband used to collect mussels here. Can I do that? If I'm hungry? I don't see anyone ever collecting them."

Aroha smiled and let the look go. "No, not anymore. There's the *rāhui.*"

"*Rāhui?*"

"In Māori culture, a *rāhui* is a form of *tapu,* and it means restricting the use of an area or resource. Wise use. You see? Self-control. For the sake of world. But if you're hungry, I can make you dinner at my place."

"Oh, no. No, thanks. I'm off to design and create!" Ammalie shut the door quickly and waved and picked up her bags. No, she could not make a friend, or more-than-a-friend, if that's what Aroha was intending.

SHE WANTED TO be bold, but not stupid. For example, she didn't want the few locals seeing her on the beach all the time, so she woke when it was still dark and went for her first walk before sunrise, so that when the morning walkers were out, she was already back at the picnic table, working on jewelry. Never having been much of a morning person, she'd seen more sunrises on this trip than she'd seen the entire rest of her life, and she knew that Venus appeared in the west in the evening and in the east in the morning. She tracked the Southern Cross, and she learned about dark constellations, much more common in the southern sky, and which were patterns and shapes defined by the *absence* of stars.

She even made an effort to swish away her footprints on the one path that took her to the beach, using an old paddle she'd discovered thrown upon the rocks by the sea. But she was also brazenly not invisible: During the morning walks, she began to make beach art on the side of beach farthest from her but closest to the other houses. Some days, she used the great glistening ropes of bull kelp that washed up, and other days she used the paddle, dragging it to make huge swirls and swoops inspired by the Pasifika and Māori designs she'd seen. Other days she wrote messages like CHEERS FOR A LOVELY DAY, LOVELIES, or sometimes, with a small stick, she'd write her favorite bit of poetry from Stephen Crane, which she'd had to memorize in middle school:

A man said to the universe:
"Sir, I exist!"
"However," replied the universe,
"The fact has not created in me
A sense of obligation."

It was true. It was humans' obligation to make their own existence meaningful. She believed that now. "I exist," she would sometimes write in the sand. "I exist. I exist. I exist."

* * *

ONE AFTERNOON WHEN the Lonelies got her, the Pierces had descended, and the Sea Creature was swimming sadly around her heart, she took her chances and packed a picnic and went to the beach at midday. Few people were out, and besides, who would question her? Aroha had said that Nan was traveling and unavailable, and surely the average person wasn't going to call Nan to ask about the artist-in-residence anyway. She'd stick with the story of her being a jeweler if anyone asked.

The weather was the best it had been—the wind quiet, the sky blue, the sun warm—and she wanted just a little more time before fleeing. It was simply too gorgeous to go. She read a book by Katherine Mansfield she'd found on the cluttered bookshelf in the front room and rested on a blanket and considered the clouds, which looked like hyacinths smeared across the sky.

The land that jutted out looked exactly like a reclining woman, with a face and breasts and hips and legs extending inland, and so Ammalie lay her own spine against the sand parallel to hers, so that they could be lined up, Earth Woman and Ammalie Woman, each taking in the purple hazy clouds, the salt-thick air. Her eyes followed the woman's hipbone, her breasts, her throat, all made of green forest.

These Alone Days, as she'd come to call them, built her up. She felt a very real sense that she had the ability to stand alone. Yes, she'd lost her husband, her job, her role as mother. And sure, she could spend the rest of her life looking for ways she did not belong, and she would always find them. But instead, she could look for ways to happily be alone—and simultaneously *belong*.

She sat up and turned around so as to gaze at the sea. Oddly, the waves looked like white clouds, but the real clouds looked like waves caught in the moment of curl. *The Good Life,* she thought, *is living in paradox. Key and keyhole.*

AFTER A WEEK, and many failed attempts that left abandoned scraps of silver wrapping on every surface, she had a rudimentary style of pendant worked out, one which involved wire-wrapping a large piece of sea glass with a swoop flourish. Her one epiphany was embracing a rustic look, which meant that her limited skill set matched the aesthetic. Her creations were not uniform or balanced—she wanted a messy and free look for messy and free middle-aged women. Playful. Random.

She felt, for brief moments, that she was an actual artist at an artist residency. That she was not a liar, she was just not the artist who had applied and been accepted. That person, according to the calendar Ammalie had found by the phone, would be there on February first, and her name was Brumby and she was from Brussels. Ammalie decided she had a week more, maybe even ten days of heaven. She'd leave in plenty of time. Besides Aroha, no one seemed to take notice of her, and Aroha didn't know her full name or any real details. Ammalie was invisible.

She was surprised by the lack of people in general in this community, but also by the state of relaxedness about everything, including the lack of a caretaker on the property. But she understood now that was how things operated here—a little bit hazy, much like the salt spray from the sea.

Besides Aroha, she saw only one other person regularly, a man always in an off-white shirt walking by himself. Richard, Aroha had said. He looked sixtyish and had a white trimmed beard. During the moments when lonely or lust descended—and they did most days, she feeling lustier than she had in some time—she masturbated, thinking of him or Kit or Dan or Levi rocking into her in all sorts of places and positions. Her fantasies were intense and involved lusty fucking, as opposed to softer lovemaking, probably because she was horny and it was the *act* of sex and not the *love* of sex she seemed to want, which was contrary to most of her repertoire of fantasies in her previous life. She wasn't sure why, or what was going on for her, but was glad for the release, glad her sex drive was not gone, glad to feel the sparks of desire, glad to feel a bit like an animal. Sometimes the orgasm made her feel a little wistful for a man and his actual arms around her, but still, she preferred feeling something to nothing.

It was friendship she yearned for; her chest ached for the want of it. She was cognizant of this shift—that as she came into herself, she was coming more into the world, that she was working herself out of isolation. She was nearly ready to reengage. She wanted quite badly to invite the locals over for dinner, share her true self, learn from others. Someday, somewhere, soon, soon.

SHE SPENT DAWN hours walking, mornings on jewelry, afternoons walking in the bush along an abandoned, hardly visible path, and evenings cooking and reading and talking to the cat, if it appeared. She weeded the garden out back, and, when it was raining, as it often was, she went back inside to sift through sea glass. She found the pure small lake that Aroha had spoken of and swam in it naked.

Some days she walked the six miles to the bridge with the eels in the stream beneath, past the sign that said SLIPPERY WHEN FROSTY, and she'd stare at the thick, somewhat horrifying tangle of eels floating in the shade. "Hullo, googlies," she'd say, "Oh, what a big ugly googly you are! Yes you are! You're a credit to yourselves!" and other such nonsense, and if there was one advantage to older age, it was that she didn't care what others thought of her, and if she wanted to fucking baby-talk to eels, she would. She made simple meals, usually a salad and thin bread and avocado and nuts, and a baguette from the pizza shop, where she got food occasionally, such as the little odd "takeaway" sandwiches in the display case. She'd lost weight and now looked like the person she remembered from her thirties, though with all the sunspots and sags of age. But she felt *good*. She did planks and stretched and read and dozed often and slept more hours than ever she had in her life.

Once more she went to the library to email her peeps that she was fine, and she wrote postcards to everyone, including one to the mayor in Colorado, addressing it simply "The Mayor" with the town and the zip code.

She became obsessed with the pohutukawa flowers, covered in bees. She learned that if she held her hand beneath a bunch and shook it with the other, fragrant honey landed on her palm in clear, sweet droplets. Astonishing. She also read up on New Zealand edibles—watercress in streams, beach asparagus, even puha, a type of sow thistle, which she washed, then rubbed the stalk to remove any bitterness. She always ate gingerly and only a little, but as her bravery grew, she mixed them in more often with the rice or beans she'd bought in Auckland.

Before falling asleep each night, she'd wander around the house and make sure everything was in order and confirmed that her Survival Kit was packed and ready by the door, although everything seemed to have fallen into a safe, sweet, predictable pattern. In bed, she'd take stock of her day and take note of what she'd done—noting how opposite her days here felt from her days in Chicago, where she'd been forever astonished by how little she'd done, how the hours had blurred together.

She dreamed of designing necklaces. It reminded her of the puzzle she'd done in Colorado, how her brain had continued the work of the day. She dreamed of colors, of gems and glass and the sea, and she often dreamed in the color green. This felt rather stunning: Her mind *had* changed. Once upon a time, it had circled around daydreams of relationships that did not exist, or around bitterness or anger or frustrations or fears. Now she was presenting it with a worthwhile challenge—how to make beauty, be in beauty, be in peace.

But life was life, which meant sometimes she took several steps backward. One night she woke to a noise, or perhaps it had been because of a ping of pain. A sudden throb stabbed at her lower left abdomen—probably a burst ovarian cyst. She gasped and rubbed at the area and then sat up. Her breathing was shallow and her heart felt weird, like it had forgotten its regular beat. When was this peri-menopause hell going to end?

Body, why? Why, body?

She put her head back on the wall. Suddenly the Sea Creature stormed anxiously through her and the silence of the room and her life buzzed more than usual. Eighteen minutes—that's how long these random anxiety attacks usually lasted. She'd have to wait it out. She got up to heat a hot water bottle, old and faded, that she'd found under the sink, wincing the whole time.

Even as she suffered through the cramp and the panic attack—which descended on her body simultaneously—a small part of her had to admit that this was the first night in so long that she'd felt this way. Finally, she fell asleep, dreaming of a car crash and a windshield that was shattered and she was trying to collect the little pieces of glass, knowing that she wanted them for jewelry. In the dream, someone was telling her, "Spend more time looking ahead, not back. Look through the front windshield; too much looking in the rearview mirror will cause you to crash. Go forward. I'm sorry a good bit of your life is over. But it is. There is no old self to find. There is only the future self to create. Create. Create your future self."

The next morning, before sunrise, without really knowing why, she skipped the walk on the beach and instead did yoga, and ended by simply standing, straightening her spine like a string of pearls, as instructed by the yoga book she'd found. Then she cleaned all the windows at the community center with newspaper and vinegar in a spray bottle she'd found under the kitchen sink. Because it was still dark, she couldn't see the streak marks, but surely the windows would be cleaner. Surely her efforts would help someone, someday, have a clear view.

CHAPTER 19

"Morning, *kia ora,* Apolena," she heard Aroha say one evening. Ammalie was sitting in the corner of the restaurant since it was raining outside, and reading *The Bone People,* one of her favorite New Zealand books thus far. She looked up, startled. Apolena. She saw a young woman, probably about twenty-five, standing at the counter ordering food. Ammalie could see her only from behind—lean and tanned legs, a long recent red cut down the back of one calf, a dark shimmery ponytail. The two women chatted and Ammalie pretended to go back to her book, but something was amiss with the Sea Creature, who was suddenly tumbling around her heart at top speed.

Then the door dinged and the young woman was gone, carrying a little paper bag filled with takeaway. She got up and approached Aroha. "Who was that young woman? I feel like I know her somehow . . ."

Aroha looked up from the till. "That's Apolena Sis. She comes in a lot; you've probably seen her. She's lived here her whole life. Loves to paddleboard. Or windsurf. She's the one you see out there most every day, just past the breakers."

"Oh! I have seen her! It's like watching an artist out there."

Aroha laughed. "Exactly. Pure grace. It's gold. To watch her."

"And her parents?"

Aroha shrugged. "Her *whanau.* The Sises. Live up in the bush. Farmers. Good people, although they do have Ponsonby tractors."

"Okay, I don't know what Ponsonby tractors are."

"Rich-people four-wheel drives. But she'll be right."

Ammalie blinked. It continued to surprise her, how the shared language of English did not always guarantee understanding. "It's an unusual name, Apolena."

"I suppose so. I like it."

"My dead husband's grandmother was an Apolena."

Aroha's eyebrows shot up and she said, "Crikey!"

"Yes," Ammalie blundered on. "I'm sorry I didn't tell you. My husband's dead. It still feels pretty fresh."

"I'm just so sorry! How horrible."

"A stroke." A part of Ammalie wanted to add, *I was going to ask for a divorce, and so it's complicated,* just to make sure she was telling an honest story, but it felt awkward and exhausting, so she went to the back room to do the dishes, being done with eating herself. She was still hoping to maintain an air of quiet awkwardness. But now, from the back, she raised her voice to ask, "Why don't I ever see you walking on the beach?"

"I actually live in Karekare, nearby, where the movie *The Piano* was filmed. You seen it?"

"Yes, actually. I hadn't realized! You drive here each day?"

"It's a beautiful movie. And yes, it's an odd drive—there's no road along the coast. You have to drive toward Auckland and then head back into the bush. That's why the café is only open Thursday through Sunday. It's a bit of a long haul for me."

"Oh, no wonder I never see you!"

"The movie," Aroha said. "It's about a unique form of love and passion and loneliness. About fantasy. Is that how you remember it too? And about flirting with the idea of love in unexpected places." Aroha leaned in and winked at her. "You know one thing I've noticed about growing older?"

Ammalie looked at her feet, who suddenly felt like they wanted to run. This sounded like a conversation she wasn't ready to have. "Um, what?"

"That older women are the most beautiful creatures on earth. When I see a twenty-year-old woman, I'm happy for her. Like Apolena. She's got that cute youthful beauty. When I notice an older woman who is strong and living well, I find her *beautiful*. We have become stronger individuals, more collaborative spirits. And more disciplined, and yet, simultaneously, more free."

Ammalie found herself smiling in a rueful way. "Hmm, well, I think that's gorgeous, but that perspective might be unique to you. My guess is that very few men see women that way."

Aroha grunted and rolled her eyes. "I wouldn't know. Not attracted to them. Don't know much about them. Seem rather incompetent and endlessly violent. But I do think *women* appreciate women. Whether they are lesbian or not, which, luckily, I happen to be." Then she added, "In the movie, I just kept wanting the main character to fall in love with a woman. She'd have been much happier."

This last bit was said with so much emphasis that Ammalie couldn't help but laugh, sincerely this time. "Believe me, I've often mourned the fact I wasn't attracted to women. They are, well, superior creatures. I have often grieved the fact that I'm not gay. But I'm not. Sadly."

At that, Aroha scowled, but in a friendly way. "Well, it's a crescive moon tonight, and that too will be beautiful, and remind us that things change."

"I'm just learning this about you. That you're a poet. And also, yes, at night I study the sky. It's a whole different starlight show down here."

Aroha smiled, a bit shyly this time, and with a blush. "That is my great endeavor in life."

"To be a poet?"

"To speak poetically about my life and my people and this place."
Aroha handed her the last of the plates to be washed. "Crescive, by
the way, is a new word for me. As in the crescent, waxing moon.
One that is growing, increasing, or developing. Like love. Or fond-
ness. How it can be crescive. Do you think I can use it that way?
Where was he from, your husband?"

"*Empyreal,* that's my favorite new word. The highest heaven.
Vincent and I met in Chicago, in college." She stared at the water
running over the soapy plates and told herself, as she had so often,
Don't share too much, don't share yourself, be invisible. "But oddly,
we'd both grown up in Nebraska. Middle of America. As white-
bread America as you can get."

"*White-bread.* That is very American." Aroha stood near her
shoulder, as if also mesmerized by the water. "Well, I'm sorry he's
gone. The Māori believe that souls fly up right near here, to the
north of us, to Cape Reinga, the top of the North Island. Empyreal."

Ammalie opened her mouth to say something, but another customer came in and Aroha left with a "*Ka kite,* see you in a jiffy," and
Ammalie breathed out, relieved. She finished the dishes quickly,
thinking of the name in the guest book—Apolena. *Just an odd co-
incidence,* she thought. Maybe there were more Apolenas than she
thought. Internationally, anyway. Vincent's grandmother had been
Czech, though the rest of the family had roots in Italy and Spain.
Family genealogy had been one of his many pursuits, a hobby that
obsessed him until some other interest took hold. The reason Apolena had stuck in his mind—and therefore hers—was that she had
been the one to come to America, speaking only Czech, and settling
into a Czech-filled town in Nebraska. She felt a swell of gratitude
for all those who had walked the earth before her, for the Czech-

speaking Apolena, who had come to America, learned English, made a life on a farm in Nebraska. Yet another regular, amazing female explorer.

THE KAURI TREES were particularly stunning and therefore their demise was was particularly heartbreaking. This was the *only* area on the planet with some left—and what kind of explorer would she be if she didn't see these giants? Plus, she'd never hitchhiked in her life, and New Zealand was famously safe for it.

She'd been on the side of the road with her thumb out for just a few minutes when a white travel van slowed and pulled over. Her delight was replaced by annoyance the moment she recognized the driver—the guy from the beach. He was the only other person in this small town who had seen her out walking, and she didn't want to deceive anyone else other than Aroha, which was bad enough. Had it been a tourist or someone from the other side of the cove, where most of the houses were, she'd simply say she was traveling around in the area. But he knew she was *around*-around.

And yet, there he was, waiting patiently in his idling van for her to approach. She zipped up her raincoat—it looked like it would be another blustery day—and pretended to fidget with something in her bag in the hopes he'd change his mind and drive off. What had Aroha said his name was? Richard. In his trademark cream-colored shirt. Her first thought was, *How many off-white tops can a person own?* and her second was, *Me and my stupid ideas.*

She couldn't just turn around and run, and her lies had worked in every location thus far, so she braced herself as she walked over and leaned in the open window with a bright smile. "I'm heading to the kauri tree preserve."

"Going right by it," he said. He had a weathered face and charming eye crinkles that deepened with his smile. He waved her in. "Glad you're going. It's really a must-see. Pure magic. To miss it would be to miss one of the most important things about New Zealand. Come on now. I'll drop you off."

As soon as she was seated and the van was moving, the question she feared came. "I've seen you walking the beach," he said. "You're staying at the residency?"

"Yep, yep. A jeweler." She trailed off and looked out the window at the jungle zipping by and touched her necklace, then turned around to face him with renewed bravery. "Sea glass."

"You don't like to be out when others are. You walk in strange places and at strange times."

"I keep strange hours, I admit."

"I had a friend who couldn't walk in the daylight because of a cancer treatment. I thought the same might be true for you."

"No, no, it's just my habits. I am a shy person who prefers solitude." Then she added more solemnly, "I'm very sorry about your friend, though."

"Ah, he's fine now."

Not only was this lying situation terrifying, but so was his driving, and she could not hide her wince as he took a corner fast. "Wow, these roads," she ventured. "They can really make a person carsick, plus them being so narrow and you drivers on the wrong side and all." This had the intended effect of his decreasing his speed, though having any more time with him than necessary didn't seem wise. On the other hand, she wasn't yet ready for the grave.

He chuckled. "It's you *Americans* who drive on the wrong side of the road."

She laughed too, and then because she feared he'd ask another question, she blurted, "And you? What do you do?"

"Citizenship." He looked over at her, and she wished he'd put his brown eyes back on the road. "Surveyor. Explorer. Geologist. Spent the first half of my career working for mining companies, spent the second half fighting them." He took in a loud breath. "I'll be honest. I've been keeping an eye on you. I saw you out walking and thought you might be a scout or a surveyor. But you don't look the type. And Aroha said you're a jeweler, arrived early."

"Oh!" She felt her heart do a skip. "I don't understand. What kind of scout would I be?"

"Real estate developer. A year or so ago, the community fought off a proposed development, in the jungle above the houses on the other side of the cove, which is where I live. But they'd love Nan's property too. It's even better, being so remote and all. Indeed, it's prime location. One big stretch of private lands, right in the best location possible. They're eager to talk a woman, or her heirs"—he made a tsking sound—"into selling their heritage."

"Oh, that's sad," she said.

"It's more than sad. It's evil. They're sharks."

She relaxed. The road was less curvy now that they'd crested the first mountain. "I feel sorry for actual sharks, being always used to represent the bad guys," she said, and to again prevent any questions about herself or her work, she rambled on. "I've been thinking about how there's two kinds of adventurers. The let's-discover-and-change-this-place kind. The colonialists, for example. They find places with the intention of 'improving' them, or extracting from them, or taking them over. Then there's the second kind. The let's-go-see-what's-out-there, just-to-appreciate-it kind."

He smiled broadly. "You're the second type of explorer."

"I hope so."

"That's why you don't look like a surveyor."

"And how do surveyors look, anyway? Well-dressed and rich?"

"No, like they want something from the place."

"Well, I *do* want something," she ventured. "But not to change it. To have a place change *me*."

"I'm glad to hear it," he said with an inflection that indicated he really meant it, and again, he looked over at her to catch her eye and she internally winced again. "It's true, what you say. There are two types of people in this world. The kind who want to *create and add* something, and the kind who want to take."

Then his blinker was on and he was pulling into a park of sorts with astonishingly enormous trees towering into the sky like wild skyscrapers. She could not help but gasp. He said, "Right? Thrilling, those buggers. And those are only about seven hundred years old! Which makes them teenagers! These are not only some of the largest trees on earth, they're also the longest-living."

"Astonishing, really. And thank you sincerely for the ride," she stammered, stepping out. "I enjoyed it. I'll enjoy this too."

Before she turned, he leaned toward her and spoke through the open window. "My pleasure. But first, I never asked your name, and second, I want to confess something. I often fly my drone to find and map the big kauri trees. They're not *all* in this reserve—there's some hidden up high on Nan's land. I'm mapping the forest to document ecological values for any legal fight we have ahead of us. I saw you walking up some little-used trails."

Her heart fluttered. "You saw me with a drone?"

He shrugged. "I followed you—"

"With your drone?"

"Sure. To see if you had any surveying equipment or some such thing."

"I didn't see any drone!"

He shrugged. "These are not kid drones. They're high up. You probably heard it."

"Ah!" she yelped, turning back to the car to fully face him. "Do they sound like a big hummingbird?"

He tilted his head, considering. "I suppose so."

"You were following me!" Her voice was higher and harsher than she intended.

Now he furrowed his brow. "Not in a creepy way, I'll have you know! But if you were out with surveying equipment or flags or maps or anything, then, hell yeah, I'd want to know. I thought you were here to . . . ruin the place."

She was a bit sick to her stomach. Apparently, she wasn't as invisible as she thought. "I keep hearing a bird that sounds like a bee. Or a huge hummingbird. There I was, being all dreamy-nature-girl, imagining some strange bird. A *drone*." Then she started to laugh. "It's pretty funny, actually."

He smiled, clearly relieved. "I also spent some time looking for my cat. Goes missing from time to time."

"Mink brown? Cutest cat alive?"

His eyes lit up, the crinkles deepened. "Sable. That's her name and her color."

She tried to silence her body's reaction, but she was mesmerized. Such kind eyes. Such an open face. A well-trimmed beard with a smile. Such a quiet sincerity about him.

"I confess the cat has often been with me," she stammered. "Helping me with the jewelry. And by the way, I'm glad she has a bell."

"Ay, well, yes, all outdoor cats should have bells. Especially in a bird heaven such as this. So a shy jeweler, huh? That's what Aroha said." When she only shrugged, he added, "I kept the drone at a distance. Just to be clear, there was nothing untoward. No *spying*. I just did enough surveillance to make sure you were who you said you were. Then I went away and left you alone. These developers are nasty. Nothing is beneath them. They want that property, and I figured you could have been . . . well, *pretending* to be an artist. That would be crazy, I know. But not impossible, right? But I've seen your tools out on the picnic table, seen your work. I wanted to come clean with you. Seemed like the right thing to do."

His look was now so open and sincere that she felt her cheeks flush and, terribly, tears come to her eyes. She was so lonely. But no, it wasn't that—it was that he was so attractive in the way that someone can be so *attractive*. As a human being. And also, wasn't it better to dive right into danger, rather than to try to avoid it? Safer in the end. It had worked so far. So she put her hand out to touch the top of the window. "I don't know where you're heading today, but I don't suppose you want to join me, do you?"

THE KAURI LOOKED exactly like huge broccoli florets skyrocketing above all the other tumble of bizarre greenery. The tree in front of them looked monstrously healthy to her, though she knew that wasn't the case—the KAURI DIEBACK signs and gates had warned her otherwise.

"I can't believe they're dying of a *fungus*." They were stopped at a yellow gate, required to scrub and spray their shoes before entering the natural area.

"A fungus spread by a mere pinhead-size amount of dirt," he said, brushing his hiking shoes with the bristle brush that had been provided. "This scrub station always feels like . . . I don't know . . . like a gong, a mindfulness reminder. Right? Some small bit of action to prevent future catastrophe. A reminder that small things can kill."

"And inattention. That can kill too," she mused.

They walked onto a wooden plankway designed to keep humans' feet off the ground and followed this path as it meandered through the forest. A few tourists wandered by—there were more people than she'd seen since arriving and she'd forgotten what even a small crowd felt like. She and Richard ducked away from most of the visitors and stopped to consider the bark of a large kauri tree, blue-gray and smooth. She didn't know quite how to articulate it, but seeing the bark hurt her heart. *Haunted* her heart. To know she was witnessing something that at some point would literally not be on Planet Earth anymore.

She spread her arms so as to feel small—the trunk of this tree was wider than she was tall. By a lot. They stopped to read more from the signage: The kauri were a species of conifer that was widespread during the Jurassic period but was now found only here.

"Colorado has signage like this, but it's about a beetle," she said. "They call the dead forests *beetle kill*. Both words imply action, an ongoing situation, you know? Verb-like! Beetle kill, dieback . . . It makes me sad." As she said that, he simply and strangely touched her shoulder and pulled her toward him, so that they were side by side, staring at the tree.

She breathed out and did not move, either into him or away from him. She tried not to tense up. Oh, god, what was she doing? What was happening here? Was this a New Zealand thing?

Luckily, a young ranger in a khaki uniform and with red curls tucked into a ball cap approached. "You okay, loves?"

Ammalie blushed and wiped away a tear that had suddenly streaked down her face. "Oh, yes. We're just feeling sad. About the trees."

The woman nodded, unembarrassed and unflustered by the show of grief. "Yeah, no joke. Now they die. And they were so strong. Their life span being one or two thousand years. That's huge. You realize how huge that is?"

"It's like looking at the stars. Or sea," Richard said, pulling Ammalie slightly closer.

"Yes," she agreed, trying to relax into his shoulder. "We're so small."

The ranger looked up at the tree with them. "The Māori built *waka taua*—war canoes—and a single trunk could hold a hundred eighty warriors. The wood is very water-resistant. So. They were used to build ships—first for the Māori, then for the English, who cut down most of them."

Richard cleared his throat. "A fungus! It takes very little things to change the world."

The ranger nodded. "It's easy to catch predators like the stoats, possums, rats, and feral cats, which kill birds around here, even to extinction," the ranger said. "But a fungus, that's tough."

Ammalie wanted nothing more than to run away from everything, but squeezed her eyes shut and begged herself for bravery, if only to bear witness to the grief. "Does washing the shoes really help?"

"Maybe," the ranger said. "Sure, it might be greenwashing—some people argue so, even my boss—because the wild pigs spread the fungus too, and by closing certain areas to all humans, including hunters, the situation might just get worse, because there would be more pigs, you see?"

"I wish it were easier to know what to do," Ammalie said. "With so much in life."

"Aye, living on earth these days is hard and complicated, but it's easy to know we could do better." The ranger's red curls bounced as she nodded her head, and then she bid them farewell.

They continued to stand, Richard's arm around her. She tried to breathe calmly. Then, she leaned more fully into him. Richard squeezed her shoulder in acknowledgment. Such a small moment, such a grand thing communicated.

She wasn't ready to turn her face toward him and look into his eyes, and so she kept her face forward, pointed at the bark of the tree. "I guess I wonder about my own greenwashing. In my life. Like, my own struggle to square my gratitude for nature . . . with . . . with, I dunno, my basic knowledge that I'm underestimating the required action. Does that make sense?"

"Yes," he said simply.

"I've been changing a lot lately, but it's not enough. Humans are not changing fast enough."

"No."

"It gives me a queasy feeling. I felt like this once when standing on a bridge in New Mexico, a bridge over a very deep gorge, so very deep, and it makes you feel queasy about everything. It's like that, but bigger. I'm queasy about my treatment of the planet. I flew to New Zealand, after all! Does that make sense?"

"Sure," he said. "I suppose that is the conundrum of eco-grief. How do we mourn something that hasn't happened, but instead is *happening*. The severity of what happens next is dependent on how we act now. And yet we do almost nothing. Because it's hard to know what to do. It's hard to change."

"Exactly," Ammalie said, and now she reached out her hand so that it was touching his stomach in a sort of half hug.

Richard, she realized, was tense too. They needed to stand side by side like this for a moment, to get their bearings.

He breathed in and put his hand on hers, both hands resting over his stomach now. "A scientist friend recently told me, 'We might be living in the coolest year of the rest of our lives. Try to remember what it feels like.' Can you believe that? It was so hot last summer. So many fires. And then floods. But what if this is the coolest one forever?"

"The coolest year . . . for the rest of my life? God. I hope not." And it did shock Ammalie—the very idea ripped at her heart.

"I no longer wish to be a dutiful descendant—but rather a good *ancestor,* you know?" He pressed lightly on her hand. "What kind of ancestor do you want to be? That should be a guiding question for us all."

"Not a lazy one, that's for sure."

"One who tried his damnedest to do right," he said.

She turned to face him then, so that they were pressed against each other. His hands slid to her waist and he pulled her to him at the same time that she reached up and touched the back of his neck and brought his head down, so as to be clear that *she* was the one kissing *him.*

CHAPTER 20

What was more fun than lusty sex in the back of a van? It conjured the frantic fumbling of teenagers needing secret spaces. Not to mention the romance of a misting slender waterfall outside, cascading down from a mountaintop in this secret place he'd known about. A green jungle dripping with rain. A sunset sending shafts of light through distant clouds.

Her three orgasms were fed by the sensation she was getting away with something, getting away from the boringness of sex-in-beds, of middle-life routine, of old patterns. Fed by the energy of them both getting something too long withheld. Both obviously *hungry*—there was no other word for it. And for her, of having the first new body naked next to her in decades. And his lovemaking! Different. Attentive. But not in a ridiculous formal and serious and silent way, but rather punctuated by humor and laughing and complaints about a cramp in his leg and the other atrocities of getting older. She hadn't felt so much pleasure in bed for . . . Well, she couldn't remember; she didn't have time to remember.

For the first go-round, her brain was still yakking away, wondering if this was wise or not, worrying, worrying, trying to deal with the zillions of things that surely zip across most people's brains at such moments, if the truth were told, but finally, finally, finally, it went silent. Her body reigned. Her mind went as quiet as the sky, interrupted by only small twinkles of thoughts.

They rested, snuggled, napped, commented on the stars, kissed and talked more, made love again. Richard was dozing and she was staring out the window at the moon, her hands between her legs to better feel the swollen pleasure, when her brain registered one clear thought: *Finally.*

Her life had been rife with incomplete and unfulfilled touch. Levi in her dreams. Kit and Dan's kisses. Even the somewhat disconnected and distracted sex of the later years of her marriage. What she had needed was rolling around and laughing and gasping and gentle bites and serious glorious fucking. *Finally, finally, finally.*

Her body was chilled with cooling sweat and she was coming back into the challenges of reality. She'd have to think this through—but later. Not while resting, not on the drive home, not when he pulled up at the base of the driveway.

"I'll walk you up," he said.

She shook her head no. "I'd like to go the rest of the way, if you don't mind." He opened his mouth as if to say something, but she interrupted. "How about we'll clarify all this later? This is perfect as is, let's let it be."

He nodded, handed her a scrap of napkin with his number. As she was walking away, she looked in the window at him. "That was deeply human, deeply amazing, you know."

He nodded his assent, and his smile was that of someone human and kind and relieved to have been seen, and to have seen someone else. She felt the same way. She turned to hike up the mountain toward her little shack of a home, moonlight and headlamp guiding her way.

FIRST LIGHT WOKE her. She pulled on clothes, grabbed her day pack, and was out the door into the dull light of a new day. Something

Richard had said triggered a suspicion. Last week, when she'd gone to swim in the pure lake that Aroha had told her about, she'd hiked until the thin path disappeared into the jungle. Conveniently, this is when her lungs wore out too. As in Colorado and Arizona, she'd wanted to do one hike that pushed her to her max, and as she stood there catching her breath, she'd noticed some light pink plastic ties circling the base of trees. She had assumed it was the work of some previous artist, the remnants of some installation of some sort, but in the middle of the night, she'd startled awake: The pink ribbons had not been battered or old or faded.

Why pink ties? Why new?

The hike was easier this time, perhaps because she was clear on her purpose. She stood, panting, above the lake and very far above the sea, in a swath of pink plastic ribbons floating on the breeze. Not an art project. She had only assumed that because that was what was in her purview. Now another idea had been introduced; her worldview had been widened.

Oh. Oh, oh, oh.

She had her phone out and was taking a lot of photos, including one that showed the pure lake downslope in the distance, so that the location could be gauged. Then, for the first time since being in New Zealand, she took her phone off airplane mode. She breathed in deeply and texted the photos to the number Richard had given her with a hopeful look. But this was not the type of communication he'd hoped for. Now everything would change. She knew this. Now she needed to leave. She'd crossed some invisible line into becoming visible. But she also knew now that she'd proven herself to *herself* that day of leaving water. She'd proven herself to *community* during the snowstorm. Now she was proving her selflessness. "Once you find yourself, it's your obligation to lose yourself," she said to no one, watching the pink ribbons flap.

* * *

WHEN RAIN STARTED lashing down from the sky upon her return, she hardly noticed. Did not really register, even, the faraway siren going off, signaling some accident. She packed her bags and tidied the place—she'd leave first thing in the morning, or perhaps even today, if the rain let up. It was only because of a change in the light—a streak of lightning?—that she stopped, startled. The image of the doe in the forest flashed into her mind—a creature on alert, ears raised, nostrils flared, body ready to run. She moved to look out the window, curious now to see what was sounding like an explosive storm.

She felt her eyebrows quirk. *Oh, oh, oh.*

In the flash of lightning, she could see two dark figures, heads bent against the onslaught as they trudged up the path, which was now more like a stream. One smaller and one larger. Then it went dark again. Then they were lit again. Dark, light, dark. The larger one slipped and the smaller helped him up and they paused for a moment, turning to look back down the hill, presumably where they'd parked. The rain was coming down in fierce sheets now. As they stood, uncertain, Ammalie did the same at the window, willing them to turn back. Surely, they were wondering if they could simply come back another time. Why walk in such a storm?

As they turned and resumed their hike toward her, she ducked away from the window. Exhaled in the quietest breath of her life. Here it was. Her eyes went to her backpack and duffel and shopping bag, sitting in a tidy bundle by the front door. Complete, ready to go.

The moment is now, Ammalie.

She turned to face the sliding glass door, all that green lush behind, the beach and ocean and path to freedom. Her escape route clear, rehearsed. But she'd made one mistake—she'd assumed access to the front door. They'd be there too soon. She bit her lip and considered her options.

The sliding glass door? The jump from the deck to the ground seemed so far. It was possible, even, that bones could be broken.

The living room window? Probably just on the verge of too small.

The bathroom? No, what good would locking herself inside do?

Hide in a closet? It had worked in Colorado! After all, people couldn't just break into people's homes, though, true, there was no working lock, there had never been a working lock. It was rusted away.

Fight, flight, freeze, or fawn?

Or face it?

Her eyes went again to the sliding glass door and the deck outside, hanging over the forest. Yes, that was best. A loud rapping sounded from the front door. She stood equidistant between the two doors and wondered in which direction her body would instinctually move. She even looked down at her hips, waiting for them to start some initial movement. Which is when the thought struck her: I am a person of interest. I am. a. person. of. *interest*.

An exhale of giddy delight escaped her lips. She had come so far. So very far. At the same time, the gravity of the situation registered. After this moment, everything would be different, no matter what she did next. So she closed her eyes to focus on her breath and to make a decision. She heard the crashing waves of the Tasman Sea, she heard the wind shift, the rain smack windows.

She picked up her bags. Put the backpack on her shoulders, a duffel in one hand, a shopping bag in the other. Then she put them back down. Right where they'd been, by the door.

She felt her resolve in her spine, and stood straight and strong. She felt the resolve in her gaze, steady and ready. She could still feel the play of a smile at the corner of her mouth. She knew now what she'd do. "Just a moment, please," she yelled in the direction of the front door. "I need a drink of water."

When she opened the door with one hand, holding the glass of water with the other, they looked nearly as surprised as she was. As she had suspected, it was not Richard and some friend, though she'd held out hope. It was the police, a man and a woman. The man looked past her, as if to ascertain that she was alone, sitting in the dark, and then, after some rustling and flipping of raincoats, they each produced a badge. "We're trying to clear something up. Can you tell us your name, please?"

The question seemed to ricochet back and forth between them for several seconds, and meanwhile, the officers stepped, uninvited, into the home to get out of the rain. They stood just inside the door, drenched and dripping, the wind and rain whipping in until the woman turned around and, with some effort, shut the door, then leaned against it with a sigh of relief that reminded Ammalie of her own struggle to shut the door in the snowstorm of Arizona.

"Oh, hullo, cheers," Ammalie said, and then in a quiet, trailing-off voice added, "I'm an artist. And I assume you are the police!" She took a long drink of water. Swallowed. Stood even straighter. "Ammalie Brinks."

"And where are you from?"

"Chicago."

"And you're here on a visitor visa?"

"Yes."

"May we see that visa and your passport?"

"Of course." She went to her bags. So packed. So ready. Something she'd done every night, whether or not she'd wanted to, because that was called discipline. To be ready to *go*. She started unzipping and zipping things, pretended to look, though she knew exactly where her papers were. Zip, unzip, zip. She needed time to think, and they needed time to pant and recover themselves. Her eyes went to the back deck—the rickety *dick,* she could still hear Aroha calling it—but no. She probably could manage to rush past the police—they wouldn't be expecting it—and run into the bush, but evading the police was a whole different matter altogether. Plus, they knew the bush and tracks much better than she ever could—this was their *home.* Their real home.

Finally, because she was out of time, she stood. Though the man had his dripping arm outstretched and was reaching for the papers, she handed them to the woman. Her fingers wouldn't let go of them—of their own accord, they clutched, until the woman gave a sharp tug.

"Shackleton," she said.

"Excuse me?" The woman huffed at her.

"You win," Ammalie said, but not to the woman. To the universe. To her life. To herself. Then she added, "I did it," and she meant it.

Yes, she had taken over someone else's identity. But it was to form one of her own!

Yes, she had believed the best thing to do was to run from her life, but it was to find a place to stop.

She wanted to explain it all, but that was too complicated, so she stood quietly in the very long silence as the police examined her passport and the man went into the bedroom and was presumably looking around as he called something in. The woman stood in front of her, blocking the front door, arms crossed.

Now it strangely seemed as if Ammalie had all of time to think. Her last few months had been filled with lies, but it was so she could discover some *truths.* She had found freedom, and now she was about to go to *jail.* Out of nervousness or release or giddy joy, she didn't know, she started to laugh. She turned to get her things, which now both officers were indicating she should do with nods of their heads. The laughter bloomed out of her mouth, like butterflies. She was not invisible after all.

She'd done it. Lived a life full of adventure. Explored the most interior regions of her heart, like any good explorer. She'd found passion and saved trees and creatures and herself. She could now die in peace. Not that she wanted to die anytime soon. But she was content—if that time came. And that was an excellent way to live.

The two officers looked worried now, and shared a glance which she knew meant *We might be dealing with a crazy here.* She thought they might handcuff her, but they only asked that she walk between them to their vehicle, parked down by the community center. They seemed disappointed in her, and cautious, and a bit sad, and resigned to the fact that Americans were strange. So as she walked in the cold rain, still hiccupping from her laughter, she felt the play of a smile at the corner of her lips as she turned to look at the gray shack one last time.

Refugia.

THE STATION WAS a rectangular cinder-block building with just one main room, though she assumed there were some smaller rooms and holding areas farther back, because she heard a door clang and saw one man come out alongside an officer who walked him down a hallway. The man was joking with the officer—clearly they knew each other—and clearly, the officer was annoyed in such a way that Ammalie could tell these two had a long history. This was nothing like what she imagined America's hustling-bustling police stations to be.

She was politely asked to sit in a chair, given a towel to dry off, and then a cup of hot tea. She put one hand on her necklace, running her fingertips over the greenstone. She watched an officer doing paperwork at a desk, the two that had arrested her conferring over in a corner, the rain sheeting down outside a window, and then her gaze repeated the same circle. She was left alone for a long time, apparently as the officers attended to some other business— the rain was causing some flooding and she overheard that a car had gone into the stream with the eels. Or perhaps they were doing a search on her. She stared at a photo of a family on a desk and tried to think of who had turned her in. Aroha? Richard? Was it the photos? Or had she simply been seen?

She put her hands on her head. Glory, glory. Her brain. Her breath. Her heart. If only they could slow down.

Eventually, the same two officers sat in front her, put a folder on a nearby desk, and sighed. They'd changed clothes but still had the look of people who had recently been swimming. "You're not the jeweler that Nan was expecting," the woman said. "That jeweler comes later and is not American. So. The question is, why are you here, living in Nan's house? Nan who says she does not know you, by the way?"

Ammalie opened her mouth, closed it, and opened it, and then decided to . . . just tell the truth. She took a big breath in. She told of Vincent's death, her son moving out, her loss of her job—the three main keys of her life gone!—and then of her need to move, to prove she could find new keys to a new life. Ticking them off on her fingers, she explained that she wanted to visit three places, one a place that she and her husband had been to together, and two—Arizona and here—that he had been to but she had not. She told them that he'd been here as a wwoofer in his early twenties, and she knew it had been *the* greatest trip of his life, and they'd meant to come back here together.

She left out the part about breaking in and the keys, but the rest of the story was true.

They blinked at her, and then the woman said, "So, you just thought you'd let yourself into Nan's place? And settle in like it was home?"

"The sound of a key turning in a lock is one of the most beautiful sounds," she said randomly. "And it's the opposite when a key doesn't turn. You feel so lost! My life was like a key that wouldn't turn. Silent. No potential."

The woman's gaze softened, and Ammalie could have sworn she heard her murmur, "Maybe she's mentally unstable."

"I'm not," she piped up. "I'm okay in the head. I knew what I was doing. But seriously, my life was all locked up."

The woman tilted her head and mumbled, "I suppose I know something about that."

Ammalie shrugged. "I'm so sorry. But it's true. I did sneak into Nan's place. Knowingly. And no key was needed at all." She took a big breath in and winced at her thumping heart. "Vincent had described it to me. He'd done work here and on a nearby farm, gardening and taking care of the artist at the residency, who had been a painter from South Africa. It's just that . . ." and here she paused. "It's just that he talked about it so much, and sent so many postcards, and showed me so many photos upon his return, that I felt like I knew the place. I guess I just showed up . . . I just showed up and . . . the door was not locked and . . ."

"And you decided to pretend to be an artist."

"Well, not exactly. But Aroha down at the café thought I was, so, well, I just went with it."

"Aroha thought you were an artist?"

"Yes. A jeweler."

"But you're not a jeweler at all?"

"No. I'm a waitress. Mother. Wife. Or, I was. By the way, who . . . How'd you know?"

The officer pursed her lips. "We're not at liberty to say. But those necklaces we brought in? Those are yours?"

Ammalie bowed her head again. "Yes. I was just learning. I just wanted to try."

"Well, we are arresting you for breaking and entering," the man said.

"They're quite beautiful," the woman officer said casually, as if she'd already made peace with the whole situation, or as if she dealt with fake artists all the time. "Sea glass."

Ammalie smiled at her. "Thank you! That really means a lot. Please feel free to take one. Or all of them. Or, but, wait. Can you give one to Aroha? And Richard? And one to Nan, if she'd take a gift from a thief? It's her sea glass, by the way. I found the pieces in old jars with her name on them. I stole them. Tell her I'm sorry. Also, she can unwrap all the silver and have her sea glass back, just the way it was when I found it."

And then suddenly she was struck with regret. Deceiving three good people. And with the sharp, piercing guilt of that came a cramp. She winced and grabbed at her side. "I need to go to the bathroom. My period started this morning. Although we'd all rather believe otherwise, bodily life continues to go on despite other stuff! Ha! Hollywood and books always make it seem as if we are not living in actual *bodies*. Do you have any supplies here?"

When she got back, the man had left, ostensibly to fill out some paperwork, and the woman, who now introduced herself as Lara, leaned back and put her hands behind her head and dug her fingers into her ponytailed blond-gray hair and sighed. "Would you like some painkillers?"

"Yes. Thank you."

"It's a dumb setup, these bodies."

"Yes! Exactly." Ammalie took the offered pill. "I'd like to have been done with this years ago. But it just keeps going and going. No one told me quite how bad it would be."

"It's crazy-making," Lara agreed.

"Absolutely," Ammalie said with an inflection that meant: *See, maybe* that's *why I did it*.

Lara nodded. "Are you the one who left the beach artwork? Did you not think someone would notice you living in a house? That we don't know our neighbors?"

Ammalie winced and grabbed her side. "No, I kinda thought they wouldn't. It's so hidden, after all! I swear, I'm not a bad person. Not really. I mean, this was wrong. I admit it. But overall, I'm not a bad person."

Lara bit her lip. "It went pear-shaped."

"Sorry?"

"Your plan went pear-shaped."

Ammalie touched her necklace. "Okay. I'm sorry, but I don't know what that means."

"Pear-shaped. It means, things didn't go as anticipated. Turned out a little wrong."

"Like, not a round apple," Ammalie said, understanding.

"Right."

"Pear-shaped. That's my life."

Lara quirked her eyebrows together. "That's most of our lives. Nothing special about *you*. So, Nan will be here tomorrow. She's just flown into Auckland for the summer. She was in England, visiting family. She doesn't drive anymore—she's getting older—so she's waiting for a friend to drive her here. As the owner of the property, and a quirky one, and a generous one, and a curious one, she wants to see who this person is who just decided it would be okay to move into her home."

"And take her sea glass."

"Yes, that too. I'll tell her that." Lara seemed unfazed by it all, and Ammalie had the notion that this woman could carry on through most anything.

"It's so beautiful, what the ocean spits up at us. Shells. Driftwood. Sea glass."

Lara smiled. "My mother told me they used to pick it up by the bucketful. In fact, one of my most treasured items is a red perfect smooth circle. My father said it was from an old Ford. Never broken."

Ammalie heard herself making an oooh sound. "Amazing. I'd love to see it." At the same time, though, the pain in her left side was increasing, and she felt herself buckle over. Her eyes sought out the nearest trash can, in case she had to vomit. Years of bursting ovarian cysts had made her an expert in seeking out available receptacles for pain-induced sudden vomiting.

Lara tilted her head. "Hopefully the painkiller kicks in soon, eh? And no wonder Aroha likes you. You're one of the more interesting criminals we've brought in lately, I'll tell you that. Perhaps the most interesting . . . *ever?* You are a person of interest in a couple of counties in Colorado, it seems. I've left a message with a sheriff there, letting him know you're here."

Ammalie put her fingertips to the necklace again. "Oh . . . that's minor. A minor thing . . . a dog I had to rescue . . . or maybe trespassing . . . or maybe it was a car I donated," she mumbled. Then she really looked down at her necklace, since Lara was looking at it. "My dead husband gave this to me. From his trip here. I think jewelry making has been some deep-seated unconscious effort to bring him back, to talk, to say goodbye. Or to bring the old me back. This was our engagement ring."

Lara paused. "Someone else is coming too. Nina Sis. Do you know who she is?"

"No."

"That name doesn't ring a bell?"

"No." Then Ammalie added, "Well, I heard there was an Apolena Sis. Looks to be the same age as my son, Powell. Is Nina her mother?"

Lara nodded. "Yup. Nina is her mother." She tilted her head and softly added, "Nina wears the same necklace as you. Is that why you really came? She knew your husband? Perhaps—"

Ammalie blinked. "No, I'm sorry. That also would be too Hollywood. That would be a predictable story. But it's not the story here." She said it with conviction. Vincent could be a lot of things—checked out, for one—but he wouldn't have lied about a lifelong secret of such import. He did not have a child in New Zealand.

CHAPTER 21

The Sea Creature lodged in her throat as the idea spread. Vincent did have a lover here; she'd always known that. So, what this policewoman was saying was: Nina had been his lover, and Apolena his . . . *child*? Powell had a half sister?

No. Impossible.

She doubled over with a cramp and gasped. Her uterus felt like it had acid in it, as if it were tearing away from the walls of her body, and the Sea Creature dove down into her pelvic region and exploded. She heard a loud yelp come out of her mouth, and then she felt the vomit rise, and then Lara was saying, "What's going on here? How bad is it? Do you need medical attention? Do you need a doctor?"

Ammalie now had the trash can in her lap, but the pain subsided. "No, no, not necessary." Ammalie heard her voice coming in fits and starts with the cramps. "It's just perimenopause. It's just being . . . a woman. No one talks about this."

Lara tilted her head and got up and brought her a glass of water, which made Ammalie wince once again. Something was breaking inside her, tearing inside her, and suddenly she was scared. More scared than she'd been walking in the desert, more scared than in the freezing snowstorm, more scared than during the housecleaner incident back in the cabin, which seemed years ago.

"I'm taking you to the clinic," Lara said. "No, I'm not. I'm calling an ambulance to take you to Auckland. They have imaging."

"I don't have the money . . ."

"What are you talking about?" Lara was grabbing her shoulder, as if to steady her body and spirit. "Oh, god. I forgot. You poor Americans! For the love of any god. No wonder you do weird, weird, *weird* things."

A vague disassociation descended on her, and she felt her body slump and Lara's voice float away again and the room warp and wave as if she were looking through a thick piece of sea glass. Then she was being helped down to the floor by Lara and was curling into a fetal position. She closed her eyes to try to stop the dizzy wave hitting her, and what she saw in her mind's eye was the Sea Creature. The actual Sea Creature, made manifest. The Sea Creature had always been her name for this force, a noncorporeal, disembodied energy that moved around her body—from her heart to her throat to her uterus, swimming all over and causing various types of chaos, sometimes surging around in joy, lighting her here and there, sometimes a heavy weight. But now she saw it, tentacled, like a glowing octopus, pinging and zinging. It was behind her belly button but with arms in every direction, electrocuting her. She was vaguely aware that tears were streaking down her face with a force that reminded her of storms.

THE FEMALE BODY existed in silence. Muted. Made invisible. Even in the best of books and movies and conversations, the topic was mostly avoided, rarely fully revealed or made manifest, even now, even with supposed access to open and forthright media and medicine. For that reason, women of all ages suffered in silence and confusion, without much recourse, without much relief. This was Ammalie's thought as she waited in the hospital bed, staring at a white ceiling, her legs in stirrups.

As the vaginal ultrasound beeped, and the doctor rotated the wand this direction and that, and mumbled something about not finding the left ovary, Ammalie's clear thought was: *This world simply, simply, simply needs to be a more honest and vocal place.*

The doctor came and went and someone new came in. This doctor was young—so young that Ammalie wasn't sure how she could be a doctor already—and Ammalie had a quick vision of blond curly-headed Lulu someday walking into a room with such authority and grace.

"There is a prominence of left adnexal vessels," the woman said, looking from a computer screen to Ammalie. "There is a presence of follicles. Those are the findings. But good news. Your uterus measures eight by five by five, and there is no discrete mass."

Ammalie nodded. The silence stretched on for a long time, so she added, "Thank you. I have no idea what that means."

"You don't have the thickening that would suggest uterine cancer."

"Excellent," Ammalie said, resting her head back.

"But it sounds like you've been going through years of pain?"

"Yes."

"How long?"

"A lifetime. But it's gotten worse."

"So, I am seeing what we'd call suspicious pelvic congestion syndrome. It's like having varicose veins, but inside, and it can be very painful. There's some medical dissent about what this is, what to do, only because, well, I'm sorry to say, it hasn't been studied much," to which Ammalie felt her eyes rolling of their own accord.

"What can you do?"

"Well, I'd suggest you wait till you're back home to discuss the pelvic congestion. It won't kill you, but I know it's very, very painful. So I'm sorry you've been dealing with that. There are several options. They could try to regulate your hormones a little better. You're a little too old for birth control, in my opinion. Blood clots and all. Leads to stroke. So you could try an IUD, an ablation, or, if you feel like it's gotten too bad, a hysterectomy, though of course that's extreme, but on the other hand, this pain seems extreme. There are other treatments, but I'd prefer you talk with your primary doctor back home." And patting Ammalie's foot, she added, "I need to leave to have a consult about this, and to check another patient. I'll be back."

When she was gone, Ammalie lay panting in pain, then roused herself and asked a passing nurse if she could make a call. She took the offered phone and called the restaurant, hoping for Aroha, who did indeed pick up after the odd buzzing ring.

"I lied to you," Ammalie said first thing. "I am not the artist. I'm a fake."

There was a sigh and silence.

"I'm so sorry," she rambled on. "I'm so very sorry. You always felt so genuine and real. And I deceived you."

"Crikey," Aroha finally said in a voice that felt like tempered anger. "I guess I don't understand."

Suddenly Ammalie felt another sharp pain on the left side, and gasped. She screwed up her face tight in order to bear the pain and push down the vomit, and then panted, "Listen, I understand if we never speak again, but before you go, can I ask you one thing? What do you daydream about?"

"Oh, stone the crows! Where are you?"

The tearing pain passed, and now she felt the echo of it thrumming. "I've been noticing. Here in New Zealand, my daydreams are about my real life, about *reality*, about the me I am now, not a younger version of me. Because my life here is more real. My daydreams have substance, because my life has substance. If you know what I mean?"

"Not sure I do." Aroha's voice was confused, but felt softer now. "Why do I hear beeping? Why am I getting another call from the police?"

"Thank you for your friendship, your *whakahoahoa*," Ammalie panted. "I need to go. But I wanted to say. Because of you, I've learned words like *whanau,* family. *Whenua,* land. *Moana,* ocean. Thank you for expanding me. I'm"—and here she gasped with a shooting star of pain—"I'm truly sorry for lying. I . . . I had to take over other people's lives until I could find my own. You are a wonderful person."

She gasped out the last words and grabbed her left side and hung up the phone just before accordioning on the bed and emitting a high-pitched animal sound. She found herself thinking, once again, *How very animal I've become!* As she continued moaning, somewhere far away she heard the dog's yelps, the gasp of the freed tree, the cry of humans and animals everywhere.

THE YOUNG DOCTOR was back, was asking her about her pain in her left side, was pressing on the right. "Rebound tenderness?" the doctor mumbled, and then there was another doctor, both hovering, and one was slowly pressing her fingers on the left side, then quickly letting go, which is when her right side started shooting pain. "Contralateral rebound," and "Yes. Yes, that's what threw me."

"Not ovary—"

"Not this congestion syndrome—"

"Appendix!"

"The two-fer rule. Two things at once."

"A keyhole surgery now."

"Yes."

"Let's move—"

"Prep keyhole."

Then suddenly an IV was being put into her arm. Again, the doctor was there saying something about *acute appendicitis . . . spread to the peritoneum? We'll see,* and then another doctor came in and asked about allergies to anesthesia and smiled and told her she'd be drifting off. As she did, she could feel the wet on her cheeks and she could hear herself whispering, "Powell. Mari. Apricot. Please. I need you."

Then, dark came.

SHE OPENED HER eyes, closed them, rested, opened them to see a dark-haired young woman. The same one from the café was sitting beside her bed, eyes closed.

"Apolena?" Ammalie whispered.

The young woman startled. "You know who I am? God, are you okay? You don't look so fab—"

"Are you Vincent's *daughter?* Are you my step—"

The young woman scowled, but her voice was very kind. "*What?*" Then a soft look of understanding spread over her face, and she smiled. "Noooo, no, no," and then she laughed a beautiful liquid laugh. "That would have made a very predictable story, no? Life is more complicated than that. But no, I am not. I am Erik's daughter. But I do know about Vincent. He was my mother's great love before Erik. Then Erik was her great love. Vincent was here one summer, at my grandparents' farm in the bush, and, yes, he and my mother were lovers. And then he went off and married you! And life went on."

Ammalie felt blurry. She blinked her eyes hard, as if that would clear her brain. "But . . . did you go visit Vincent in Arizona?"

"I did."

Ammalie felt a gasp escape. "But you're not his daughter?"

"No, no. Listen. No. My mother, Nina, married Erik, and they had me. No affairs were had. I look just like my father, don't worry. But my mother found Vincent on Facebook years ago. She sought him out because I was in trouble. I happened to be in the States, traveling across the American West, my big OE adventure—Overseas Experience, you know?—and it was harder than I thought it would be. I was lonely and tired and broke. Guidebooks make it seem so easy! Everyone else seems to make it sound so fun! But, you know, it is *not* easy. It's *not* always fun! Life is scary! Everything costs so much! American buses are . . . creepy! A man showed me his . . . Well, it doesn't matter. Well, it does, actually. I was having a panic attack in Tucson. I was pretty down-and-out. So my mother was frantic and found Vincent and put us in touch and then bought me a Greyhound bus ticket. I went to see the Dark Sky with him. He picked me up at the bus stop in Portal, Arizona."

"But your name—"

"It was a family name, on Vincent's side, I know. My mother heard it and loved it. She asked my father, and he loved it too. It's unusual. It's pretty. That's all." Apolena laughed her liquid laugh again and shrugged. "I was born a year after your son. Who is on his way to New Zealand, by the way. With your sister and your friend."

"*What?*" Ammalie tried to sit up, but her abdomen roared with pain. The Sea Creature was cowering there, full of pricks and needles and nervy blasts.

"Nan's driver is picking them up at the airport when they arrive."

Ammalie made a gargling, gasping sound that surprised even her. "Why . . . for the love of the universe, why would Nan do *that*?"

Apolena shrugged. "Because Nan is Nan. As she puts it, she gets a 'kick out of you.' She went to the house and saw how you had taken out all the pots and pans and cleaned the cupboards, which is something she's wanted to do for years. Or hoped someone else would do. She said the residents loved your beach designs. She said you left necklaces everywhere. She said that obviously, you were a good and strange soul. And, as we all know, the world needs more of those. The problem with this planet is that we don't have enough of those sorts."

Those words, said so kindly, made Ammalie start to weep a gentle weeping—her body was in too much pain and too traumatized to do much more—but the tears leaked and Apolena sat nearby, holding her hand.

THE NEXT DAY came and went in a haze. A haze fostered by pharmaceuticals, by a body injured and healing, by her own exhaustion. A haze that reminded her of sea spray. A haze she clung to because it was safe. But the morning after that came, and it became clear that *she* was supposed to be clear. She tried to concentrate—information on painkillers, rest, incision instructions, bloating—but all she really heard was the doctor's final words: "Though it was an emergency, it was, after all, only a minor surgery. You can go home soon."

Ammalie blew out air. "No, thank you." Then, "Really? I'm in too much pain for that. Also, I don't *have* a home."

"I think you can. We'll watch you tonight, though."

She was too groggy to think it through, but heard herself venturing, "Do you know where my necklace is? I had one on . . . from my late husband."

The doctor shook her head no. "I'm sorry. Later, I'll ask the ambulance drivers."

With her words came a memory—oh, god, how had she forgotten?—the man in the back of the ambulance had been Richard! He'd been hovering over her, stroking her hair back from her forehead. If she remembered right, his fingers had paused on her two scars, and his eyes had shown real concern. It had felt so good, just to have that touch, that moment of someone seeing her hurt. Maybe what humans want most: another human to see the hurt borne. To see it and to care.

And yet. She had hurt him. And she felt a deep pain echo in her chest. Surely he was angry—their real and beautiful moment had been built on a foundation of a lie.

Later that night, she woke and shuffled to the bathroom in her hospital room. She knew that much would happen in the light of the new day:

She'd be *dis*charged from the hospital, then *charged* with crimes.

She'd face Nan.

She'd face her Three Keys.

She'd face her dead husband's ex-lover.

And she'd need to apologize to several people.

She figured she might as well examine herself tonight, the self she was before this upcoming day, because she'd be a different Ammalie before tomorrow ended.

She looked in the mirror. At the two scars, one at her hairline from the restaurant long ago, one across her scalp from Arizona. Her hair was light gray, and she found it pretty, contrasted with the tan of her skin and her flushed cheeks. Her eyes looked bright and clear and calm, as if full of bigger thoughts, as if she had forgotten herself, in a good way. As if she was less Ammalie and more a part of the living, breathing creatures of the world. More a part of the birds, trees, stone, glass, stars, shells, curls, braids, patterns of the world.

THE NOISE OF feral happiness: When Powell walked in, she heard herself yelp in joy. He bent over and was saying "Oh, Mom." Then Apricot and Mari were there. The two women looked the exact same as when she'd last seen them—Mari's long white-black hair pinned up, Apricot's blond dyed hair precisely cut, her lips plumped and covered with thick pink lipstick. But Powell looked different. Really different. He had an actual beard, scruffy-looking. She'd never seen him with facial hair at all. He'd filled out and muscled up a surprising amount for only a few months. Before she could comment, they were turning and shaking hands with Apolena, who had just walked in, and suddenly . . . What was that?

The air changed.

She could feel it radiate through the hospital room, clear as an approaching storm. Oh, how things happened all at once! She could not help but smile. As Powell shook Apolena's hand, the air vibrated with the invisible but powerful electricity that happens when two people catch each other's eye—and are surprised to discover something there. Attraction. It was an amazing thing to witness. And yes, it could happen just like that, in a moment. Ammalie's eyes darted from Powell to Apolena and she laughed, startling everyone, but she said nothing.

There was an awkward silence, so she cleared her dry throat. "You all three came? You dropped everything . . . and came?"

"Of course," Apricot said, reaching down to brush Ammalie's hair from her face.

"Sure, Mom," Powell said. "But I had to put it on your credit card."

"I'll pay you back for any other expenses. I'll pay you *all* back," she mumbled. "You're here!"

After more gentle hugs—she was still hooked up to an IV—Mari lifted Ammalie's shirt to stare at her scar. Apricot looked embarrassed but peered under too and said, "Ouch," and Powell said, "Mom, Mom, Mom," the way she had once said, "Powell, Powell, Powell."

She became aware then that they were all staring at her.

"You're so . . . muscly," Mari said happily. "But have you been eating enough?"

"And tan and actually kind of burned." Apricot was scowling. "You could get your hair done. I'll take you! We'll do it together."

"She looks beautiful," Mari corrected.

"Your hair turned white!" Powell's voice was soft, as if in awe. "You look good, Mom."

Ammalie smiled. "I feel lousy. No, I mean, I feel good. Temporarily lousy but overall good. But thanks. And it started turning gray years ago. Dye is an amazing thing, but I'm glad it's gone. I feel more me now."

Powell touched her arm, a bit awkwardly. "Mari caught me up on some stuff. I took a literature class too, you know. You're like on a hero's journey." He sat on the bed and put his hand on her shin. "A heroine's journey."

"Exactly," Ammalie said. "And it went pear-shaped."

They all stared at her blankly.

"It's a phrase they use here. Like, 'Cheers,' and 'Done its dash,' which means something has died. Pear-shaped."

"Like a woman's body." Apricot patted her round rump, but Ammalie noticed with a start that it wasn't very round at all; indeed, Apricot looked thinner than she ever had before, and in a way that didn't look healthy. Ammalie felt a zing of worry; she'd ask about it later.

"Your life doesn't seem so pear-shaped to me," she heard Mari mumble. "Actually, it sounds quite interesting." Then she leaned over and whispered into Ammalie's ear. "I'm getting a lot of calls about you. From Levi. And from a sheriff wanting to do a well-being check. They called your work; your work gave them my number. Your car was found in Wisconsin. No plates but they tracked the VIN. And something about a possible break-in in a cabin? But then the homeowner dropped charges, took back his story. Seems the place was left in better condition than it had ever been, including some jewelry left there, and also, ya know, who wants to deal with the law when you don't have to?" Mari pulled her face back and quirked an eyebrow. "Damn, Ammalie. When I told you to go forth and kick ass, I didn't expect you to become an *outlaw.*"

Ammalie winked at her. "I've had the best adventure ever, my friend."

NAN DID NOT press charges. "Not only did you clean my cupboards and windows," she said, "but some people reported seeing you picking up trash on the beach." Then she added, "I like your jewelry. You can stay as an official artist in residence next year, if you wish." She sat in a chair next to the hospital bed, more elderly and hunched than Ammalie had imagined, closer to the end of a life than she wanted to consider. Still, Nan was beaming a calm, unmistakable energy or life force or whatever it was that made humans glow.

"What a gift you are. What a gift you offer others." Ammalie reached out to hold Nan's thin hand. "That you help the world in that way, I mean. Thank you."

"With great wealth comes great responsibility. I was gifted wealth. My grandfather made money chopping down kauri trees, and he was part of a society that took land from the Indigenous peoples. So I try to intelligently gift back my fortune by giving it to others in one form or another, and I could not be happier about that. I hope soon to be rather poor, in fact. I hope to die with nothing, as all people truly do. I remember your Vincent, a little. I'm sorry he is gone. He seemed a good man."

Ammalie paused. "He was. It was complicated, but he was."

Nan sat back. "Your son looks like him. I have a daughter. And I worry. How sad the future might be. And what should we do? Shall we sit now in the evening hours and simply take note? Shall we lodge the cool days into our memory, so as to conjure them up later?"

Ammalie tried to pay attention through the drugs. This woman seemed to talk in wisps. "Yes. I can't . . . I can't see what to do. Beyond that."

But Nan was still on her own train of thought, distant eyes focused on the view out the window. "If we had new words and new stories, maybe we wouldn't treat the planet so." Her words were broken into fragments, as if she were lost in thought, or half elsewhere. "The smoke from Australia chokes us, those poor people. And then we got such heavy rains that the roads caved in. Floods caused septic tanks to spill into streams . . . landslides . . ."

She drifted into a silence, and to fill it, Ammalie ventured her newest thought. "I've been considering . . . the three wisdoms of growing older. One, if you feel irrelevant, well, what the hell, *become relevant*. Two, if you feel lonely, *fall in love*. Three, I forget three . . . Oh, to caretake. Yes. *Caretake*. That's the word. Yes. Lose yourself and caretake. That's what you do." Perhaps it was the pain, or the painkillers, but she couldn't quite complete a clear thought. But she did manage to get out the one most important truth. "I'm so very sorry I stole from you—you of all people! I took your sea glass . . ."

Above her, Nan fingered her necklace, which Ammalie could see was one of hers, and she thought it beautiful, more beautiful than any object she'd ever made.

In the quiet half hour before Ammalie left the hospital, while waiting for the doctor to sign papers, she shooed everyone out of her room so that she could jot down a new list.

Things to Do Now

Go visit Apricot.
Spend time with Mari and Powell.
Apologize to Richard.
Call Levi.

After all, there *was* something with Levi. She wanted closure of some sort she couldn't explain. She wasn't a damsel in distress. She didn't *need* him. He didn't occupy her daydreams anymore. Perhaps she just wanted to tell him goodbye, one human to another, and in tribute to all the mealtimes they had sort-of shared.

Finally, she added:

Sell the house.
Buy Cave Valley Cabins.

Besides operating it as a rental property, she was going to do three things:

> Offer free rooms to others seeking to learn about the natural world.
> Offer cabins for artists or activists.
> Offer a cabin to people working for humanitarian reasons on the border—volunteers doing water drops, for example.

The rest of the rooms would cover the taxes and insurance and upkeep and employees, she hoped. In this way, it would be a small society of sharing, based on community and care for the planet and her people. She would plant trees for future generations—and help others do the same.

Refugia.

She had to admit it now, finally, even if just to herself: She had money. She'd gone into a state of denial, pretended it wasn't there. All those cheap cans of beans! All that homemade Chex mix! All the scrimping and saving on this trip! She could have *rented* three vacation homes. *Fancy* homes! But the wealth seemed so unfamiliar it was scary. It didn't feel rightfully hers. And she hadn't spent a cent of it.

Vincent had been Vincent, after all. A careful planner. A detail-oriented, responsible guy, and surely, some of those nights in the basement he had been tracking finances. Which is why he had a million in retirement, a million of life insurance. The life insurance would go to Powell. And the retirement would go to her, and she'd share it, which, she felt sure, Vincent would be smiling at. He would like this new her. Even though, contradictorily, their dynamic might have been what tamped down this version of herself.

Forgive him, forgive self, move on, do good. Her mantra for the rest of her life.

With the support of the others, she'd find a manager, a book-keeper, a lawyer to help her get going. She'd buy Cave Valley Cabins and would study hard to learn how to best run such a nonprofit. Rita and Rex would help. Nan had agreed to advise.

How best to provide a welcome, safe home—*that* was her purpose in life.

To hand out keys to others.

CHAPTER 22

While Powell and Apricot went to hike among the kauri trees—something she couldn't do with her stitches—Ammalie took Mari on a very slow amble across the black sand beach. As they meandered along the shore, she caught Mari up on everything, although some of it was so hard to explain that Mari only laughed and shook her head at what she referred to as Ammalie's "lovely lack of logical thinking."

They stopped to stare at the swells and the waves peeling from the sea, and Ammalie gently drew a mandala in the sand with her walking stick. "Look, there are purple tones to the black sand, aren't there? It looks metallic."

"The natural beauty here is really amazing, I'll grant you that. And it's so quiet! Not like Chicago! It's really freaking out my ears. And my eyes."

"Ha! I know. The green."

"Yes! The silence and the green." Mari touched her shoulder gently. "Friend, you had me listed as your emergency contact."

"Yes."

"That's how they contacted me."

"Yes."

"Not Vincent?"

Ammalie looked over at her. "That's telling, isn't it? I changed it to you years ago. You'd be the person I'd want to come."

Mari sighed, understanding. "I'm sorry he wasn't more there for you. I often wondered if his emotional absence would make you slowly kinda . . . well, *crazy*! Loneliness can do that." But then her eyes lit. "You are a new person. Tell me what you've learned here."

Ammalie tilted her head onto Mari's shoulder, and mumbled, "I've been reading so much. I know about the kawakawa, which is used for tea. *Hangehange,* which are young leaves you can eat raw, and karamu, orange berries with a lot of vitamin C. I know to beware of the karaka berries, which are poisonous, but which have the most fruity, perfumy smell. And Mari, the manuka—oh, the smell of manuka! And the harakeke, which is a flax, those tall orange flowers that the tui love. And did you know, the riroriro bird, a gray warbler, has a mournful sound that signals imminent rainfall? And don't you love the names? And I'm happy."

Mari had real wonder in her voice. "You've gone and turned into a natural-history sort of person."

"See these little holes in the sand? I thought that's where the waves just aerated it, but it's also sand hoppers burrowing out. And in the really early morning, right at the tide line, you can see all the nocturnal activity of insect tracks."

"And that beach grass stuff? Those golden spiky globe things?"

"Spinifex. Kowhangatara grass. The seed heads are everywhere now; it tumbles around the beach, swaths of it resting at the tide line or floating in the streams. Also *pingao*—that's another dune grass which dries a deep golden orange. Prized for weaving of precious *kete* in Māori culture. And look here, see this hard thin crust of sand? That's called *biscuit.* And up there? That rock. The remains of the rim of the ancient Waitakere volcano."

"Lovely. All this is lovely."

"Mari, my body is aging—boy do I feel it. But the real Ammalie is getting younger. More playful. More free. More accepting. More childlike. It sounds so cliché, but clichés are clichés for a reason, no? I couldn't have done it without this journey."

Mari opened her mouth, closed it. "I'm not sure I should say this, and I don't intend any hurt. But I wish Vincent could see you now."

Ammalie laughed. "I know. Frankly, and egotistically, I wish *everyone* could see me now. And yet, I don't need to be seen anymore."

"Well, sorry, but we're all here, seeing you. It's important that Powell see you this way."

Ammalie nodded. "Yes, I guess you're right. And you *came*! I needed you, and you came."

Mari put her arm around Ammalie's shoulder. "I finally got to be the companion fated to go along! I adore you, adventurer! I suppose that back home, I've been on my own journey. You were right all along. This last arc of life? We better do it right. We only have so much time. And you know what you've taught me? It's not so much *pressure* to do it right. No, it's more like a *challenge* to do it right."

Ammalie turned so she could hug her friend full-on, and she rocked Mari back and forth, back and forth, back and forth as the sea thundered and echoed.

That evening, Ammalie found herself alone with Aroha in the restaurant—the others had needed to sleep off jet lag at their holiday rental. Aroha slid a plate of fish-and-chips close to her, peered out from behind her black-rimmed glasses, said, "For you, love," and held her gaze with warmth and steadiness. Then, sitting, she took a piece of fish and took a hearty bite. "Don't mind if I do. This is very good food."

"Yes. I'm so grateful."

"Richard is very angry with you. He was hoping to . . . you know . . . well. He said that one thing you learn in older age is to be direct, honest, open, and reach out while the iron is hot, and so he did, and now he feels betrayed. He was right all along. You were a fake. He can't quite forgive you. That you were lying to us all."

Aroha arched her eyebrows playfully. "But I can. First, I have to say, I have been friends with Nina Sis all my life. So when you said that Vincent had a relative named Apolena, and was from the Midwest, I remembered. 'The summer of love,' we called it. That summer, Nina fell in love with an American wwoofer, and that is the same summer I realized I liked women. *I* was sleeping with the artist who was here at that time. She was much older and a perfect first lover. But I was so confused: What were the chances that Vincent's widow would show up here? But then I began to understand—you'd come here because he'd been here. And you knew about the residency and the house."

"Yes."

Aroha flashed her gorgeous smile. "What a world we live in. Pear-shaped all the way."

Then she grew serious. "I was not the one who called the police, by the way. Richard called Nan to tell her about the pink ribbons. Amazingly, she answered her phone. I suppose he wanted to speak with her to, well, find out more about you, to tell her that he'd been delighted to discover you weren't a surveyor for a real estate company. And she didn't know who or what he was talking about! So he called the police."

Ammalie felt a flush in her cheeks. Anger or embarrassment, she wasn't sure. "I wish he'd—I don't know—"

"I know."

"It feels like a betrayal to *me*. I *was* trying to help him, after all."

"Yes, but you have to understand. It was out of a love for Nan. And you did pretend to be someone you were not."

Ammalie ate a fry slowly and let her gaze linger on the view outside the window, all the greenery and birds and sky. "Yeah, I get it. I understand, I do. I feel terrible. I probably would have called the police too. Well, maybe not. But I *do* owe him an apology. I didn't tell him the truth. I let the lie float around. And . . . it's not right."

Aroha reached over to touch her cheek. "No, it's not, but he'll heal. And how *are* you, love?"

Ammalie knew her to mean health-wise, but she responded in a truer way. "I feel . . . free. Not problem-free, just free."

"Well. If you had no problems, I think that means you'd be living a lazy life."

Ammalie snorted. "Exactly. I have some regrets. I also have *confusions*. About the way I grew up in a culture that . . . I dunno, *assumed* the male gaze, how maybe much of what I did was to attract that gaze, want that gaze, depend upon that gaze, whether I was conscious of it or not. I'm a little jealous of women growing up now. I think the world has been opened up to them in various ways."

Then she winked at Aroha, who laughed and said, "This is why I like you."

Ammalie felt emboldened. "I grew up in a family and in a time when heterosexuality was, you know, assumed. Or at least encouraged. Looking back, I now see that some of my female friendships, well, maybe that was *romance*. But I didn't experience it as that! It didn't even occur to me to call it that. Or explore that. I . . . I . . . There's a lot to unpack here for me. All the assumptions I've made! All my blind spots! I need another life!" But then she added, "But I will die loving the life I've had." She gulped in a breath, feeling as if she'd been talking for too long. "Do you have regrets?"

Aroha considered the question. "No, I have no regrets. I would have liked to be born in a different world, though. One that was more honest. More kind. More accepting. Of other cultures, of other sexual paths, of identities, of everything."

"Yes. Yes. I know." They held each other's eyes, acknowledging what all the *yes*es meant, the paths not taken, and then Ammalie said, "I feel like my heart awoke so very late. The other day I was thinking that maybe only now, as my womanhood fades, has my heart become a woman."

"That sounds as it should be, the natural order of things." With that, Aroha stood up enough so that she could lean across the table to kiss Ammalie's forehead, near her scar. Then, intentionally, she leaned down and kissed Ammalie briefly on the lips, and Ammalie kissed back, closed her eyes, and felt the pure perfection of this one moment.

NAN HOSTED A dinner in her Auckland home to celebrate the solstice, for now they were near the day that signaled the longest, lightest day of the year in the Southern Hemisphere. A time, she reminded everyone, to rededicate oneself to bringing the most light that you could into the world, working right alongside the sun. While everyone else was celebrating other holidays, she said, she would always celebrate the *original* one that inspired them—the full arc of the sun's journey.

Ammalie looked around the room, noting how nearly everyone was as odd and beautiful as sea glass, tumbling together in old and ancient ways. Nan and Aroha remembered Vincent from thirty years ago. Nan had been middle-aged then, and Nina a young woman. Nina described her and Vincent's passion with obvious joy and Ammalie felt only happiness in hearing about it, in remembering her own limerent time with Vincent. Erik seemed to take it all in with acceptance and happiness too. Ammalie was relieved that something about middle age brought depleted jealousy and replenished joy for anything that had been beautiful.

Powell loved hearing stories about his father at the age he was now, and how his father had "wwoofed it through New Zealand," as everyone there put it, and it became clear he was going to apply to do the same. He was checking into getting an extension on his visa, and he'd been invited to stay with the Sis family. It also was apparent to everyone in the room that he and Apolena, sitting near each other on a blue couch, had a crush on each other, and that all their lives would now be further linked.

Mari was trying to extend her stay as well. After all, she and Powell were over here, and it was gorgeous, and they were awed by the tui birds and the pohutukawa trees and the Tasman Sea.

Aroha arrived last, whispering, "Hi, love." Ammalie touched her own lips, remembering their kiss the night before, tentative and brief and yet brave and curious too.

Also in attendance was Lara the policewoman and the actual jeweler, Brumby, who had arrived early for an arts festival in Auckland, and who wore scarves and big jewelry and a flowing dress and was delighted by the whole story—and confessed to being glad about clean cupboards. "Peace, justice, homes, and art for *all,*" she said after a few drinks, hugging Ammalie with real force.

The one person who refused to come was Richard, who was still angry. Ammalie had written him a long letter, and would follow up with a call later. "It wasn't right," he had told Aroha. "It simply wasn't right to go around breaking into a private home, pretending to be someone else—who does that?" Ammalie felt the sting of that truth—he was right; she deserved his anger. The sliver of muted shame that ran through her was something to be borne.

Simultaneously, though, she felt delight, especially when she

Zoomed in Lulu and Dan, Rita and Rex, with Lady bounding around in the background. Together, they toasted Vincent, who, although absent, had brought them all together. Though she didn't say it aloud—some emotions were meant to be kept private—Ammalie had the clear knowledge that the marriage would have faltered and ended. Yet it had been a worthy journey overall, and she felt a great sorrow for the fact that he was not alive, heartache for the fact that Powell would not have more time with his father, and a real worry that Powell would be affected in ways which neither of them could foresee.

It *hurt*. It hurt and it was complicated—and it was okay.

"We must age and die, because that is our debt to nature. *Debitum naturea*," Nan said. "Our debt to nature is to die!" She raised her glass in a toast.

Everyone did the same, and then looked to Ammalie, as if she was meant to say something. So she cleared her throat and breathed in. "Uh, so, well . . ." she started. Then she straightened her spine and faced them all. "So, here's the deal. A few months ago, I piled a bunch of stuff in my car and started driving west. I left the three keys of my life behind—Powell, Apricot, and Mari—but only temporarily, so that I could make new friends, new keys, such as Rita, Lulu, and Aroha, all of you here. I've had three adventures in three places. I've felt three times as if I might die—once getting hurt in the desert, once being unimaginably cold in a snowstorm, and once of a body gone haywire. But I have never felt more alive. I feel so very alive. I found the key to my life; I've unlocked my life. With the help of you all."

As they cheered, she handed out necklaces to everyone, so that they could all wear some frosted sea glass around their necks. She'd never found her old greenstone necklace, so she replaced it with a long green sea glass oval on a black cord, similar to the one she'd just given Powell. She'd miss the old one, but also, attachment to things . . . Well, the time for that was over.

When she found herself standing next to Lara near the end of the party, she said, "I happen to know a few people who *should* be in jail. I daydream about it all the time. Won't you please arrest them for me?"

Lara looked confused. "Who?"

"You know those people who make first aid kits with nothing that's actually helpful?"

Lara paused for a moment and then burst out laughing. "Yes. You think they should be put in jail for stupidity? Yeah, I'll agree with you there."

"And those who make videos on how fun it is to live in your car?"

Lara's eyes lit up. "Okay, yes, and those who tell non–New Zealanders that it's okay to come and freedom-camp wherever you want!"

"Okay, sure!" Ammalie said, laughing, and then wincing, because her abdomen was still tender.

Aroha, who had come over to listen, chimed in. "American drivers on the wrong side of the road!"

"Snotty divorce lawyers," Mari said.

Powell made a noise of surprised hurt. "You're getting divorced?"

Mari reached over and touched him on the shoulder. "Naw. Maximo and I almost did, but decided it was true-if-sometimes-bored love. And that we can do better. And we will."

Powell nodded, then bounced onto his feet, full of energy. "Grocers who leave spoiled fruit out on purpose, hoping you don't notice, which you don't, and you get home to find your plum is gross! And also, an economy that makes it impossible for young people to get a start in life."

"Ooof, that's a biggie," Ammalie said.

Lara elbowed her teasingly and said, "Lots of people should be in jail. But not people who break into other people's houses to make jewelry."

"Absolutely not! Not them," Ammalie said, to which everyone cheered again.

LATER, SHE CAUGHT Apricot's eye and signaled with her head to a corner of the room. She braced herself for an impatient sigh or a roll of the eye, but on approach, Apricot said only, "I'm glad I came. A good adventure for me too. You inspire."

Ammalie felt her eyebrows shoot up of their own accord. "Well, that's a nice thing to say. But, Apricot, you look . . . so thin." The moment she said it, she winced; surely, Apricot would be annoyed.

But her sister only frowned and turned to look out the window. "Okay. Yeah. It caught up with me." The look on her face was grave, but she brightened a little and added, "There's still a lot they can do. It's not the end-end, but I do need to get serious."

"Damn." Ammalie's eyes burned with tears. "Damn, damn. Damn. I'm so sorry, Apricot." Then she reached out to hold her sister's hand and swung it, just as she had done so often as a child. "You have so much living to do! And what about *me*? Selfishly, I need you! You are the person who has known me the longest, and Vincent was the other one, and I just lost him. No, it's not fair to you. It's not *right*. You deserve . . ."

Apricot sighed a calm exhale. "Don't I know it. I think it all stinks, frankly. Cancer. This mortality business. But that's just how it goes."

Ammalie pulled Apricot into a hug.

"Come back, spend some time with me," Apricot said, and then, pulling away, held Ammalie's shoulders. "This adventure of yours reminds me of that game we played as kids. Remember? How we'd pretend we were being chased by bad guys, and had to hide out? But at the end of the day, we always went home."

"I've thought of that often." Ammalie then took both of Apricot's hands in hers. "Thank you. For those games. For being such a wonderful big sister back then. And yes, I'll come."

"And then you can do Cave Valley."

"Yes."

"Is it a cave or a valley? I don't get it."

"Exactly."

"Maybe I'll come visit you."

"I'd love that."

"I want to see one of those things. A . . . ringtail?"

"Yes. There are ringtails and there are coatimundis. And cactus!"

"I want to be of more *use*. In whatever time I have left."

"Excellent. And Scrabble. I want to play one game of Scrabble with you."

Apricot looked confused, but shrugged. "Sure thing, sister. Whatever strikes your fancy."

SHE HAD TALKED with Mari and Apricot—and now, Powell. He broached the topic bluntly and without preamble as they walked slowly down the black sand beach the next morning. "So it sounds like Dad stayed in touch with the Sis family here and never told you about it?"

Ammalie bit her lip. "Your dad was a good man and he loved you an insane amount."

"I know it."

"And I don't ever want to dis him. He was your father, and a good one. But there were lots of things, really, that he never included me in on."

"Or me." He stopped and kicked at the sand and looked out at the waves crashing in. "You don't think I noticed all the nights in the basement? All the times he was reading about geology or stars or Vikings and not, ya know, upstairs doing homework with me? Doing dishes with you? You don't think I noticed how much time he seemed to need to himself?" Now Powell was as angry as Ammalie was surprised. "That's the thing about this that's hard, Mom! I grieve him and he's dead and yet I am also angry. Or maybe sad. And it's weird having so many contradictory emotions!"

His voice was bitter, but Ammalie couldn't help the bark of laughter that escaped her. "I'm sorry, I'm sorry," she said right away. "I only laughed because what you say is so true. That's exactly what I've been having a hard time with myself. Exactly. *Exactly.*"

"No one really talks about that!" Powell said. "What the hell am I supposed to do with all that?"

Ammalie turned and looked at the waves, so steady as they unfolded and glided to shore, one after the other. "I dunno," she whispered. "Feel it all. Talk to me about it, I guess. Also, look at those waves. They're like the regular heartbeat of the planet, no? Let them be soothing?"

Powell turned too and seemed to seriously consider the waves for a long time. "It's not like Dad was a *bad* guy," he finally said. "He was a good guy. But night after night after night . . . the basement. I *hate* it down there. I hate that I hate it. And then I want to walk down there and talk to him. I miss him. It's so fucked."

She reached out and hugged him, rocking him back and forth. "Me too. Me too." She almost told him the full truth—that she had come to hate the basement and the silence so much that she'd been ready to leave Vincent, was only waiting for Powell to be established, was still trying to wrap her brain around the logistics of a divorce. But she let the words die in her throat. Maybe someday. What would they help now? It sounded as if they both had to struggle with grieving someone while letting some anger dissipate. It was complicated enough.

When they quit hugging, Ammalie reached out and scratched Powell's scruffy cheek and then put her arm around his shoulder as they continued walking. He was taller and broader-shouldered than she was, but she could still manage, the zings and plings of joy lighting her heart with every step.

On her last night, Ammalie placed her packed bags in a tidy bundle at the door. Everything was in perfect order. So many nights she had done this, ready to flee. So many nights, she had stood above them, considering various escape scenarios. But tonight there was nothing sneaky about her routine.

Mari and Powell were staying a little longer, charmed by both New Zealand and the possibility of missing some Chicago winter. Ammalie was flying back to New York with Apricot for a new round of doctor appointments and treatments. Then, whenever it made sense, she'd go back to Chicago, then to Cave Valley. What happened next would be convoluted and complicated and heartbreaking and glorious, to be sure—that's how life was.

Right before heading to bed, she stood in front of the mirror and brushed her hair with the brush she'd stolen from the Colorado cabin. She thought of Fluffiest Red and Dude-the-Stove and the Holy Trinity first aid kits. She thought of the fork in her hair in Nebraska. She thought of all the pears she had eaten on the road, and how her life had gone pear-shaped in the most wonderful ways.

What, she wondered, would be the fourth key? And the fifth and sixth? Who knew? But she could easily imagine herself holding a jumble of different keys in her palm, considering their potential.

EPILOGUE

She sat at Cave Valley Cabins in the warm sun watching an absurdly tiny house wren belting out a melody which seemed aggressively directed at a blue jay, as if the wren were defending her home via song. Though so little, wrens were fierce—almost too fierce, on the crazy side of the bell curve of crazy bird behavior—which is why she loved them the most.

Because Levi was still sleeping, Ammalie had time to let her mind wander to their first kiss. He'd met her at O'Hare after she'd flown in from New York, and as she walked out of the airport, he'd walked quickly up to her, eyes fixed on hers, and flashed a gorgeous smile when he saw her smile, which he took as an invitation to pick her up and swing her around, plonk her back down, and kiss her on the lips. They somehow walked themselves backward so as to find privacy against a wall and communicated solely by kissing, without speaking. They did not need to; so much of communication between humans did not depend upon words. She smiled into her coffee, remembering all the kisses since, and Kit's and Dan's and Richard's and Aroha's kisses before, how different they all were, and how each had felt right.

A person should listen to her daydreams, she reminded herself. Hers had occupied her night after night for a reason. She had wanted to connect—and he had wanted to connect with her. As simple and as glorious as that.

Levi had retired from work early—ready anyway, he'd said—

and moved without hesitation to join her in Arizona. He would help when asked, but would otherwise stay out of her affairs, knowing this adventure was hers. They would find a way to be in partnership—companionship was one of the great joys of life—but he was aware of her insistence on autonomy in her life.

Powell had already come for a long visit which was, hands down, the best month of parenting in her life, mainly because it involved less parenting and more friendship. He then flew back to New Zealand to spend a year working, and, she presumed, kissing Apolena. And Apricot, pending her doctor's okay, was going to come in November, her least favorite month to be in New York, and perhaps, she admitted bravely, her final November. Aroha and Nan were coming in December, a one-year anniversary of their meeting Ammalie. Lady was happily living with Rex in Mexico, and both were doing well, and Rita was off exploring Alaska. Mari and Maximo had come for two weeks as part of their redo-honeymoon, from which they relaunched their marriage, with more honesty and oomph. The Grey Goose had been recovered and donated to NPR, and Ammalie couldn't find any stories about anyone arrested for obstructing the oil and gas development near Chalk Canyon or anywhere else. She'd received a postcard from Wisconsin with an *All well, work continues, the Grey Goose flew me home, love to you, lady,* and Dan had written a long letter detailing Lulu's adventures, the family reunited now, and ending with *Sending you a hug and a wink, you badass adventuring woman.* Even Richard had been in touch, sending a short but friendly-enough email, telling her that Nan had put all her land into a permanent conservation trust, thereby ending all developers' plans and pink ribbons.

And Levi. He was stirring now, and soon he'd come out and sit on the bench next to her and they'd lean into each other in the sunlight. They'd have coffee and watch the coatimundis eat the birdseed. The Sea Creature swam happily around her chest, the sun warmed her face, and the house wren sat on a branch belting out a song in the direction of his home, which was a birdhouse built to look like a travel trailer. She'd painted it to look like Dart, and from its small hole, three fledgling wrens were about to launch. The parent wren seemed to be encouraging them to leave by offering an exuberant melody of joy, which sounded to Ammalie like a chant: *Adventure forth and onward, friends! We got this. Let's do it together.*

ACKNOWLEDGMENTS

Special thanks to Karye Cattrell, Laura Resau, Todd Mitchell, Claire Boyles, Alyson Hagy, and Beth McMurray for being fabulous readers. Thank you to Michael Heiner, Mary Lea Dodd, Aaron Abeyta, Nancy King, Claire Inwood, Linda Pretty, Jim Davidson, and Marina Richie for offering advice on birds, storms, locations, stars, and life. Thanks to Alex Hunt for making me a beautiful lap desk of maple, cherry, and walnut, so I could write this book from the comfort of my couch.

Huge gratitude for the Aldo and Estella Leopold Writing Residency in New Mexico, the Earthskin Trust Residency in New Zealand, the Ucross Residency in Wyoming, and Lara Richardson of Colorado for providing me with remote places to work and inspiration of places for Ammalie to break into. Luckily for me, I was invited.

Thank you to Susanna Porter for being an editor extraordinaire and to Peter Steinberg for being an agent extraordinaire. To have someone believe in your book—and provide a key and a home for it—is a true gift. Likewise, thank you to all former teachers—there are too many to name—who believed in my writing ever since I was a kid who went around insisting that I'd write books someday. Thanks to all readers and book lovers everywhere, of course, because without you, there are no book adventures to be had.

One of the great honors of my life has been the opportunity to develop and direct the MFA with a concentration in nature writing at Western Colorado University—one of the few graduate writing programs in the country dedicated to place-based writing. So I'd like to thank my students and colleagues for this particular vital door. Several of the characters are named after students in the first cohort in gratitude for helping me get it all going. Onward, Shackletons!

In Chapter 17, I quote *Natural Rearing of Children* by Juliette de Bairacli Levy, a wonderful book I came across while at my writing residency in New Zealand.

Thank you to Eliana and Jake and Michael for being my hooligan adventure partners—and for understanding the quiet time it takes to write a novel. You are my Three Keys.

THREE
KEYS

LAURA PRITCHETT

A BOOK CLUB GUIDE

Dear Reader,

At a remote writing residency in New Mexico, I sipped coffee, considered the Sangre de Cristo Mountains, and thought about the likelihood of being able to break into certain places without being noticed. This was all a hypothetical daydreamy delight, mind you—I had no plans to really break into homes. But by the end of the sunrise, my character Ammalie did!

Like me, she's going through the transformation into middle age—and confronting the accompanying invisibility situation. Our culture does a fine job of erasing older women—an impulse that must be met with resistance, of course. How satisfying, then, to be playing around with the anonymity a person might want, and the kind she *gets,* whether she wants it or not.

Soon after the pandemic hit, I became increasingly interested in the ways we adapted to isolation, in our newfound awareness of the fragility of what we'd taken for granted, and how the outdoors served as a safe haven.

All these themes—remoteness, invisibility, middle age, self-sufficiency, adventuring, the glory of nature, and the responsibility of caretaking of our planet—came together in *Three Keys*. Ammalie takes "an Awfully Big Adventure," as Peter Pan puts it, traveling across the United States and breaking into homes in Colorado,

Arizona, and New Zealand. She discovers that by breaking into other people's lives, she can find her own.

I hope you enjoy her trip—both literal and metaphorical—as much as I did writing it. And may we all find our own ways of adventuring forth with humor and mindfulness and grace.

For the wild,
   Laura

THEMES AND DISCUSSION QUESTIONS

The Feminine Heroic Journey

Women have gotten short shrift in adventure tales. Cultural narratives celebrate the solo male adventurer, but we all know that women have also explored the farthest reaches of our planet and space—all while dealing with body stuff that would send many men to their knees!

1. What are some of the "hero's journey" narratives that come to mind? These tales are often individualistic, external, and violent. (Think Odysseus and Luke Skywalker.)

2. More important, what *feminine* heroic journeys do you know of? These tales involve journeying inward—while often exploring community, outreach, the lifting of others. Are inward journeys less prevalent? Or just written and talked about less?

3. What barriers prevent women from taking solo adventures? How can that be changed for the better?

Living in Deeper Relationship with the Natural World

Ammalie is falling in love—with the planet, that is. And when we love something, we yearn to protect it.

4. In what ways do you presently engage with nature? What brings you delight? Birds? Clouds? Stars? The sea?

5. Has your relationship with nature changed over time? If so, what triggered that change?

6. How would you answer Richard's guiding question: "What kind of ancestor do I want to be?"

Survival Course, Anyone?

Who doesn't like a good survival story? Especially now! Enrollment in survival courses has increased dramatically since Covid—including urban survival, naturalist schools, and outdoor survival camps—and this novel attempts to capture the common human impulse to feel safe in a time of uncertainty.

7. Do you try to be prepared for the unexpected? Is this something that you think about regularly, or not at all?

8. Have you ever been caught in a storm that scared you? How did it affect you, at the time and afterward?

On Being Invisible

Let's face it: TV, magazines, books, and society largely erase the middle-age woman—ugh!

9. If you have experienced this, how so?

10. Have your roles changed over time? If so, how did that feel?

11. In what ways have your priorities shifted?

12. How have friends helped? Ammalie and Mari discuss some big questions. How do we get better, not bitter, as we age?

13. Finding joy and relevancy—that's what many people report worrying about as they age. What does that (or will that) look like for you?

Adventure On!

14. What adventures do you want to take (both external ones that involve your body and internal ones that involve your mind and emotions)?

LAURA PRITCHETT is the author of seven novels and two books of nonfiction. Her work is rooted in the contemporary American West and has been significantly influenced by her life in Colorado. Both her fiction and nonfiction often focus on issues of ecology, conservation, climate change, and social justice. She has been awarded the PEN USA Award for Fiction, the High Plains Book Award for fiction, the Milkweed National Fiction Prize, several Colorado Book Awards, and has been shortlisted for many other honors. She is the editor of three anthologies, all on environmental topics, and writes regularly for magazines. She directs the MFA in nature writing at Western Colorado University, and teaches around the country. She is often found watching clouds, stars, birds, or looking for sea glass.

laurapritchett.com
Facebook: LauraPritchettAuthor
Instagram: @laurapritchettauthor

RANDOM HOUSE BOOK CLUB

Because Stories Are Better Shared

Discover

Exciting new books that spark conversation every week.

Connect

With authors on tour—or in your living room. (Request an Author Chat for your book club!)

Discuss

Stories that move you with fellow book lovers on Facebook, on Goodreads, or at in-person meet-ups.

Enhance

Your reading experience with discussion prompts, digital book club kits, and more, available on our website.

Join our online book club community!

f **g** randomhousebookclub.com

Random House Book Club ™

Because Stories Are Better Shared

RANDOM HOUSE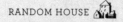